Advance Praise for *The Silver Candlesticks*

"For a generation, Linda Chavez has provided a clear, courageous voice in our national discourse. Now, as it turns out, she's also a novelist of grace and skill. Inspired by 500 years of her family's remarkable history, she tells a story of hidden identity but unfaltering faith. *The Silver Candlesticks* is compelling, readable, and particularly pertinent at this moment of surging, worldwide antisemitism."

—Michael Medved, syndicated radio host, author of *The American Miracle*

"One of the most satisfying aspects of *Finding Your Roots* is unveiling hidden mysteries on a guest's family tree, and political commentator Linda Chavez's ancestral revelations were among the most astonishing that we have ever uncovered. Chavez has transformed the fascinating raw material of her long-hidden family saga into a brilliant novel about the Spanish Inquisition. Linda's family migrated to the American Southwest from Spain more than 400 years ago seeking adventure but also escaping persecution for their religious beliefs: secretly, they were Jews! Chavez has masterfully woven a story of love, intrigue, and the meaning of faith into a page-turning novel that takes the reader into the home of one of Seville's prosperous merchant families in the late sixteenth century. The novel's heroine, Guiomar Péres, must fight her own inner demons while staving off the city's new Grand Inquisitor, obsessed with entrapping her into the cells of his medieval torture chambers. *The Silver Candlesticks*' characters are complex, the plot exciting, and the prose evocative of an exotic

place and time. Extremely well-researched, Chavez has marvelously transformed the historical facts of her own ancestry into fully-imagined, luminous fiction. It is a stunning accomplishment."

—Henry Louis Gates, Jr., Harvard University

"This immersive, haunting, richly detailed historical novel of the Spanish Inquisition tells the story of Guiomar, a young woman whose future is forever changed when she learns her family's dangerous secret: they are Conversos, or secret Jews, their heritage embodied in a pair of silver candlesticks. Set in 16th Century Spain, and told in Linda Chavez's steady, assured prose, *The Silver Candlesticks* is a haunting—and unforgettable—story of the secret Jews of Spain, as well as a gripping tale of love and friendship, and of how faith endures in the face of persecution."

—Susan Coll, Author of *Bookish People* and *Real Life and Other Fictions*

"What an electrifying feat to go from discovering your hidden Jewish heritage to producing a richly elaborated novel about your ancestors and their mortal fear of being exterminated for their faith. Linda Chavez has done just that in *The Silver Candlesticks*, taking us on an epic journey from the horrors of Spain's Inquisition to the aftershocks in colonial Mexico. Throughout, she evinces a razor-sharp skill for vivid storytelling."

—Marie Arana, Prizewinning Author of *American Chica, Bolívar: American Liberator,* and, most recently, *LatinoLand*

THE SILVER CANDLESTICKS

A Novel of the Spanish Inquisition

LINDA CHAVEZ

WICKED SON

A WICKED SON BOOK
An Imprint of Post Hill Press
ISBN: 979-8-88845-497-8
ISBN (eBook): 979-8-88845-498-5

The Silver Candlesticks:
A Novel of the Spanish Inquisition
© 2025 by Linda Chavez
All Rights Reserved

Cover Design by Jim Villaflores

This book is a work of fiction. People, places, events, and situations are the product of the author's imagination. Any resemblance to actual persons, living or dead, or historical events, is purely coincidental.

This book, as well as any other Wicked Son publications, may be purchased in bulk quantities at a special discounted rate. Contact orders@posthillpress.com for more information.

No part of this book may be reproduced, stored in a retrieval system, or transmitted by any means without the written permission of the author and publisher.

Post Hill Press
New York • Nashville
wickedsonbooks.com
posthillpress.com

Published in the United States of America
1 2 3 4 5 6 7 8 9 10

For my grandparents
Ambrosio Chavez de Armijo and Petra Armijo de Chavez

Table of Contents

Preface 9
Sevilla: 12 February 1481 16

PART I - 1587

Chapter One: Benita 21
Chapter Two: The Choice 28
Chapter Three: The Banquet 40
Chapter Four: The Bedchamber 53
Chapter Five: Esperanza 63
Chapter Six: Castillo San Jorge 72
Chapter Seven: The Sacraments 84

PART II - 1594

Chapter Eight: A Birth 97
Chapter Nine: A Confession 106
Chapter Ten: The Letters 117
Chapter Eleven: Alfonso 134
Chapter Twelve: The Deluge 143
Chapter Thirteen: The Easter Repast 154

PART III - JANUARY 1597

Chapter Fourteen: The Baptism 169
Chapter Fifteen: The Trap 180
Chapter Sixteen: La Giralda 191
Chapter Seventeen: A Death 203
Chapter Eighteen: A Decision 215
Chapter Nineteen: The Rumors 224

PART IV - APRIL 1597

Chapter Twenty: The Archbishop 239
Chapter Twenty-One: María Luísa 249
Chapter Twenty-Two: A Death 259
Chapter Twenty-Three: The Trap 271

PART V - AUGUST 1597

Chapter Twenty-Four: Francisco's Return 285
Chapter Twenty-Five: Barrio Santa Cruz 290
Chapter Twenty-Six: Homecoming 302
Chapter Twenty-Seven: At the Docks 314
Chapter Twenty-Eight: The Dilemma 328
Chapter Twenty-Nine: A Sudden Decision 336
Chapter Thirty: A Gift 347
Chapter Thirty-One: The Farewell Dinner 355
Chapter Thirty-Two: An Escape 363
Chapter Thirty-Three: Within Reach 370
Chapter Thirty-Four: Deliverance 377

About the Author 384

Preface

When I was a growing up, I often wondered why my grandmother Petra turned her only plaster saint to the wall on Friday nights. A statue of Niño de Atocha is a common feature in New Mexican homes, but I knew of no one else who did this. Spanish conquerors who settled the area in the late 16th Century brought the medieval *santo* with them. In a legend from 13th Century Spain, then under Muslim rule, the Christ Child visited prisoners and protected travelers, carrying a basket in one hand and holding a staff in the other. He sat on a carved chair and wore a blue velvet gown and broad-brimmed hat with a white plume in it, a distinctive image unlike other depictions of the young Jesus.

I hadn't thought about my grandmother's odd practice in many years. But I recalled it when a producer contacted me from the PBS series *Finding Your Roots*. Created and hosted by Harvard historian Henry Louis Gates Jr., the show is famous for uncovering secrets in the ancestry of his guests. "Are there any family mysteries you'd like to solve?" the young woman asked. My grandmother's odd behavior was the first thing that came to mind.

I'd been picked to round out an episode featuring three people whose backgrounds reflected the diversity of the 65 million Americans who claim Hispanic heritage. The other two were both actors: Michelle Rodriguez and Adrian Grenier. Gates chose me because he'd followed my career as a political commentator, columnist, and Reagan White House official; but also because I represented a segment of the Hispanic population who were not descendants of recent immigrants.

The Chavez branch of my family came to New Mexico in 1601 as part of the Juan de Oñate expedition that founded the territory. The Armijo branch came a hundred years later when Diego de Vargas reconquered the territory after the Pueblo Indian Revolt of 1680. It was a story I had often heard growing up. But I was soon to discover it wasn't entirely what I'd been taught to believe—a journey driven by a thirst for adventure and riches.

During the research and filming, I traveled to the Spanish city of Sevilla to meet with Gates and a film crew. I'd been there twice before but had no idea that my family had lived there for hundreds of years before embarking for the New World. What I learned there planted the seeds of this novel.

At the time, I was pursuing an MFA at George Mason University. At the age of sixty-five, after a career of writing on politics and public policy, I wanted to write fiction. I published short stories about North Korean prison camps, inspired by work I had done on a United Nations human rights commission, and intended to turn a collection of the stories into my MFA thesis. But my thesis adviser, Alan Cheuse, quickly convinced me that I should write the surprising story Gates uncovered.

The morning after I arrived, Spanish genealogist Matthew Hovius showed me numerous documents in the Archives of the Indies, including records of the family's journey to Veracruz in 1597. It was thrilling to see the four-hundred-year-old wills, estate sales, and passenger logs bound in large leather folios. But the biggest surprise came from a page in a contemporary book by Juan Gil, a Spanish historian. Listed among the secret Jews living in 16th Century Sevilla was my 10th great grandmother, Benita Orozco. Was this the clue to my grandmother's odd behavior? I was soon to find out.

An engaging storyteller, Gates in our final interview wove a fascinating tale of my family's history. Benita's daughter, Guiomar, had married a young neighbor, Francisco Armijo. This was not

THE SILVER CANDLESTICKS

unusual except that Francisco was a candle maker and she came from a wealthy family. Marriages across class lines would have been uncommon in the highly stratified Sevillian society. But Gates' researchers found more intriguing clues.

In 1597, Francisco, Guiomar, their children, and their household slaves abruptly departed for the New World. This was a period of great adventure when many Spaniards set off to strike it rich in the colonies. But most were single men, or married ones who left their families behind. As historian Rick Hendricks pointed out on air, it was rare for a wealthy family to risk the dangerous and difficult journey. Meanwhile, *Roots* researchers discovered another clue that pointed to the unusual circumstances of the family's departure.

In 1492, after defeating the Muslim rulers who had governed parts of Spain for some eight hundred years, King Ferdinand and Queen Isabela had expelled not only Muslims but also Jews who had not converted to Christianity. The Edict of Expulsion forced them to liquidate their property, often at great losses, and they were not allowed to take gold or silver with them. Doubtless many wealthier families remained and converted, but some continued to practice their religion in secret. Even a hundred years later, the law still required sworn witnesses to attest that those who left for the New World were not Jews. These witnesses were usually neighbors or business associates. But in the Armijo family's case, foreign ship captains signed their exit documents, leading Gates to speculate that perhaps they'd been paid for their testimony.

Meanwhile genealogical analysis showed that 21 percent of my DNA is shared with people of semitic origin from the Middle East, a surprisingly high percentage since my mother's family came from Ireland and Great Britain. "Linda's DNA indicates that the Orozcos were not her only Jewish ancestors," Gates explained on air, noting, "several of her lines had Jewish roots, possibly linking her even more strongly to the crypto-Jewish community in New Mexico." Indeed, the Chavez and Armijo branches of my family had intermarried for generations, and my grandparents Ambrosio Chavez and Petra Armijo were first cousins. These marriages may have been more about their secret Jewish ties than preserving wealth or the status that came with being white. As it turns out, about 6 percent of my DNA was Native American. Finally, I had some explanation as to why my grandmother Petra was turning her plaster saint to the wall. She would not display an idol on the Sabbath.

I knew when I began writing *The Silver Candlesticks* that I would have to find out as much as I could about the customs and religious practices of the converso Jews of Spain, and what it was like to live during a time of great persecution. Antisemitism has taken many forms over the centuries, but the Spanish Inquisition—which lasted from 1478–1834 in Spain, Mexico, and Peru—was the longest, most systematic, and organized instance. While there are hundreds of books about the Inquisition, fewer studies of converso Jews exist. I read some two dozen books and many more articles about the Inquisition, including transcripts of trials, descriptions of the ritual burning of Jews, known as autos-da-fé, and converso life in Spain and the New World. I drew from these sources in writing my novel. But ultimately imagination is what puts flesh and blood on the skeleton of any historical fiction.

Over the decade I spent writing it, I traveled a half dozen times to Sevilla, walking its streets and visiting the sites in the book, including many hours at the Iglesia Santa Ana in Triana, where my ancestor Benita Orozco lies buried. Castillo San Jorge, the Inquisition's local headquarters, is the gateway to the Triana neighborhood where my family lived across the Guadalquivir River from the historic center of the city. It looks much as it did five hundred years ago, a neighborhood with narrow, winding streets whose houses are hidden behind iron gates that guard elaborate tiled courtyards overflowing with flowering trees and colorful plants. I marveled at the familiarity I felt when I heard the trill of canaries coming from the gardens, a sound I'd grown up with in my grandmother's home. Petra kept canaries on her porch in the family compound near Old Town Albuquerque, where the Armijo family settled in 1701.

I also felt the pull of Judaism awakened by my research. At nineteen I had converted to marry my husband, as did my younger sister Pamela—though neither of us knew of our Jewish roots at the time.

In creating Guiomar, the novel's heroine, I decided to have her "discover" her Jewish origin in the course of the story, in much more dangerous circumstances than mine. I imagined her as a spoiled young woman born to a rich merchant family, whose world is turned upside down when she discovers that her parents are secret Jews. Reluctant at first to accept her Jewishness, the threat of persecution leads her to accept her identity and ultimately embrace her new faith.

Her husband Francisco is modeled on my ninth great-grandfather, who came from an Old Catholic family of modest means, and I created the character Esperanza (which means Hope in Spanish) from the description of a slave by that name who was part of Benita's estate when she died. Esperanza is the heart of the novel, helping teach Guiomar her dead mother's secret Jewish customs and sharing in her heartbreak at being abandoned early on by a man she loves—invented out of whole cloth—who also becomes a key character.

I've used many names of family members, but their characters are pure invention, as is the villain of the tale, Padre Diego Dominguez, inquisitor at the Castillo San Jorge. Dominguez's masochistic practice of flagellating himself with a whip in his private quarters has deep roots in Spanish Catholicism and many Spaniards brought the practice with them to northern New Mexico. Even today, a small religious fraternity known as *Hermanos Penitentes* make an Easter pilgrimage to Santuario de Chimayo, north of Santa Fe, carrying crosses and whipping their backs along the dirt road. Inside the small adobe church sits the familiar Niño de Atocha perched above an open pit of dirt, which pilgrims believe cures diseases and makes the lame walk again. (A pile of discarded crutches lies against one wall in the church.) Though Petra turned her *santo* to the wall each Friday evening, she also kept a small burlap pouch with the miraculous dirt at her bedside, apparently hedging her bets.

Writing *The Silver Candlesticks* inspired me to continue pursuing my family's history. Among Guiomar's and Francisco's descendants were adventurers, merchants, bootleggers, and gamblers, including the last Mexican governor of New Mexico, Manuel Armijo—the man responsible for losing one-third of Mexico to the United States in the Mexican-American War (1846–1848). Their stories deserve telling. I hope to pick up the Armijo family's journey when their descendants leave Zacatecas, Mexico, in 1698 for Santa Fe, New Mexico, to help recapture the settlement after the Indian Pueblo revolt drove out most of the Spaniards. What happened along the way? Did the first Armijo in the New Mexican territory carry with him the Jewish traditions of his great grandmother Guiomar? And did he find others already there who had established their own crypto-Jewish communities? I'm anxious to find out and I hope readers will be, too.

My agent, Josh Getzler, helped shape the story and its characters during early drafts. My editor, Adam Bellow, took great care refining the prose, catching mistakes, and improving the novel's pacing, while Ashlyn Inman did a wonderful job copy editing the final draft and Aleigha Koss saw the project through to publication. But the novel might never have been written had my teacher and mentor, the late Alan Cheuse, not encouraged me to take it on, while my husband, Chris Gersten, patiently endured the hours spent at the computer. I owe each my thanks.

Note on Spanish Names

I have chosen to use Spanish spelling for place names throughout and to sprinkle a few Spanish words and phrases in descriptions and dialogue for their lyrical quality. Most, I hope, will be clear from the context. I have also chosen to follow the Spanish naming conventions, which consists of two surnames. Men and women

THE SILVER CANDLESTICKS

both take their primary surname from their father's and their secondary one from their mother's paternal surname. When women marry, however, they retain their paternal surname followed by their husband's name, often preceded by the preposition *de* (of) or the conjunction *y* (and). When Guiomar Péres marries Francisco Armijo, she becomes Guiomar Péres de Armijo on legal documents and in formal situations or to distinguish her from another married woman with the same paternal surname. But in everyday parlance she remains Señora Péres, while her children are Antonio and Ursula Armijo Peres. To make matters more confusing, the honorifics *Don* and *Doña* are used along with the person's given name to designate respect, status, or advanced age, thus Guiomar's parents are Don Pedro and Doña Benita. I have tried to lessen the complications by using given names as much as possible.

Sevilla

12 February 1481

Juana weaved through the crowds storming the Plaza San Francisco, hoping she could remain on the fringes. The young woman had become separated from her husband outside the silversmith's shop. She clutched the candlesticks to her breast as the angry Christians surrounding her shouted at the secret Jews.

"The gates of hell await!"

"Burn them!"

"Repent and accept Christ before it is too late!"

The screams were deafening. She wanted to cover her ears, but her hands weren't free. She wished she had given the heavy candlesticks to her husband Ambrosio to carry.

Juana leaned back against the wall of a shop as the procession passed in front of her. First the bishop, his gold staff glistening in the noonday sun. Then the inquisitor, two dozen priests, and a handful of city officials. At the end of the line of dignitaries, the tall, hooded executioner led the yellow-robed prisoners by a long rope that bound them together.

The crazed crowd fell in behind, shoving Juana along through the narrow streets of Sevilla to the walls encircling the city. At the Torre del Oro on the banks of the Guadalquivir, the stampede halted. Bodies crammed against her until Juana thought she would suffocate. A bony hand grabbed at her elbow, the long nails digging into her flesh. She twisted her torso to see whose hand it was, but a large man with a protruding stomach forced the fingers to release their grip as he trampled the person underfoot.

Slowly, those nearest the gate squeezed through the stone archway and Juana was again driven forward until she too emerged on the other side. Before her stood a large wooden platform erected along the banks of the river on a stack of tree trunks stripped of bark. She stared up in horror at the six men and six women, bound to tall stakes by thick ropes that barely concealed their emaciated, near-naked bodies. She shut her eyes tight but could not block out the voice of Inquisitor Alfonso de Hojeda shouting from the platform.

"Sevillanos, have I not warned you of the corruption in your midst? They who would defile the image of the Savior, are they not the sons and daughters of those who crucified Him?"

She opened her eyes as the inquisitor paced the length of the platform, his black and white robes fluttering in the wind. Behind him, the white-haired priest of Iglesia de Santa Ana approached the first prisoner. Juana strained to hear his words, but they were lost in the roars of the crowd. The old priest stopped before each man and woman, leaning into them, his hands folded in prayer. The executioner, whose face remained hidden under his black hood, followed behind. In his fist, the man carried a stick attached to a short cord. His immense hands reminded Juana of the butcher from whom she purchased meat.

"Do you see, my friends? We offer mercy to the Judaizers," the inquisitor bellowed from the edge of the platform. "If they would but reconcile themselves to the Church, the executioner's garrote would spare them the pain of being burned alive. But they refuse."

"Let them burn!" screamed the woman next to Juana.

"You're not so high and mighty now!" yelled a man.

Someone behind Juana threw a stone toward the platform, nearly hitting her instead. She desperately wanted to run, but the press of bodies prohibited her escape. Her eyes now fixed on the stage.

"Stand back," the executioner shouted, the garrote replaced by a torch. Screams went up from those closest to the platform. Juana felt herself falling backwards, as if pushed by a gigantic wave propelling the whole of humanity. But with the crowd packed so tightly together, she remained upright.

When she looked up again, the twigs and branches piled around the prisoners' legs had begun to burn, first the outer edges progressing inward until the flames caught the prisoners' rags. The sky filled with blackened smoke and the air with shrieks of agony from the condemned. The flames reached higher, whipped by the wind. Still, she could not turn her eyes away until the smoke blinded her and the stench of burning flesh made her gag.

"Move back, move back, for the love of God," screamed those closest to the platform as the heat scorched their faces. Again, she struggled to get away but was hemmed in by those who wanted to stay until the last cries were silenced by the smoke and flames.

In a matter of minutes, the intensity of the heat drove the crowd to disperse, their raucous shouts replaced by eerie quiet as the chill February wind carried clouds of smoke and greasy soot across the river. Juana pulled her shawl tightly over her breast to better conceal the silver candlesticks and retreated across the wooden bridge to Triana.

There she would live for the next fifty years, every day expecting the brutal knock upon her door that never came.

Part I

1587

Chapter One

BENITA

Benita lay on her bed, a black velvet robe wrapped tightly around her despite the stifling midday heat that filtered through the curtained windows. Her skin's feverish glow made her face, heart-shaped with black eyes and aquiline nose, appear younger than her forty-nine years. A black girl, hovering next to the bed, flicked a lace fan back and forth over her mistress, whose eyelids fluttered as the air touched them.

"Bring me the wood box from the cabinet in the hall, Esperanza," Benita said, lifting her body off the pillows. "And ask Guiomar to come in. Quickly, child." The words brought on a fit of coughing so violent it shook the posts of the heavy carved bed.

Esperanza stopped in the doorway, unsure whether to return to her mistress's side or comply with her orders.

"Didn't you hear me? Bring the box. Now." Benita raised her voice as best she could before another paroxysm overcame her.

Esperanza returned with the dark mahogany box, placing it next to her mistress on the bed. The woman's wheezing sounded as loud as the bellows the girls used on the fire in the *cocina*. It had become much worse in recent days, and Esperanza feared her mistress's end was near.

"Well, what are you waiting for? Bring Guiomar," Benita said, her voice raspy. After the girl closed the door, Benita took the key she wore on a long chain around her neck and inserted it in the metal lock. She lifted the lid. Inside were two silver candlesticks wrapped in a lace mantilla the color of old ivory. Her mother, Inés, had given her the candlesticks before her marriage to Pedro Péres de Fonseca. They had been in the Orozco family for generations, passed on from mother to eldest daughter in an unbroken chain that linked her to all the generations of their sojourn in *Sefarad*. As a small child, Benita had watched her mother lighting the candles on Friday evenings, strange-sounding words coming from her lips, "*Barukh Attah Adonai, Elohaynu, Melech Ha'olam…*" And when Benita was older, her mother taught her to do the same, covering her hair with the lace mantilla, holding her palms in front of her face as she intoned the ancient prayer.

But she had not followed in her mother's path after her marriage to Pedro, who took no interest in such rituals although he was a secret Jew too. Sometimes she mouthed the words silently when the family dined alone on Friday evenings, but never with guests at the table. She trusted no one—not even those she suspected might also practice her ancestors' faith.

A century had passed since the Holy Office of the Inquisition had set up its tribunals in Sevilla. Benita's great-grandmother, Juana Gonzales, had been present at the first auto-da-fé in 1481, along with most of the conversos of Sevilla, who feared their absence might raise suspicion. Juana had been only eighteen and newly married when she watched in terror as the blaze consumed the six men and six women accused of Judaizing. When she'd returned home, she ordered all the fireplaces tiled shut so that she'd never again witness tongues of fire lapping the air or feel the scorch of their heat on her skin.

As a result, all the Orozco women who followed were obsessed with keeping warm. Juana's daughter Catalina complained of chills her whole life. And though Benita never heard the story of her great-grandmother's ordeal, she remembered her own mother drawing her chair so close to the fireplace she feared her skirts would catch fire. "Be careful, Mamá," Benita would warn. But now

THE SILVER CANDLESTICKS

she too drew close to the flames in winter and wrapped herself in shawls even in the heat of summer.

With the last Jews expelled a century earlier, their books burned, their synagogues destroyed or converted to churches, few of the descendants of those who remained remembered enough of their religion to practice it. But the Inquisition continued; though in her lifetime, Benita had heard of more adulterers and sodomites than Jews imprisoned in the Castillo. So it came as a surprise when she learned that the Dominican from Llerena who'd recently taken charge of it was filling the cells with Jews.

Surely her family was safe, she thought. Wasn't that why their only son had become a priest? But of course, one could never be sure.

As she waited for Guiomar, she anguished over what she was about to do. Her husband had forbidden her from teaching their daughter the rituals of their faith. Before leaving on his latest trade mission, he reminded her of the risk: "We are only a stone's throw from the Castillo. Do you want her to end up there? No. Forget these superstitions. The best thing is to marry her to the Armijo boy, Francisco. They're pious Catholics and hardworking. Her dowry will provide a good life for them. And she will never have to fear the Inquisition."

Benita didn't want to disobey Pedro, but what else could she do? Her time on earth was short. She'd begun to cough up blood and had grown so weak she spent most of her days in bed. She'd already waited too long. She could wait no longer.

Guiomar entered the room with her usual exuberance, pushing the heavy oak door open, which caused a gust of air to rustle the closed curtains at the large window across the room.

"Mamá, how are you feeling today?"

"Better, *m'hija*. But what's the occasion?" Delicate and long-limbed, with thick black curls surrounding her oval face, Guiomar wore a dress of red and black taffeta that shimmered as she moved. The design accentuated her tiny waist and full bosom, but Benita worried the girl's beauty was a curse as much as a blessing.

"I've been invited to dine with María Dolores this afternoon," she said, as she walked toward the tall window. "May I let in some light?" she asked, pulling back the thick burgundy velvet.

"Leave the curtains shut, please. I have something I need to discuss with you."

Benita stared into her daughter's eyes, hazel like her father's but fringed with long, dark lashes. She knew that the visit to María Dolores was merely an excuse to spend time with the Herreras' youngest son, José Marcos. The boy was handsome but careless, and Benita feared he would break Guiomar's heart. In any case, the match was impossible, as she must now explain.

"Come sit next to me, dearest," she said.

Guiomar sat on the edge of the bed, her full lips pressed together tightly. "Please, Mamá, don't talk to me of José Marcos. I know you and Papá are opposed to the match. But I love him."

"You think I don't remember what it's like to be in love?" Benita asked. "But we aren't always free to do what we want. Maybe you'll understand better when I explain this," she said, laying the lace-wrapped candlesticks gently in Guiomar's lap.

Guiomar looked down with confusion. "What is this?"

Benita pulled back the ivory-colored mantilla that covered the candlesticks. "My most precious gift, Guiomar. Worth more than everything else you will inherit when I die," she said. "My mother gave them to me, as did my grandmother to her. They go back generations."

Guiomar frowned at the heavy candlesticks in her lap. Her mother had many sets of candlesticks: gold from Peru, blue and white porcelain from China, silver from Zacatecas, all of them more delicate and valuable than these.

"They're lovely, but…"

Benita stroked her daughter's hair. "Didn't you ever wonder, Guiomar, why we only serve pork when we have guests? Or why we use olive oil for cooking, never pig fat?"

Guiomar put up her hand. "If you're about to tell me what I think, I don't want to know. You'll ruin my life." She shoved the

THE SILVER CANDLESTICKS

candlesticks off her lap onto the bed as if the metal were burning her flesh. "Does Papá know?"

Benita took her daughter's hand. "It's what drew us together, dearest." She hesitated. How could she explain? Perhaps it was too much at one time. And what she had to say next would be even more difficult. She took in a breath and let it out slowly.

"When possible, we marry only within our own people. But even that has become too dangerous."

"I don't understand."

"The Holy Office compiles lists of New Catholics, and when the families of both a bride and groom appear on the list, they're assumed to be secret Jews."

"Surely you aren't suggesting…"

"No," Benita shook her head. "I doubt they're Jews."

"So what's the problem? He'll accept me no matter what. We're in *love*, Mamá. Besides, his family aren't especially devout."

"Precisely. I know it may not make sense to you, but it's because the Herreras are so lax that we cannot permit a marriage to go forward." She squeezed her daughter's hand, which lay limp in her lap. "If one of them were accused of blasphemy at some point, or even adultery, the Holy Office could launch an investigation and who knows where it would end. Our family can't afford that kind of scrutiny."

"So now you're going to sacrifice my happiness out of fear that one of the Herreras might fail to genuflect at the proper time and bring the Inquisition down on our heads?" Guiomar's voice rose. She stood up and paced the room, arms folded tightly across her chest.

"Sit down, Guiomar." Benita lifted her torso with some struggle and made room for her daughter near the head of the bed.

Guiomar hesitated, her body rigid beneath the soft taffeta. Slowly, she lowered herself next to her mother, picking up the candlesticks and placing them on a small table nearby.

Benita stared into her daughter's eyes, which had begun to fill with tears. She wished that her husband were with them. He had a way of pacifying Guiomar, even when her strong will made it impossible to reason with her. He would put his arms around her and kiss her cheek until tears replaced anger, and then gently wipe them away. He had done the same with Benita in the early years of their marriage, pulling her toward him in bed when her crying awakened him, gently stroking her face with the back of his hand until the tears stopped.

"I am not a Jew. You cannot force me to accept this burden."

"I can't force it," her mother agreed. "But you can't run away from it either. If the Dominicans come looking, they won't care that you didn't choose your family. And what will you do? Betray your father? Your brother? I'll be long dead, but they could still burn me in effigy."

"Stop it, Mamá. Please, I beg you. No one is going to betray anyone. This is just your fever talking," she said, leaning over to wipe her mother's brow.

"Do you think when God chooses you, you can turn your back on Him? You violate a holy covenant…" Benita's words were barely audible.

"He did not choose me."

"You're wrong, Guiomar," she said, reaching to grab her daughter's hand. "We have lost many words of the Torah, but not these: *It was not with our fathers that the Lord made this covenant, but with us, the living, every one of us who is here today.*"

Guiomar sat dumbstruck as she listened. Had she missed the signs? She remembered her mother refusing a slice of pork once; she wouldn't have recalled it but for the clever remark her mother made. *A woman must be careful what she eats, or she'll end up resembling the source.* Maybe there were other hints she hadn't fully recognized. Her mother worried over everything, even good fortune, as if too much happiness would somehow court disaster.

"There's more I must tell you," Benita said.

Guiomar stiffened.

"Your father has chosen a husband for you," she said bluntly. "Our neighbor's son, Francisco."

THE SILVER CANDLESTICKS

Guiomar leaped to her feet. "How could you, Mamá? A candle maker's son? He stinks of tallow. I will never agree to it," she shouted, stomping her shoe on the thick carpet, which muffled the sound.

Benita began to cough. She pulled a handkerchief from her bodice; it was already stained with dried blood.

"Mother of God," Guiomar screamed when she saw the crimson sputum on her mother's lips. She grabbed her mother's hand, which was cold and clammy even though the room was stiflingly warm.

"I don't have much time left. We must begin now if I'm to teach you what I know." Benita wiped her lips and stuffed the cloth in her bosom again.

"Enough, Mamá. I won't hear another word." Tears streamed down her face. In a matter of moments, the happy life she had envisioned had come crashing to an end. She was now a prisoner of a faith she didn't understand or want. She stood abruptly, turning her back on her mother, and walked out the door.

Benita picked up the lace mantilla and covered her head, placing her hands over her face, softly muttering the words her own mother had taught her. She prayed there would be time enough to teach them to her daughter.

Baruch Attah Adonai Eloheinu
Melech Ha'olam Asher
Kideshanu Bemitzvotav
Vetzivanu Lehadlik Ner Shel
Shabbat

Chapter Two

THE CHOICE

The large courtyard appeared deserted in the mid-afternoon sun as everyone, even the servants, rested from the unseasonable heat. In the middle, an orange tree blossomed, its heavy fragrance mixing with the pungent scent of the animals in their stalls at the back of the property.

At the west side of the house, Guiomar emerged from a doorway on the second-floor portico and slipped down the stairs into the courtyard. As she started across the yard, the door to the *cocina* opened and Esperanza appeared, carrying a large wooden bucket. Guiomar hid behind one of the pillars and watched Esperanza attach the bucket to a rope and lower it into the well, then pull it up again, splashing water on her ebony arms. The slave's broad shoulders seemed incongruous with the delicacy of her long, slender neck and small oval face. Guiomar waited until Esperanza had returned to the *cocina*, then she slipped out the iron gate into the empty street, making sure the metal latch didn't clang.

Cautiously, she pulled the corner of her black lace mantilla across the lower part of her face. It was unusual for a woman to walk the streets alone, especially a rich one. Her striped taffeta skirt dragged along the cobblestones as she quickly made her way through the narrow alleyways along Calle Santa Catalina. She wished she'd changed before sneaking out, but there was no time after the confrontation with her mother, whose words echoed in

THE SILVER CANDLESTICKS

her head as she made her way to Santa Ana's. José Marcos would be waiting near the Virgin's statue.

Refusing a mother's last request was no trivial matter. But once away from the sight of her fevered face, the sound of her strained wheezing, the shock of the blood-stained handkerchief, Guiomar's resignation turned to anger. *Your father has already chosen a husband for you....* And all to carry on customs and beliefs she'd only learned of that day. No, she thought. She wouldn't accept her parents' decision as easily as they imagined.

The acrid smoke from the nearby pottery works stung her nostrils and tears welled in her eyes. Not even the oleander from the courtyards could mask the stench that permeated Triana, smoke billowing from its tile and pottery factories. A gitano plucked his guitar from one of the houses as she turned the corner of Calle de la Pureza, staying in the shadow of the stone wall. She glanced back over her shoulder. It wasn't beyond Esperanza to follow her and report back to her mother.

Guiomar clenched her jaw. She'd been jealous of Esperanza since childhood when her father bought the young slave—the same age as her—as a gift for her mother. But she shook the emotion away. She had no time for such distractions. Her father's ship was due in at any moment, and Guiomar had been hopeful that she could persuade him to accept José Marcos. Now the hurdle was much higher.

The sun beat down and she slowed her pace. She didn't want to arrive at the church wilted from the heat. She pulled a lace fan from her skirt pocket and stopped in front of a wrought iron gate. Inside the courtyard, caged canaries trilled their melody. She listened, flicking the fan with her wrist as she tried to compose what she would say to her beloved. She felt suddenly ashamed. How could she tell him her family were Jews? She fanned herself more furiously, but she could feel her cheeks burn. Would he love her less? And could she trust him? She knew he sometimes drank recklessly. What if he were to reveal her secret in such a moment, even unwittingly? She risked not only her own life but her parents' and brother's.

She snapped the fan shut and began walking again but bumped against the wall after a few steps. A layer of fine, grey dust settled on her dress and she brushed it away. She was letting her fears overcome her resolve. She should pay more attention to her own carelessness, which, she reminded herself, could betray her just as easily. She must put aside her doubts. If she couldn't trust José Marcos with her secret, why would she want to marry him?

She stopped short of the plaza in front of the church, its single tower rising high above the district's ochre walls and red-tiled roofs. Her family had lived within a short walk of Santa Ana's since the church was built in 1276, when her seventh great-grandfather on her father's side had fought beside Fernando III to rescue Sevilla from the Moors. It was one of the oldest churches in the city, and unlike the much grander cathedral across the river with its towering Giralda, Santa Ana's had never served as a mosque.

Still, the architecture was in the Moorish style, as was much of Sevilla, for the Moors had occupied the territory for over half a millennium. Guiomar had been baptized in the church's font, *La Pila de los Gitanos*, as had her mother and grandmother before her—something she had taken for granted until that morning. Now, as she looked across the empty sunbaked plaza, she wondered how they had managed to fool not only strangers but their own daughter as they knelt before the saints in apparent devotion.

She quickened her pace across the plaza until she stood before the brass door of the church. She pinched her cheeks to bring color to her pale skin. Pulling on the iron handle with both hands, the door opened, and she slipped inside. It was cool and dark except for the sanctuary lamp before the main altar and the red glow of votive candles in the smaller side alcoves. The smell of melting tallow reminded her of the candle maker's son she would be forced to marry if she couldn't come up with a plan. She crossed herself as she caught sight of José Marcos kneeling before the Virgin, his wavy, fair hair falling loosely to his white collar.

"My dearest, you look as if you've been crying," José Marcos whispered as he stood to face her, the sharp features of his handsome face set off by a short blond beard that followed the line of his prominent chin.

She looked about. They were entirely alone, and she hoped it would stay that way until she could explain what had happened. "It's my mother," she said, averting her eyes.

"Has she taken a turn for the worse?"

"No…well, yes, but it's not that."

"What then? Tell me."

She blurted out a reply before she had time to reconsider: "They want me to marry Francisco Armijo. My father has already arranged everything." She reached out to grab the rail in front of the Virgin, unsteady on her feet. José Marcos put his hand around her waist and guided her to one of the pews. She sat down, gathering her full skirts to make room for him beside her. The sound of rustling taffeta echoed through the cavernous silence. She waited for him to speak, but he said nothing. Only took her hand in his, squeezing gently.

After a long moment, he twisted in his seat to face her. "I know they don't approve of me—but why that one? He's beneath you. It will make a scandal."

"Surely you don't think…" she couldn't finish the words.

"It's not what *I* think but what others will suspect. You've been childhood friends—" He loosened his grip on her hand, searching her face for signs of deception.

"As God is my witness, no man has laid a hand on me. How can you imagine such a thing?" She pulled away. She'd never let José Marcos violate her chastity, even though he often pressed her for more than the few passionate kisses he could steal in rare moments when they were alone.

"Forgive me, Guiomar. It's just that I am stunned by this news. Is there nothing we can do to dissuade them?"

She hesitated before speaking further. His reaction was not what she had anticipated. She wanted reassurance, but he seemed instead to question her virtue. "Nothing," she said.

They sat awkwardly, side-by-side, staring up at the gilded altar piece. Finally, she broke the silence. "Perhaps there is something we could do."

José Marcos turned towards her, closely studying her face. "What do you mean?"

Her hands trembled as she reached into her pocket searching for her kerchief. "We could run away," she whispered.

José Marcos looked at her incredulously. "Where to? And with what? Without your dowry, we wouldn't have anything to live on. I'm the younger son. I have nothing to offer you."

Again, he disappointed her. Her tears flowed freely now. She wanted to run from the church, but she had no place to go except home. Her body crumpled, and José Marcos reached out to comfort her.

"Don't cry, my sweet," he said. "We'll figure out a way. Perhaps the best thing is for me to talk directly to your father. Is he back yet?"

"He's expected today. The other ships from the Antilles have arrived at the port. His is the last." For a moment, she let herself believe that José Marcos could indeed convince her father. After all, he wasn't the one who'd insisted on retaining the rituals that put them all at risk. It was her mother's doing, provoked by fear of her impending death. But Guiomar had often been able to convince her father to side with her. Perhaps it wasn't too late to do so again.

She rested against José Marcos's shoulder and glanced back up at the altar. The magnificent hanging sanctuary lamp of silver and gold, brought back from the New World, cast shadows on the rich retablo. She could barely make out the statues that stood in the golden alcove, the Virgin and Child with Santa Ana, their red brocaded robes almost black in the dim light.

How many times had she knelt here, whispering prayers that her parents' hearts might open to her love for José Marcos? Yet her prayers had gone unanswered. Her mother's earlier condemnation of worshipping false idols crept into her thoughts like worms eating their way through her skull. She pressed her hands against the slick taffeta, rubbing it as though she might find an answer in its folds. The words stuck in her throat, but she knew her only hope was to tell José Marcos everything and pray he would agree to her plan.

She slowly began to unfold the scene in her mother's bedroom from earlier that day. José Marcos clenched his jaw when she mentioned that her mother had given her a pair of candlesticks that had been used in their family for generations for the Friday meal. His eyes moved down her face, examining every feature. She felt the tiny hairs on her arms rise in response to his cold appraisal. Was he searching for clues to her Jewish blood—in her eyes, her lips, the bridge of her nose? She was about to describe her mother's prayer in a tongue she had never heard but stopped short.

"Is there more?" he asked. He pulled back ever so slightly.

She wanted to reach out and plead with him again to take her away, but she feared his answer. He buried his head in his hands. She waited for him to speak, this man who had never been at a loss for words, who had wooed her with poetry and romances, made her blush when he recited lyrics comparing her breasts to pomegranates, her body to a graceful cypress. His silence chilled her. Her lips moved, mutely intoning the prayer that had always brought her peace, *Ave Maria, gratia plena....* But now, she felt nothing.

"This is more serious than I feared, my love." His words startled her. He turned toward her again, his brows knitted. "Even if we were able to sneak away, we'd always be on the run, not just from your father but from the Holy Office." As he spoke the words, their meaning settled deep in her brain.

Guiomar was suddenly afraid, knowing she'd need to somehow undo the damage she'd done by hinting at her family's secret. She had expected José Marcos to embrace her and promise to protect her. Instead, he had grown distant and suspicious.

"You misunderstand. My family is innocent. They are good Catholics," she said, looking directly into his eyes. "They have done nothing to warrant an accusation that they hold to their family's old faith," she lied. "But all New Catholics are suspect once again with this new Inquisitor in charge. My parents believe that my marriage into a devout Old Catholic family is important for my safety."

"But why did she keep the candlesticks?"

Guiomar could feel her pulse quicken, but kept her eyes steady. "They've been in my family for generations. There's nothing unholy about a lump of silver. They've never been used by my family for any religious purpose, nor do I plan to start using them in that way."

He reached out to stroke her face, grazing her moist lips with his fingertips. *What is he thinking?* she wondered, watching worry transform his face.

"Perhaps there's a way," he said, finally breaking the silence. "No one could track us to the New World," he paused, "if we had the means to get there."

So he did love her after all. But it wouldn't be as easy as he imagined.

"How can we get permission to leave Spain? My father's connections at the House of Trade would surely expose us if we tried. And who would vouch for us?"

"Silence can be bought. As can testimony that will allow us both to travel."

"Bought with what?" She studied his face. He reached down to the pearl pendant around her neck, nearly as large as a grape.

"My father has been very generous with me." She reached up to touch his hand as he rubbed the pearl between his thumb and fingers. She shuddered slightly, his touch arousing desires she knew to be sinful. He said nothing as she held her breath once again. She would miss the life she'd known—her family's status, the jewels, the beautiful dresses, even the servants—except for her rival, Esperanza. But it was the only way to buy her freedom. "We could sell my jewels," she said, finally.

"I know a Jew…"

She winced.

THE SILVER CANDLESTICKS

"Forgive me, I meant nothing by it. I only meant to say that in the Old Jewish Quarter I know someone willing to give money on collateral without asking questions."

So it was true, what her parents had said, that José Marcos was a gambler and had debts he couldn't pay. She felt queasiness in the pit of her stomach, but she couldn't pull back now. His eyes were downcast, whether from embarrassment or hesitance to go through with the plan, she wasn't sure.

"We'll have to bribe our way at every step," he said, looking again into her face. "We'll need more than this," he touched the hollow of her throat where the pearl nestled. "And these," he tapped the small diamonds that hung from her earlobes. "Once we embark on this journey, I'll be in as much danger from the Holy Office as you, my dear."

His words stung sharply. She started to stand, but his hands pulled her towards him for a passionate kiss. She clung to him, wishing to stay in his embrace forever, sheltered, protected from her fate. But the loud creak of the sacristy door surprised her.

The old priest padded softly across the marble floor, stooping like a hunchback. He seemed not to see them in the darkened nave. Guiomar slid along the pew until she was at some distance from José Marcos, who was now kneeling, head bent in prayer. She wished she could hear his pleas, whether he sought guidance to aid them in their flight or deliverance from the destiny her blood imposed. Then he stood abruptly and stepped into the side aisle, drawing the priest's attention.

"My son, you startled me," the old man said. "Do you wish to confess?"

"No, Padre, my sins are too long to enumerate and would keep you from your task."

"I see." The priest nodded as his gaze shifted to Guiomar. She burned with shame.

José Marcos's boots echoed loudly in the empty church as he made his way towards the door. He looked straight ahead, never glancing back at Guiomar, who followed his movements with her eyes despite the priest. She bent her head, but not in prayer, pushing her knuckles hard into her forehead to drive away the frantic thoughts that raced through her mind.

Don Pedro returned home while Guiomar was out. He'd sent word that he was coming, but Guiomar had already slipped away. His was the largest ship in the fleet, which had arrived that morning after a three-day journey up the Guadalquivir from Cádiz, the gateway from the Atlantic to Sevilla, Europe's busiest port. He'd spent hours supervising the transport of the gold and silver he'd brought back from the Americas to the *Real Casa de Moneda* where it would be minted into the doubloons that financed Europe's economies. The servants waited in the hall patiently, forming two lines to greet their master. Miguel, who was as strong as a bull, held his head high as he balanced a silver goblet of wine in the palm of his hand. The younger male servant held a large bowl of fruit to his chest, and the three females bore dishes of figs, nuts, and flowers. Esperanza stood at the end of the line, holding a bouquet of lilies in front of her face to conceal the worry she felt over Guiomar's absence.

Pedro opened the door, his large, imposing frame blocking out the sunlight. He stood in the doorway, his hands on his hips and a broad grin on his sunburned face. But when he did not see his wife or daughter, his smile quickly disappeared. Esperanza stepped into the middle of the hall as the others stood stiffly at their stations. He could tell by the frown on her dark, comely face that something was wrong. He strode towards her, waving away Miguel, who thrust the goblet toward him, and nodding silently to the others.

"Has something happened to the Señora? Where's my daughter?" he asked, his deep voice unsteady.

Esperanza bowed her head, trying to hide her tears. "Doña Benita has taken to her bed. She's too weak to greet you."

Don Pedro rushed towards his wife's bedchamber, which had been moved to the ground floor before his departure to save her from climbing the stairs. The girl followed quickly behind him as the others shook their heads sadly and retreated to the *cocina* with their welcoming gifts. There would be no celebrations in the Péres household that evening.

After returning from the church, Guiomar had spent most of the evening in her mother's room alongside her father. Pedro had tried to cheer his wife with tales of his adventures, but with her husband now safely home, Benita soon drifted off into a deep sleep. When Guiomar finally retreated to her room, she tossed in her bed, endlessly replaying in her mind the conversation with José Marcos. No matter how many times she tried to recall his words, the expression on his face, the timbre of his voice, she couldn't be sure her memory served her well. One moment she was sure he would save her, and the next she was convinced he would abandon her. She imagined what she would say to him the next time they spoke, then gripped the bedcovers in terror that they would never speak again. The murmur of doves outside her window finally lulled her to sleep just before dawn.

In the mid-morning, noise from the hall awakened her as the household came alive. Guiomar threw open the windows to let in fresh air. The faint sound of bells from Santa Ana struck the half hour. She hoped the day would bring word from José Marcos that he would run away with her. But even as these thoughts occurred, she felt pangs of guilt imagining the pain it would cause her parents.

Guiomar spent the morning unpacking the huge wooden crates the sailors had carried from Don Pedro's ship. Inside were bolts of white cotton and linen and colored silk in saffron, crimson, green, and several shades of blue from the azure of the morning sky to the indigo of evening. The seamstresses in Santa Cruz would turn the cloth into garments in the latest style for Guiomar and the farthingales worn by her mother. The servants stocked the larders under the house with salted meats, fish, and yams, as well as dried maize, which they would later grind into coarse flour. Spices—cinnamon, cloves, coriander, mace, nutmeg, and ginger—filled the house with their aromas.

Guiomar had picked up a bolt of emerald silk and was holding it up to her face before the gilt mirror when Pedro came out of Benita's room. His demeanor had changed from the previous evening. He smiled, running his fingers through his disheveled hair. Then he thrust his hand into the pocket of his breeches to pull out a small leather pouch.

"Good morning, Papá," Guiomar said, dropping the bolt of silk back into the wooden cart with the others. "How is Mamá?"

Without answering, he gathered her in his arms and lifted her off her feet.

"I didn't give you a proper greeting last evening, my child. I was too concerned about your mother. But her fever seems to have abated, and she's anxious to get dressed this morning," he said, his hands still on Guiomar's shoulders.

"Do you think that's wise?"

"I've warned her she must proceed cautiously. But you know your mother. She's intent on supervising the preparations for the banquet in two days."

"But I can easily take over those tasks, Papá. She really must rest if she is to regain her health."

"The best help you can provide is to be by her side to observe when she is getting tired. Esperanza, too, will keep watch." Her father watched the expression on Guiomar's face change at the mention of Esperanza's name. His daughter couldn't hide her jealousy of the slave, and it troubled him. He took her hands in his. "I have something for you. It will go nicely with that silk you were just admiring, which brings out the green in your lovely eyes," he said, handing her the small pouch.

She untied the thin leather that secured it and pulled out a square emerald ring the size of man's thumbnail. It was set in a thick gold bezel that tapered down to a thin band with intricate carvings. The stone felt as heavy as the lead pellets her father used in his musket when he went hunting bear. She kissed him and danced around like a child. "Papá, it is the most beautiful ring I've ever seen." What she did not say was that she felt her prayers to the Virgin had been answered. This ring alone might pay for her passage to the New World with José Marcos.

Doña Benita appeared, Esperanza at her side. She looked frail, clinging to the servant's arm to steady herself, her dark hair with its few streaks of silver falling loosely over the shawl she held closely to her chest. Pedro rushed to her. "Benita, my dear, let me take you to the *sala* where you can rest and still oversee everything for yourself," he said, picking her up in his arms.

She rested her head against his broad shoulder as he carried her to the large chair in the corner of the room, from which she could observe the servants unpacking the crates and her daughter looking far happier than she had the day before. For that one moment, at least, Benita could put aside her worries and enjoy the company of her husband and daughter, the family safe and together, if only for a while longer.

Chapter Three

THE BANQUET

Guiomar stood near her bedroom window examining the brilliant emerald ring on her finger, but her heart felt heavier than the gem. It had been three days and she still hadn't heard from José Marcos. She closed her fingers tightly around the ring until the edges of the stone dug into her flesh, replacing one pain with another. She'd do whatever was necessary to escape, even if it meant sneaking into her mother's room to secure more jewels. She wondered how much the candlesticks her mother had shown her would fetch in Santa Cruz. At least in Marranos' hands—the secret Jews—they would have some meaning. For her, they represented only a symbol of her burden.

A knock on her door interrupted Guiomar's thoughts. She slipped the ring into her bodice and opened the door. Esperanza stood in the hallway, her head bowed.

"Yes, what is it?" Guiomar spoke sharply, annoyed that the servant would not look at her.

"I'm sorry to disturb you, but a boy from the Herrera family asked that I deliver this."

Guiomar grabbed at the note in Esperanza's hand. "Give it to me," she said.

"I would have brought it earlier, but I couldn't get away from the kitchen—or your mother's watchful eyes," Esperanza said. She turned to go, but stopped, looking over her shoulder at Guiomar.

THE SILVER CANDLESTICKS

"Your mother asked me to follow you if you left the house the day your father returned, but I didn't. I know what it is to love someone when it is forbidden."

Esperanza's words shocked Guiomar. She reached out and turned the servant toward her. She stared into Esperanza's black eyes, puzzled. For the first time, she didn't feel the pangs of jealousy she'd experienced since childhood. Perhaps the servant wasn't her enemy after all. "I am indebted to you," Guiomar said. The girl bowed her head and turned to leave, closing the door softly behind her.

Guiomar clutched the letter to her breast, afraid to open it as she walked to the edge of her bed. She sat down, placing the letter in her lap. She turned over the folded paper with its red seal to examine it. José Marcos had not marked the wax in any way, which seemed wise in case the letter went astray. She breathed deeply as she slipped her finger between the folded page and slid it along the edge. She paused a moment, hoping the letter would answer her prayers and mark the beginning of a new life. She could barely focus her eyes on the dark ink in José Marcos's familiar, elegant hand. The message was short, which she took as a good sign.

> *You will be forever in my heart and prayers, but I cannot do as you ask.*

There was no signature. Nothing else. Only the one sentence. Her tears fell on the paper, hot and copious, blurring the ink so that the message was barely decipherable. She felt her heart constrict as if it would shrivel into a black and bitter pit beneath her breast. She'd betrayed her mother's trust—only moments earlier she'd contemplated the theft of her jewels—for the love of a man who feared to face her in person or even sign his name.

How had she been so deceived by his promises of love? She meant nothing to him. When it came time for him to choose, he chose himself. He was a coward. She remembered that he couldn't even look at her as he left the church. How had she ever allowed herself to be put in this position—she who was one of the wealthiest and most desirable young women in Sevilla?

She crumpled the vellum in her hand, twisting it until the fibers began to shred. She pulled the emerald from her bodice and held it to her lips. The stone felt cool against her burning skin. She closed her eyes tightly, squeezing out the last tear, took her kerchief from its place between her full breasts and dabbed it against her face. She must put this behind her, bury deep within her the memories of his kisses and caresses, his flowery words. She must bury her own emotions deeper still. He'd meant everything to her, but these feelings were already turning to bile. Somehow, she'd make José Marcos pay for the insult he'd inflicted.

She walked across the room to pull back the thick curtains. She couldn't see the Armijo house from where she stood. But the orange trees, where she and Francisco had played as children, now bloomed in full, their delicate white blossoms fluttering in the afternoon air. She was too young then to understand the difference in their stations. She knew only that Francisco was a kind boy who made her laugh. Perhaps one day she would learn to love the candle maker's son—and he, her—and if not, she would still have her home, her parents, and in time, children on whom she would lavish love. Again, her tears began to flow, but now they were tears of shame at her own foolishness.

In the grand *sala*, the immense walnut table was set for twenty guests. One continuous cloth of deep blue damask covered its entire length. At each setting, the servants had placed handsome blue and copper-luster plates from the Triana pottery works and silver forks forged in Zacatecas, which her father had carried back on his previous voyage. Over the table, a wrought iron candelabra hung from the vaulted ceiling, adorned with forty long white tapers, signaling that the dinner would last well into the early morning hours.

Guiomar surveyed the room, wondering who her parents had invited. Of course, her godfather, Don Enrique Gomez, her father's partner and oldest friend, would be there, as well as the ship's captain. But the table was set for far more than that. Surely, they wouldn't have included the Armijos in this gathering. No, she thought, it would take time and preparation for her father to explain to his wealthy trading partners why he'd chosen to give his daughter in marriage to a mere artisan. And the matter would be tricky. The last thing her parents could afford was gossip. Not that any among her parents' circle would ever question Don Pedro's motives outright. He was too powerful, and many in Sevilla benefitted from his business. Until her conversation with her mother three days earlier, Guiomar had never questioned her family's privileged place in society, assuming it would be hers to enjoy forever. Now she understood the cloud of suspicion that hung over them all.

"I see you've deigned to join us." Benita's voice was still weak but bore an unmistakable note of rebuke. Guiomar was slow to turn around and face her mother. She wore a plain black dress and her familiar shawl though the room was warm. A large gold cross, embedded with small colored stones, hung from her neck on a heavy chain. It was a piece she always wore on special occasions, but it was unusual that she had it on now, before she'd changed into her evening dress.

Benita's face softened as soon as she saw the pain in Guiomar's eyes. "Have you been crying, child?" she asked. Benita walked feebly around the large table and took Guiomar's face in her hands. Guiomar didn't look up but nodded. "I hope it's not over the Herrera boy. When will you see that he's not worthy of you?"

"I am beginning to see that," Guiomar answered, hoping that her mother wouldn't press further.

"Good. So, for now, forget whatever it is that has reddened your eyes. Tonight is a time of joy and celebration. Your father is home, safe and in good health. And with a surfeit of goods from the New World that will ensure he need not venture across the oceans again for a long time. We should all be happy."

"I cannot promise my own happiness, Mamá, but I won't ruin yours—or father's."

"Your happiness will come in time, Guiomar. I know you can't see it now, but trust me, it will. Now, I need your help."

Benita took her daughter by the arm and led her to the *cocina*, leaning heavily on Guiomar for support. The room was large, with a massive stone fireplace that ran along one wall. Inside the fireplace, big black cast iron pots hung from swinging brackets that protruded from the stones. Near the door that led to the courtyard, a stone basin ran half the length of the wall, and over it, a window looked out on three spits turning a side of beef, a lamb, and a suckling pig. The three servants—Esperanza, Concha, and Margarita—sat on a bench at the long, rough table in the center of the room removing the internal organs of more than two dozen small headless fowl.

Guiomar rarely ventured into the *cocina* while preparations for a meal were in progress. But soon enough, her mother's duties would be hers. She watched as her mother went to each servant, observing how they handled the birds.

Benita pulled Esperanza aside. "Did you slaughter the guinea hens as I instructed?" she whispered.

"Yes, Señora, and I have separated those that were not cleanly killed for the servants' consumption."

"Good. And you may take, as well, any of these whose lungs aren't perfect," she said, motioning to Guiomar to come to her side. "There, you see, that one's lung is deformed," she thrust her chin forward indicating the grey organ on the table where Esperanza had been sitting. "You must learn to detect such signs, Guiomar, so that when you have your own home, only the healthiest meat reaches your table."

Guiomar knitted her brows as her mother spoke. Why did she have to learn such things, she wondered. The servants attend the animals' slaughter and cooking.

Benita looked at Guiomar gravely, as if reading her daughter's thoughts. "Some families are careless in the *cocina*, but our family's customs are more exacting," she said. "There was a time when we could obtain our meats from a special butcher, who ensured the animals were properly slaughtered. But that's no longer possible, so we must do the best we can." She lowered her voice to a whisper. "Under the laws of our people, animals must not suffer needlessly when they're killed and their blood should be drained fully before it reaches the table. That's why we soak the fowl in saltwater, which also makes it tastier."

Guiomar pondered her mother's words. She'd always attributed her mother's preoccupation with cleanliness and diet to an anxious nature. The family changed its linens and undergarments each week and bathed as often, even though in the winter months it sometimes caused Benita pains to sit in the large copper tub while Esperanza poured in scalding water. And when Guiomar had become a woman, Benita had insisted that she bathe as soon as her bleeding stopped each month.

Guiomar had overlooked this fastidiousness over food preparation, perhaps because she wasn't interested in what went on in the *cocina*. Now she suspected it had something to do with Jewish practice, though exactly what she didn't know. Even her mother's disdain for pork had never raised questions. The animals were disgusting, wallowing in mud and filth. When she was a girl, her grandmother had told her a tale about a servant's child who wandered into a pigpen and was partially devoured before the servants discovered the body. She shuddered recalling the story. But now she wondered if it was even true—or simply a way to instill an aversion to pork.

Guiomar wandered over to the basin. The sight of dead fowl made her feel the need to wash her hands. She opened the window wider and the smell of roasting meat from the courtyard drifted in. Outside, two of the male servants were turning the spits. Miguel basted the lamb and beef, while Manuel kept watch over the piglet a short distance away. The dripping fat sizzled in the embers, throwing up thick, dark smoke. Guiomar closed the window and turned to her mother, who was studying their movements with great care. She thought to herself that she should observe whether her parents avoided the pork at dinner. She hadn't paid attention before, but she worried now that if she noticed, so might the guests. She made up her mind that she would eat a healthy portion of roasted pig, no matter what her parents did.

    The women discarded the hens' entrails into a large bowl, which Guiomar suspected would find its way onto the servants' plates later that evening, smothered in lard. The thought made her queasy. She recalled the greasy layer of lard that coated her tongue after every meal at the Herreras' table. Her throat constricted, but not because of the unpleasant taste the memory evoked. Until that moment, she hadn't even considered that in addition to losing José Marcos, she'd also lost the friendship of his sister. They'd been inseparable since they were girls. Now she'd have to refuse María Dolores's invitations. How could she share a meal with José Marcos sitting across the table? Even if he had the decency to be absent at such times, María Dolores would sense that something had happened and would want to know the details. Perhaps he had already shared her deadly secret with his sister. And who knows who else. Guiomar shuddered, even in the stifling heat of the *cocina*.

Guiomar sat in the middle of the long table with two women on either side. Her companion to the left was almost deaf, which made mindless chatter avoidable on an evening when Guiomar's mind was elsewhere. On her right, the daughter of her mother's oldest friend, María de Jesus, prattled on about her difficulties finding a new seamstress. Opposite sat her father's business partner, Enrique Gomez y Duran. He was godfather to the Péres children, but Guiomar had always been his favorite. When she was little, he would come to their house with his carriage and take her for rides in the countryside. He had no children of his own, so when he called her *m'hija*, the endearment expressed his paternal affection. Next to Don Enrique sat the ship's captain, Fabián Lopez de Sosa, a slight man with thinning hair, who nonetheless looked proud and vain.

    Pedro sat at the head of the table, his impressive frame dominating the gathering. His was taller than everyone else by nearly a head, a trait that had served him well as a leader. Handsome despite his advancing years, his dark, curly hair was now threaded with silver. He'd celebrated his fiftieth birthday shortly before he left for the Antilles.

To Pedro's left, the captain's pretty young wife looked up at him coquettishly as he described her husband's masterful sailing through a storm off Hispaniola. He was flattered by the woman's attention but couldn't help focusing on Benita at the opposite end of the table. She was dressed in an elegant blue dress that he hadn't seen before. But the brilliant color made her seem even more pale as she picked at her food without appetite. He'd impressed her with the three-pronged forks he'd brought back with him. She'd seemed eager to introduce them at her table, but now she merely used the tines to move the meat around her plate.

"My friends!" Pedro's deep voice stopped the lively conversations as he pushed back his heavy chair and stood. "I thank Our Lord that he has brought me home to be surrounded by my family and by all of you, who've been as dear to my heart as my own blood." He glanced at his wife, whose faint smile suggested his charms still worked. His gaze alighted on each person around the table, stopping for a moment to marvel at his daughter's lovely face. She had grown from a pretty girl into a beautiful young woman in the fifteen months he'd been at sea. He thought he could detect tears in her eyes, but she quickly lowered them. Benita had told him about Guiomar's unhappiness over his decision to wed her to Francisco Armijo, but it couldn't be helped, especially with the announcement he was about to make. He had kept it from his daughter, telling only his wife of his decision.

The silence around the table grew awkward. Pedro cleared his throat and lifted his goblet. "To you, Enrique, my oldest friend, my partner, you have been like a brother to me. Without you, I could never have had the courage to venture across the seas, to risk everything—and to be so richly rewarded for my temerity. Thank you, my friend." Pedro held the goblet out toward his friend, who bowed his head in recognition. Everyone lifted their goblets—even the women, who only touched the vessels to their lips—as both men tilted their heads back to down the contents in one gulp.

"So," Pedro began again, his voice now faltering, "my decision to make this voyage my last comes with a heavy heart, since I know that it affects not only my own future and that of my family but all of those who are with us tonight."

Cries of protest went up from both men and women. Benita's face remained placid. But Guiomar looked stricken, her eyes darting back and forth between her parents before resting on Don Enrique. His face had turned bright red, his eyes clouded in anger. Guiomar hid her hands under the table, pressing the edges of the large emerald into her palms. She looked back toward her father, who remained resolute, raising his large, powerful hands to quell the dissent.

"Now, now," Pedro said in the tone of a man chiding his children. He leaned forward and rested his hands on the table, looking from one guest to another. Guiomar felt the tension rising and glanced anxiously again at Don Enrique. She couldn't read his face. He had covered his emotions behind a small impenetrable smile, his lips slightly pursed and his eyes staring directly at her father as if he were a neutral stranger. Her father's announcement clearly came as an unwelcome surprise. Since before she was born, her father had sailed the oceans trading goods from Sevilla and other ports of call. The riches he brought back not only provided the family with luxury but cloaked them in power that Guiomar feared would be lost. She squeezed her hands together more tightly until she winced.

Enrique rose to his feet. "I say we should congratulate our dear host," he said in a voice that could easily be mistaken for loving friendship. The others looked around quickly to judge how they should react. Then the captain and the other men lifted their glasses to toast, first Don Enrique, then their host. But before the wine could travel down their throats, Enrique slammed his goblet on the table, startling even the deaf woman at Guiomar's side.

"He has the good sense to get out before the ocean claims him or another of his ships," he said, his eyes hardening.

Pedro smiled at his partner, despite the gall in his throat. It was a low blow. He knew that Enrique still blamed him for the loss of one of their galleons, loaded with Zacatecas silver, in a storm off Havana on a previous voyage. He had suffered severe financial losses. But hadn't they all? And he'd more than made up for it in subsequent voyages. But Enrique had yet to forgive him. Pedro had thought it would be best to announce his retirement publicly, but now he wondered whether his judgment had been wise.

"Come, let us have some more wine and put aside our disappointments," he said, ignoring his partner's challenge. The servants moved forward to replenish the wine, their faces registering no sign that they had heard, much less comprehended, the harsh exchange of words. Enrique moved his chair back to take his seat, the noise of it scraping the floor drawing all eyes to him. As if to turn their attention back to himself, Don Pedro loudly commanded Miguel to start serving the suckling pig and, when the platter finally came to him, speared a thick portion of the flesh with the tip of his knife.

Guiomar was relieved that he did not hesitate to eat the forbidden food. She used her new implement, the fork, its three prongs far more adept than a knife in getting the meat from her plate to her mouth. The meat was succulent and rich, the servants having studded the brown skin with cloves and ladled on stewed plums that enhanced its natural sweetness. Guiomar savored the taste. How could the Lord forbid something He'd made so delicious?

Don Enrique ordered Miguel to bring him another slice of pork, but as he was about to put the dripping meat in his mouth, he stopped and pointed the knife towards his partner, a wide grin on his face. "Tasty, my friend, don't you agree?" Enrique nodded and picked up his empty goblet, holding it aloft until Miguel could put the platter down and pour wine from a large pitcher. Guiomar watched the whole charade, wishing she could ask for more wine to calm her nerves, but she didn't dare.

Just as the tensions of the evening had abated, Benita's fierce hacking silenced everyone. Esperanza rushed to her mistress's side from the hall, where she'd been waiting unobserved. Pedro, too, moved quickly to his wife, whose chest convulsed in spasms no manner of soothing quelled. He lifted her into his arms as if she were a child, which, in truth, she'd come to resemble in her frailty. A general murmur arose around the table, the women crossing themselves, the men exchanging worried looks. Several guests seemed on the verge of leaving. Guiomar watched as her father carried her mother from the room, wanting to follow him. But it was her duty to remain and calm the guests.

"Dearest friends," she said in a voice as commanding as she could muster. "Please, finish your meals. My mother will be fine."

"That is not at all clear, my dear," Enrique replied. "It appears your mother is gravely ill. I believe your father's decision, which surprised us all, was a recognition of her condition."

Guiomar was confused by Don Enrique's sudden turn of heart. A few moments earlier, she'd have sworn he was incensed by her father's announcement. But perhaps she was mistaken.

"We should all wish for husbands so devoted they'd give up adventure to be with us in our time of need," the captain's pretty wife said from the other end of the table.

"When we're as rich as our host, we'll gladly do so, Consuela," her husband retorted, provoking awkward laughter around the table and breaking the solemn mood.

"With your father no longer leading us, we may never be so lucky," the ship's pilot, Alberto Torres, ventured. The laughter subsided with the pilot's remark. Torres's grey beard and weathered face showed he had acquired more years than wisdom, Guiomar thought. She frowned at him, pointedly, hoping Don Enrique would notice. Such talk was dangerous, especially now. All the men present knew it was her father's genius for striking a good bargain while treating those he traded with fairly that had allowed the company to reap riches from the natives time and again. She glanced anxiously at Don Enrique, but he didn't return her gaze.

After a brief awkward silence, the guests seemed eager to resume their private conversations. Guiomar engaged the women to her left and right, speaking loudly and simply for the old woman and discussing fashion with the younger. All the while, she worried about what was happening in her mother's chamber and continued to cast furtive glances at Don Enrique, who seemed to have settled into lively conversation with those nearest him. The servants brought out cheese and dried dates, figs, and apricots, as well as fresh plums. Guiomar eagerly watched for the dripping of excess candle wax overflowing the silver candelabra onto the blue damask, which would signal a close to the evening. By the time she'd finished her first plum, a large white spot appeared in the middle of the table.

"It appears our evening must end," she said, commanding all the strength in her voice. She'd never assumed this role, which was her father's when he was present or her mother's when he was at sea.

"Our beautiful Guiomar has proved herself a worthy hostess," Enrique offered from the other end of the room. "Soon, I expect she'll be honoring us at her own table, and fortunate will be the man who wins her hand."

Guiomar felt the color rise to her cheeks. Little did her godfather know how soon that might be—or how surprising the choice.

As Guiomar said her goodbyes, Don Enrique stood at her side, waiting until the last guest had left. She felt uncomfortable with him lingering, but she could hardly encourage him to leave without appearing rude. And perhaps his intention was to wait for her father to return. When the door closed behind the captain and his wife, he turned to Guiomar. "I am deeply concerned not only about your mother's failing health, *m'hija*," he said, "but also with your father's decision and what it will mean for this family." The deep folds beneath his eyes appeared darker and the long creases at his mouth's edge took on a more sinister look. Guiomar was tempted to look away but held her gaze steadfast.

"As you could see tonight, Godfather, my mother isn't well—"

"Yes, I saw blood on her handkerchief," he interrupted.

"Well, then, I don't need to tell you that Papá cannot leave her in this condition."

"I understand, of course, but his announcement didn't suggest this is a temporary measure."

"How could he say so in front of my mother? It would imply he must wait for her to die to resume his life." Guiomar's words tumbled out before she could consider whether they were wise.

"He should have spoken to me privately," Enrique snapped. "I hesitate to say these things to you, Guiomar, but his manner was a public affront, one that another man who didn't feel such affection for your father—and his family—would have been unable to ignore. You're like a daughter to me, child, so I am telling you this so you might act to heal this wound before it festers."

Enrique leaned over and kissed her on the forehead, squeezing her hands in his. "You're young to carry such a burden, my dear, but you're up to the task. I place my trust in you," he said and reached for the metal door handle, pulling the heavy door toward him before Miguel could intervene. Guiomar looked anxiously at the servant. She'd forgotten he was there, waiting at his post in the corner. She worried he'd listened to her conversation with Don Enrique, but the slaves were privy to all sorts of family secrets, including perhaps the most dangerous secret of all.

Chapter Four

THE BEDCHAMBER

Esperanza wiped Benita's brow as she lay on her bed struggling to breathe. Pedro stood by helplessly, hands clasped behind his back. Benita's chest moved up and down in an increasingly erratic rhythm. Her lips had already turned blue.

"How long has she been having these episodes?" he asked the girl.

"For at least a month, Don Pedro. She has good days and bad. Since your return, she's seemed better. But tonight's festivities were too much for her."

"Dr. Garcia should be here momentarily. Manuel will bring him through the back as I requested?"

"Yes. Manuel is reliable."

"We can't be too careful. I don't want the vultures hanging about waiting for her…" he cut his words short. He didn't know how much his wife could understand in her present state.

He paced back and forth at the foot of the bed, helpless to do anything but wait. Perhaps he had provoked her attack with his announcement, though she hadn't objected when he told her his intentions that afternoon. More likely it was Enrique's outburst that brought on the coughing fit. It had been unwise not to warn his partner in advance. But he feared Enrique might try to talk him out of his decision. Surely he had made it clear before they left that this was to be their last voyage. He'd promised to bring back their most profitable cargo yet. And he had. Enrique had no reason to complain.

The knock on the door was barely audible, but Pedro quickly opened it and motioned the grey-haired physician into the room, signaling for him to talk quietly. Garcia was slightly stooped, burdened by the large satchel he carried. Manuel stood behind him, near the door.

"When did she fall into this state?" The physician approached the bed and Esperanza quickly moved aside.

"She began coughing at the dinner table and by the time I carried her to her bed, she was as you see her. Is there nothing we can do?"

"I should bleed her if she is strong enough. I haven't seen her for the past month, and she seems even thinner than the last time I was here. Have you been feeding her as I directed?" he asked Esperanza in a tone that suggested mistrust.

Esperanza wrung her hands. "I've done exactly as you directed, Doctor, but it is not possible to force her and she has little appetite."

"And have you rubbed her chest with lard and camphor each night as I instructed?"

Pedro watched Esperanza carefully to see if she understood the necessity of dissembling on this point.

"Faithfully, Doctor." Esperanza looked unflinchingly into the doctor's eyes.

Pedro wondered whether Benita had confided in the girl, whom she loved almost as a daughter, or if the slave was wise enough to be discreet. Either way, he worried that the servant might compromise the family secret, which could become more dangerous as the days passed. He consoled himself with the thought that he'd always treated his slaves well. They had no cause for discontent. He provided decent shelter, good food, and had interfered very little with their family life. One of the women had borne a child, a boy, but he had no plans to sell him, though he would bring a tidy sum. Still, one never knew what secret resentments they might harbor. And perhaps the girl remembered that he'd almost sold her when she turned thirteen. He determined to make sure she knew that whatever happened to his wife, her place in the family was secure.

The doctor bent over Benita, pressing his ear to her chest as he held her wrist in his hand. When he had finished, he turned to Don Pedro. "She is too weak for me to bleed. Her heart is beating rapidly but unevenly, and her lungs sound as if they are filled with fluid. We can do nothing now but wait. Either she'll recover her strength and we can bleed her again or…"

Esperanza dropped to her knees beside her mistress's bed. Her lips moved in silent prayer. Pedro looked on enviously. He wished that he shared a belief in an eternal being. Who was this Hebrew God that couldn't comfort him when he needed it most? He felt, as he often did, like a man caught between two worlds: the familiar one in which he'd lived his entire life as a secret outsider, and the unfamiliar one to which he was tied by blood but felt little affinity for. The latter now threatened to destroy the former, and there was little he could do about it. The important thing was to protect his family, especially Guiomar.

After drifting off to sleep in the large chair in the corner of the room, Pedro awakened to the sound of whispered voices. Guiomar sat on the edge of her mother's bed, stroking her head gently, while Esperanza rubbed a foul-smelling ointment onto Benita's exposed chest. Her bones were clearly visible through the pale, translucent skin, which he recalled had once felt as soft as the silk he brought back from the Orient.

"What is that stink," he demanded.

"It's what the doctor ordered, Papá."

"You know your mother wouldn't approve, Guiomar."

"I know, but there's nothing else we can do to relieve her suffering."

"If she were awake, my child, what you're doing would cause more pain than her disease." He glanced at Esperanza to see if she comprehended why he was criticizing their efforts, but the servant's eyes showed no recognition that the discussion was anything but meaningless jousting between father and daughter. Esperanza dipped her fingers into the greasy mixture made that morning from the suckling pig fat from the feast. She spread it evenly across Doña Benita's chest, finally covering her nakedness with a white cloth and pulling the bedcovers over her although the night was warm. His wife's wheezing continued, but her breaths seemed steadier and less shallow now. Maybe the medicine was working after all, he thought. But the room reeked of camphor and pig fat, which made him want to gag.

"Esperanza, you may leave your mistress now. You should rest. You'll have many days and nights ahead nursing her back to health."

Esperanza nodded, wiping her hands on a piece of muslin that she then draped over the bowl with the ointment. She didn't want to leave Doña Benita's side, but she knew better than to argue with Don Pedro.

When the servant had shut the door behind her, Pedro joined his daughter at his wife's bedside, reaching out to stroke her soft curls.

"I'm sorry to have left you to the vultures, dear. But judging from how late they stayed, you must have been a success."

Guiomar looked up at him with accusing eyes. "I wish you or Mamá had warned me of your intentions. I was as stunned as everyone sitting around the table—including my godfather."

"Enrique will get over it. I have made him more money than he can spend in two lifetimes. And he has no heirs to leave it to when he dies."

"Surely you know, Papá, that for some people there is never enough to be satisfied."

"When did you become so wise, little one?" He tried to tousle her hair, but she twisted away from his touch.

"He stayed behind to speak to me after the others left. He feels you insulted him by announcing your intentions in public, without paying him the courtesy to tell him in advance. I must say, I sympathize with him, Papá."

"He would have tried to talk me out of it, with threats if need be. He can be a ruthless man, Guiomar, no matter how much love he's shown you over the years."

"Then he is even more dangerous now."

"Perhaps. But though it wasn't planned, your mother's sudden collapse will surely soften his heart. Even he can understand that I can't leave her as she is."

"And if she goes quickly, what then?"

"Guiomar, do not speak of it. Your mother is a strong woman, stronger than you know. She's withstood much in her life, a great deal of it unknown to you. But let's not talk about this now. We have other matters to discuss."

Guiomar stiffened as he said the words. She dreaded what would come next.

Pedro observed his daughter's anguish. He wished she didn't suffer so. He knew she had her heart set on the Herreras' youngest son. But even if the family's situation didn't require the match with Francisco Armijo, he would never allow her to marry the other one. She was too young to understand that the boy would bring nothing but sorrow. He'd known many men like José Marcos—handsome, charming, full of guile—who suddenly wanted something new once they obtained what they initially wanted.

"I suppose you want to talk to me about my betrothal to our neighbor's son," she said finally.

"Yes. Your mother told me she has explained why it is necessary."

"And you? Is this all Mamá's doing, or are you part of this deception that has been going on—how long?"

"We have no choice, Guiomar. We were born into this, as were you. Do you really believe we'd be safe if we had chosen to fully abandon the faith of our ancestors? I know you pay little heed to such matters, but Sevilla is in thrall to a dangerous group of men who turn neighbor against neighbor, friend against friend, child against parent, all in the name of God."

"But how does my marriage to Francisco protect me? I'm still your daughter."

"In itself, it wouldn't be enough. But it will buy time—and our wealth will buy more. We've lived carefully—not just in this generation but for many. Our families have given generously to the Church, with uncles and aunts in the religious orders as well as your brother, gold and silver to adorn parishes and line the pockets of the clergy. Were it not for the present fanaticism, we'd be beyond suspicion."

"How many of us are there?"

"Secret Jews?"

"Yes, if that is how we call ourselves."

"Who knows? Many conversos still practice our rituals, but others don't. I doubt there are as many as the Holy Office suspects. And that's the danger. The Dominicans distrust all New Christians, no matter how faithful they seem. And they'll use every means to root them out."

"But I don't understand how marrying Francisco will make any difference. Will it change the blood that runs in my veins?"

"It will change the blood that runs in your children's veins. And it may delay the Inquisitors' investigations. We are not on their lists, at least not yet. My partners are Old Christians. We live outside the old Jewish quarter. And our family has been scrupulous in its Catholic observance. And need I remind you, your brother has devoted his life to the Church? We might avoid detection for as long as the present persecution lasts. In the past, they've come and gone, some bloodier than others. This one can't last forever."

He felt exhausted by his long defense. The hour was late, and he wanted to retreat to his bed, though he feared that if he left Benita's side, she might expire in the night.

Guiomar sat silent, stroking her mother's brow. He wished he could ease the girl's pain. It was at times like this a young woman most needed her mother—and she would soon lose hers.

"When can the marriage be arranged?" Guiomar spoke finally.

Pedro was stunned by her response. "So, you won't protest?"

"Would it matter if I did?"

THE SILVER CANDLESTICKS

His daughter's demeanor saddened him. She'd always been a willful child but now she looked defeated. He leaned over and kissed her cheek. She'd become a beautiful young woman with her dark hair and fair skin, like her mother. The Armijo boy was fortunate beyond words to marry such a girl. Though low-born, he had impressed Pedro with his ambition and intelligence. And he remembered that the two had played as children, running about the yard in the afternoons. He'd even warned Benita they would have to keep an eye on them as they grew older. They could never have imagined that they would desire such a union.

"You were friendly with Francisco as I remember." He wanted to hear his daughter out, even if there was no chance that any other path lay open to them.

"It was a long time ago, Papá. We've exchanged no more than brief pleasantries since we were children."

"He's not a bad looking young man," he offered. Although not handsome, Francisco was tall and well built. Guiomar smiled, ruefully. He thought she must be imagining Herrera, who was both handsome and vain. Pedro knew from experience that handsome men were often the most trouble, but his daughter was too young to understand such things. "Francisco will never give you sorrow, Guiomar, as many men do. He's quite devout, I am told, and will never be unfaithful."

"You haven't answered my question. How soon will the marriage take place?" Guiomar grabbed her father's arm. She would force him to deal with her as a grown woman, not the child he imagined her to be, compliant to his wishes and obedient to his commands.

He gently placed his hand over hers. "I'd like it to take place while your mother is still with us," he answered, looking directly into her eyes. "It will raise fewer questions about why we moved so quickly. Everyone will understand that a mother wishes to see her daughter wed before she dies. I considered announcing it tonight, but when your mother became ill, it was impossible."

"Without warning me?" Guiomar raised her voice so loudly her mother stirred.

"Hush, Guiomar. I said I thought about it—in truth, not until Enrique became angry. It occurred to me that it might be a way to distract the conversation."

She pulled away from him and stood defiantly, arms across her chest. "And does Francisco know?" she asked.

"He is overwhelmed with joy. I think he's loved you for many years, my dear. Who wouldn't?" he replied with the tenderness he'd always felt for his younger child.

"I'm not asking if he knows I'm to be given to him, with or without my consent. What I'm asking is, does he know my parents are Jews?" She spat out the words.

Pedro tightened his jaw. "You must never speak that way, daughter. You act as if you're ashamed of who you are." He wasn't a religious man, but he wouldn't countenance such disrespect. It was one thing to remain silent when Old Christians accused the Jews of greed and deception, but he wouldn't have his daughter follow suit. "Who do you think gave the world the belief in one, almighty Creator? Your carpenter from Nazareth? It's the Christians who've violated the commandment to worship one God with their superstitions about Holy Ghosts and their deification of a man who was no more than a prophet."

Guiomar covered her ears with her hands. "I will not listen, Papá," she said.

He grabbed her arms. "The Holy Office will make no distinction whether you believe or not, Guiomar. Don't you see? Your mother and I are trying to protect you in the only way we can. It may not be enough, but it's the best we can do." He felt his chest constricting. He loved this child and would do anything to keep her safe. If he could denounce himself and save her, he would. But that would only hasten her torment. No, the solution he'd come up with was the only way—and even that might be difficult.

Guiomar's shoulders heaved up and down, but her sobs were silent or nearly so. Pedro looked anxiously to his wife, whose eyelids fluttered as if dreaming. He hoped that her dreams were happy, perhaps of her youth, the love he felt for her from the moment he met her in her father's house, a shy young man with much ambition but little fortune. They'd shared thirty-two good years together; she'd borne him four children, two of whom died; and he'd been loyal to her in body and spirit.

Guiomar stood, mutely observing her father as he, in turn, stared at her mother now breathing restfully. Her father's words wounded her deeply. He was right; she did feel ashamed to be a Jew. She felt it when her mother uttered the strange words, which sounded harsh and ugly to her ears. She had felt it when José Marcos examined her so coldly in the church, as if she would suddenly sprout horns. Why would she want to be one of these despised people? They had been driven from Spain because they were a danger, spilling the blood of Christian children in their rituals, cheating even their friends to increase their wealth. The proof of their perfidy was displayed on every altar in the kingdom, Christ crucified by the Jews.

She'd heard these accusations for as long as she could remember—from the priests, her teachers, her friends, repeated even by the slaves in her own household who'd rejected their foreign gods to accept Christ. Yet, as she thought about it, she couldn't remember her parents ever uttering a word against the Jews, or even her grandmother Inés who had few kind words for anyone outside the immediate family. Guiomar slipped out of her mother's room, trying not to disturb her father, who seemed lost in his own thoughts.

Pedro looked up as the door closed behind her. He knew his daughter suffered at the moment, but the girl was sensible. It wouldn't take long for her to adjust her expectations. And he thought it entirely possible that she'd find happiness with the candle maker's son. The Armijo family had become prosperous over the years, with both father and son displaying a keen eye for business. He often had to drive a hard bargain with his neighbor when trading large shipments of candles for wares from New Spain. The old man had insisted on paying him less than what he received in Sevilla. "I know my customers in our neighborhood," Armijo had argued when Pedro made his last purchase. "I know they'll be back for more. How do I know these *Indios* will ever buy from me again—or that the goods that will pay for my hard work will ever make it across the seas to my doorstep?" His son had let out a hearty laugh at his father's bickering, and Pedro smiled as well, though he wondered at the time whether the candle maker had been referring to the loss of the *Santa Cátalina*, the only tarnish on his reputation in his long seafaring career. Few men in his profession could say the same.

He would deal with Francisco's father in the morning, provided Benita lasted the night. He lay down beside her. It had been many years since he had shared her bed. Her body was warm next to his. He leaned on his side to look at her face. He could still see the beauty that had once enchanted him despite her fevered pallor: the long, thin nose, the lower lip slightly fuller than the upper, the fine arched brows. It pained him to think he would not spend the rest of his life with this woman. He'd always believed that he would be the first to die, lost at sea or the victim of some New World disease. Now it was she who lay dying, and there was little he could do.

He looked up at the niche on the wall opposite Benita's bed. The Virgin looked down benevolently, her hands outstretched. At that moment, he wished he could believe as others did, but he did not. It wasn't even that he believed in the other. He simply lacked any faith.

Chapter Five

ESPERANZA

Esperanza entered the casita behind the main house, which she shared with the other female servant, Concha, and her son, Juanito. The room was stifling, the only air coming from a small window adjacent to the door. Juanito was asleep on one of the narrow beds, the hair sprouting under his long arms a sign of his impending manhood. Soon he would have to sleep in the loft over the stables with Miguel and Manuel. Esperanza was hungry despite the worry that consumed her and thought about going back to the kitchen where she could feast on the remains of the rich banquet. But she did not want to be pulled into the servants' gossip. They would ply her with questions, and even if she didn't answer, they'd assume she knew more than she was willing to share. Their resentment might lead them to gossip to others outside the Péres household.

She reached into the pocket of her dress for the handful of figs she'd taken when she helped clear the plates. Don Pedro had kindly sent her to rest, but she couldn't leave the main house before helping Concha and Margarita without making them deeply angry. They already resented her favored treatment, the way Doña Benita always asked for her when she wanted someone at her side, the little gifts and sweets her mistress bestowed. Only Guiomar's obvious dislike protected Esperanza from greater jealousy on the part of the others.

"You better watch out for that one when Doña Benita dies," Concha had warned her often enough. And Esperanza indeed worried that she might be sold off or perhaps end up with Guiomar, who would treat her with contempt or worse. But she had another reason to worry. When the household became smaller through her mistress's death or Guiomar's marriage, she was likely to be parted from Felipe. Don Enrique's anger at the table could spell trouble for the family's fortunes. Unlike herself, Felipe, who was of mixed race, wasn't owned but indentured to Don Pedro until he paid off what he owed for his training as a cooper for the fleet.

She popped the last fig into her mouth and savored its sticky sweetness. It would hold her until morning. She'd be the first one up to get the oven fires started and could eat more then. Lately, she had been ravenous no matter how much she ate. She unlaced her sleeves and bodice, slipped out of her skirt and hung them on the hook beside her bed. She ran her hands along the front of her shift. Her belly was no longer flat but had begun to bulge just below her navel. Soon she'd have to tell her mistress, who would no doubt be as disappointed as she was angry.

Esperanza wished the baby would go away. She had heard the other women talk about how to get rid of a child. There were herbs that could be put in the place between her legs, which would cause cramping and then much blood. But she feared it was too late for that. She'd felt the child quicken as she caught sight of Felipe two days earlier. She hadn't told him yet—and she feared doing so almost as much as she dreaded telling Doña Benita.

She splashed water from the large ceramic basin onto her face and under her arms. The water offered no relief from the heat since it had become warm from sitting so long in the hot room. She wished she could lie under the orange trees dressed only in her thin cotton camisa. Perhaps Felipe would wander out to make water in the night and find her there. Then they could lie together on the cool earth, as they had a few moons before. Maybe then she would have the courage to tell him of the child.

It was foolish to think such thoughts. Don Pedro had been home two days and Esperanza noted that Felipe had seemed to avoid her the whole time. Maybe he was just being cautious, for her sake as well as his own. Yet, she feared there was another reason. Could it be that he was planning to return to the Indies, where he had traveled with her master on an earlier sojourn? Perhaps Don Pedro had brought back word from his latest voyage that would draw Felipe back there. She had heard that many men, even those with wives and children in Spain, established families in the New World. The women there were said to walk around half-naked and offer their bodies to the sailors for a piece of cloth or a broken mirror.

She clutched her arms around her thickening waist. What had she done, giving herself to Felipe before they sought permission to marry? Now he might be forced to marry her, not for love but because the master ordered it. And what if he already had a wife in the Antilles or Veracruz? She tried to remember what he had said that night several months ago when he made love to her in the garden after everyone in the household was asleep. *Do you not think I would marry you if I were free?* Those were his words. She had assumed that he meant he could not do so until he earned his freedom from servitude. But perhaps he meant that he already had another wife. She felt suddenly angry. He had deceived her, and now she would have to bear the consequences alone.

"You're still awake?"

Concha's voice startled her. She hadn't heard the door open.

"It's too hot to sleep," she replied.

"So, tell me what happened in Doña Benita's chambers? You know I'll learn sooner or later, with or without you." Concha set the candle on the table next to the basin. The flickering light made her head appear like a shriveled plum, the features dark and evil. Esperanza distrusted Concha, who had one way of behaving in front of her masters and another when their backs were turned. She'd bow and smile sweetly when Doña Benita asked for a cup of tea and then spit on the floor as she went to fetch it. Esperanza wouldn't put it past her to spit in the cup before she served it.

"Doña Benita is resting. The banquet was too much for her."

"She'll be dead before Holy Week."

"Don't say that! It's as if you wished it."

"Why shouldn't I? She's done nothing for me but lock me in this hovel."

"You know as well as I that she treats us well. You've gotten fat on her food. And she never said a word when you gave birth to Juanito."

"It's easy for you. You're her favorite. They'll never sell you. Me, my boy, they'd get rid of us if they weren't afraid we might talk about what we've seen here."

Esperanza moved toward Concha until barely the width of a hand separated them, her clenched teeth, her eyes fixed on Concha's. "You've seen nothing. Do you hear me?" she said, reaching out to squeeze the woman's plump arms. Concha pulled herself loose and spat.

"I know what I've seen," she said. "And I know that you help them. Like today in the *cocina*. The Holy Office would be interested to learn what goes on here. Who knows, I might even gain my freedom as a reward." Concha's lips curled into a menacing smile, her teeth white against her purple lips.

"If you spread one lie, you'll get your reward in Hell," Esperanza moved toward Concha, her hand balled into a fist. She wanted to hit her, but she knew better than to provoke further talk of the habits of the Péres family. She wondered whether she should say something to Guiomar. Until this evening, it would never have occurred to her to confide in the Señorita. But it was important that the family be warned of the treachery lurking in Concha's breast.

The rays of the sun came too quickly. Esperanza had been unable to sleep most of the night, the loud snores from the woman and the boy interrupting her each time she drifted off. She reached down and touched her stomach. She'd felt a movement like a small flutter from within. *Mother of God*, she whispered to herself, *protect me*. She slid her legs over the side of the bed and sat up. Her camisa stuck to her with sweat. She must move quickly and quietly if she was to avoid rousing Concha. The boy would sleep no matter what.

It irked her that he was so lazy—even more that his mother made excuses for it. She was not helping him by allowing him to become slothful. One day, he would pay dearly for not having been taught well, but by then, the habits of a lifetime would already be set. She was glad Doña Benita had helped form her, favoring her but also teaching her the importance of work. "Why should he work?" Concha had replied when Esperanza complained that the boy did nothing for his keep. "They claim to own him, but I'm the one who paid in blood and pain to bring him into this world."

Esperanza didn't dwell on her plight as one owned by another. As a girl, she had felt no more loss of liberty than does any child. Guiomar's movements were hardly freer than hers when they were children. Doña Benita kept a watchful eye on her daughter from the time she woke up to when she went to bed. True, Guiomar could play outside under the orange trees in the afternoon while Esperanza had to work sweeping the rooms and preparing the meals. But in the evening, when Don Pedro was at sea, Doña Benita would often sit in the grand *sala*, both girls resting on pillows on the wood floor in front of her, as she read aloud from one of her romances. Esperanza had often wished that she could decipher the marks on the page and envied Guiomar's time with the tutor, though the girl complained incessantly of the old man's foul breath and the trials he put her to. Still, Guiomar was free to learn, and Esperanza was not.

But it was only since she had come to love Felipe that she understood what it meant to lack freedom. His indenture would end when his ten years of service had been fulfilled. He would then be free to live where he chose and make his own profession, though he knew nothing useful but serving others and the life at sea. Esperanza would be unable to follow him and would instead be tied to the Péres family until death—or until she was sold.

But she pushed the thought from her mind. It did no good to worry about matters she was powerless to change.

Entering the *cocina*, she was startled to find Don Pedro sitting on the bench before the large refectory table in the center of the room. He held his head in his hands and did not seem to realize that she had come in. Esperanza hesitated to approach or speak to him, thinking he might have fallen asleep.

He lifted his head slowly, surprised that he was no longer alone. "Esperanza, you're up early," he said.

"Doña Benita..." Esperanza struggled to make the words come.

"She's alive. In fact, she awoke just before dawn and was able to speak a few words. I came in here hoping to find the ointment you applied last night. I think it may have helped. Her breathing is much steadier this morning." He smiled at the pretty servant. He was glad his wife had talked him out of selling her, though that had been his ultimate intention when he bought her from a Portuguese captain ten years earlier. It was always a financial mistake to bring a slave into the home at too young an age. It was impossible for a woman like Benita not to become attached to a smiling child, no matter her color.

Esperanza let out her breath, slowly, as her master spoke. "I keep it in the shed. Doña Benita would not want it in the *cocina*. I'll fetch it," she said with great relief.

"Yes, do, but wait a moment. I wish to talk to you, Esperanza."

She took in a breath and clasped her hands together. She didn't like the sound in his voice—she feared it would be bad news.

"You have been with Doña Benita since you were just a tiny girl. I know she has been almost like a mother to you—and she loves you almost as if you were of her own flesh. But she will not be with us for much longer...." He watched the servant's face grimace. "I know my daughter has sometimes been unkind to you, Esperanza. But she's a good girl, and she will be as good a mistress as you're likely to find. Guiomar is soon to be married and will need a trustworthy servant to help her run her household. It is Doña Benita's wish that you serve Guiomar. In her will, she's bequeathed you to her."

Bequeathed. It was a word Esperanza hadn't heard before, but she sensed its meaning, and more. So, this is what it meant to be the property of another. She could be given away as well as sold. If she were still a child, it might be an act of kindness, so that she would be taken care of until she could provide for herself. But she was a grown woman now, and one who carried a life within her. Yet she had no control over her own life, much less that of her child. Though she had never uttered the wish, even to herself, she'd hoped that she would earn her freedom when Doña Benita died. For the first time, she understood the depths of Concha's bitterness.

"Do you understand, Esperanza?" He watched the girl's face for signs of defiance in addition to pain, but he knew she was too obedient—or clever—to allow her true emotions to be seen.

"Yes, Don Pedro. I understand. I will be in service to your daughter," she brushed away the single tear that had run down her face to her chin. She turned to leave but felt his hand on her arm.

"It's because she loves you both that Doña Benita wants you to be together. You will make each other stronger." He hesitated a moment, his hand still gently holding her bare arm as she faced him. "And you will protect each other if the need ever arises." His eyes stared deeply into hers, conveying more meaning than his words.

Esperanza searched Don Pedro's face. He had rarely spoken more than a few words to her but now, despite her disappointment, she felt the urge to warn him of Concha's threats. She wasn't sure if it was wise—he might be so angry that he'd do something that would make matters worse. But she couldn't tell Doña Benita, and she feared Guiomar would be helpless to do anything.

"There's something I need to tell you," she said, her voice barely above a whisper.

"Yes? Speak." Pedro's eyes narrowed as he let go of her arm.

"I've had a bad talk with Concha. She's a bitter woman. And not to be trusted."

"Does she steal from us?"

Esperanza shook her head.

"What then?"

She wondered whether she should she go further. Raising the matter could make things difficult for her as well. "She's been making certain…threats."

Pedro snorted in contempt. "How could a slave possibly threaten her master? Will she attempt to kill me in my sleep? She'll be out of this house—with her bastard son—before sunset," he said, his voice rising to the point it could be heard beyond the *cocina*.

"Don Pedro, it is not my place…"

"Speak up, Esperanza. If you know something I should know, it's your duty to tell me. Everything." He was growing impatient.

"She's made certain accusations." She watched his face go almost white. "I know there's not a word of truth in them," she added quickly. "She said that if you were to sell her or her boy, she would go to the Holy Office. She thinks by telling lies, she'll earn her freedom."

He stood up, straightening his back to his full, towering height as he faced her. "Did she say anything specific? She cannot make accusations against a family such as ours. It's she who'll be subject to the rack if she makes false charges."

Esperanza didn't know what to say. If she told him what Concha had said, she'd be betraying Doña Benita's confidence in her. Had not her mistress warned her many times that the instructions for the slaughter of animals weren't to be shared with anyone—even her husband?

"You know more than you're saying, Esperanza. As I have told you, my wife regards you almost as a daughter. If you hope to return her love—and trust—you must tell me everything you know." He reached out for her hand and patted it gently, though the crease in his brow betrayed his worry.

She let out her breath, which she barely realized she'd been holding. She pulled back her hand, which went, as if of its own will, to her face, her fingers brushing against her forehead. She wanted to cross herself, but she realized that her master might misinterpret her gesture.

"She knows nothing, Don Pedro. She's a spiteful woman with a lazy son. What could she know? There's nothing to know." She looked steadily at Don Pedro, her eyes concealing the fear she felt toward the man who held her future in his hands. "May I get the ointment now?"

"Of course. Go," he said, the smile on his face as false as the reassuring look on hers.

As she pulled open the door, he called after her in barely a whisper, "And of course, you won't speak of this to Doña Benita. You would only cause her worry."

"I wouldn't think of it. Nor to anyone else," she added.

She walked toward the shed where she kept the ointment along with the butchering tools and other implements needed in the home. The embers still smoldered in the pits from the evening before, giving off a sour smell. She heard voices from the men in the stables and listened closely for Felipe, but it was only Manuel and Miguel arguing. She clenched her fists, terrified at what she had done, which jeopardized not only her future but that of her unborn child. But she had little choice. If Concha went to the Holy Office to accuse Doña Benita as a Judaizer, the woman might accuse her of being a disciple. Her only hope to avoid torture, even death, would be to turn witness against Doña Benita. She could never do that willingly. But there was no way she could be sure of her resolve should she end up behind the walls of the Castillo.

Chapter Six

CASTILLO SAN JORGE

On the western bank of the Guadalquivir, the tall grey towers of Castillo de San Jorge soared above Triana, casting late afternoon shadows across the river like fingers reaching out to ensnare its enemies. The Castillo had been built on the foundations of the Moorish Castillo de Triana, which was destroyed by Fernando III when he recaptured the city from the Moors in 1248. It had stood ever since as a symbol of Christian triumph, and within its walls, the Holy Office had waged war against heretics for the past hundred years. No one crossing the *Puente de Barcas*, the pontoon bridge that connected Sevilla to Triana, could avoid passing the Castillo. For those unfortunates who ended up in its dungeon, one large windowless room held terrors few could imagine. Manacles and chains lined the damp stone walls, and hooks hung from the ceiling so prisoners could be suspended by ropes with weights attached to their limbs. In the center of the chamber was a wooden structure, the *potro*, on which prisoners were laid, their arms and legs tied to rollers at either end. When turned, the rollers dislocated limbs from their sockets until the prisoner confessed or passed out. But such a fate could be avoided, so long as the prisoner reconciled with the Church to save his immortal soul.

It was this mission to save souls that had driven Padre Diego Dominguez to become an inquisitor. Dominguez came from Llerena in the adjoining province of Extremadura, where he'd assisted Francisco de Soto in the prosecution of the Alumbrados, a local group of mystics, until the bishop was poisoned by his own physician. During his investigation into de Soto's death, Dominguez developed his real passion: to root out the secret Jews who still held to their old faith. For he believed that de Soto was one of those men led astray by Judaizers.

His zeal had taken its toll on Padre Dominguez. He had been a man of average build and height when he entered the Order, but everything about him seemed to have shrunk with the years. Though only forty, most of his hair had fallen out, and what remained was nearly white.

Now, he sat across the broad table from the slave who was nervously tapping her foot against the tiles. She was fat but neat in a clean muslin frock, her skin as black as a ripe olive. Her wide nostrils flared even as she kept her head down, resting her chin on her large bosom. He had seen many such women since he'd arrived in Sevilla: eager to expose Judaizers to the Holy Office in hopes of gaining some advantage. Often, they were servants or slaves, like this woman, who felt mistreated in some way. Sometimes it was a woman who had had a falling out with her neighbor or became jealous when the accused had caught her husband's eye.

He knew he should be careful as he listened to the woman's story. His resources were limited, and his priests couldn't investigate every piece of gossip. He needed evidence, not hearsay or fantasy. He wouldn't allow attacks like the ones that had occurred in the early years when men and women were dragged from their homes, their property looted, accused of murdering Christian children and spreading the plague. His was not a mission of revenge, but to save souls.

"What have you observed with your own eyes? I want specifics," he said, his voice so low Concha strained forward to listen. He stood up from the table, placing his hands into his floor-length black scapular robe above the cincture that held the outer garment to his white tunic. The large rosary hanging from his waist hit the table as he swayed back and forth on his heels. The sound created a contrapuntal rhythm with the woman's tapping foot, echoing off the stones of the castle.

"I've seen things, Padre. Just yesterday, Doña Benita came into the *cocina* to inspect the guinea hens we were serving at the banquet to celebrate Don Pedro's return. She gave me a perfectly good hen for the servants' meal because she didn't like the look of its lungs." She lifted an eyebrow, looking directly into the priest's pale eyes.

"She has been ill, correct?" Dominguez asked. "You told me she spent much of her time in bed, coughing up blood on occasion."

"Yes, it's true."

"Maybe she feared a fowl with bad lungs would worsen her condition. You didn't consider that, did you?" The woman had looked for the worst explanation, one that didn't even make sense, because she obviously hated her mistress. He wondered why, but it would be difficult to get her to tell him honestly.

"What else was served at the meal?" What meats?"

"A roasted lamb and a suckling pig, Padre."

"A pig you say?"

"Yes."

"And did your mistress eat the pig?"

"She ate almost nothing. And then she started one of her coughing fits and had to be carried to her quarters."

"And others? Did Don Pedro Péres eat pork?" Concha bowed her head. She began to whimper, shutting her eyes. "Did he?" he asked. His upper lip quivered. He had caught her in a lie. She was nothing but an ingrate who wanted to smear her mistress.

"I think so," she sniffled.

He walked around the table until he stood next to her. He pulled his bony fist from under his garment and slammed it on the table. "I want to know what you *know*, not what you imagine. Do you know the Eighth Commandment? 'Thou shalt not bear false witness against thy neighbor?'"

"But, Padre, I came with the best intentions. I felt it was my duty."

"Go. I cannot waste my time with false accusations. Doña Benita has been a generous benefactress to the Church. Did you know her son is a member of our Order?"

"Yes, but…" Concha faltered.

"Out of here, before I decide to investigate *you*," he shouted.

Concha left the room in a state of terror. She'd been mistaken to come without further proof. She would find some in time, so long as she kept her eyes open and her mouth shut. Especially in front of Esperanza, who didn't have the good sense to realize that she was still chattel, to be sold or traded like the rest, no matter how well they treated her.

Padre Dominguez retreated behind the table and sat gripping the edge of the wood. The woman had left a rank odor. Was it menstrual blood? He shuddered, recoiling at the woman's sensuality, her piercing eyes, full lips, and ample breasts. No doubt she had led many men astray. Perhaps even Don Pedro Péres. That might explain her anger toward Doña Benita. Why were men so frail? Even those within his Order. He looked out the bars of the window but saw no trace of the woman on the street.

He felt the need for prayer and mortification after his encounter with the woman. His cell, down the long hall from his office, was directly over the small room where prisoners were brought throughout the day to reconsider their obstinate refusal of Christ's mercy. He'd decided on this particular cell so he could be reminded of his duty. Day and night he could hear the anguished cries of those who suffered the turning of the rack, their limbs stretched until their bones broke or they confessed, as well as the muffled whimpers of those administered the *torca*, whose voices were too weak from their near-drowning to give evidence against themselves until later. He wanted to experience their pain so that he might never forget the heavy responsibility that rested on his shoulders.

He knelt on the floor of his cell and untied the cincture around his waist. The dark leather was worn and supple, its edges frayed. He lifted the scapular over his head and laid it on the ground, then untied the strings that secured his tunic and slipped his arms out of the garment so that his back and chest were bare. He usually waited to begin his self-flagellation until he heard the screams from the chamber below him. He would pray then that his suffering might be joined with that of the heretic to open the unfortunate's soul.

But his purpose today was more urgent. He must cleanse himself of the unchaste desire that now consumed him. Her very name, Concha, conjured impure images of the pink flesh between a woman's legs. The first sting of the leather brought tears to his eyes, but he didn't stop until he had completed praying the rosary of the Blessed Virgin to purify himself of all carnal desires. Afterwards, he lay prostrate on his pallet, the damp air of his bare cell inflicting yet more exquisite pain across his flayed flesh.

A loud knock roused him from a deep sleep. He didn't know how long he'd been lying there, but the banging at his door suggested he had missed some important duty. "Wait!" he shouted, gingerly pulling his tunic up over his raw back. He hoped the blood had dried so that the cloth wouldn't stick to his wounds. He'd never performed this act of mortification at such length. He didn't want the friar who washed his garments to wonder what awful sins he was trying to purify. It could cause gossip among the others, whose vows of obedience were as loosely kept as their vows of poverty and chastity.

"Yes, what is it?" he asked the young friar, Ignácio, who stood shaking before him.

"There's a problem below. One of the accused has hanged herself." Ignácio's smooth face was white with fear, his small hands nervously fingering his beads.

"When? Who was she?"

"It was the young girl whose mother gave witness against her. I found her just a few minutes ago when I came to deliver her food. I thought to tell you first, Padre."

"But how did she do it? Haven't we made sure there are no means available to the prisoners to harm themselves?"

THE SILVER CANDLESTICKS

"We have, Padre, but the girl was so small—almost a child, really—she used her shift to hang herself from the bars on the window. If she had been a little bit taller..." the young friar began to tremble.

"Lord have mercy on her soul. She has committed the sin against the Holy Ghost, despairing of God's forgiveness. But why, Ignácio? Didn't she understand we'd show her mercy if she repented and returned to the faith?"

Ignacio couldn't answer. Instead, he began to cry like a woman, wringing his hands, unable to catch his breath. Dominguez reached out and patted the friar's shoulders. "Come, my son. Show me."

The two men walked down the dank staircase to the area of the castle where the prisoners were held. Torches burned at intervals along the way, filling the long hallway with acrid smoke that stung the padre's eyes and choked him. Dominguez covered his mouth with the corner of his habit to avoid the stench of human waste as he peered into one of the cells that held multiple prisoners. Old, crippled men huddled alongside younger ones whose bodies were nearly as disfigured. These were the hard cases, the ones who had been subject to tortures but still hadn't confessed.

He prayed day and night for these heretics. Why would they not repent, even as the turns of the rack stretched their bodies beyond human endurance? It was all he could do to keep from screaming out when he attended the *tormentos*. And yet he was bound by sacred duty to witness the most important interrogations to ensure justice. He needed to listen with his own ears to the confessions of those put on the rack. How else could he be sure nothing had been left out when the prisoner was asked to repeat their confession before the tribunal?

But it was not always possible, and he had failed to be there during the girl's mother's ordeal. He wondered what would happen when she was asked at trial to attest that her child practiced the Law of Moses. He'd seen many prisoners recant their testimony, especially when they'd accused family members. He prayed the woman would choose to save her own soul now that her daughter's was lost for eternity.

They came to the girl's cell. The fat jailer who stood guard outside smelled of garlic and stale wine. The man leaned unsteadily against the wood door, his head blocking the small grate that allowed a glimpse into the darkened cell. As soon as he recognized Padre Dominguez, he stepped aside.

"Has anyone been in here?"

"No, Padre. Brother Ignácio said not to allow anyone entry."

"Good. And you? Have you been inside?" The man shook his head, but Padre Dominguez didn't believe him. He lifted the heavy bar that secured the cell and pulled the door open. At the far end of the cell, the late afternoon sunlight through the tiny window cast a glow above the girl's head. If he didn't know better, he might have thought it was a halo. *How the devil tries to trick us*, he thought. It was so dark that he couldn't make out any details, just the silhouette of the body against the dark walls. He stood still, wary of moving forward until his vision adjusted to the dim light. Brother Ignácio's sobs irritated him. Why was he crying? For this girl whose sins could never be forgiven now? The boy had a kind heart, but his pity was misdirected.

Slowly, he could make out the figure before him. Dominguez shielded his eyes from the vision before him. The girl's naked body hung from the grey camisa wound tightly around her neck. Had she planned this final sinful act: to expose her body in defiance of all natural modesty? "Ignácio, quickly find something to cover her," he yelled, though the friar was so close their habits were almost touching. The boy grabbed a filthy blanket on the pile of straw in the corner, which sent two black rats scurrying for a crack in the damp walls. The priest grabbed the blanket from Ignácio's hands and wrapped it around the corpse, which had already begun to stiffen.

"Cut her down," he said to the guard who'd stepped into the cell. The man pulled a long knife from his belt and cut the tattered cloth attached to the window bars. The body fell against

THE SILVER CANDLESTICKS

Dominguez as he held the blanket around it. He staggered backwards, not because of the weight—which was less than a large sack of beans—but because he felt the presence of evil around him.

"Take her away. And make sure no one sees you," he growled at the guard through clenched teeth. Brother Ignácio fell to his knees on the filthy floor, but the priest grabbed him by the cowl of his habit and jerked him up. "And you," he said, putting his long, skinny finger into the young man's chest, "keep your mouth shut." Ignácio recoiled from the priest's tone and grasp.

When he returned to his office, Dominguez summoned his chief inquisitors, Padre Yañes, a Dominican, and Padre Jaramillo, a Franciscan who had only recently arrived at the Castillo. The men stood before him, visibly shaken by the news of the suicide. Jaramillo's lips moved in silent prayer while Yañes swayed forward and back, clutching his rosary.

"Well, what have you to say?" Dominguez demanded. "What transpired at the *tormento*? Do you have the scribe's notations?"

Padre Yañes was first to speak. The priest was nearly the same age as Dominguez and came from a smaller town in Extremadura. But unlike his superior, Yañes was swarthy-skinned and built like an ox, with broad, well-muscled shoulders that strained against the strictures of his habit. "Nothing unusual happened," he answered. "Inés Mejia gave witness under moderate torture against her daughter Paloma. It was our intention to question her again today."

"But she recanted it as soon as the ropes were loosened," Padre Jaramillo interrupted. Yañes threw the younger priest a quick look meant to silence him. But Jaramillo couldn't remain silent. He had objected when the mother was tortured, to no avail. She willingly confessed she was a secret Jew, but it was clear from her answers throughout the many interrogations he'd witnessed that she knew almost nothing about Jewish ritual or teachings.

"How many turns of the rack did she endure before giving her child's name?" Dominguez asked.

"I believe it was four," Yañes replied. "I'd have to consult the secretary's transcript before giving a definitive answer." The procedures to be followed were meticulously observed. The interrogators did not make the rules, but they obeyed them to the letter.

"But she's a small woman," Jaramillo interjected. "Four turns would inflict more pain on her than on a larger person." He'd made the same point before his fellow inquisitor ordered the guard to turn the wheels a fourth time, but Yañes ignored him.

Dominguez took note of Jaramillo's vehemence. He would have to question the Franciscan alone to get to the bottom of what had happened with the girl's mother. It was possible that the Franciscan simply had no stomach for the work. He might even by sympathetic to these secret Jews, which would necessitate closely watching his behavior at future tribunals. But another explanation worried Dominguez. What if the girl was innocent? A sweat broke out on his brow. He wanted to be alone, to pray for guidance.

"I want the transcript. Do you hear me? And I had better not find it different from what you've told me. We have a dead girl—how old was she? This incident could endanger our whole purpose here. Do you think we're monsters who drive mothers to make false accusation against their own children?" he shouted.

"Forgive me for speaking, Padre, but I've seen it before. I know our purpose is to elicit the truth, but fear of pain can cloud the mind…" Jaramillo said, his voice trailing off to barely a whisper.

"Which is why the accused must swear freely, under no duress, at trial that her confession is truthful." Yañes spat out his words.

"There's no point in arguing among ourselves," Dominguez interjected. "We want the truth here. Which is why I will begin an inquiry into this matter. In the meantime, it's important that this be kept quiet. Pray that word has not already spread among the cells below. The mother must be isolated immediately."

"She was twelve." The young Franciscan's voice trembled with emotion.

"What?"

"You asked how old the girl was. She was twelve."

Padre Dominguez clutched his knees, driving his fingers deep into the flesh through his garments. Holy Mother of God, why had he not taken time to attend the *tormento*? Had he been there, would he have stopped the turns of the winches that pulled the limbs from their sockets? Was it possible, Dear God, that pain had driven this woman to utter such a terrible accusation if it weren't true? But what else could one do with these Judaizers and their secrets? He must examine the records of this case. Who were the witnesses against Inés Mejia? He couldn't remember. He was overworked. There were so many to investigate and so few resources. The Judaizers who'd been found guilty had too often been simple artisans and storekeepers with little property to seize. He must petition the Master of the Order again to send him another priest. And if he couldn't count on his own Order to support his work, he'd seek the intercession of the bishop.

"You may go, Padre Yañes," he said. "Padre Jaramillo, stay for a moment." Yañes turned abruptly on the heels of his sandals and left wordlessly. The man was angry. It was not a good thing, Dominguez thought. "Have a seat, Padre," he said, motioning the younger priest to sit in the chair the slave Concha had earlier occupied. "I wish to talk to you as your Confessor. I must know what you observed. I regret that I wasn't there myself." He wondered what had kept him from his duty the day before but couldn't recall.

The Franciscan remained reticent. The rough brown fabric of his habit was threadbare and shabby, and his face was gaunt. Father Dominguez wondered whether the man's former superior had transferred him to Sevilla to get rid of a troublemaker. If the man couldn't answer a direct question, his word might not be trustworthy. "Speak, Jorge," he said, hoping the use of the priest's Christian name would loosen his tongue.

"I wish to tell you everything, Padre, as God is my witness. But I must also tell you that I have grave doubts that I'm fit to continue in service to the Holy Office." The man shuddered as he spoke.

"We all have doubts, my son. Have you prayed to the Holy Ghost about this?" he asked, mustering all the kindness he could inject into his voice. It was important to earn the young priest's trust, especially if he turned out to be an enemy. "You must ask that your doubts be lifted so that you may continue your work here. You are vital to our mission in a way that Padre Yañes cannot be."

Dominguez stopped speaking briefly as he held the priest's gaze. He raised his pale eyebrows and nodded benevolently to assure the man of his sincerity. "We must approach each accusation with skepticism," he continued. "It must be proven through our canonical process. We are careful. We take testimony. We provide a lawyer to the accused."

Dominguez paused again to see if his words were having the desired effect. But Jaramillo remained mute, his eyes betraying nothing. After an awkward few seconds, Dominguez began again.

"Like you, I worry that men like Yañes are too willing to accept the testimony of those who bear some grudge against the accused," he said. He knew he should tread carefully in case the man used his words against him in the future. But he needed to find the truth. "The Holy Office has enough priests who follow Yañes's path. We need more like *you*." He reached across the table for the young priest's hands, which were folded as in prayer.

"I don't approve of torture," the Franciscan said, withdrawing his hands. He looked directly into his superior's eyes, which suddenly flared in anger.

"But Rome has sanctioned its use." Dominguez slapped the table with his open palms, staring back at the priest. "What's worse, a few moments of earthly pain or an eternity in the fires of hell? Our mission is to save souls," he said, his voice rising again.

Padre Jaramillo fingered the knot on the rope belt tied around his habit. The fibers had begun to unravel. "She begged for mercy, the mother. I should have intervened." He hesitated again. "Shouldn't torture be reserved for the most extreme cases?" he asked in a voice barely louder than a whisper.

"There were many witnesses who came forward against her," Dominguez said, growing impatient with the young priest's insolence.

THE SILVER CANDLESTICKS

"Inés Mejia was accused of turning her eyes away from the Host when the priest raised the ciborium last Easter. Does this prove she was a Judaizer?"

Dominguez's jaw tightened. "And the girl's suicide? Isn't it further proof that the Mejia family are heretics?"

"She's not been in her right mind since she was brought here. I warned Padre Yañes against putting her in a solitary cell. Gregorio told me earlier that she has barely eaten anything in the last two weeks."

"What does that stinking drunkard of a jailer know? He's probably lying to protect himself. He should have been more vigilant in making his rounds. He might have stopped the girl before she condemned her own soul to damnation."

Dominguez stood up, his slight frame shrinking in upon itself. He would get nothing more from the priest today. "Let's talk further when you've had time to examine your conscience," he said. "Meanwhile, I will add you to my prayers so that you may know your duty and serve Our Lord."

The young priest bowed his head and retreated from his superior's office. Padre Dominguez vowed to find out from Brother Ignácio whether the man had told the truth about the girl's refusing food. If so, he should have been informed sooner. These priests and monks were an unreliable sort, used to lax obedience, unlike the strict discipline that prevailed in Llerena.

The bells announced Vespers. He'd missed both Sext and None while he dealt with the dead girl. He must hurry if he was to take his place in the chapel for the chanting of the Hours. He stood up from the table with difficulty. He nearly lost his balance from the pain of his torn flesh. He would offer up his suffering for Padre Jaramillo. The priest might yet come to recognize the Church's wisdom in ridding the kingdom of these Judaizers who jeopardized the souls of all New Christians, not just their own.

Chapter Seven

THE SACRAMENTS

The two black Arabians, their manes braided in white ribbons, coats shining in the bright morning sun, lifted their forelegs and impatiently set them down on the dusty narrow street. Don Enrique stood beside the carriage, waiting to assist Doña Benita and Guiomar into the compartment, hidden from sight as they traveled the short distance to Santa Ana's. Felipe held the bridles, looking almost as nervous as the horses. Finally, the gate opened, and Benita emerged in her husband's arms. She looked almost childlike in a blue satin dress that enveloped her tiny frame. Don Pedro nodded at his partner, who stepped back to allow him to place her on the carriage seat. Despite her frail body, it was still a struggle to fit her in with her hoops bumping against the front and burying her in fabric.

"May I help, my friend?" Enrique felt a surge of pity for Pedro despite his recent betrayal. It couldn't be easy to watch your beloved waste away before your eyes. His own wife's end had come quickly—and he had spent fewer years at her side. He still thought of Beatriz occasionally, always with regret that she had given him no heirs. He might have married again, but his business had monopolized his passions—and now Pedro was risking even that.

"Thank you, Enrique, but I think she's settled now. Aren't you, my dear?"

"I'll be fine. I've prayed to the Blessed Virgin to give me strength," she said, looking into her husband's dark eyes. She clasped a crystal rosary in her hands, which she lifted to show to Enrique. Everything she did now would reflect on Guiomar. She must observe every ritual of the Mass. This would be the last time she'd hold the host on her tongue, filling the long moments until it dissolved with prayers asking the God of Moses for forgiveness. When the priest came to administer Extreme Unction, she planned to feign choking so as not to taste the blasphemous wafer again.

"We'll walk together to the church," Enrique said to Pedro. "There's not enough room in the carriage with the women's gowns."

Pedro nodded. Their talk after the banquet a few days earlier had resolved nothing. Enrique insisted his partner owed it to him to return to the seas once his wife was in her grave. But the man had been obstinate. Was he hiding something? He seemed reluctant to return to Veracruz. Was there some woman who would expect him to marry her now that Benita was gone? He'd heard no gossip to that effect, but one never knew.

The door opened again and Guiomar appeared on the steps looking more beautiful than ever, her slim shoulders held back, her long neck taught, accentuating the soft line of her jaw. An old lace mantilla, which had turned the color of wilting camellias, covered her thick, dark hair. The yellowed lace made the white of her satin bodice and skirts appear even more brilliant. She had not yet covered her face, which looked unnaturally pale despite the rouge on her cheeks and lips. Behind her, Esperanza carried the long train of her gown. Guiomar's hooped skirt, like her mother's, would prove difficult to fit into the carriage. Her father stepped forward to take her arm, bending to place a kiss on her brow.

"You look lovely, my child," he said as he lifted her hand to his lips. She was wearing the emerald he had brought back from his voyage, the facets catching the sunlight. He was pleased that he could give her such a gift. There might not be many like it in the future.

Pedro walked her around the carriage and helped her up onto the stool so she could step in. Esperanza stepped forward awkwardly trying to fit the satin train in the carriage at Guiomar's feet without soiling the fabric or encumbering her mistress's movements.

"We will have to send you ahead so that you can be there at Guiomar's side when she arrives," Pedro said. "Felipe will go with you."

Esperanza looked pleadingly at Guiomar, who seemed to sense her discomfort.

"I think we can squeeze her in here," Guiomar offered. "She can crouch at our feet. "Do you mind, Esperanza?" The servant looked relieved.

"It's time," Enrique said. Your father and I will walk in front. Felipe will lead the horses.

Esperanza had only caught a glimpse of Felipe as she carried the train around the carriage. He looked more handsome than she'd ever seen him, wearing a burgundy jerkin and britches, his white stockings showing off the strength of his calves. She wondered if he had even noticed her behind the bride. She, too, was dressed more elegantly than ever before, thanks to Doña Benita's generosity. Her mistress had given her an old blue velvet farthingale. A bit heavy for the season, but it fit her well, even with her thickening waist. She'd never possessed such an elegant gown. She couldn't help hoping she would wear it on her wedding day. But Felipe hadn't spoken to her in weeks.

The scent of white roses and melting candle wax wafted through the church. The altar was arrayed in white, the statue of the Virgin in rich white and gold brocade. The guests had been waiting restlessly for Mass to begin. In the rear of the church, two people seemed especially eager. The first, Padre Dominguez, wearing his stark black and white robes, looked around him, observing everyone already in the pews. The second, the handsome José Marcos, faded in and out of the shadows.

THE SILVER CANDLESTICKS

Padre Dominguez scoured the faces, looking for the servant who had visited the Castillo. He didn't expect to find her at Mass. But if she were, he'd decided not to acknowledge her. He was there to observe the bride and her mother. He had little doubt that his initial instinct was correct—they were loyal and true to the Church. But he would be derelict if he didn't witness them perform their religious duties. Sometimes, a Judaizer would give a sign: failing to look at the Host during the consecration, refusing communion, being slow to kneel. It was not proof they held to their heretical faith. Even he found his observance faltering after a bad night's sleep, like the ones he'd suffered every night since the girl's suicide at the Castillo. But it was a piece of evidence he could use if needed.

Two young boys emerged from behind the sacristy curtains, one holding a gold censer by its long looped chain and the other the silver-bound prayer book. Two priests followed, the hems of their black habits showing beneath their white cassocks. Both men wore the tonsure of the Order of St. Dominic. The younger one's hair was black, the thick curls cut close to the scalp so that he looked like a shorn lamb on the way to the slaughter, an effect the solemnity his face reinforced. Behind them followed the old priest, Padre Saavedra, his ancient shoulders stooped beneath the heavy white and gold vestments.

In the front pew, Francisco Armijo, his father, and two uncles stood up as the priests crossed the altar. Francisco and the older of the uncles stepped out into the aisle. Francisco was of above-average height, broad-shouldered, with a short-cropped beard whose color was lighter—redder—than the chestnut on his head. His thick brows gave him a serious look, though his lips were curled in a smile of anticipation as he glanced toward the main door. But in the back of the church, just behind the point where he would greet his bride to accompany her to the altar, he spied Guiomar's lover. Francisco started down the aisle, unsure what he would do when he stood face-to-face with Herrera. The man's presence was an insult. But as he reached the end of the nave, Herrera stepped behind a priest. The fellow was a coward. Still, if Guiomar loved Herrera, she would never love him. He pushed the thought away.

Outside, the bridal party entered the square in front of the church. Felipe pulled the horses' reins, bringing them to a halt, while Enrique and Pedro flanked the carriage. Esperanza struggled to stand up, nearly losing her balance until Don Enrique reached in to give her his hand. She took it haltingly, unaccustomed to being assisted by anyone other than her fellow servants, and even they rarely helped. She stepped down onto the stones of the plaza, holding her dress above her ankles. Behind her, Guiomar leaned forward, taking her godfather's arm. Esperanza positioned herself to grab the long train of Guiomar's gown as the bride stepped out, making sure the white fabric didn't touch the ground.

Benita sat patiently waiting until her husband could help her. She worried that she wouldn't be able to walk down the aisle, but she didn't want to be carried. The sun shone brightly in a cloudless sky, but she shivered as her husband reached in to slip an arm under her legs and the other behind her back. She leaned against him, allowing him to bear her weight. The hoops of her gown flew up, indecorously exposing her white stockinged calves. She pushed the skirt down with her hands, but no one looked her way in the plaza, empty except for the wedding party.

"Can you walk, *mi corazón?*" Benita nodded and feebly squeezed his arm. Pedro helped her around the carriage toward Enrique. "My friend, will you do the honors?"

Enrique quickly came to Benita's side and put one arm around her thin back and laid her arm over his other. "Lean on me, Benita. I will not let you fall," he reassured her.

Pedro then took his daughter's arm to lead her into the church. Guiomar let the front of the mantilla down to cover her face. The church loomed in front of her, obscured in dark shadows through the lace.

"Be strong, *m'hija*," her father whispered. He hoped she would accept Francisco. The boy was no fool, and with his daughter's generous dowry, he would quickly become a prosperous merchant. His

THE SILVER CANDLESTICKS

ambition, as he had explained to Don Pedro, was to take his trade to Méjico where labor was plentiful and cheap, available for the cost of shelter and food. He could make his candles in the Indies and ship them back to Spain for more profit than he'd earn simply selling them in Sevilla. And, of course, he would expand his products, making not only the candles but candelabra and candlesticks.

But Pedro understood that his daughter could see no farther than the next few hours and days. He believed Francisco would prove a gentle and loving husband who would bring his daughter happiness, but at the moment, Guiomar looked as if she were going to a funeral.

Felipe pulled open the heavy church door, and they stepped across the threshold as the congregation rose to greet their arrival. Esperanza bent to lay down the long train as her mistress moved forward, then slipped into a pew at the back.

Guiomar's eyes searched the crowded church as she moved slowly from the side door. At first, she did not see him hidden in the shadows. But just as she reached the center aisle, he stepped forward, and she knew it was him. She had hoped María Dolores would come, but she had never imagined José Marcos would be so reckless. She gripped her father's arm, fearing José Marcos had come to expose her before she could take her vow. She was so distracted, she didn't notice Francisco, beaming, as he walked toward her. Her father patted her hand and gently moved it to the groom's.

Francisco slipped his arm underneath hers, the weight of her arm as light as a bird's wing. He couldn't see her face clearly, but the warmth of her body aroused him. He'd never been so close to her before. Soon he would be closer still.

Guiomar instinctively shrank from his touch, then caught herself. When she looked up again, José Marcos had stepped back into the shadows. The walk down the aisle, though no more than fifty steps, seemed interminable. She was glad for the veil that covered the pain in her face so that no one could see it.

At the altar, Guiomar was barely aware of her groom. Instead she focused on her brother, Alfonso, who stood smiling next to the old priest. She hadn't seen him since he had taken Holy Orders more than five years ago. He'd seemed happy then too. She felt bitterness that her family's secret had been kept from her so long. If she'd known about it earlier, her expectations would have been different. She would never have permitted herself to fall in love with José Marcos or dream of a life she could never have. Her parents believed they were protecting her, but instead they'd made life unbearable. It was far more painful to know love and be deprived of it than never to have experienced it in the first place.

Alfonso nodded at her, his eyes, dark and deep-set like their mother's, glistening under the large sanctuary lamp. She would rather her fate had been the same as his, locked in a convent somewhere, never to marry. If she could study the sacred texts, then maybe she would understand why it was so important that she sacrifice her personal happiness to protect a despised people. She was so distracted she barely heard the priest's words.

"Francisco and Guiomar, have you come here freely and without reservation to give yourselves to each other in marriage?"

She breathed deeply, forcing her words out as she exhaled. "Yes," she said, but her voice was barely audible compared to Francisco's strong assent.

"Will you love and honor each other as man and wife for the rest of your lives?" Padre Saavedra asked, staring intently. She closed her eyes briefly before replying yes, but in her heart, she vowed she would never be his. Her parents could force her to marry this man, but they could never make her love him.

Francisco felt a chill go through him. He had dreamed of this day since he and Guiomar had played in the Péres' yard as children. He hadn't understood at first why his dream could never be fulfilled. He remembered being turned away by a servant at the door to the Péres' *cocina* when he was twelve. One day he was allowed to chase Guiomar around the orange trees in a game of hide and seek, and the next day it was forbidden. His father tried to explain it to him. "You are getting too old to be playmates. And you can never be lovers, my son. Her parents won't take that chance, so you must

THE SILVER CANDLESTICKS

learn to stay away from her. Forget her, Francisco, she is too far above our station. No matter how much wealth you accumulate, you will never be worthy in Don Pedro's eyes." Now the words that he'd uttered as he'd lied to his father were again coming from his lips. "I will," he said, turning to look at his bride.

The priest turned again to Guiomar. "Will you accept children lovingly from God and bring them up according to the law of Christ and his Church?" the priest asked each in turn. Guiomar felt the words choke in her throat. Yes, she would raise her children as honest Christians. She would not curse them with the burden her mother had imposed. Her parents had insisted she marry a faithful Christian, and in return, she would give them Christian heirs. It would serve them right.

When each had assented, Padre Saavedra took the groom's hands and laid them on the bride's. Alfonso Péres stepped forward and walked behind the couple, handing the old priest one end of a strand of long brightly colored ribbons, which he then unfurled over their shoulders, placing the other end in Saavedra's right hand. The priest tugged on the ribbons, drawing the couple closer together, as he uttered the words that would bind them until death: "I unite you in wedlock." He blessed them with the sign of the cross and leaned forward to give the groom a kiss on both cheeks. In turn, Francisco lifted the lace mantilla and was about to convey the same sign of peace on his bride's tear-stained cheeks when a cry went up from the pew behind him.

By the time Doctor Garcia arrived, Benita was barely breathing. She lay on her bed, still wearing the blue bodice of the gown she had worn to the wedding. Esperanza, tugging and pulling, had removed the hooped underskirt so it wouldn't fly up to expose her mistress. Don Pedro knelt next to the bed, his head buried in his hands. Guiomar knelt beside him, her husband resting his hands gently on her shoulders, while Esperanza stood against the bureau, weeping silently. Padre Saavedra stood on the opposite side of the bed, his gold vestments replaced by a simple white surplice and purple stole. With him were two Dominicans, the dying woman's son, Alfonso, and the inquisitor from the Castillo, Padre Dominguez, who had asked if he could attend out of his great respect for "a great benefactress and faithful servant of the Church." Saavedra didn't like the look of the fellow, whose eyes burned with a fanatic's zeal. But it would be dangerous for a simple parish priest to offend such a powerful representative of the Church.

Standing stiffly next to the inquisitor, Alfonso held a silver tray with a small bowl of water, six pellets of cotton, and a piece of bread. At that moment, he wanted more than anything to put down the tray and lean over to kiss his mother's dying lips. But he must play the role of priest, not son. If she were awake, his mother would understand. When he'd objected that he couldn't become a priest in good conscience because he would have to affirm his belief in the Trinity, she reminded him of Jacob's deception of the Patriarch Abraham. "God's will sometimes requires us to deceive our fellow man. Didn't his mother Sarah persuade Jacob to cover himself in animal skins so that he could receive his father's blessing instead of Esau?" He smiled at the memory.

Padre Dominguez gripped the small flask of holy oil in its purple silk pouch in one hand, and in the other, the round silver vessel that held holy water. He looked over at the Péres' son, whose lips conveyed levity rather than the pain of his impending loss. He wondered what the man could be thinking to make him smile at such a solemn time. He knew that men as handsome as Péres had many worldly temptations and resolved to speak to the priest's superior about his reputation.

Padre Saavedra lifted the crucifix from the small table next to the bed and took the holy water from the sour faced Dominican, sprinkling it on all those assembled. "Purify me with hyssop, Lord, and I shall be clean of sin. Wash me, and I shall be whiter than snow. Have mercy on me, God, in your great kindness," he chanted in Latin. Esperanza moved closer so that the droplets would fall on her though she could not understand the prayer. Alfonso pressed his hands together. If only his mother could hear the words the

THE SILVER CANDLESTICKS

priest uttered now and know that they were David's plea for forgiveness after he had sinned with Bathsheba.

Benita flinched as the water touched her skin, a movement Padre Dominguez noted. Perhaps it was merely the body's reaction to something cold and wet, he thought. But other explanations were possible as well. He would watch for any other signs until the woman took her final breath.

Saavedra lifted his right hand and made the sign of the cross: "In the name of the Father, and of the Son, and of the Holy Spirit; may any power the devil has over you be destroyed by the laying-on of our hands and by calling on the glorious and blessed Virgin Mary, Mother of God, her illustrious spouse, St. Joseph, and all holy angels, archangels, patriarchs, prophets, apostles, martyrs, confessors, virgins, and all the saints." He pulled a small silver flask from his pocket, applied a drop of oil on his thumb, and made a small cross in holy oil on Benita's eyelids, which fluttered at his touch. "By this holy anointing and by His most tender mercy, may the Lord forgive thee whatever thou hast done amiss by sight."

Then he blessed her earlobes, nostrils, lips, and hands, invoking the same plea for God's mercy. He walked to the foot of the bed and motioned the servant to approach. Esperanza moved swiftly to his side, not knowing what was expected of her. She glanced at Padre Alfonso, who pointed with his chin toward the bed. She realized then that the priest had blessed the hands but not the feet and bent to pull back the heavy blanket. Doña Benita still wore her white hosiery. Esperanza gently reached under the cotton underskirt and pulled down the stockings, exposing her mistress's thin ankles and tiny feet, which had already turned blue. The priest poured another drop of oil onto his thumb and blessed the soles of both feet.

Alfonso moved toward Padre Saavedra, who had baptized him and heard his first confession as a boy. How innocent he was then, how devout in his Catholic faith. He felt a surge of affection for the priest who wished to usher his mother into heaven cleansed of her sins, but also pity that the man worshipped false gods. Yet this was no more Saavedra's fault than it was Alfonso's that he must hide his Hebrew faith under the cassock of a priest. He looked toward his sister, whose bowed head rested on her clasped hands. Francisco's hands lay lightly on her shoulders. Alfonso nodded as Francisco looked up to meet his gaze. They were brothers now, bound together by law and their love for Guiomar.

Padre Saavedra reached out to Alfonso who moved the silver tray closer to the priest. The old man's gnarled hands shook faintly as he dipped his fingertips into the water and dried them on the piece of bread, which he then dropped into the bowl. The pellets of white cotton still lay on the tray and the priest sighed. He had forgotten to wipe the excess oil from the woman. "Son," he whispered softly to Alfonso, "will you take care of blotting the consecrated oil from your mother?" Alfonso nodded and put down the tray, gathering up the small cloth balls in his right hand. He knelt beside his mother and gently touched her forehead. "Baruch Attah *Adonai*," he prayed silently. When he touched his mother's lips, she was no longer breathing. Standing up, he looked at his father and sister. "Rest in peace," he said aloud. "It is over."

"Forgive me, Mamá," Guiomar cried as her husband lifted her into his arms.

Part II
1594

Chapter Eight

A BIRTH

Guiomar lifted the infant from the cradle. The tiny face was shriveled and red, its eyes shut tight and its mouth sucking the air. Her arms felt heavy, as if she were holding a stone instead of the little girl she had just given birth to hours before. Esperanza had wanted to take the child into the servants' quarters so she could be nursed. But Guiomar had insisted on keeping the baby near her for the first night, knowing her room would be warmer. The fire burned brightly, throwing off a red glow along with its soothing warmth. She put her finger into the baby's tiny mouth and felt the gums clamp down around it, instinctively sucking. Her breasts began to drip milk. She thought of putting the child to her breast, but she knew that it would only make it harder for her milk to dry up if the baby suckled even once. Her womb contracted, bringing sharp pains. It had not been like this with the first child.

Francisco had not yet come to see his daughter. Guiomar felt a pang of guilt. She had acted coolly toward her husband throughout her confinement, though he tried his best to be attentive, bringing her sweets and the dark, warm liquid made of the ground cocoa beans her father had brought back from the New World. Don Pedro no longer accompanied his fleet on its trade missions, keeping the promise he'd made to her mother three years earlier. But he remained an investor in Don Enrique's company, and she feared that he might yet be enticed aboard ship only to die on some foreign shore. Tears welled again as the pain in her womb overwhelmed her.

"Esperanza," she called, her voice barely more than a whisper. Withdrawing her finger from its mouth, she put the baby back in its cradle. She would not be a beauty, this child, especially with that wine-colored stain on her cheek. But perhaps that was a blessing. After all, what had her own beauty brought but disappointment? Guiomar reached for the bell on the nightstand. The clang of brass awakened the baby, who began to wail. Propping herself on her elbow, she leaned over the cradle, putting her finger back in the infant's open mouth, which quieted her.

Esperanza pushed open the door and rushed to lift the baby as Guiomar slid her finger out of the child's mouth. "Señora, forgive me. I must have fallen asleep." Guiomar envied Esperanza's soothing ways with children. Her own son had been born only a few months before Antonio, Guiomar's firstborn, and she had nursed both boys, who now toddled around after her, tugging at Esperanza's skirts until she lifted first one, then the other into her arms. Francisco, too, adored the boys, treating Esperanza's son as his own. But Guiomar had warmed to her own son no better than she had to his father. Francisco was a good man, a good husband, but he did not stir the passion she had felt for José Marcos. She wished that she felt differently, but every time she felt tenderness for her husband, José Marcus would creep unbidden into her thoughts.

"My husband is asleep?" Guiomar asked, trying not to convey her disappointment.

"No, Señora, he has asked me to alert him as soon as you asked for him. I think he was afraid to disturb you…"

"No matter. He can come of his own accord or not at all." She sank back against the pillows, grimacing as the contraction came again, nearly as bad as it had been during her labor.

"You are in pain?"

"Yes, it is not like the first."

"They say the second birth brings more pains. But if you wish, I will call for Doctor Garcia."

THE SILVER CANDLESTICKS

"Not yet. A good night's sleep will cure me. Can you bring me a cup of chocolate? And take the child to my husband so he can see her."

"And if he asks for you?"

"I will not refuse him," she said. Although she feigned indifference, her voice betrayed her. Despite her own lack of desire, she still expected him to want her. Her mother would have chided her for being spoiled if she were alive, she thought, and vowed to try harder to love Francisco.

Esperanza wrapped the infant tightly in her blanket and carried her down the hallway to Don Francisco's rooms. She tapped lightly on the door in case he was sleeping after all. It was already past eleven, and the day had been a long one as everyone stood about waiting for her mistress to deliver. Esperanza had not cried out when Benito was born, but the Señora's cries could be heard as far as the servants' quarters during the new infant's birth.

"Enter," Francisco called out. He sat in the same chair he had been sitting in most of the day, a blanket over his feet and a thick book in his lap. As soon as Esperanza came into the room, he jumped to his feet, which sent the precious volume flying.

"Your daughter," Esperanza said, placing the infant into his arms.

"She is beautiful," Francisco cooed, his love for the child blinding him to the reddened skin and puckered lips that made the infant appear more like a wizened crone than a newborn. "We must choose a fitting name for such a princess," he beamed. He had felt great pride when his son was born, but he felt something different now, an instant love that he had experienced only once before—the first time he spied Guiomar through the gate when she was only four or five and he was barely older.

"And the Señora? Is she recovered enough to let me see her?" he asked, his voice plaintive.

Esperanza hesitated a moment. "She is in much pain, Señor, but I think a visit from you would warm her heart." Her master smiled, taking his eyes from the baby for the first time. "I am just on my way to prepare her some chocolate. Perhaps you will take it in my place?"

"Yes, yes, a good idea. I have another gift for her, but who knows that she may not prefer yours." He held the infant in the crook of his arm and reached with his other hand into the pocket of his muslin shirt for the delicate pendant he'd had made for Guiomar at the goldsmith's shop in Barrio Santa Cruz. It was unlike most of her jewelry, gifts from her father that were heavy with large stones set in ornate gold. The pendant he had asked the Jew to make was small, no bigger than a rose petal, but inlaid with tiny colored stones that sparkled as it moved. The chain was as fine as woven strands of silk and so short that the pendant would hang just at the small concave part of her throat. Francisco regarded that place as among the dearest on her body. Sometimes when she lay beside him in the moonlight, he would watch her pulse beating there and it would cause him great longing. But his desire was rarely reciprocated, and she performed her wifely duties with little passion or pleasure.

He had yet to tell her that he was to travel to Veracruz in a few months' time in place of her father, who Don Enrique continued to pester to return to the trade missions. Perhaps she would miss him and might even learn to love him in his absence. Though his hopes seemed less likely to be fulfilled with each passing day.

Esperanza went to the *cocina*, which was dark and cold. She lit a fire in the hearth and filled the kettle with water from the pitcher, which had a thin layer of ice floating on its surface. She wrapped her shawl around her for warmth and sat on the bench at the table. Her eyelids felt heavy, and she wished she could be in her bed next to her son, for she would have to be up again at dawn. Her mistress was demanding, though she had softened a bit after Doña Benita's death. Esperanza felt some bond with her mistress: they had both been denied the right to share their lives with the men they loved. It was clear to her that the Señora did not love her husband, though she was never unkind to him in Esperanza's presence. But it was equally clear that the Señor adored and doted on her, even if his actions seemed occasionally to annoy her.

Esperanza watched the kettle as the flames leaped up around it. She stood and moved closer to the fire, both to keep warm and to fight off sleep by remaining on her feet. She almost forgot to fetch the dark powder to make the drink. She had prepared a large stock of it early in the winter, mixed with the sweet *azúcar de caña* and *la canela* that Don Péres had first carried back from the Azores, and it had now become a popular beverage in Sevilla. She went to the cupboard and reached for the earthen jar she kept the mixture in, but in her sleepiness, she knocked it over and most of the contents spilled on the ground, splattering her skirt with the fine residue. The sound of breaking crockery echoed off the pantry walls, but there was no one else to hear the racket. She bent down and shoved the powder into a pile and then looked around for something to hold the precious mixture. Finding a small red and yellow bowl, she scooped the pile into the container.

Had Doña Benita been alive, she would never have dared such uncleanliness, but the household no longer followed the old rules. The cooks prepared meat without first examining it. No longer did she have to remove the vein from the lamb's forelegs and shoulder or discard certain parts of the meat. Even the slaughtering of the chickens and lambs had become careless. Guiomar had given no specific instructions to abandon her mother's practices, but neither did she often enter the *cocina* to ensure their enforcement. Esperanza did not want to risk Concha or one of the others going to the Dominican, who occasionally dined at the household at Don Pedro's invitation, so she let Doña Benita's rules go with her to the grave.

Esperanza poured the hot water over the rescued powder in a large cup for her mistress. She sipped the liquid, which scalded her tongue. It tasted sweet and bitter at once. She carried the cup brimming with the steaming chocolate to Señor Francisco's room. When she opened the door, she found him rocking the sleeping infant in his arms.

"I will trade my sweet for yours," he said.

Esperanza placed the cup on the trunk at the foot of the bed and stretched out her arms. "She is sweet, Señor, like her mother and grandmother before her."

Francisco laughed. "You are a flatterer, Esperanza." He sometimes cringed when Guiomar spoke harshly to the servant, especially when their son, Antonio, followed her around the house, imitating her sweeping the floors. But the servant's affection for Doña Benita seemed to color her feelings for his wife, even when she did not deserve it. He carried the warm cup the short distance between their two rooms and knocked softly in case she had fallen asleep.

"Enter," Guiomar commanded, though her voice was still weak from her exhausting labor.

"My love, I have brought you something to give you strength," he said, moving swiftly to her side. The cradle took up much of the space next to the bed, so he stood at the head and leaned over to kiss his wife. "Was it terrible, *cariña*?"

"Not so bad as the first, though the pains now are as strong as before the child came."

He put the cup to Guiomar's mouth. She took tiny sips, like a child, the warm drink making bubbles as it passed through her parted lips. "Careful, *mi amor*," he said as he withdrew the cup. "I don't want you to burn your sweet mouth."

She fell back on the pillow. His attentiveness merely reminded her of her own shortcomings. "So, you've seen her?" she asked.

"Yes. She is beautiful, like you," he stroked his wife's cheek.

Guiomar's lip curled before she caught herself. The child was anything but beautiful, resembling Francisco's family with its swarthy complexion and dark spot on the cheek. She had almost forgotten that Francisco had such a stain when he was younger and they played in the garden, but it had faded so that it was barely visible now. "What shall we name her?" She tried to force a smile, but her lips fought her as she spoke.

"I was thinking we might name her after my mother, María Úrsula."

THE SILVER CANDLESTICKS

"Yes, she looks like your family. I think that would be fitting."

"We should baptize her on Saturday, if you're well enough."

"And who will be *padrino* and *padrina*?" She had hoped to ask María Dolores and her husband-to-be, Jorge de Madrid, but she hesitated even to suggest it to her husband, who might see it as an effort to keep José Marcos close. But she had already mentioned her desire to her father. He had advised her instead to consider Don Enrique, but she was still resentful that Don Enrique continued to pressure her father to sail with the fleet, and she had no desire to flatter him until he came to his senses.

"It should be your choice, my love. I chose Antonio's godparents, now it is your turn." Francisco reached in his pocket and pulled out the pouch with the pendant. "This cannot make up for your suffering, but it will be a reminder of the gift you have given me with our daughter." The chain and pendant slipped into the palm of his hand. He kissed it and put it in his wife's palm.

Guiomar looked at the pendant with its tiny, multi-colored stones. It was unlike her father's gifts, large, ornate pieces that bespoke her wealth and class. But there was a certain delicacy about the necklace that reflected great care in its creation.

"Here, let me put it around your neck." Francisco unfastened the tiny clasp and draped the pendant over her throat.

Guiomar's fingers touched the oval, which fit almost perfectly into the small indentation above her collarbone. "It was very thoughtful of you, Francisco," she said. No doubt he had used his own money to buy it. There was something admirable in his actions, which she vowed to remind herself when she grew impatient with his sometimes-rough manners.

"I have something to tell you, Guiomar, which I hope will not distress you," he said.

Her thick brows came together forming a crease above her nose. "What is it?"

"I will be going away when the fleet sails again. To Veracruz…"

"What are you talking about? You are leaving me here? Alone?"

"No, my love, not alone. Your father is here, and you have the whole household to care for you and the children."

"But why, Francisco?' Her voice reflected hurt as much as shock. Had she been such a bad wife that he was abandoning her? And with two babies to care for?

"I must make my own way in the world, Guiomar. I cannot live on your wealth or your father's generosity. And there are many opportunities in Méjico, as your father has demonstrated. I will be gone for a while—two years, three at the most. And when I return, we will make our own lives, dependent on no one."

Guiomar began to shake, her chest heaving up and down, but no sound emerged from her throat. Francisco lifted her into his arms and held her, feeling the warm tears flow down her cheeks. He was surprised at her reaction. He had thought it might be a relief for her if he were gone. And he hoped that she would understand his need to forge his own path. He could never live off another's inheritance, especially a woman's, even if it was his right. He had always worked to earn his bread, and he must do so again. If he could not win her love, he would at least earn her respect.

"My dear, you must be brave. It is for our future. And our children's. I will not leave until Úrsula is six months old. It will give us time to prepare. Your father has already agreed. And it will finally relieve him of his duty to Don Enrique. "

He held her at arm's length. Her tear-stained face made her dearer to him. Perhaps she loved him a bit after all. She was a proud and willful woman. He knew she had never wanted to marry him; her parents had insisted on it for her protection. They had never spoken of it, but he knew that her parents were Jews. It did not matter to him. He had seen no evidence that the family practiced the old customs. But the Holy Office struck terror in the hearts of many New Christians who were faithful to the Church.

Her fingers went to her throat. She rubbed the little pendant between her thumb and forefinger. As she suspected, he had paid for it with his own money. She must work harder to love him…

"Do you like it, my sweet?"

"Yes. Very much. I will wear it always," she said, though she was not sure she would keep even that trivial promise. "I am tired now. I must rest."

"Of course. How thoughtless of me." He kissed her forehead and then her lips. "I will tell Esperanza not to disturb you until the morning."

She let out a moan, clutching the bed covers.

Francisco was already at the door but turned quickly. "Should I call Dr. Garcia?" he asked, his face showing his concern.

"Esperanza says it is normal to have such pains after the second child." The pains came sharply again, and she could feel the warmth of liquid seeping between her thighs. She pulled back the covers to see the dark stains spreading over her gown. Francisco yelled for Esperanza, who came running, the child still in her arms.

"*Madre de Dios*," Esperanza gasped, quickly laying the infant in its cradle and going to her mistress's side.

Francisco rushed from the room and did not waste time summoning one of the other servants. He ran to the stable, grabbed a set of reins, and put them on the large mule. He mounted the beast and gave it a kick in the ribs, urging it forward through the door that led to the narrow street. He made for the doctor's house near the Guadalquivir as fast as the animal could be prodded. Sweat drenched his shirt and he began to shiver. It was only then that he realized that he had not put on a coat and there was frost still in the air. He could not afford to be careless. Guiomar needed him, as did his children. He would ask at the doctor's home for something to cover him on the way back.

He couldn't stop thinking of the blood seeping through Guiomar's gown, spreading wider and wider. He kicked the mule harder to hasten its pace, smothering the scream in his throat.

Chapter Nine

A CONFESSION

Padre Dominguez paced the hard, stone floor. His spine curved now so that he looked like a hunchback. Some said his chest caved in because his heart had shriveled to nothing, leaving a hollow space that his bones bent to conceal. He heard them telling such tales behind his back. They all despised him—his own priests, the inmates whose souls he tried to save. It was God's punishment for the carnal desires that still burned in his loins. He had tried everything to cleanse himself, but when he slept, the images crept in. And when he awoke, his seed soaked his pallet.

Last night's dream was like the others. The image of the young girl's body. Only she was not hanging in her cell, as he had first seen her, but alive and smiling, beckoning him.

The girl was the devil's maiden. Had she not corrupted her own mother? He wished he could save the poor woman, Inés Mejia, who continued to waste away in the dungeon below. But she would not accept his help. And he could not release her for fear that once out among the faithful, the girl's soul would take possession of her to work evil in others. The city had become a den of iniquity. The Judaizers' ranks had been thinned in the Plaza San Francisco, but their filth continued to pollute Sevilla, inspiring new evils that wracked the city, especially among those men who sought out their own sex to satisfy their depraved desires. Had there not been stories of such debauchery in the first book of the Old Testament? God had rained down fire and brimstone on Sodom and Gomorrah, but their wickedness had not been destroyed and had found fertile soil in Sevilla.

The loud knock on the door jolted him.

"What is it?" He opened the door, annoyed at this interruption when he was about to perform his penance.

"Pardon me, Padre, but a servant from the home of Doña Guiomar Péres de Armijo has come with an urgent message for you," the young brother said, his voice breaking. "It is the Señora. She is on her death bed and will have no other administer the Sacraments."

Dominguez nodded. It had been some time since he had been invited to the Péres home. He had heard that she had given birth again. But she was young and strong. The news that she was dying troubled him. Since her mother's death a few years earlier, Guiomar and her husband had become generous benefactors of Santa Ana's. It was rumored that Don Pedro Péres, who still lived with the young couple, was the source of the money that regularly found its way into the church coffers, for Francisco had yet to make his own fortune. But why then did the woman insist that he administer the sacraments instead of the parish priest?

The priest stepped out into the street, which had become unseasonably frigid as the sun disappeared behind the tiled roofs of the neighborhood. The chill seeped through the frayed seams of his well-worn cape. Perhaps the woman's father would notice how poorly dressed he was and make a gift of a new cape to the Holy Office. He gripped the small leather satchel he carried until his long nails dug into the palm of his hand. He should not be thinking about his own comfort at such a time.

The distance was short, but Dominguez reached the front gate out of breath. He felt under his cape and robes for the vessel that carried the Host. The ciborium hung near his heart, against his sunken chest. His fingers caressed the silver, which was warm to the touch. Here was the power of salvation. In his pocket, he carried holy oil to anoint the woman, but it was the gift of the Body and Blood that would bring her eternal life.

He was about to knock on the heavy wooden door when it opened.

"You're here. Thank God," Don Pedro pulled the priest across the threshold, his still strong hands nearly dragging the man down. "She is fading quickly," he said, as he led the priest along the dark corridor.

They entered the room, which glowed eerily from the candles that had been lit and the fire in the hearth. Guiomar lay on the bed, her cheeks flushed, her damp hair plastered against her head. Her eyes were closed, but Dominguez could see that she was still living by their rapid movement beneath the blue-veined lids. He walked toward the bed and was about to make the sign of the cross when she opened her eyes and stared into his.

"Send him away," she whispered, her voice shaking.

"*M'hija*, it is Padre Dominguez, whom you asked for," her father leaned over and touched her forehead gently. She opened her eyes widely and stared about the room as if she did not recognize its inhabitants, though her husband and servant were the only ones there besides the priest. She shut her eyes again, and for a moment, Dominguez thought she was about to expire. He pulled the small flask of oil from his pocket and looked around for the necessary implements.

"Where are the cloths? Have you not prepared the way for me to administer the sacraments?" he shouted.

Guiomar writhed on the bed and let out a deep moan like the lowing of a cow.

"You are upsetting my wife," Francisco interrupted. He moved toward the priest, but his father-in-law reached out to grab his arm.

"Forgive him, Padre. We are all distressed at my daughter's illness," he said, his eyes belying his apologetic tone. "Esperanza, get Padre Dominguez what he needs. "

THE SILVER CANDLESTICKS

The servant left the room quickly, but as the door closed behind her, the wails of an infant could be heard echoing in the hall. Again, Guiomar opened her eyes.

"My baby," she cried, lifting her body up. "Bring me my daughter," she called out to Esperanza. "And my mother's candlesticks…" but before she could say more, Francisco lifted her frail body into his arms.

"Do not speak, *mi corazón*," he said, burying her head in his chest. "You must rest."

Pedro observed the quick movement of his son-in-law. He was sure Dominguez saw it too. He must distract the meddlesome priest before he became too curious. "Padre, would you lead us in prayer," he asked, touching the priest's robe. The man startled, turning to him with his pale eyes opened wide, his upper lip quivering, whether in momentary fright or anger, Pedro did not know. "My daughter is recalling your last visit to this room, when her mother lay in this very bed, surrounded by candles. Let us pray that she will remain with us a bit longer so that she may at least see her daughter baptized in the one true faith." Pedro hoped the priest had missed the reference to Benita's candlesticks.

Dominguez stared at Don Pedro, judging his sincerity. What could it mean, her mother's candlesticks? But there would be time to investigate later. For now, his duty was to save the woman's soul. He lifted the crucifix from the rosary hanging from his cincture. "*In nomine Patris, et Filii, et Spiritus Sancti*," he said as he made the sign of the cross over the two men and the woman, whose rapid breaths had slowed when her husband released his grip and placed her head back on the pillow. She opened her eyes and smiled faintly.

"Padre Dominguez, you have come," she whispered.

"My love, you must save your strength," Francisco bent over to quiet her.

The priest observed the action carefully. The husband seemed intent on silencing his wife.

"Perhaps she would like to confess," the priest said, looking directly at the husband. He had seen this behavior before around the deathbed, a spouse afraid to leave the priest alone with the dying partner. It was only on death's door that some were willing to divulge their real sins. What was told in the confessional never struck the heart of the matter. *Father, forgive me, I broke my master's cup and hid the pieces. Forgive me, I stole a peach from the market. I spread gossip about my neighbor I knew was untrue.* So many sins, and none so numerous as those of the flesh. *Forgive me for I let a man rub against me in the public square. I peeked through a hole in the wall as the servants were bathing. I snuck a look while my brother made water.* He had heard it all, every lewd fantasy, every indecent act.

No, he would hear nothing new from the woman on this score. But, with death so close, perhaps she would reveal something greater than the lascivious litany he had to endure in the confessional. Might she be the key to exposing the secret sect of Judaizers whose corruption infected the city? He had ignored the accusations of the fleshy servant who came to him around the time of the mother's death. Perhaps he had made a mistake.

Guiomar reached out to take her husband's hand. "Yes, Francisco. Padre Dominguez is right. I want to confess." She must make her confession before it was too late, though the bleeding seemed to have stopped. She no longer felt the slow trickle between her legs. Perhaps it was the bitter herb drink Esperanza administered earlier, which had forced large clots of blood with much pain. "I am better now, Francisco. It will be all right," she said squeezing his hand.

Francisco worried what she might say to this priest. They had never once spoken of her mother's revelation. It was a secret too dangerous to acknowledge. Nor had he spoken about it with Don Pedro, though his own father had told him of the problem before the betrothal. To utter the words, however, would have increased the danger. If the words were never spoken, they need never be denied.

Francisco stroked Guiomar's forehead, which was cooler to the touch. Her fever had finally broken. He caressed her face. She was more beautiful at this moment than on their wedding day. If only

THE SILVER CANDLESTICKS

he could arouse in her the same deep love he felt. He remembered when they played together as children, her sweet temperament and laugh, like the tinkling of bells. Once when he skinned his knee, she'd bandaged the wound, kissing her fingertips and touching the cloth as she muttered a prayer. It was sometimes difficult to recall that tenderness when his wife was cold or distant, but he saw glimmers of the young Guiomar in her eyes as she looked up at him now.

Esperanza entered the room, carrying a tray with three small bowls and several small strips of white cotton.

"Thank you, my child," Don Pedro said. "Put them on the table. My daughter wishes to confess. It is a good sign. If she is strong enough to request the sacrament, she does not need anointing after all. We may have wasted the Padre's afternoon for no good reason."

"To hear the confession of a good Christian is never a waste of time, Don Pedro," the priest said. "It may be some time before the Señora is able to attend the sacraments at Santa Ana. I am happy to administer them now—without, of course, the anointing. She seems to have made a miraculous recovery. It was, no doubt, His Presence," he said, pulling out the small ciborium from under his robe.

"Yes, Padre, I want Holy Communion. I have not been able to receive the sacraments since my confinement," Guiomar said. She looked quickly at her father and nodded, almost imperceptibly, but the gesture did not escape the priest's notice.

"If we might have some privacy," Dominguez said, stretching out his arms to clear away the husband and father and the young servant, who seemed as anxious as the others. Was she the one the other slave had referred to when she made accusations against the Péres family? He had not seen the other dark buxom creature on this visit—what was her name? Concha? The very image of the shell's pink underside repelled him. Perhaps they had sent her away. He must make inquiries. Discreetly, however. There was no point in antagonizing a rich family unnecessarily. Or putting Judaizers—if that is what they were—on their guard.

"We will leave you," Don Pedro said, bowing his head to the priest.

When the door shut behind the others, Dominguez approached Guiomar's bedside. She felt a cold chill despite the heavy blanket that covered her. His face was grey, his eyes almost as pale as the thin wisps of white hair that stuck out around his tonsure. For an instant, she imagined she had died after all and descended into Hell. She clutched the blanket more closely around her. She watched as he removed the black cape and laid it across the chair next to her bed.

"God has been merciful, Señora. He has given you another chance at life. You must use it wisely to save your soul and those around you." His eyes bored into hers, hoping to ferret out her secrets.

"I have done my best to lead a good life, Padre," she said with as much conviction as she could muster. But she knew it was not true. She had been unfaithful to her husband, if not in body, in spirit, loving another man for all the years of her marriage. A night did not go by when she did not think of José Marcos as she closed her eyes, her chest pierced with such longing that she felt almost crushed by the pain. Perhaps if she unburdened herself to this priest, God would give her the grace to forget José Marcos and embrace her husband fully. She would confess without naming the object of her desire. The Dominican would not be able to guess as Padre Saavedra, her parish priest, might. She recalled the shame she felt the afternoon, so long ago it seemed, that she had knelt praying to the Virgin at Santa Ana to give José Marcos the courage to flee with her when the old priest interrupted their tryst. She could feel the color rising to her cheeks even now. Why did she continue to love this man who had abandoned her? Why could she not push him from her memory, allowing him instead to hurt her again and again with his cowardice?

THE SILVER CANDLESTICKS

The priest opened the small leather case he carried and pulled out the silk stole he had received at his ordination. It remained beautiful still, despite the years and use. His mother had embroidered the crosses at either end and had tied the fringe to the garment herself. He kissed the crosses and draped the stole over his shoulders. "*In Nomine Patris, et Filii…*" he intoned again as Guiomar touched her fingertips to forehead, heart, and shoulders.

"Bless me, Padre, for I have sinned," she replied, her throat constricting with fear of what she was about to confess. "It has been one month since my last confession," she said, her hands trembling as she clasped them to her breast. "I have sinned many times, Padre, in my thoughts if not in my deeds." Tears began to stream down her face, and she feared she would not have the courage to continue.

"Do not be afraid, child," the priest's voice took on a sudden sweetness that comforted her as she struggled to form her words. "It is better to unburden yourself of your secrets," he said. He took a deep breath. He wanted to probe into her strange cry for the candlesticks, but he must tread lightly. If he seemed too eager, she might withdraw. "Our Lord will forgive you so long as you repent."

"Oh, I do repent, Padre. Every day I pray for the will to resist the thoughts that creep into my head unbidden." She hesitated before going on. She could hear the priest's breathing. Did she imagine that his breath had quickened? She didn't want to go on, but she had opened a door and had no choice but to go through it. If she was truly dying, she should unburden herself, just as Padre Dominguez instructed. But there were others to consider. "I do not love my husband," she said finally.

"Is there another?" he bent closer to her. He watched her chest heave up and down, heavily, but her lips remained still. This was not what he was hoping for, but it might prove that she flouted the Church's teachings on matrimony, and who knew where that might lead.

She dared not look at the priest, whose shadow fell across the bed, dark and threatening. "No," she lied, but surely God would forgive her, though which God she was unsure—the faceless God of her mother or the gentle Jesus who forgave even the adulteress who was about to be stoned.

"Have you desires for others?" he asked, his voice breaking, like a boy's. He cleared his throat.

She must be strong. She turned toward the priest. "I want to love my husband, as is my duty."

He was disappointed. "You have two children, Señora. Surely this is proof you have performed your wifely duties," he scoffed. She was no more than a common *puta* despite her wealth and station, expecting pleasure in the marital bed. It was his sacred duty to press her for the truth. "There are other ways of acting on desire. Have you ever…touched yourself in an impure way?' he asked, his voice now barely audible.

Guiomar gasped. It was unthinkable. "Never!"

The priest cleared his throat again. Guiomar tried to lift herself higher on the pillows, unsettling the blankets. The stench of blood rose to his nostrils. He could feel his lips curl involuntarily and tried to conceal it by coughing into the threadbare sleeve of his habit. Why had God formed woman from Adam's rib if only to lead man into sin? Even the Virgin Mary was the source of temptation. *Forgive me, Father. I stared at the Blessed Mother's breasts during Mass.* Had he not heard that and worse from his own priests?

"For your penance," the priest leaned in close to Guiomar's face, "you must come to El Castillo San Jorge when you are well enough." He watched closely to judge the effects of his words.

Guiomar's eyes opened wide. She had been wrong to confess to this man. Better that she had faced the rebuke of Padre Saavedra. She tried to lift her upper body to a sitting position. If she was to protect herself—and her family—she must show strength. "What has the Castillo to do with me, Father?"

The priest smiled. She was afraid. His suspicions had born fruit. "There is a woman there I want you to speak to. She is a difficult case. Perhaps you can persuade her to renounce her sins as you have your own." His eyes held hers so she could not turn away. "Now make a good act of contrition," he said.

Guiomar recited the prayer for forgiveness. But it was not God's forgiveness she sought but her husband's. She closed her eyes as she uttered the words.

"God, father of mercy," the priest intoned.

He lifted his right arm above Guiomar's body as she shrank back against the pillows, her eyes still closed. "*Et ego te absolvo*," his voice rose as he absolved her sins making the sign of the cross in wide gestures above her. He was pleased. The idea to have her come to the Castillo was an inspiration. One confessed Judaizer and another suspected one—he would have their interactions closely watched for any signs that they still practiced their Hebrew faith in secret. And if Señora Péres de Armijo could be caught doing so, he could save two souls or see them both burned.

He reached inside the ciborium for the thin wafer. "You must try to sit up, my child. Do you need assistance?" he asked.

"No. I can do it," she said, struggling to lift herself upright.

A sickly-sweet odor of milk rose from her body as the covers slipped from her shoulders. Padre Dominguez drew back, but his eyes lingered on the stains on her nightdress, which seemed to spread before his eyes, the wet cloth outlining the shape of her full breasts. She pulled the blanket up to cover herself, but it was too late. The vision would linger in his memory, as did so many others, coming back to taunt him when he was at prayer, as he was drifting off to sleep, in his dreams, where it would torment him until he woke in a sweat. He should never have instructed her to visit the Castillo. Now he would be forced to see her again, perhaps many times. How had he imagined the penance was Divinely inspired? He could already feel the Devil at work in his loins. His hand trembled as he placed the Host on Guiomar's outstretched tongue. He closed his eyes quickly as his fingertips brushed the moist flesh.

The priest walked back to the Castillo slowly. The sun had not yet set, but the smoke from the ceramic works darkened the sky prematurely and burned his nostrils. It would be almost time for Vespers when he got there. He looked forward to the cleansing he experienced as the monks sang the Hours. Their voices were not as beautiful as those among whom he'd lived in Llerena, but the Castillo's monks chanted with great vigor, and the stone walls of the chapel seemed to magnify the sound. He had hoped this afternoon would bring him closer to Don Pedro and his son-in-law, which might result in some adornment for the bare chapel. But they had been wary of him, too much so for innocents, he thought. Well, if they would not open their purses, the Holy Office had other means to get at their wealth. Especially if his suspicions bore out.

He thought back on the woman's confession. Was it really something so common as lust that she was trying to hide? He would have to make inquiries. Perhaps it was more than her lack of desire for her husband's attentions. He should have pried more into her history. Had there been another man before Armijo? Not that she would necessarily have told him. Perhaps the old priest at Santa Ana knew. That would explain why the woman did not ask for him when she thought she was dying. What did the husband know? he wondered. He, too, might be an avenue to the truth. The marriage had been an odd one to begin with. Francisco Armijo was a candle maker, not exactly the match Don Pedro Péres must have wanted for his daughter. They had married in haste, yet no child was forthcoming for more than a year, so pregnancy had not forced the decision. He must get to the bottom of this. And, who knew, his prodding might loosen those purse strings. The small house that was being built for him within the walls of the Castillo could use the generosity of the Péres family. He would begin making inquiries about Señora Péres' previous lovers immediately.

Chapter Ten

THE LETTERS

*G*uiomar read the note again. *It has been three months since the birth of your daughter. I pray that you have recovered enough to come to the Castillo to assist me in the matter we discussed when you were ill. The woman of whom I spoke is in danger of losing her immortal soul. Yours in Christ, Padre Dominguez.*

She folded the paper and put it in her pocket. She could not avoid the request for much longer without arousing suspicion. She wanted to confide in Francisco, but he had become more aloof in the months since her recovery, and she had no one to blame but herself. Perhaps she should discuss the matter with her father. She stood up from the desk and was about to seek him out when Esperanza came into the room with Úrsula.

"Señora, the child seems a bit feverish today. Would you like me to send for Doctor Garcia?"

Guiomar looked at the infant nestled in Esperanza's arms. The girl had a sickly pallor. She was not pretty to look at, her dark eyes too large for her tiny, shriveled face. She wished that she could love the child. But she felt little, even when she held her. Esperanza seemed to care for the infant as if she had given birth to her, just as she did Guiomar's son, Antonio. Perhaps it came more naturally to one who nursed the child. But that was not always the case, as she knew from her own childhood experience. Her mother had not nursed her, yet Guiomar's earliest memories were of sitting in her mother's lap while she showered her with *besitos*. How she missed her mother at times like this. She must work to love the infant, just as she tried to love the child's father. Why was it, she wondered, that what came naturally to most women eluded her?

Esperanza waited for the Señora's response, but her mistress was distracted. The baby began to cry, a soft mew like a kitten, her mouth puckering with barely any sound escaping.

"The child is not strong. Perhaps she is not eating well. Have you enough milk?" Guiomar asked.

Esperanza felt the blood rise to her face. It was true, her milk had begun to dry up. The child would not suckle enough to keep up the flow and it had been too long since she had given birth to Benito. "We should consider bringing in another wet nurse, Señora. I will make inquiries."

"It is not a criticism, Esperanza," Guiomar said. "But for the health of the child we should do what we can."

"And Doctor Garcia?"

Guiomar stared at Esperanza. If the child was too sickly to survive, it would perhaps be a blessing that she die before her father became too attached. He already spent as much time in the nursery with his two children as he did in her company. She was surprised by her jealousy of her own children. Perhaps it was true what some said of her, that she must always be the center of attention. "Not yet. If she isn't better by morning you can send for him."

Esperanza left her mistress sitting at the desk and returned to the nursery. The infant continued to cry softly as she rocked her in her arms. It had only been an hour since she had nursed but perhaps she was hungry. She pressed her fingers to her breast, but they sunk into the flesh so that she could feel the bones beneath. The milk had not yet time to replenish.

Her son Benito played in the corner of the room stacking wooden blocks as little Antonio watched. The Armijo boy always seemed to be studying what was happening, waiting before he entered into play or touched his food, as if looking for what was expected of him. Yet the boy was a quick learner, and though quiet and somewhat shy, he knew many more words than her own son. She loved them both, even though Antonio was not her flesh. After the birth of Benito, she had worried that Don Pedro might send her away. It would have been easy for him to persuade her mistress to do so since Guiomar had never cared for her before her mother's death. But the Señora had grown kinder after her marriage. Or perhaps it was not the marriage but the loss of her lover that had softened her. They shared that in common, after all.

Esperanza placed the infant in her cradle and went to the window, which looked out on the courtyard. She had tried to remove Felipe from her mind. Don Pedro had chosen not to send either of them away. Perhaps he thought that Felipe would one day acknowledge the child and give the boy his name. It was her hope as well. Felipe would soon be able to buy his freedom, Esperanza calculated. He had told her in the courtyard that last night they had lain beneath the orange tree, which seemed so long ago, that he had nearly enough money put aside to strike out on his own.

Of course, he had not been able to accompany Don Pedro on the voyages to the New World that earned him much of what he'd saved since the master retired. But there were rumors that Señor Armijo would be travelling to Méjico soon. He would not lead the expedition, as Don Pedro had. But perhaps he would take Felipe with him as his servant, and he would finally earn his freedom.

She felt her stomach tighten at the thought. She knew Felipe had a woman in Las Indias, perhaps another son. Why would he choose to return to Sevilla when he could make a new life in Veracruz? Her throat constricted as she fought back tears. She must not think of him. She must not imagine that one day he would return her love or accept his child. In the three years since Benito had been born, Felipe had not once paid the boy any heed in the *cocina*, and his glances toward her had been cold, as if he barely saw her. At one time, he had only secret smiles for her, his voice low and intimate when he spoke her name, even when others were present. But he had not spoken to her directly in some time and rarely raised his eyes when she entered the room.

Tears stung her eyes and she quickly wiped them away. When she turned toward the boys, Antonio stared up at her, his solemn face taking hers in. He was far too young to understand what he saw, but his gaze seemed to linger.

"Antonio, do you want something?" Esperanza walked toward the corner where the boys were seated on the ground. She leaned over to place a small block of wood on top of the tower her son had built, but it infuriated the boy, who knocked the blocks to the floor with his fist. Antonio did not turn his eyes from Esperanza's and she thought she saw a tear form. The noise startled Úrsula in her cradle and she began to cry, her tiny voice like the bleating of a young lamb.

"Is there something wrong with her?" Francisco had entered the room without Esperanza's notice. He stood near the doorway as if he needed an invitation. Both boys jumped to their feet and went running to him.

Francisco reached down to lift Antonio into his arms while Benito held tight to his leg. He felt sorry for Esperanza's boy with no father to claim him, though it was apparent just looking at the boy's lighter skin and the shape of his eyes that he was the groomsman Felipe's child. What man would not be proud of such a spirited boy, he wondered.

Francisco's eyes lifted to Esperanza. Her ebony skin and high cheekbones looked to be carved from stone, cold to the touch, he imagined. But her eyes were kind, and she showed his son much love, which the boy needed. Antonio had failed to win Guiomar's heart. He was hoping Úrsula would do so, and perhaps his wife would eventually warm to the boy.

He put Antonio down and the child retreated to the blocks, but Benito still clung to his leg.

Esperanza pried the small hands loose and walked him back to the corner where the blocks lay spread out randomly. Only then did she turn to her master. "She is warm to the touch. I spoke to the Señora, but she thought we should wait awhile before sending for Doctor Garcia." She lowered her eyes. The Señora would not be pleased.

"Why should we wait? If the child is ill, the sooner he examines her, the better."

"There is little to be done for one this young, Señor. They cannot bleed her and what medicines can he prescribe for one who can barely muster the strength to suckle?" She did not wish to frighten her master, but infants often did not live beyond their first year and she must make him understand.

"I see," he said. He walked to the cradle where Úrsula lay on her back. He bent over and stroked the infant's cheek. The mark had already begun to fade but was still visible. *Poor child*, he thought. She did not resemble her mother but had his features. Still, it was difficult to tell what she would look like. All infants looked similar, he had observed, with different coloring perhaps, but all with heads too big for their small bodies. The infant's eyelids fluttered, and her lips formed a tiny bubble. "Keep me informed, Esperanza," he said as he headed for the door. "And the Señora? Where is she at the moment?"

"She was at the desk in the *sala mayor* a few moments ago, Señor." Esperanza hoped he would not ask why her mistress was at the desk. It was not a place she was often found. She wondered if it would be wrong to reveal that Señora Guiomar had received a letter from the Castillo. But Francisco only pursed his lips and nodded.

Guiomar was not in the *sala*, which was flooded with light from the large windows. Francisco walked to the desk and opened the drawer, but there was nothing but a few sheaves of paper inside. He lifted the quill from its stand to test the tip, but it was dry. He clenched his teeth. Why was he suddenly so suspicious? His wife had given no hint of infidelity, though she was cool to him, more so since the birth of the second child. But could he blame her? She had not wanted to enter this marriage. He was beneath her.

He shoved the quill back into the stand too harshly and heard the tip break.

"Here you are. I've been searching for you," Guiomar's voice came from behind him.

He turned around abruptly. "And I you, my love," he said.

"I received a letter this morning." Guiomar reached into her pocket and handed him the single sheet, waiting while he read the priest's words.

"What is he talking about? You have not mentioned this to me." Francisco kept his voice calm, though he could feel his heart pound rapidly. The letter suggested that Guiomar had made some promise to the priest when he came to administer the last rites. He had been opposed to inviting the inquisitor at the time, but Guiomar insisted. Now, he feared the priest had his wife in his sights. Was this how it would begin, an investigation into the family? He knew the day might come, but he was not yet ready. He had hoped that his trip to Las Indias would prepare the way if it were ever necessary to leave. But the trip was still six weeks away, and he would be gone for two years, maybe more.

"He wants me to visit an old woman in the Castillo, as his letter says. He talked to me about her when he came to administer the sacraments after Úrsula's birth. He believes he can save her with my help."

"Why you? This could be a trap." He reached out and grabbed her arm. She grimaced, and he loosened his grip. "I am sorry, my dear. I don't want to frighten you. But you know these men are dangerous. They see Judaizers everywhere—" he hesitated, watching her eyes for some sign. "Even in the most devout Catholic families, such as this one."

Guiomar looked anxiously into her husband's eyes. They had never spoken of her family's secret, but there was no doubt he knew the truth even though she had done nothing to raise suspicion. Her mother's ornate candlesticks remained locked in the mahogany box, along with the lace mantilla. She remembered her mother's words and felt her heart clutch. She could not even recite the prayer her mother tried to teach her: *Baruch? Adonai?* It was gibberish in her mind. "How can I refuse, Francisco? My failure to appear would signal fear or guilt, either of which would be dangerous, as you have said."

"We must be careful. We should consult your father—and perhaps your brother. We could invite him for Holy Week and put off your visit to the Castillo until we can discuss the matter with Alfonso."

"It would be wonderful to see Alfonso, if he could be allowed to travel at such an important time. Would it not seem strange though?"

"Strange? To invite your brother for Easter? He has not been in our home since the wedding…and your mother's death. Who better to guide our actions?"

Guiomar did not think about her brother often. She had been a child when he left for the seminary, and they were never close. But her mother had said that the decision for Alfonso to enter the priesthood was to protect him from the Holy Office—and to allow him to learn their own faith by studying the Old Testament. She wondered whether it would be wise to involve him. Perhaps he had changed his mind in his years in the priesthood. Might he not betray her to save himself? She would have to approach him carefully, seeking only his advice on dealing with a difficult situation.

"Help me draft a letter to Padre Dominguez. And to my brother," she said. She walked to the desk and pulled the drawer open. Francisco hovered over her as she sat facing the blank sheet. When she reached for the quill, her husband's hand intercepted her own.

"I seem to have broken the quill, my dear. Let me fetch another."

Guiomar was sure the quill was untouched when she had been there earlier. She picked it up and examined the tip, which was nearly severed, as if it had been used with great force. A good quill was valuable. What had made Francisco so angry that he ruined the quill, she wondered.

"Here, my love," Francisco said, handing his wife the new quill he had retrieved from the drawer of his dressing table.

"You're out of breath," she chided.

"I'm getting fat. If I don't occasionally run up the stairs, I'll soon be unable to," he said, noticing the disapproval of her arched brow. He knew she didn't like his habit of doing things for himself instead of relying on the servants, but it was one he had acquired honestly. And who should complain that a man could care for himself?

He put his hands on her shoulders as she bent over the paper. "Dear Padre Dominguez," he dictated, "I am eager to assist you in the Lord's work as soon as I am able. My daughter Úrsula is ill, however, and I must attend to her. I have sent for the doctor and will advise you when he says I am able to leave her side." He marveled at how quickly Guiomar formed the words on the page. His own hand was clumsy and ill-formed.

Guiomar bristled as Francisco called out the words too quickly for her to write before another followed. She did not look up until the last letter was laid down. How had he known of Úrsula's illness? And had he already sent for the doctor against her wishes? She touched the blotter to the page, being careful not to smudge the fresh ink.

"Let us hope that this will hold him off," she said turning to look her husband in the eye. "Have you sent for Doctor Garcia?" She struggled to control the accusatory note in her voice.

"No. Esperanza said there is little to be done." He squeezed his wife's shoulders gently. His fingers sank into her flesh, which had finally begun to plump after her illness. She moved away, almost imperceptibly, and he quickly dropped his hands. *Why was she so cool to him, even after bearing him two children? There could be only one explanation.*

"We must reply at once," Guiomar said, folding the letter and handing it to her husband. "Will you seal it, my dear?"

Retrieving the small tin spoon he kept in one of the desk slots, he broke off a tiny piece of red wax, then lit a taper at the candelabra and held it under the spoon. "Now you should write your brother," he said as he poured a small drop onto the paper's folded edge and waited for it to cool. He stared at the block of unused wax, taking in its contours. He would watch to see how quickly the wax disappeared. If Guiomar was sending secret letters, he would confront her. It was one thing to deny him her love and another to cuckold him.

He looked down on her as she bent over the paper, quill in hand. He wanted to lift her up and shake her until she told him the truth. How could he leave her to sail to Méjico not knowing whether she would be faithful in his absence? He would sit down with his father-in-law and tell him of his concerns. They had made a bargain, one that risked his life. He had done it out of love. But there was a limit. Did she not understand how risky this was?

"I have asked Alfonso to come for Easter, but we are very late in making the request. He will have to seek permission from his superior. Perhaps a gift…" she hesitated.

"An excellent idea," he said. "But perhaps we should also invite the inquisitor so that he can see with his own eyes there is no reason for suspicion." She took a fresh sheet and rewrote her response to the inquisitor, adding that they would be honored by his presence at their Easter dinner.

Francisco took the letters and looked in her eyes. "Do you understand, my love, how dangerous the situation is? We must live our lives beyond reproach." The melting taper singed his fingertips, and he blew it out before applying the wax.

"What are you accusing me of, Francisco?" She felt her face flush.

"I am not accusing you. I am simply warning you to be careful. It isn't only the things we do but what is in our hearts that can betray us. I cannot make you love me, Guiomar, though I have tried my best." He reached out and touched her arm. She shook it off, stiffly.

"I have done nothing to warrant your suspicions," she said, her cheeks growing red.

"I am leaving for Méjico when the fleet departs. I will be gone for a long time. I cannot leave without being able to trust that you will do nothing to…harm my name or endanger our children." His voice betrayed more than he had intended.

It was as if a cold wind had blown into the room. He had never spoken to her in such a tone. The tears welled in Guiomar's eyes. She brushed past him without answering. He wished he could take his words back. Where had they come from? She had given him no cause to be suspicious. She rarely left their home, and never alone. But his father-in-law had warned him that she had considered asking María Dolores Herrera and her *prometido* to be Úrsula's godparents. He should have confronted her at the time, but she never raised the issue, so he remained silent.

Why was she still friends with Herrera's sister? He could feel the bile rising in his blood. He had been foolish to think that he could ever win her love. He recalled his wedding day and the insolent look on José Marcos Herrera's face as the coward hid in the alcove of the church. He had never said a word to Guiomar about the incident, but it rankled still. Every time his wife shrank from his touch, he wondered if she was thinking of the other.

He let out his breath through pursed lips. If he could not trust Guiomar, it was better that she fear him. He took up the tin and grabbed another taper, holding it beneath the lump of wax until it bubbled. He poured the red wax onto the letter to Alfonso. It was impossible to unseal his fate. The best he could hope for now was that he would be successful in Veracruz. A few years in Las Indias and he would reap enough riches to bring Guiomar and his children to the New World, where neither his rival nor the inquisitor could touch her.

Don Pedro returned from the Casa de Contratación tired from the long walk. The streets were crowded, and it irritated him that he saw so few faces he knew. In the last few years, as Sevilla became the hub for trade with the New World, people from everywhere, not just neighboring towns and the Kingdom itself but foreign lands, flocked to the city. The streets were packed with sailors, traders, and thieves. Then there were the prostitutes, many of them women

THE SILVER CANDLESTICKS

whose husbands had departed for Las Indias and never returned, leaving them to provide for their hungry children the only way they could.

Pedro no longer carried more than a few copper coins for fear he might be robbed. Today, two men accosted him in an alley near the Alcázar. They would have harmed him had it not been for one of the sailors from his last trade mission, a small man whose only advantage was his relative youth. Pedro's pride was damaged by the incident, and he was tempted to act rudely to the sailor for having interfered, but he thought better of it. There was no point in creating enemies, and the sailor probably saved him from a beating when the thieves discovered only the handful of coins. At one time, Pedro's size would have deterred such scoundrels, but he had shrunk within his skin, his broad shoulders curving downwards, his midsection heavy from too many rich meals on land. He felt weary, defeated—alone. It was times like this he missed Benita most.

"Papá, I must speak with you," Guiomar said, without waiting for her father to remove his cloak. His frown surprised her.

"Can it wait?"

She could see that something had happened, but what? It was not possible Francisco had already spoken to him. "Of course, Papá. We can speak after you have rested. You look..." she hesitated, "like a man who has had a busy day. Did all go well?" Her eyes searched his face for clues. Perhaps he had encountered Don Enrique, who still harbored resentment against him.

Don Péres could see the disappointment in her face. Like a child, she pushed her lower lip out. He couldn't resist. "All right, tell me what is troubling you *m'hija*."

"I received a letter," she said, waiting to make sure she had his full attention. "From Padre Dominguez." Her father's eyes widened, and he took a step closer to her.

"Tell me," he whispered. He took her by the arm and led her toward the room he used as his study at the end of the corridor. The curtains were drawn and no lamp was lit so it was difficult to see. He pulled the door shut and only then did he walk to the window and pull back the drapes so that a sliver of light fell across the carpet. "Proceed, but keep your voice low. My hearing is not what it used to be, but we can take no chances."

They sat, and Guiomar pulled her chair close so that their knees were touching. "The Dominican has asked that I come to the Castillo to help with a woman he says is a difficult case." She wished there were more light in the room so she could judge the effect of her words. "It was something he spoke to me of when he came after Úrsula's birth."

"I don't understand. It sounds like a trick."

"Yes, I am fearful as well. Francisco has suggested we consult Alfonso, so I have invited him to visit Easter Week."

"When did this happen? I was only gone a few hours…"

"The letter arrived this morning. Francisco helped me draft a reply. We have put the priest off, pleading Úrsula's health."

Pedro let out a deep sigh. "And how is she?" It was lamentable, but Benita had also lost their second child.

"Esperanza suggests that we get a new wet nurse. And we will ask Doctor Garcia to come if her fever has not broken by tomorrow. Esperanza says there is little we can do."

"Well, it may hold the priest off for a while. But what of this woman he talks of? Who is she?"

"The Dominican mentioned the woman the night Úrsula was born, but I hoped he would forget. I have never met her. She is accused of Judaizing and denounced her daughter, a girl of twelve or thirteen, while under the *tormentos*." She shivered uttering the words.

"Yes. I know the story. The girl hanged herself." He took Guiomar's hand in his. He wanted to tell her he would never betray her, no matter what was done to him. But his words would only frighten her more. "What does he want you to do?"

"I don't know exactly. I think he wants to find a way to absolve himself of his own guilt in the girl's death. But how I could play a role is unclear. Maybe even to him."

THE SILVER CANDLESTICKS

"Francisco is right. Your brother may be able to guide us. He has spent enough years as a Dominican to understand these men better than we ever could." He had come to respect his son-in-law more than he had imagined he would when he chose to give him his daughter's hand. Yet, he was worried about Francisco's impending departure. The timing was bad.

"There's something else," Guiomar said, squeezing his hand. She felt the swollen knuckles and the loose skin, and her throat constricted.

"What is it?"

"Francisco suspects me…" She couldn't finish her words.

Pedro pulled his hand away. *What was the girl saying? The man knew the family's origin and he had married her anyway. Was there more?* "The matter was settled before your betrothal. Is he claiming ignorance now because of the letter?"

"No. You misunderstand me." Her lips trembled and she reached out for her father's hand again. "He is worried…" again the words would not come. How could she even speak of such things to her father? "About what will happen when he is gone. He is jealous."

Pedro bent towards his daughter, lifting her face so he could see into her eyes. "Have you given him reason?"

"None," she said, though she knew it was not entirely true.

"Well, I will speak to him. He has no right to accuse my daughter," he said, stroking her cheek with his thumb. It was natural for a man who marries above his station—especially one as beautiful as she—to worry that he will not keep her love. Had he not had his doubts about Benita long ago, though it was he who had strayed with her cousin, if only one time? Perhaps his daughter still had feelings for Herrera. But they would fade in time, as his had done.

"Don't worry, *m'hija*. I will take care of it. Now, let us put these worries aside. I want to see my grandchildren," he said, lifting her up from the chair. "And I am as hungry as a bear. The next time I go to the Casa de Contratación, I will ride a burro. I am getting too old to cross the river on foot."

Padre Dominguez unfolded the letter, breaking the red wax seal. It was about time the woman finally fulfilled her promise, he thought, when he glanced at the signature. But as he read her words, he saw that she was once again avoiding her duty. She had promised to assist him with the Mejia woman, yet made excuses as to why she could not come.

He crumpled the paper in his fist. She had added insult to injury by inviting him to her house for Easter dinner with a member of his own community. Why had he not been informed that Alfonso Péres was coming to Sevilla? And why was the priest not staying with his brethren at the Castillo? Did the man not accept that he had given up his earthly family when he took his vows?

Discipline within the Order was becoming lax. The Dominicans, who had once embraced their vows of poverty with passion, now dined on meat daily in some abbeys and were frequent guests among the wealthy of Toledo and Castilla. But Dominguez had made sure that those under his supervision adhered faithfully to the Order's Rule. He led by example, refusing even fish during Lent. He would, of course, accept the invitation, if only to check on the family's piety.

In truth, he had not thought much lately about Inés Mejia, despite his letter to the Armijo woman. He had not visited her cell in months. Now that his own house was nearly complete, he spent less time sleeping in the small room above the prisoners' cells. From his old room in the castle, it was easy to slip down the hall to the dark stairway that led to the cells below. He could come and go anytime, day or night, without drawing attention. The guard outside the women's quarter could observe him, of course, but the man was usually asleep at his post or too drunk to notice.

But now that he had his own house a short walk from the tower, he worried that his nighttime visits would be seen by the groomsmen in the stables, the families of the guards, and others who lived within the Castillo's walls. He sensed that he was not well liked by the workers, though they fawned on him whenever they needed something. He could see the disdain in their eyes and the way they sometimes avoided physical contact, shrinking from him on the paths within the Castillo walls, drawing their children closer as he approached. *What had he ever done to these people that they treated him like a pariah? Perhaps it was God's effort to ensure his humility, though he had never considered pride his particular weakness. No, lust was his cardinal sin*, he thought, clenching his teeth.

"Brother Tomás," he yelled from the top of the stairs that led from the courtyard down to the ovens where the monk baked bread. He wanted to send Señora Péres de Armijo a reply that accepted her invitation but expressed disappointment that she had time for dinner parties but not to save a dying woman's immortal soul. But no. That was not the best way to accomplish his goal. He must be patient. If he offended Guiomar Péres, she would be on her guard. He should flatter her, make her believe that she had been chosen by God Himself—and wasn't it true? Hadn't the idea to enlist her help come to him while he was administering the Sacraments? He was merely God's instrument, delivering a Divine message. But then, from nowhere, the image of her milk-stained shift appeared before his eyes, and he shuddered. *Why could he not wipe this sinful apparition from his memory? Was God testing him, like Job? Or was it the Devil?*

Brother Tomás appeared at the foot of the steps, wiping his hands on a white apron that stretched across his wide girth. "I am sorry, Padre. I was baking bread—for the children," he said. He observed Dominguez screw up his nose as if he had encountered a rotten smell.

"Your street urchins would be better served by your prayers than your pastries," he said. He had warned the friar against feeding the children who hung around the Castillo walls, many of them the offspring of those held in the cells.

"I pray for them, too, Padre, but surely we are supposed to suffer the children to come unto us, as Our Lord instructed."

"Yes, well, I have a message to be delivered to Señora Péres, that is, if you have time to attend to more mundane duties," he snapped.

Tomás nodded. "Of course, Padre. I've just put the loaves in the oven. Would you like me to deliver it now?"

"Listen carefully. I want you to repeat my words exactly as I say. Do you understand?" Dominguez walked down the stairs until he was face to face with the friar. The smell of yeast stuck to Brother Tomás, like a woman's scent, sweet and damp.

"You must deliver the message to the Señora personally. Do not let the servants give any excuses. Tell them you will wait as long as necessary."

"But…" Tomás started to interject that the bread would burn unless he could be back within the hour.

"Do you have some objection?" Padre Dominguez leaned into the fat friar, so close he could smell the man's breath. He had been eating anise, no doubt adding the sweet spice into the loaves for the beggars.

"No."

"So this is what you are to say: 'Padre Dominguez asked that this message be delivered only to you, Señora Péres, because of his high regard for you.' Make sure you put emphasis on the latter—let her know that I am concerned for *her* especially. Can you convey that?"

"I think so. Yes," he said, his voice wavering.

"All right. Then go on: 'He accepts your gracious invitation to join your family to celebrate the Paschal Sacrifice.' Do you have that, Brother Tomás, 'the Paschal Sacrifice?'"

The friar again nodded, though the request was odd.

"And, one last thing. Since it is Easter and we are breaking the Lenten fast, you might drop a hint that I have not tasted roast pig since I have been in my post at the Castillo and that you know I am partial to it. Be subtle about it. Do you understand?" Dominguez searched the friar's face to see if the suggestion shocked him, but his wide, fleshy countenance showed no change. "Then be on your way, Brother. We don't want your bread to burn." Dominguez squeezed Brother Tomás's thick arm as he pushed him from the stone landing onto the hard dirt of the courtyard. The man stumbled slightly before regaining his balance and headed toward the Castillo's main gate. "Don't be in too big a hurry that you forget your manners," he yelled, "and take off that apron!"

Padre Dominguez was pleased with himself. His reference to the Paschal Lamb would no doubt be repeated by the woman to her brother, the Dominican. Alfonso Péres would recognize the allusion, even if his sister did not. It would set the family on edge if they were, in fact, Judaizers. The symbolic significance of the family's invitation to celebrate the Easter meal had not been lost on Padre Dominguez. He would use it to his advantage. If they served up roast pig, he could feel reassured that the family were indeed pious Catholics. But if they chose to ignore Tomás's mention of his superior's taste for pork? Well, that would spell trouble. He licked his lips. Judaizers were clever, but how would they resolve such a conflict? He could barely contain his eagerness to see if the Péres family would pass his test.

Chapter Eleven

ALFONSO

The *cocina* bustled with preparations for the homecoming of Padre Alfonso, who was arriving that day on the eve of Maundy Thursday. A cauldron of stewed vegetables and dried fruit bubbled on the hearth, filling the room with the sweet scent of cinnamon and cloves. In the yard, Concha was beating a large carpet to remove the dust, her face set in a menacing scowl. Esperanza watched from her spot at the long table where she sat peeling potatoes with the two boys on either side, while Úrsula slept peacefully in her cradle. She had survived the fever that wracked her small body just a week earlier, and Esperanza's milk had not yet completely dried up, so she continued to nurse her.

Benito grabbed a handful of peels and squeezed them in his small hands, dripping starchy liquid on the table in a pattern. Antonio watched his playmate but kept his hands folded in front of him.

"Careful, *m'hijo*, you are making a mess," Esperanza chided half-heartedly, for she was pleased that her son was enjoying himself. She wished Antonio would play as freely as Benito, but the boy had a serious nature. She pushed a pile of peels toward Antonio. "Can you make a picture for me?" she asked. The boy looked puzzled. "Like this," she said, taking four long pieces and forming a diamond with them. He nodded solemnly, searching through the pile until he came up with four shorter pieces, which he formed into a rough square. "And you, Benito, can you make a circle?"

THE SILVER CANDLESTICKS

Her son stuck his hands into the large pile and pulled out two handfuls of peels, dumping them in front of him. He looked up at her, his eyes narrowed as if expecting disappointment. "Very good! You made two spheres, which are better than circles." The boy's rivalry with her mistress's son pained her, but Antonio seemed not to notice as he made other shapes from the slivers of potato skins. She enjoyed afternoons when the boys could join her in her work. She worried that her mistress might not approve of Antonio's presence in the *cocina*, but she scarcely seemed to notice the boy when she happened upon them together.

Concha came into the *cocina* panting heavily, carrying a large rug over her shoulder. She threw it onto the floor, casting a vicious look at Esperanza. "I see who does the work around here," she said, pointing her chin at Benito. "Maybe the boy will grow up to be a ship's cook and travel the world like his father." She liked reminding Esperanza that everyone knew the circumstances of the boy's birth despite her denials.

"And where is your son? He should be helping you with that heavy load," Esperanza replied.

"He's got his own work to do. There's more than enough to go around with Padre Alfonso coming. It will be like the old days when Don Péres returned home from Las Indias," Concha said. "A feast for everyone."

"The Señora has asked me to keep things simple. Padre Alfonso is a pious man who has no appetite for elaborate meals."

"What, no suckling pig on Easter?" Concha's eyes widened.

"I am told he eats no meat," Esperanza replied.

Concha grunted. She had been looking forward to the scraps from the Easter meal. She missed the grand parties Doña Benita had thrown. Even though they had meant more work, the feasts ensured a hearty meal afterwards for the servants. She had no taste for the stews Esperanza cooked, though they too had been favorites of Doña Benita. Señora Guiomar was indifferent to what went on in the kitchen, which Concha could have accepted as a blessing. But she resented it, as she did much else that went on in the household. She wished that they had sold her when she was younger. She might have done well in another family, one with a master who appreciated a woman with flesh on her bones, not a scrawny chicken like Esperanza with her haughty manners.

"And will the Dominican from the Castillo be coming?" Concha asked.

Esperanza stood up, dropping the potato she was peeling. "Why is the guest list a concern of yours?" she asked, still holding the knife in her hand. She moved toward Concha, who stood defiantly with her hands on her hips.

"The priest has not been invited to the house since the Señora's sickness. He will be insulted that a member of his community is here and he has not been asked to join the family for a meal. It is not how things are done. Doña Benita would have known better. Doña Guiomar listens to you. You must warn her."

Concha spoke her words carefully. She did not want Esperanza to become suspicious, but she hoped that she would have an opportunity to see the priest again. Their meeting years earlier had not ended well, but he could be useful to her, and she must find a way to let him know that she could be useful as well.

Esperanza laid the knife on the table. No matter how devious Concha was, the woman was right. She must ask her mistress if the Dominican had been invited. "Thank you, Concha," she said, forcing a smile. "I will ask, though I am quite sure she has her reasons whatever she has decided." She knew she must warn the señora of Concha's inquiry, but in the meantime, she must keep Concha off her guard. "Let me help you," she said as she bent to lift the heavy rug.

Concha's eyes burned with hate as she stared at Esperanza's back, where the muscles strained against the weight of the rug. Even after the birth of her son, the woman retained her tiny waist. But Esperanza's beauty would not save her if Concha could prove that she helped these Judaizers.

THE SILVER CANDLESTICKS

Guiomar walked out into the courtyard and drew a deep breath. The orange blossoms had come late this spring, though they had already fallen and lay on the ground, the white flowers turned to brown. But their scent was still strong. She walked up the stone stairs that led to the second-floor veranda. Alfonso's old room, the one he had occupied as a boy, was at the far corner of the house. She had not had a chance to speak with him alone since he arrived. She knocked on the door.

"Come in," Alfonso called. He stood up from the red velvet kneeler, holding his prayer book.

"Have I disturbed you?" Guiomar asked shyly. She still found her brother's presence intimidating, his severe brow and dark habit making him look foreboding even when he tried to set her at ease.

"Not at all, my dear sister. You could never disturb me," he said, putting the book down on the table next to the bed. "But you look worried. Tell me, is something troubling you?"

She frowned. "When I received word from Padre Dominguez that he would accept my invitation to join us for dinner on Easter, I found his reply puzzling." Guiomar and her father had spoken with Alfonso soon after he arrived, expressing their concern over the Dominican's request that she assist him in rehabilitating a Judaizer at the Castillo. Alfonso tried to reassure them that the request was not so strange and might even be a testament to the inquisitor's faith in her piety. She was sure Alfonso was wrong on that account. But she did not wish to share her reasons. Perhaps he could make sense of the priest's words, relayed so carefully by the florid friar.

"He said that he would be pleased to join us in the celebration of the 'Paschal Sacrifice.' I had never heard the phrase before, but Brother Tomás, I think that was the man's name, said it so carefully it was as if there was some special meaning to it. I thought I should tell you," she said, blushing like a schoolgirl.

Alfonso pursed his lips. "Christ is the Paschal Lamb, who was sacrificed on Calvary and rose on Easter," he finally replied. "But there is another meaning, too, I fear." He let out a breath through his lips, slowly. "Sit down, Guiomar. We must talk frankly, *mi her-*

mana," he said, motioning his sister to the chair beside the bed. He too sat and took her hand in his.

"Padre Dominguez surely knows that this year, the Gregorian calendar overlaps the Hebrew calendar. Sunday, which is of course Easter, also marks the last day of Pesach," he paused to see if Guiomar showed any recognition of the term. Her pretty face remained pensive, but she showed no sign that she understood the significance of his words. "By referring to the Paschal Lamb, he drew attention to the Jewish Passover. Do you know the story?"

Guiomar shook her head. Her mother had told her something about a special feast commemorating God's mercy and deliverance of the Hebrews, but she had not paid close attention. At the time, the only thing that mattered to her was that her mother's revelations had put an end to her hope of marrying José Marcos.

Alfonso was disappointed in Guiomar's ignorance. It seemed unlike his mother to have neglected her education in such matters. But perhaps she hoped to spare her youngest child the pain of persecution. "You remember the story of Moses leading his people out of slavery in Egypt?"

"Yes, of course. Moses received the Ten Commandments in the desert. The nuns at the convent school taught me as much. I can still recite them, if you'd like to hear," she replied eagerly.

He smiled. "Before the Jews went into the desert, God punished the Egyptians with ten plagues because Pharaoh did not want to let the Hebrews go, even after their four-hundred-year captivity in Egypt. And the last of these plagues was the most terrible—the slaying of the firstborn."

Guiomar vaguely remembered the tale, but like so many of those Old Testament stories, this one had struck her as especially cruel. Why would God kill innocent children to set the Hebrews free? "Yes, now I remember. He spared the Hebrews," she said.

"But do you remember how the Angel of Death knew which were the houses of the Hebrews?"

She didn't like being tested by her brother. "What does this have to do with Padre Dominguez's reply?" she interjected.

"The Hebrews marked their doors with the blood of a lamb. And during the time of Christ, a sacrificial lamb, known as the paschal lamb, was sacrificed in the Temple. The feast is called Pesach, which means 'to pass over,' but it also suggests the sacrificial lamb," he said gently. "The Last Supper, which Christ celebrated with his apostles the night he was arrested, was a Pesach celebration, and in Christianity, Christ Himself becomes the sacrificial lamb." He paused to see if his sister was taking in his words, but her lips revealed her impatience, pursed tightly together as if she was forcing them shut, much as they had when she was a child and he had tried to teach her the psalms. "Did the friar say anything else?"

"Only that the priest had a special taste for..." she stopped herself.

Alfonso dropped her hand. "He expects roasted pig. Am I right?"

He stood abruptly and paced the floor, head bent in contemplation. The inquisitor was testing them. No matter how elaborate a feast they might prepare, if it did not include that which was forbidden to Jews, he would assume the worst. But his deviousness was even bolder. By drawing attention to Pesach, he was taunting them. Not only would they be forced to serve pork, they would have to do so on the last day of Passover. And Dominguez would be watching—all of them—to see if they consumed it.

Alfonso shuddered. It had been easy to avoid disobeying the dietary rules in his Order simply by refusing to eat meat. Doing so had earned him a reputation for great piety. He could use this excuse at the dinner on Sunday. But his father and sister would have no choice. He bridled at the thought of sitting at table on Passover with Dominguez, who would blaspheme it. He sometimes wished his family had followed the example of others who fled to distant lands instead of hiding their faith, sending their sons into the priesthood and their daughters into convents. How many generations could a religion survive under these circumstances?

Guiomar lay in her bed, sleepless though it was after midnight. On most nights when she couldn't sleep, it was the face of José Marcos that haunted her dreams. How could he still cause her such pain when it had been four years since he abandoned her? But tonight, it was her brother's words that troubled her. Perhaps he was wrong. The priest from the Castillo did not strike her as a scholar who would know the Hebrew calendar. It was possible that Alfonso was reading too much into the message.

But there was more in her brother's behavior that distressed her. He was disappointed in her. She could see it in his eyes when he told her the story of the Jews' flight from Egypt. Her mother had tried to teach her the Jewish prayers and customs before her death, but every time she brought it up, Guiomar had found a reason to cut her short. It pained her to remember how disrespectful she had been, especially on the day her mother informed her of the family's secret.

She threw off the blankets and got up. The full moon made the room nearly as light as day, but it would still be many hours before the rest of the household was up. She threw a shawl over her shoulders, put slippers on her feet, and went out onto the veranda. Outside the air was cool with a breeze blowing off the Guadalquivir. Dark clouds gathered, blackening the moon as they passed over it. She feared a storm was brewing.

When she was younger, she worried whenever thunder shook the skies, fearing for the safety of her father. She did not understand then, as he explained later, that the skies over Sevilla were not the same that he experienced at sea. "Look, *m'hija*," he said, pointing to the clouds overhead. "See how they cross the sky from west to east? The winds you feel now would have lashed my boat hours, even days ago if I were on the ocean. The world is vast and time itself is fluid." She had listened patiently and tried to understand. But even now, she was not sure she fully apprehended his meaning.

She tiptoed down the stone steps into the courtyard as the wind whipped up. The first drops of rain struck her head, sending shivers down her body. She tried the door into the *cocina*, but it did not budge. She leaned into it with her shoulder as the rain, which was now falling hard and blowing sideways, drenched her thin gown. It

THE SILVER CANDLESTICKS

gave way suddenly, nearly causing her to fall. She was surprised to see Esperanza before her, Úrsula at her breast.

"Señora, what are you doing up?" Esperanza asked, frowning at the sight of her shivering mistress. She placed the child in its small cradle, rocking the infant gently so she would not fuss.

"I couldn't sleep. I thought to make myself some chocolate," she said.

"I'll make it, but first we must get you dry," Esperanza said, giving the cradle one last push. She took her own wrap from her shoulders and put it around her mistress, removing the wet one. "Let me start the fire and you can sit and warm yourself." She moved to the large hearth and lit the firewood, which she had placed there earlier, blowing gently on the tiny flames that licked up from the bottom of the pile.

Esperanza wondered whether she should bring up her conversation with Concha from the previous day. It was difficult to know how much she should say, and the immediate worry about the Dominican had already been resolved. Señor Armijo had informed Esperanza that she must secure a suckling pig from the butcher as well as a lamb to serve at the Easter meal in honor of Padre Dominguez.

"You are good to worry yourself about me," Guiomar said. "And I see my daughter is doing much better. You have a way with the children." She put her hands out near the flames and was surprised at how quickly the warmth spread through her body. "I have not always been kind to you—or to the others," she said in a voice barely above a whisper. "My mother was better suited to running a household. I fear I did not learn enough from her when I had the chance."

She turned to face the servant, who was pouring water from the pitcher into a black pot. Esperanza turned, her brow furrowed as if fearing what might be said next. But Guiomar felt compelled to go on. "It is a very lonely life I lead," she said, hesitating.

Guiomar walked over to the cradle and peered in. The fire threw shadows on the child's sleeping face, which twitched as if in a frightening dream. She sat on the bench and gently pushed the cradle so it began to rock again.

"I know my mother taught you many things." Guiomar stopped herself briefly. "Are you willing to teach me what you learned of our family's customs?"

Esperanza turned to hide her distress and hung the water to boil over the fire. She moved to sit beside the Señora on the bench. Her mistress's face was more open than she could ever recall, her eyes curious, almost like a child's. "There is something I must talk to you about, Señora," she said, her voice tremulous.

"Yes, go on," Guiomar responded, suddenly unsure whether she should have opened this door.

Esperanza reached out to take her hands. "The woman Concha remains a danger to you and your family. I fear that she will do something on Sunday when the padre is here."

Guiomar squeezed the servant's hands. So she knew. How could she not? Wasn't that the very reason she had asked Esperanza to teach her what she had failed to learn from her mother? She stood up from the bench and approached the boiling pot. "Then we must see to it that Concha is never alone with the padre," she said firmly. "But you haven't answered me. Can you help me learn what I need to know about…" she looked at Esperanza for some sign if she needed to be more explicit.

"I will, Señora. I loved your mother with all my heart. And I hope to repay the love she showed me by serving you faithfully, all my days."

Guiomar reached out to embrace Esperanza when the child began to cry. The servant turned toward the cradle, but Guiomar grabbed her arm gently. "Let me do it, Esperanza. It is time I get to know my daughter," she said as she bent to lift the infant in her arms.

Chapter Twelve

THE DELUGE

*P*adre Dominguez returned from the chapel drenched by the sudden heavy rain. His habit stuck to his body, inflaming the recent self-inflicted wounds on his back and shoulders. His new abode was more comfortable than the small cell he had occupied in the Castillo, but the trek between his little house and the chapel to pray the Divine Office in the middle of the night made living there a penance.

His teeth made an unpleasant chatter as he shivered in the harsh wind. He lifted his eyes as a large bolt of lightning lit up the night sky. The last time it had rained this hard, his first year in Sevilla, the Guadalquivir had flooded its banks, the water seeping into the foundation of the Castillo so that the always dank cells oozed moisture. Many of the inhabitants died. It was regrettable. But what could he have done?

He wrapped his arms closely around his chest, vowing to speak to the groundskeeper. He would order bags of sand to be placed around the Castillo walls if the rain lasted into the morning. The prisoners could perform the task within the walls, he thought, though he would have to make sure that only the most trustworthy guards would be allowed to participate.

He pushed against the door to his house, leaning his shoulder into the wood, again feeling the raw welts from his scourging. The new wood had expanded with the rain, but with the second shove, it gave way and swung open. The candle in the far corner of the room burned brightly as he had left it. He thought to snuff it out and retire for a few hours until the sun rose, but stopped in his path. Water had seeped in from the joint in the walls and puddled on the wood floor.

"What idiots," he shouted, though there was no one to hear his words. "Incapable of making even a simple hut." He looked around the room for something to sop up the pool at his feet but, finding nothing, took off his cloak and used it. He walked to the corner where the water seemed to be leaking in and got down on his knees. He pressed his fingers into the walls, which crumbled into mud at his touch, exposing a small hole from the force of the water that grew as he watched in disgust.

He lifted his body with some effort. He was exhausted. But instead of the slight rest he had hoped for, now he would have to wake the groundskeeper to come inspect the damage so that it could be repaired before it turned into a calamity. Was this more punishment for his carnal desires? Had he not already paid the price with the welts on his back and shoulders? What more could the Lord want from him?

He picked up his wet cloak, which would be of no use now against the torrential rain outside, and threw it on the table, nearly knocking over the flickering candle. He had hoped the Armijo family would reward him with a new cloak when he visited the young Señora after the birth of her child. But they had made their donation in silver to the Holy Office instead. Had they not noticed the threadbare condition of his garments? Did they think his visit was part of his official duties? Were they simply like other Jews who lined the coffers of the Holy Office in hopes of fending off inquiry? He had witnessed such bribery in Llerena.

No, Señora Péres requested him as her confessor out of her high regard, or so Don Francisco had professed. Surely he knew that such a favor required a personal reward. Yet they had shown indifference. And now they wanted him to sit at their table on Easter. He would be lucky if his cloak and habit dried in time, even though it was three days away. Perhaps they would notice if he showed up chilled and hacking from the cough that he would surely have by then.

He headed back into the night, the wind whipping through his wet garments so that his very soul was frozen.

Inés Mejia moved away from her corner of the cell into the middle of the room, where a dozen women huddled. The water, which started as a trickle, had now grown to a steady stream coming from the place where the stone floor met the bricks of the outside wall. She moved slowly in the dark, afraid she would slip on the slick stones. But when she reached the others, all but the one called Marta moved away towards the door with its iron grate.

"We will drown if they do not let us out of here," Inés whispered. "And even if they do, disease will surely follow this flood as death follows life. I have seen it before." She shivered as the water, now half-way up her calves, soaked the edge of the blanket she clutched.

Marta reached her arm around the old woman and wrapped part of her tattered shawl around Inés's shoulders. "Surely they will not let us die. If you sent word to…Padre Dominguez—" Inés stiffened at the mention of the name—"he would not refuse you. You need only call out to the guard," Marta said, emboldened by her fear.

"I will do it for you. And the others," Inés responded, moving toward the women who were now pressed flat against the door.

"Let us through," Marta said, grabbing the old woman's hand and pushing against the others. "The Señora is our only hope for survival." The women parted, leaving a clear path to the grate.

Inés was nearly a head shorter than the small barred opening, but she stood on her toes and called out as loudly as she could.

"For the love of God, send word to Padre Dominguez that the sinner Inés Mejia wants to see him!"

The women waited in silence, hoping to hear some response, but none came.

"Call again, Señora, *por favor*," several uttered the same plea at once.

Inés pushed her face against the door, but she knew that it was useless. She could not be heard unless her lips could reach the bars. "Help me," she said, turning to Marta. "You and the others must lift me up. Otherwise, the guard will not make out the words and he will ignore it."

"You heard her. Help me raise her," Marta said, and two of the biggest women stepped forward and put their hands on the old woman's waist. They lifted her with ease, as the woman was light as a child.

"For the love of God, I pray you, send for the priest. It is Doña Inés Mejia who requests it," she shouted, her voice breaking. She pushed her fingers through the slats, holding tight, and tried to peer into the dark hallway, but she could see nothing. "It is Doña Inés Mejia. I wish to confess my sins to Padre Dominguez," she shouted again. But there was no way to know if anyone heard. The women's fingers dug into her ribs, but the pain was nothing to her. She put her ear to the grate hoping to hear footfalls, but the silence was accompanied only by the sound of running water. "Let me down," she said. "There is no one to hear our pleas."

"Will they let us drown here like rats?" one of the women cried out.

"The guard has probably fled to save to his family," said Marta.

"Surely someone will come before the waters rise too high," another said, as others began to weep. "*Madre de Dios*," the cries went up as the women began to push against the door, screaming for help.

Guiomar woke with a start. The room was bright as day, lit by the flashes of lightning outside. The thunder was deafening, shaking the very foundations of the old house. She threw back the covers, wishing Francisco had come to her in the night. He had not done so since the birth of Úrsula, and he had been especially indifferent to her since their encounter over the letter to Padre Dominguez.

THE SILVER CANDLESTICKS

She would never understand her husband. What had she done on that occasion to warrant his jealous behavior? It was as if he could read her mind. Well, he would be gone soon enough to Las Indias. She had better get used to sleeping alone every night, perhaps for the rest of her life. He could easily find another to warm his bed in Méjico, but she needn't worry that he might not return like many others who established new lives in the New World. His son would ensure that he came back to Sevilla, if not to her bedchamber, she thought. She laughed bitterly. She was becoming jealous too now that Francisco had cooled to her.

A large branch from the tree in the courtyard hit hard against the window. She could see sheets of rain in the glow of the lightning. She had barely slept at all, especially with her visit to the kitchen a few hours earlier. She clutched the shawl closer as she stepped into the hall, holding a candle to light the way. No doubt Esperanza would soon be up as well, and the baby. The servant's words that evening still troubled her.

"You are up early, my dear." Francisco said when he encountered Guiomar in the hallway. He was surprised to see his wife at such an hour, but no one could sleep through the storm. He had thought of going to her room in the night. He knew she would be restless. But he hesitated. He could not throw off the suspicion that she still harbored feelings for Herrera, though he had no more evidence than his fears.

"You scared me," she said as he drew nearer. The candlelight threw a sinister shadow over his features, but his eyes showed concern, even love. "I couldn't sleep. Who could through this thunder?" she said, a small smile forming on her lips.

"Let us get some *café*. Surely the servants will be up soon." He put his arm around her shoulder and took the candle from her hand as they continued to the end of the hallway.

The *cocina* was dark when they entered, so Francisco was startled to see his brother-in-law sitting at the long table. "Alfonso, you are up too. We will have to fend for ourselves since the servants seem to be the only ones able to sleep through this storm." He put the candle on the table and saw that Alfonso had a small book open before him. In the dim light, he must have been reciting the prayers from memory.

"I do not recall such a storm," Alfonso said. "It is as if God has unleashed his wrath on the poor sinners of Sevilla. Though in truth, the innocent will suffer along with the guilty."

"I will fetch Esperanza," Guiomar said, touching her brother's shoulder as she passed.

"You cannot go out there," Francisco said, grabbing her arm. "Let me."

"Yes, let him," Alfonso said, looking up at his lovely sister. "Sit with me awhile. We have barely talked since I arrived."

Guiomar watched as Francisco ran across the courtyard to the servants' small *casita*. "I am glad we are alone, brother. There are so many questions I wish to ask you." When she had returned to her bed after her midnight talk with Esperanza, she'd made up her mind to learn more about the Jews, even if she did not feel that she was one of them. If she was to live in fear that one day the blood in her veins might cost her freedom, even her life, she should at least learn what it meant to be a Jew.

"Can you teach me..." She couldn't force the words out, but Alfonso seemed to understand. He slid the small book he'd been reading across the table. "This may answer some of your questions. But you must be careful no one sees it. Not even Francisco."

Guiomar pulled the candle closer to the book, which was crudely bound, with no writing on the cover. The pages were covered in dense script that was difficult to read. There were some drawings of animals being slaughtered—a fowl, a sheep, a cow—that looked like a child had made them. There was a picture of candlesticks like her mother's and words she could not read in letters she guessed were Hebrew. At the back of the book were a series of these letters.

She looked up at her brother. "How am I to learn this in a few days?"

"I will help you. You need not learn all of it, only the part that deals with the home. When it comes time, I will prepare Antonio to become a man of our people. It will be easier for you than for some. You had good training in the convent and know many of the stories of our people, including the most important one, which we are celebrating this week."

"Easter?"

Alfonso could not help but smile. But he could see that he had offended her. "I am sorry, *mi hermana*. It is just that Jesus was a Jew, despite what we have been taught. The Last Supper was a Passover feast, as I told you. The Christians have appropriated our story—the story of the Jewish people. So you already know much of it."

Guiomar slipped the small book into the pocket of her skirt. "I will study it, I promise." Despite herself, Guiomar felt a certain pride in this possession, not of the book itself but the knowledge that it was up to her to carry on so ancient a tradition. Who were these Jews that they felt singled out by God, she wondered, and what did it mean that she was one of them? The thought had frightened her at first, even repelled her. But perhaps this book could help bind her to all those who had come before her, not just her mother and grandmother and the rest of their family line, but others, like herself, who must carry on this tradition in secret and great peril.

"Why did our family not leave at the time of the Expulsion? I mean if it was so important to them to retain their faith," she asked.

"Many did. But even those who fled sometimes returned. It was easier for those to leave if they had little to keep them here. The Jews were not allowed to bring anything with them but a small sum of money and what they could carry. Our family was perhaps more prosperous than pious. I think many Jews believed that time would pass and they would be allowed back. They were once very important to the Crown."

Francisco pushed open the door accompanied by Esperanza. "As you can see, we need your assistance," he said, motioning to

Guiomar and Alfonso, who were seated just as he had left them. Despite her intelligence, he wondered how his wife would survive if left to her own devices. She had not even moved to start the fire under the kettle.

Padre Dominguez made his way down the dark steps to the cells where the women were held. He was angry that the guard had deserted his post. The water rushing down the stones made the stairs treacherous. He held a candle in one hand while the other tightly gripped the metal rail. He could hear the voices of the women crying out in terror, but without the key to open the cell door, there was little he could do.

The water was cold and moved rapidly, nearly knocking him down. It was as if he had stepped into a stream. The stench of excrement and rot was nearly unbearable. He heard a high-pitched squeal and realized that a rat was drowning in an eddy where the water was being pulled down through a grate into the sewer drains that ran beneath the floor. As he approached the cell, the shrieks of the women ceased. He held the candle high and peered into the murky cell. The women were pressed against the heavy door, their eyes reflecting the candlelight like cats—or maybe devils.

"*Madre de Dios*," one of the women screamed out. "Save us, please, Padre."

"I have no key. Where has the jailer gone?" he asked.

"You must help us, Padre," Inés raised her voice, "for the love of God."

The dark was suddenly filled with light and the sound of voices coming from the stairwell. Brother Ignácio waded through the dirty water holding a ring of heavy keys, followed by Padre Jaramillo, who held a burning torch aloft.

"Quickly. We must get them out of here," Dominguez said, dropping his candle in the water and grabbing the keys from the friar's hand. He fumbled to get the key into the slot but found that even when the lock was turned, the heavy door did not budge. The wood had swollen from the moisture, like the door of his casita.

"Push. Push hard," he told the women, but the door still did not move. "We need a lever, or an axe," he yelled. The voices of the women were growing hysterical. "Quiet. Your screams will not help. Pray to the Virgin to save you!"

Padre Jaramillo stuck the torch into a sconce, grabbed hold of the bars in the grill and pulled with all his might. He felt the door move enough to slip his fingers in the gap, allowing some of the trapped water to spill out. "Help me," he said to the priest and the friar, who tried to maneuver their bodies so that they too could tug at the door. Slowly, the door moved until one of the women was able to squeeze through the opening.

One after another, the dozen women pushed through the opening. The last was Inés Mejia. They stood shivering, their filthy rags soaked through.

Padre Dominguez looked at the sorry lot, unsure what to do with them now that he had saved them from drowning. "Come, we must get you dry clothes," he said, pointing toward the stairs.

Jaramillo took the torch from the sconce and led the way while Dominguez brought up the rear. The women struggled against the water on the stairs, stumbling, unsure of foot. When all finally reached the hall above, Dominguez led them toward his old cell. It was smaller than the one that had held them, but it was dry and could be locked.

"Get them something to cover themselves," he directed Brother Ignácio, who stood with a confused look on his face. "Well, move," he said, shoving the friar.

"But what, Padre? We have no women's clothing," the friar muttered.

"Go to the laundry. Bring some habits if you can find nothing else," Dominguez ordered. He should send one of the friars to the convent near Santa Ana's, but in the meantime, the women must be made warm and decent.

Inés Mejia approached the priest. She was shaking, both in fear and because of the cold. She looked at the Dominican, who was nearly as soaked as she. "I called out for you, Padre," she said, feebly. "I wanted to confess." The words were out of her mouth before she could consider what she was saying.

"There will be time for that, Señora. But I must attend to the needs of all at this moment." He looked down on the wizened face, bewildered. For months, she had refused everything—better food, clothing—and now she was ready to confess without prompting. "Are you feeling sick?"

Inés shook her head, but she felt suddenly weak and light-headed. Marta put an arm around her shoulders. "May she sit, Padre?" she asked motioning toward the chair behind the table.

"Yes, of course. Sit. Rest. All of you. Make yourselves as comfortable as you can. I will send blankets. For the time being, you will remain here. Now I must see that the men are safe." He pulled Jaramillo aside. "Keep watch on them. Brother Ignácio will return with clothing and then they should be fed. Bread and broth," he whispered. "Make sure the old woman eats. I do not want her to perish before I have heard her confession."

Guiomar rocked Úrsula in her arms as she paced the floor. The baby's birthmark had faded so that it was barely visible. Perhaps the child would be less homely than Guiomar feared. The infant smiled in her sleep, her tiny mouth turned up at the corners, revealing a tiny dimple in her chin. Guiomar sat on the edge of the bed, looking down at her daughter. It was wrong to think so, but she felt that José Marcos would have given her more beautiful children, fair-haired and perhaps with light eyes as well. She lay back on the blankets, the child nestled in her arms.

Francisco was unfair to suspect her. She had done everything she could to avoid José Marcos, even avoiding his sister, though María Dolores was her oldest friend. She turned down invitations to dine with those who might, unknowingly, include the Herreras among their guests. She had even given up going to Santa Ana's except on Sundays and Holy Days with her husband and father, never alone in the afternoon as she had the last time she had seen him. But it was impossible not to hear occasional word of him. It was rumored that he was heavily in debt and might soon travel to Las Indias to strike out on his own. She had heard Don Enrique mention it to the ship's captain after Úrsula's baptism, but moved away quickly so as not to overhear the details. It seemed she spent much of her time driving José Marcos from her mind. And still Francisco was suspicious.

She fingered the small pendant Francisco had given her with her free hand. She would miss him, she had to admit. He was a good husband, and generous. Still, with him gone, her time would be her own. She could amuse herself as she chose, within reason. Maybe she would even renew her friendship with María Dolores. If she stayed away from her friend's house, no one could fault her for inviting the woman to her own. She could invite several of the young women who had been in the convent with her. Many of them had children now, and some had husbands who were gone. She could turn her house into a social gathering place. With her father's permission, she could invite guests for dinner on a regular basis, much as her mother had done all her life. The Péres home would once again be the center of social life in Triana. Don Enrique would be pleased as well. The family had been in mourning too long, and with Francisco away, there would be no fear that he might do something to embarrass her.

She lifted the sleeping infant and gently placed her in the cradle in the corner. She hoped Esperanza would fetch the child before she woke, hungry, in the morning. Before slipping into bed, she pulled the small book her brother had given her from the pocket of her nightdress and quickly thumbed through it in the dim light of the bedroom. There would be time enough to study it in the morning. The rain outside had stopped. Perhaps tomorrow would bring the sun and she might even go with Esperanza to Santa Ana's to walk the stations of the cross.

Chapter Thirteen

THE EASTER REPAST

Guiomar looked anxiously at her father in his place at the head of the long table. The seating was an awkward arrangement, with her father at one end, her and her brother on either side, and her husband at the far end, flanked by Padre Dominguez and Don Enrique. Her father would have preferred that she and Francisco sit in the places of honor at each end, but she was insistent. She wished, as much as possible, to avoid having to interact with the priest. It was safer that Dominguez be seated with her husband and godfather, whose Catholic faith were beyond suspicion. She would not have to fear that one of them would make some inadvertent slip that he might seize on, and she was seated far enough away that her own interactions with the priest would be limited.

"Shall we say grace?" Don Pedro asked when the servants stood ready with the platters. "Will you do the honor of blessing our meal, Padre Dominguez?"

Dominguez made the sign of the cross, "Bless us, O Lord, for these gifts we are about to receive," he chanted, bowing his head, "through Christ Our Lord. Amen." He lifted his eyes, taking in a deep breath. "Ah, the delicious aroma of roast pork," he said, smiling toward Alfonso Péres. "What better way to break the Lenten fast, do you not agree, Padre?"

Guiomar watched her brother as he turned toward his fellow Dominican. He showed no emotion, but she sensed tension.

THE SILVER CANDLESTICKS

"The delicious smell brings back many happy memories of Easters past at this table," he answered with a smile. "Indeed, the desire to partake in this feast tempts me sorely. But I fear that I would not be true to the Rule we observe at our monastery in Ronda if I were to eat meat, even on this joyous day," he said, taking a large helping of the vegetable stew that Esperanza had prepared for him.

"Ah, yes, I had forgotten that your monastery observes the more ascetic Rule of our order," he said. "All the better for the rest of us," he continued, forcing a laugh that others took up with less enthusiasm.

"I will gladly eat Alfonso's portion," Don Pedro chimed in, spearing a large slice of pork, "although if my departed wife were here, she would chide me about my expanding girth."

Guiomar reached to pat her father's hand. "My father's appetite is a sign of his robust health," she said approvingly.

"More wine for our guests," her father called out, thumping his goblet on the table. Guiomar hoped he would not drink too much, but there was little she could do to interfere. She nodded to Esperanza, who disappeared into the hall to fetch the wine.

"I heard, Padre, that the Castillo suffered much damage in the flood," Francisco said in a voice that invited all to listen. "Was everyone rescued safely?"

"Interesting that you should mention it," he said, chewing a large chunk of meat as he spoke. "As I am sure your wife has told you, I have asked her assistance in saving the soul of one of the most difficult cases at the Castillo, Inés Mejia." He looked toward Guiomar at the other end of the table, who nodded her assent. "As it happens, God's Providence, as is so often the case, turned the flood into an opportunity. Apparently, faced with the imminent possibility of drowning, the woman confessed." He stopped himself as he caught Alfonso staring at him. "Of course, I would never break the seal of confession, but I will say that the woman's soul is no longer in danger."

"Will she be released then?" asked Guiomar.

"That is not for me to say," Dominguez replied. "There must first be a tribunal."

Guiomar frowned. "I'm not sure I understand."

"Perhaps you can explain, Padre," said Dominguez, pointing his fork toward her brother.

"I am unfamiliar with the case, as you can imagine," Alfonso answered brusquely.

"Of course, how foolish of me," Dominguez said. "But you know the role of the Holy Office," he said, smiling.

"I would not presume to know it as well as you, Padre," Alfonso said. "But, in general," he looked toward Guiomar, whose anxiety was written on her brows, "our Holy Mother Church is very merciful toward those who repent of their sins."

"But only if that repentance is sincere," Dominguez interrupted, "which is what the Holy Office must determine. And in this case, as with all Judaizers, it is important to ensure that they reveal all of those who may have been corrupted by their apostasy, so they also may be questioned and repent." He stopped to take a hefty drink of wine, which was of much higher quality than the Castillo's budget could afford. "Señora Mejia must demonstrate to the satisfaction of the tribunal that she is in no danger of relapse if she is released into society, after undergoing a trial that will determine her just punishment. At the moment, however, she remains somewhat confused on certain issues."

He motioned to the servant who stood holding the platter of sliced pork to bring him another portion. It was the same fleshy woman who had come to the Castillo years earlier. He grabbed for the wine goblet again. "And here, Señora, is where I hoped you might keep your promise to assist me," he said, his voice rising to make certain the spoiled young woman understood she could not wriggle out of it.

Guiomar leaned into the table. "I am eager to help, Padre," she said calmly. "But I wonder how I can. I don't know her. Nor do I know what to look for as a sign that she still holds to her heretic beliefs. I have never encountered a Jew, thank God," she said, making a quick sign of the cross.

"My dear sister," Alfonso interjected, "that is Padre Dominguez's point. These Jews are great deceivers. They are in our midst, without our knowledge, which is what makes them so dangerous."

"Your brother is exactly right, Señora. We grow up hearing stories that they use the blood of Christian children in their Passover rituals. But these are just wild tales meant to scare the ignorant. The danger is not to our bodies but our souls," he said. "They deny the Trinity. They refuse to accept Church law and the intercessions of the saints and the Virgin."

Don Pedro put his hands on the table. "We are getting too serious for such a joyous occasion," he said. "We are here to celebrate my son's return, if only for a few days."

"But, first, our Lord's Resurrection," Alfonso objected.

"I don't know about you," Don Enrique said, joining the general conversation for the first time, "but I am also celebrating my good fortune that Francisco will accompany my fleet to Veracruz." He raised his goblet to Francisco, seated to his left. "May you follow in your father-in-law's path and enrich not only my precious goddaughter and your children but help to fill my coffers as well," he said, draining the cup in one gulp.

"May I add my blessing too?" Dominguez said. "And perhaps a request?"

"Your blessing is very welcome, Padre, and I will do my best to honor any request," Francisco said, though he feared what might come next.

"While you are busy filling Don Enrique Gomez's coffers, spare a few alms for the Church," he said, laughing awkwardly. "We will have much rebuilding to do at the Castillo after the Guadalquivir finally recedes, I am afraid."

"Of that you have my assurance, Padre. Would any sailor refuse such a request before embarking on such a dangerous mission?" he asked, a grin spreading over his face, though inside his anger seethed. He looked down the long table to Guiomar, who had lowered her eyes.

"And since you will be gone," Dominguez said, following Armijo's gaze, "your wife will have time to supplement your family's gift by instructing the errant Mejia woman."

Guiomar lifted her eyes to meet the priest's directly. She nodded in assent, though fear gripped her. The priest's eyes burned with a cold fury that she had never encountered in anyone. Why did this man hate her?

"You know there is some irony in this year's Easter celebration?" Dominguez asked, looking to each member of the family and ending with the wealthy merchant across from him.

"Irony?" Guiomar spoke up, since she suspected the question was meant for her. "What could be ironic about our Savior's Resurrection?"

"I was referring to the coincidence that this year, Easter falls on the last day of the Jewish holiday," Dominguez said and took another drink of his wine. "Of course, you would have no reason to know that," he added. "Yet it was crucial to Señora Mejia's change of heart."

Francisco felt alarmed that the priest would not give up the subject. This was more than idle chatter. He was a man obsessed with ferreting out Jews and Francisco had no doubt that the fanatic would not hesitate to ensnare his wife.

"Tell me, Padre. How did the Mejia woman come under suspicion? Did it have to do with this feast you referred to? Which is what?" Francisco asked.

"They call it 'the Passover.' We know the story as the Exodus of the Hebrews from captivity in Egypt." He paused and took another sip of wine, which was making him more voluble than usual. He looked to the other end of the table. "Do you remember the ten plagues, Señora? I am sure the nuns taught you the story. Am I right?"

THE SILVER CANDLESTICKS

Guiomar glanced at her brother. They had celebrated the feast as best they could the evening before, when the two of them sat down alone to dinner. But she was unsure how much she should say.

"I seem to recall Guiomar was quite upset with the God of the Jews when she was a young girl," Alfonso said, his voice light-hearted, though it was true.

"Upset with God?" Dominguez asked, incredulous.

"With the God of the Jews," Alfonso repeated. *Elohim. The One God this man would never know.*

"Is it ever proper to be upset with God?" Dominguez replied.

"What upset me was the death of innocent children—what was it, the first born of the Egyptians? That seemed to me, especially as a child, unduly harsh," she said, taking a sip of wine to calm her nerves at the obvious tension growing between her brother and the inquisitor.

"In the Old Testament, God often dealt harshly with unbelievers," Alfonso answered. "Sometimes even with those who believed in Him, if only to test their faith."

"And what about the plagues? Do you remember them, Señora?" Dominguez asked again. He would not give up so easily on testing how much she knew of the Passover story.

Guiomar smiled involuntarily, remembering the previous evening when her brother dipped his fingers in the wine, calling out the ten plagues, one by one for each drop that he cast on the plate. It seemed not just peculiar but somewhat rude. She wished she could repeat the gesture now if only to see the expression on the priest's face.

"You found them amusing?" Padre Dominguez asked, noticing the smile on her lips.

"I was not the best student, Padre. But the image of frogs jumping everywhere, in the ovens, in beds, well, yes, it was amusing." She pursed her lips tightly to prevent herself from revealing more than she intended.

"And the boils? And lice?" Dominguez pushed again.

"Disgusting—and not the best talk at dinner, perhaps," Alfonso interjected. This inquisitor was clever, but he would not trap Guiomar so easily. "Tell us, Padre, what had the confluence of the two holidays to do with the woman at the Castillo?" He cast a subtle glance at Guiomar.

"Apparently, Señora Mejia knew that the Jewish holy day was approaching—it often falls within Lent—and when the terrible rains began, she believed the ensuing flood was akin to one of the curses sent by God. I suppose she thought we priests would drown, like the ancient Egyptians, and she and her fellow Judaizers would be saved, as when Moses parted the Red Sea. When it became clear that her god would not save her, any more than he would the rats who infest the cellars, she called out to make her confession. I appeared outside the cell door within minutes, though of course I had no way of actually hearing her plea far away in my casita." His face beamed as he told the story, suggesting his rescue had been a miraculous feat.

Guiomar knew she should compliment the priest on saving the woman's soul, but the look of self-satisfaction that spread across his face made it impossible. "Didn't this woman have a daughter, Padre? I heard she died under tragic circumstances. What happened?" she asked, feigning as much innocence as she could.

Dominguez felt stung by the question. "It was years ago, Señora, and had nothing to do with what we are discussing," he said. He could feel the eyes of all at the table staring at him. She pretended ignorance, this haughty woman, but he was sure she knew the story well enough. Many in Sevilla blamed him for the child's death because he was the head of the Holy Office. It was grossly unfair. And hadn't the child's hanging herself been proof enough of her demonic possession?

"It is just that if I am to help the mother in some way, it seems I should know as much as I can," Guiomar said, pleased that she had drawn blood with her words. She caught her brother's eye, which looked apprehensive. No doubt he would admonish her later, when they were alone. Like Francisco, Alfonso was fearful

THE SILVER CANDLESTICKS

that the priest would ensnare her in some plot he was hatching. But she had no choice.

"Please, I must insist," Francisco spoke up forcefully. "This is a time of joy. No more talk of curses and floods and heretics. Esperanza, bring out the sweets for our guests." He turned around to the servant, who stood behind him in the corner, immovable as a statue. Next to her stood Concha. When had this dangerous woman reentered the room, he wondered. How much had she heard? Or understood? The sooner they got her out of the house for good, the better.

Concha licked her fingers after finishing off the crackling skin of the piglet, which she had made certain was browned but not burnt on the spit. There was more food left over after the meal than during Doña Benita's time because there were so few guests. She wished she had found the opportunity to catch a moment alone with the Dominican, but Esperanza had made sure she got no nearer than shoving a platter of food in his face. She tried to make eye contact, but he refused. He knew who she was, she was sure of that. And perhaps she had planted the seeds of suspicion, judging from his strange speech at dinner, which she only half paid attention to until her mistress brought up the girl who hanged herself. Soon, none of it would matter. They were about to send her away—as punishment, no doubt. But she would have the last laugh.

Esperanza came into the *cocina* carrying another platter of meat. "We'll have quite a feast tonight. I see you have already begun," she said, eying Concha.

Concha turned around quickly, her face covered in pig grease. "Well, why not? Did I not stand over the flame turning the spit so that the meat would be tender? What's more, it may be the last time I can indulge myself in this house."

"Why do you say that?" Esperanza asked.

"I thought you knew everything that went on in this family," Concha said, picking a piece of skin from between her front teeth with her long nail.

"I know only what I need to know," Esperanza said, "which is a rule you might consider following."

"They didn't tell you?" Concha spat out a small piece of gristle. Perhaps the family did not trust their favorite as much as Esperanza believed. "I am to be given to María Dolores Herrera as her bride's gift."

Esperanza struggled to control her surprise. So this was the plan Señor Armijo had come up with to rid the house of Concha's threat. She wondered if it was wise. She hoped her mistress had not planted the idea so that she might maintain contact with the man who had spurned her. "So, when will this take place?"

"You think they consult me? I am a piece of property to be gotten rid of at their convenience. I am surprised the Señora didn't pick you. She was always jealous of her mother's fondness for you. But maybe she worried you would seduce her lover."

Esperanza moved toward Concha, the platter still in her hands. She wanted to dump it on the ugly *puta*, but she turned and placed it on the table, lifting the knife that was stuck in the meat. "If I ever hear you make such accusations again," she said, her voice barely above a whisper, "I will cut your tongue out. Do you understand?" Concha opened her mouth to say something, but instead stuffed it with another piece of meat.

Francisco knocked softly on Guiomar's bedchamber door. "Are you awake, my dear?" he whispered, opening the door slightly. Guiomar sat at her dressing table, brushing her long dark hair. She turned to face him with a puzzled look. He entered hesitantly. "I hope I'm not disturbing you," he said, sitting on the edge of the bed.

Guiomar was pleased that he had come, but also fearful. She hoped he would not pursue his line of accusations about her being unfaithful. "I'm glad you are here," she said, studying his face for signs of jealousy. "We've talked so rarely since Úrsula's birth."

"Come here, *mi corazón*," he said, patting the bed. "We must have an honest conversation before it is too late and I am gone."

THE SILVER CANDLESTICKS

She approached the bed, dreading what would come next. He moved to the foot of the bed and pulled back the covers so she could get underneath. She sat up, still apprehensive, but his face looked gentle, even loving.

"I sensed that you were not happy with the talk at dinner," she said. "The Dominican is a menacing figure. I have avoided doing as he asked for months now, but I don't think I can avoid it much longer." The evening had been fraught with tension. She worried that she may have inflamed the priest further with her questions about the girl's suicide. She wished she could speak candidly with her husband—with anyone—about her doubts.

"Do you trust me, Guiomar?" He reached out to take her hand.

It was as if her husband had read her thoughts. She wasn't sure how best to answer the question but nodded.

He smiled and kissed her fingers. "We have never spoken openly to each other, Guiomar, about your family's secret." Again, he kissed her fingertips, but he could see the fear in her eyes. "We must be able to talk about it if I am to protect you, dear. I would give my life for you, Guiomar. I have loved you since the first moment I saw you in the garden when we were children. There is nothing I would not do for you—and our children."

She took a deep breath and held it. His whole face was transformed by tenderness, but she had always found it hard to completely accept his love since she couldn't return it in kind. "I know, Francisco. You are a good man—and," she hesitated, "I don't deserve you."

"Don't be silly. It is I who do not deserve you. But let us not argue over this matter when we have important things to discuss." He stood up and walked to the door, opening it a crack to make sure there was no one on the other side, listening. When he returned, he took off his boots and slipped into bed next to her.

"I fear Dominguez is laying a trap for you," he said, facing his wife. "All that nonsense about the Mejia woman is simply a way to get his hooks in you. I may not be a learned man, but even I could see his talk of the Jewish feast was a way to test you and your father, and perhaps even your brother. Alfonso told me that the slave Concha suspects the family, which is why I was willing to send her to the Herrera household—not an easy decision on my part, my sweet." He stroked Guiomar's cheek. "You are so lovely any husband would be crazy with jealousy, even if you gave no reason."

"I promise you on our children's lives, you have no reason to be mistrustful, Francisco," Guiomar interrupted, though her secret guilt consumed her. She faced two dangers. One from the priest, and one from her former lover. And the two were intertwined, she feared.

"You know, I saw him at Santa Ana's this morning." He pulled away slightly but continued staring into Guiomar's eyes. "I was filled with jealousy at his handsome looks, his swagger. I might have accosted him on the spot had it not been for seeing Concha pursue him out of the church."

"Please believe me, Francisco. I do not love the man. That is not to say I did not once, but he proved himself unworthy. You are the better man. In every way," she said, tears starting to trickle down her cheeks. She looked at her husband, and for the first time realized she could love him, if only because he loved her so much. He did not arouse the same feeling in her as José Marcos, but that passion had brought her only misery and rejection.

"I am relieved to hear it, my love. But we must be careful now to avoid becoming ensnared in the Dominican's web. I am leaving soon, and who will protect you while I am gone?" He spoke his fears out loud when it might have been better to keep them to himself.

"My father will protect me. And Esperanza too. She will keep an eye on Concha, even from a distance." But even as she spoke the words of reassurance, she was not entirely confident in them.

Guiomar reached over to kiss Francisco's lips lightly. She had never been so bold before. "I am glad we can talk about this. About my family's secret as well as your jealousy. We may only have a few weeks together now, but we will have a lifetime when you return to get to know each other better." Francisco began to unbutton his shirt and slip off his pants as Guiomar lifted her nightgown over her head. "I love you, my husband," she said as he wrapped her in his arms. But when she closed her eyes, José Marcos's face crept in, against her will, and she squeezed them shut tighter to drive the image away.

Part III

JANUARY 1597

Chapter Fourteen

THE BAPTISM

"Do you reject Satan and all his works?" the old priest, weighed down by his heavily embroidered white and gold garments, called out from the baptismal font. Guiomar lifted her head as the two couples replied, "I do." María Dolores held her infant daughter while her husband stood beside her. Guiomar tried not to look at José Marcos or his new wife, the infant's godparents, but she could not block out the sound of the woman's voice, which stood out from the others, high-pitched and nasal.

"Do you reject sin, so as to live in the freedom of God's children?" the priest asked, and the couples assented. And once more, "Do you reject Satan, father of sin and prince of darkness?"

"I do," the four voices replied in unison.

Guiomar's eyes wandered to the woman José Marcos had married not long after his sister's wedding. The woman was attractive, though she carried herself as if she believed she was a great beauty, her auburn-haired head held high and her thin lips in a perpetual half-smile. She stood slightly taller than José Marcos, which made him seem smaller than he was.

"Do you believe in Jesus Christ, His only Son, our Lord, who was born of the Virgin Mary, was crucified, died, and was buried, rose from the dead, and is now seated at the right hand of the Father?"

Guiomar winced at the words, which she had also assented to at her children's baptisms. She no longer believed what they represented, though she had not fully replaced those beliefs with new ones since she knew so little of her ancestral faith.

"I baptize you in the name of the Father," the priest said, pouring water over the child's forehead, "and the Son," again dripping water from the silver pitcher as the child wailed, "and the Holy Ghost."

Guiomar had no remorse about baptizing her children. It was a formality only. If she did not know enough to observe her new faith, it was sufficient that she believed in one God and kept the laws as best she knew them. If she must show one face in public and another in her home, she would. In the nearly two years since Francisco had departed for Veracruz, she had slowly introduced more Jewish customs into her family life, picking up bits and pieces of information as she could, even from her visits to the Castillo. When she and her father dined alone on Friday nights, she laid out her mother's silver candlesticks and intoned the prayer she had taught her before lighting the candles. After she bled each month, she bathed in the large copper tub used for dying fabrics, which Esperanza brought to her bedroom, first removing all her rings and scrubbing under the nails on her fingers and toes and cutting them close. She fasted, as the small book instructed, even though she was unsure why she was obliged to do so or even the exact days it was required. But still she attended Mass each Sunday and Holy Day, confessed her sins to Padre Saavedra each week, and dutifully swallowed the Host when he placed it on her tongue.

José Marcos stood stiffly next to his sister at the altar, his teeth clenched as the child whimpered. Guiomar was surprised that his marriage had so far produced no offspring, and if the rumors of the woman's age were true—she was said to be at least ten years older than he—she was nearing the age when she would no longer be able to do so. But Guiomar doubted that José Marcos minded his lack of heirs. If he outlived this wife, he could always find another, younger one, and there would be no children to share his

THE SILVER CANDLESTICKS

inheritance. He glanced over at Guiomar, who looked away. The last time she had seen him, soon after his marriage to María Luísa López had been announced, she pushed by him without speaking in the hallway at his sister's house. But she would not be able to avoid him today at the Christening party.

The priest motioned to the godmother to place the baptismal dress over the child's head as the mother lifted the squirming infant. Guiomar had given the child the dress as a baptismal gift, made of the finest silk her father brought back from one of his trips. "Margarita Teresa," the priest addressed the infant, "you have become a new creation and have clothed yourself in Christ. See in this white garment the outward sign of your Christian dignity. With your family and friends to help you by word and example, bring that dignity unstained into the everlasting life of heaven." The guests and baptismal party joined in proclaiming "Amen" and rose to greet the family.

Guiomar took her father's arm as they stepped from the pew and made their way to the baptismal font. "We can forego the party, Papá, if you are not up to it," Guiomar whispered in his ear.

"No, *m'hija*, we will both go. You must stop treating me as an invalid," he said, gently squeezing her arm.

"Perhaps I just wished for an excuse to avoid it," she said, patting his hand, which was now covered in dark spots and had lost much of the strength of his youth.

Guiomar approached María Dolores, who held the sleeping baby. The child had the same fair skin as her mother, her tiny pink mouth puckered into a small circle. She was a beautiful child, so unlike Úrsula, whose swarthy complexion made her daughter look more like one of the servant's children than her own. Guiomar blushed at her own cruelty. Úrsula was, after all, a very bright and cheerful child and Guiomar had tried her best to love her.

"May I introduce my wife, María Luísa López de Herrera?" José Marcos leaned in toward Guiomar as she stroked Margarita's cheek.

Guiomar looked up to meet José Marcos's eyes briefly, then turned toward the tall woman at his side. "María Dolores speaks

171

fondly of you, so I have no doubt we, too, shall become friends," Guiomar said, kissing the woman on both cheeks.

"I look forward to that," María Luísa said, "but it is curious it has taken so long to make your acquaintance."

Guiomar wondered how much the woman knew of her relationship with José Marcos. But she responded calmly. "I regret that since my husband's departure, I rarely go out or entertain. My children keep me very busy, as does my work at the Castillo."

José Marcos frowned. "What takes you to the Castillo?" he asked.

"Padre Dominguez asked for my assistance with a particularly difficult case. A Judaizer, who has since renounced her heresy but refuses to leave the Castillo, protesting that she must atone for the rest of her days. It has been my hope to persuade her that she can be more of an example to other heretics if she returns to life outside. But I have yet to convince her."

"Such acts of charity are commendable," María Luísa interjected, "but you should not cut yourself off from society, my dear. It is not healthy."

Guiomar detected no malice in the woman's voice, grating though it was, but she suspected the implied criticism had some basis in jealousy. Perhaps she knew more than she let on. "Well, I will begin by making my way to María Dolores's home for the fiesta," she said, turning to look for her father who had moved away to talk to other guests.

José Marcos waited in the courtyard, hoping to waylay Guiomar as she made her way back through the orange garden. The fruit was in full bloom, filling the air with their sharp scent. He wanted to question her about her visits to the Castillo, which seemed dangerous under the circumstances. The servant Concha eyed him from the door. The slave made no secret of her lust, but he found the woman repulsive. He was not above bedding one of the servants, but he was not desperate enough to seek out this fleshy creature who followed him around his sister's house each time he visited. Even María Luísa had noticed the slave's attentions and let him

THE SILVER CANDLESTICKS

know that he should keep his distance. "Other men may take their pleasures outside the marriage bed," she'd told him, "but I will not stand for it." He protested the rebuke with a profession of undying love, but he could see in his wife's eyes that she didn't believe him. And why should she?

Guiomar turned the corner along the portico but stopped as José Marcos stepped from the doorway. She could not easily reverse course without being obvious, but she hoped to avoid speaking to him at length. She looked through the window and noticed Concha also lurking near the door. She tried to avoid her when she visited María Dolores, but it was not always possible. The woman was understandably concerned about her son, who had traveled with Francisco to Méjico. It had been Francisco's idea to take Concha's son with him as insurance against any plots she might hatch. And it worked, almost too well as Concha sought out Guiomar for news whenever their paths crossed.

"I hope you are not avoiding me," José Marcos said as Guiomar approached.

"Is there some reason I should?" she said, looking directly at him. He smiled in return, but his eyes conveyed something else. "I am pleased to have made your wife's acquaintance," she said with as much sincerity as she could force. "She is," she struggled for the right word, "imposing."

"She would be pleased to hear so," he replied.

His eyes wandered over her elaborate gown, and she could feel the blood rushing to her cheeks.

"You are angry with me, I know," he said, "but I only wish the best for you, my love."

Guiomar flinched. He had no right to address her with such intimacy. She started to move away, but his eyes stopped her even before she felt the pressure of his hand on her forearm.

"I must talk to you," he whispered. "I am in agony, and what you said earlier about the Castillo fills me with dread."

Guiomar could see the pain in his eyes. It was entirely unexpected. She wanted to turn and run, but she would only draw attention to their unusual interaction.

"Señora, may I speak with you a moment?" Concha tugged on Guiomar's sleeve.

Guiomar turned quickly. "Of course, Concha. I have been meaning to catch a word with you," she said, moving away from José Marcos without looking back at him. "I received a letter from my husband, who spoke fondly of your son's service," she said, though Francisco had said nothing of the kind. His only mention of the boy had come two years earlier, when he complained that Juanito was as surly as he was lazy. She could hear José Marcos's boots on the patio stones as he quickly walked away, determined to escape the prying eyes of the *esclava*. "But you will see for yourself soon enough," she said. "I expect they will return in the fall, but no later than Christmas."

Guiomar took Francisco's last letter out to reread it. She had read it so many times, the paper had become stained by the oils from her skin.

> My dearest one, the days here are long and hard. The sun is sometimes unbearable and the stench of the slave ships drift into my tiny quarters near the docks at all hours. The ships will soon be unburdened of their human cargo and filled with gold and silver from the mines, but in the meantime, I find it difficult to sleep without covering my face with a cloth soaked in cloves each night. How I miss the smell of oleander from our garden, and your scent, my sweet.

She had never imagined Francisco capable of such words, but the handful of letters he had sent from Veracruz always surprised her with their images. He painted a picture of great hardship, not so much for himself as for the workers whose products were enriching their family. She found his sympathies unexpected. Her father had never voiced concern over the *Indios* when he talked of his adventures and had never mentioned their trade in slaves at all. Perhaps it was a new phenomenon. Francisco spoke as if there were thousands arriving from Africa, and, from his description, they seemed nothing like the *slaves* of Sevilla, who were Catholics and worked mostly in homes like her own.

"They march down the gangplanks shackled at the throat and feet, their naked bodies dripping sweat and sometimes blood," he wrote. "Yesterday, I saw a woman who reminded me of Esperanza. She held an infant, who appeared dead, at her breast." She wished he would not share such stories, but she did not say so in her own letters, which she filled mostly with details of the children and her desire that he would return home soon. Well, her wishes would be granted before long.

She folded the letter and slipped it in the drawer by her bedside. She would write a response, perhaps the last letter he would receive before the fleet headed back to Sevilla. In the meantime, she could not put aside the brief encounter with José Marcos. Why had he called her "my love?" And why did he wish to speak to her? What was this "agony" and "dread" he described? It was all so unsettling. Was it some trick, or had he simply become bored with his wealthy wife? She was pleased she had been able to escape quickly, but even more that she had felt so little emotion as he poured out his own. She had picked at the scab of her hurt so many times that she had grown numb to the pain. He would not seduce her so easily this time.

She felt suddenly tired though the evening was young. Tomorrow she would go to the Castillo, the monthly trip she continued to make to fulfill her promise to the Dominican. The old woman had been moved from the cells to a small room near the servants' quarters. During the day, she scrubbed the floors of the monks' quarters and took her meals alone in her small room. Guiomar made her hour-long visits during the afternoon meal. They prayed the rosary together and talked about faith and, on occasion, Inés would describe some of the Jewish customs she had abandoned, which Guiomar would later look up in the small book her brother had given her. She had even begun to look forward to the meetings, but they were often spoiled when Dominguez intercepted her for a talk in his study afterwards. Tomorrow, she would try to draw out Inés about the life the woman had led with her daughter in their home in Santa Cruz. But she would have to do so carefully, partly to avoid suspicion if the woman revealed her conversations to Dominguez, but also to keep from reminding her of her lost child.

José Marcos retreated to his room on the second floor of the home he shared with María Luísa. The room was spacious, and the bed, made of heavy dark timber from the Orient, was large enough to accommodate himself, his wife, and a chambermaid or two. He sometimes imagined such a scene, though in truth, María Luísa never came to his bed but instead summoned him to hers when the mood suited her, which was more often than he cared. His wife was an aggressive lover, something he had not anticipated. He preferred to be the pursuer, but she flaunted her status in the marriage bed as well as outside it, to the point that he sometimes refused to perform. If she would emasculate him, he would show her the consequences, choosing to spill his seed without entering her. "It is a mortal sin," she said the first time it happened. But so long as he gave her the pleasure she wanted, she mostly kept quiet.

He had never imagined he would speak to Guiomar in the way he had at the baptismal party. He had thought about their meeting many times. In his fantasies, he was the one who avoided her, and she the one eager to attract his attention. It would be his revenge. True, he had rebuffed her when she proposed they run away together, but over time, he had convinced himself that she was the one at fault. She had asked the impossible of him, and then treated him as a coward when he refused. But as he stood beside her in the church, his old longing returned. And her mention of the Castillo troubled him. María Luísa's imperious tone had only set him more on edge. His wife could assert her power over him, but she could not control his heart.

He searched his desk for paper. The last letter he had written Guiomar had been short and hurtful. Now he must try to make her understand. He dipped the quill in ink and held it poised over the paper. A drop fell from the tip and spoiled the clean sheet, spreading across the page like an evil omen. He crumpled it and reached for a fresh one.

"My dearest, I fear you are in great danger. I don't know what I can do to help, but I am ready to try. Do not ignore my plea out of anger. I know I hurt you, but it was for your protection." He paused, considering whether he should try to make his case, adding instead, "and mine." He blew on the ink to dry it faster. "None of us are entirely free to make our own decisions." He read the words carefully. Should he add more? "Please send word when and where I may meet you. I have only your safety at heart."

He waited for the ink to dry fully, then folded the letter without signing it. He warmed the ball of green wax over a match until a drop landed on the edge of the folded paper and let it seal the letter. He must be careful in choosing a courier. It was not easy for a married man to write to the wife of another without raising suspicions, but a few copper coins could buy silence. He would attend to it in the morning.

For now, he closed his eyes and visualized Guiomar's face. Was she as attractive as he imagined or did love color his vision? María Luísa was more striking, taller, with auburn hair and large, wide-set eyes, the kind of woman men turned to look at when she entered a room. But María Luísa was too vain and self-conscious, while Guiomar seemed unsure of her own charm, which made her even more appealing. He would always have the upper hand in a relationship with Guiomar, which was as it should be. María Luísa's dominance was unnatural, and if he strayed, she was the one to blame. No man wished to think himself a woman's trophy.

The knock on the door startled him. "Who's there?" He put the letter in the drawer, hidden under a sheaf of plain paper, but the smell of wax still lingered.

"I thought I would pay you a visit," María Luísa said, standing near the open door without fully committing to enter.

José Marcos moved toward her. "What a pleasant surprise," he said, hoping to divert her attention from the desk. "I was just about to take a stroll in the garden. Would you care to join me?"

"It was not what I had intended, but why not? The evening is warm, and the moon is nearly full," she said, turning on her heels as her husband took her arm. "I couldn't help but notice your little talk with the Péres de Armijo woman at María Dolores's this afternoon," she said as they walked down the stairs to the main hallway. "You know there are rumors about her?" she said, turning to José Marcos. "One must be careful," she said.

"What kind of rumors, my dear?" He looked at his wife's face with complete innocence.

"That she is a Judaizer." She turned away. "It could, of course, be idle gossip," she added.

José Marcos walked several steps beside his wife silently.

"My family has known hers for many years, and I've never heard such a rumor," he finally said. "I hadn't thought there were many Judaizers left in Sevilla. But perhaps women are better informed on such gossip."

María Luísa smiled. "You are right, of course. We women know more than we are given credit for. Besides, her comment about the Castillo got me wondering. And the fact that she has never invited us into her home," she added, suddenly stopping to face her husband. "Considering that your families were so close at one time, doesn't that raise questions?"

José Marcos studied his wife's face carefully. How much did she know of his relationship with Guiomar? She had never mentioned it, but perhaps someone had told her that Guiomar had rejected him to marry Francisco Armijo, which was of course untrue.

THE SILVER CANDLESTICKS

"There is another explanation, my dear," he said, squeezing María Luísa's arm. "She is jealous of you."

"Why on earth?" María Luísa's voiced sounded genuinely surprised, but her eyes narrowed with suspicion.

"She was once in love with me. When I rejected her, she married Armijo," José Marcos said in as offhand a way as he could.

María Luísa let out a brittle laugh. "You are quite the catch, my husband, to have so many women in your thrall. But all the more reason you should avoid her," she said, bending to smell a rosebush in bloom.

Chapter Fifteen

THE TRAP

Guiomar closed the iron gate outside her home and headed toward the bridge and the Castillo. The streets were deserted while most residents in the neighborhood ate their midday meal and took a siesta. The bells of Santa Ana rang out Sext. She was late for her visit with Inés because she had stopped to pick fresh vegetables in her garden and a few oranges from the courtyard.

The basket she carried was heavy on her arm as the noon sun beat down. She wore her black taffeta dress and a lace mantilla, which hid much of her face. She would be drenched in sweat by the time she arrived. She pulled a small lace fan from her sleeve and flicked it open, fanning herself with her free hand. She did not have far to go along the winding streets, though the short distance belied the enormous gap between the two worlds she now occupied.

The trill of canaries stopped her in her path in front of one of the last grand houses on her route. She peeked through the iron gates to see if she could get a look at the birds, but the oleander bushes blocked her vision. She would have to be satisfied with their song alone. Perhaps she should buy a pair of the songbirds and hang them on the veranda outside her room to keep her company, she thought before continuing on her way.

She had been going to the Castillo on the first Thursday of every month since Francisco had departed. It was not something she looked forward to, even though her visits with the old woman had taught her many things she might not otherwise have learned about Jewish customs. She was careful not to push Inés too hard. Guiomar feared that Padre Dominguez might have set up the visits not as an act of kindness to the old woman, or even to salve his own conscience, but to ensnare her. Her suspicions deepened when the Dominican accosted her after the visits, inviting her into his office for conversations that inevitably left her shaken.

The stench of sewage pouring out of the Castillo into the Guadalquivir nearly gagged her as she drew closer. She was relieved that her family lived far enough away from the river not to suffer as those close by did, especially in the warm months. She pulled the mantilla over her face hoping the dry rose leaves she stored with the lace had imparted enough scent to cover the stink. Once inside the walls of the Castillo, the smell, she hoped, would not be as bad.

The guard nodded as she approached the low entrance near the bridge. She was a familiar face now, and he opened the locks on the heavy door and motioned her inside quickly. She crossed the empty courtyard and made her way to the far corner where the servants lived. She rapped on the door lightly.

"*Entrada*," Inés called out in a weak voice. She had already begun to eat the thin broth that was her afternoon meal since it was half past the noon hour.

Guiomar entered the darkened room, whose only light was from a barred window high above. The room was so cramped there was barely room for a table, two chairs, and a modest cot, with a few nails on the wall that Inés's other garments hung from.

"I am sorry I'm late, but I wanted to bring you these," Guiomar said, putting her basket on the table and pulling some oranges, carrots, and a few spring onions out. "They are from my garden. You have become so frail, my dear. I worry about you. Next time, I will bring some cheese and bread."

"There's no need. I eat well enough. Brother Tomás sneaks me a fresh loaf of bread once a week, and cheese is too rich for my stomach," she said, then took a sip of her broth.

Guiomar reached out her hand. "Inés, you are wasting away. This life isn't good for you. Why don't you leave the Castillo, as Padre Dominguez has suggested many times? Others here are not free to go as you are. Why do you remain?"

"How can I leave, Señora? I have no place to go, even if my conscience did not tie me to this dreadful place."

Guiomar hesitated. Inés rarely referenced her deceased daughter, whose dead body was not buried here but burned at the stake after her suicide in one of Sevilla's last autos-da-fé. "Have you no one? No friend or relative?"

"No one. The Holy Office confiscated my humble home, and what few relatives I had all fled before they ended up here as well."

"Perhaps you could live in my home," Guiomar offered, the words escaping her mouth before she had time to consider the complications.

Inés looked up at her. "I could never impose on you, Señora. You have been too kind already."

Guiomar patted the women's gnarled hand, the knuckles red and swollen. "You should not be on your knees all day scrubbing floors. I will talk to Padre Dominguez."

"Be careful, Señora. He is the devil himself," Inés said. She reached for an onion, peeling it back and taking a bite.

Dominguez was surprised to find Guiomar Péres waiting outside his office when he returned from the chapel. He had looked forward to a few precious moments to himself and had forgotten this was the day of her usual visit.

"You wish to see me?" he said as he approached the supercilious woman.

"Yes, Padre, I brought you a few oranges from my garden. They are said to be as sweet as those that grow in the Alcázar. I hope you don't mind the intrusion."

"Of course not, my child," he said, opening the door and motioning her into his office. "I take it you have come from your visit with Señora Mejia? Please tell me of your conversation." It

THE SILVER CANDLESTICKS

was odd that the woman had sought him out. He had always been the one to initiate their conversations. She must have something important to discuss, he mused as he took his seat behind his large desk.

"I am worried about Señora Mejia, Padre," Guiomar began, hesitating.

"Worried? Do you think she is relapsing into her old ways?"

"No, no," she said emphatically. "Nothing of the sort. She is very devout in her faith."

"Do you pray the rosary, as I instructed?"

Guiomar frowned. She was so surprised at the direction their conversation had taken that she had forgotten to pray with Inés. She dared not lie to the priest. What if he questioned Inés, and she admitted they had not prayed?

"I was remiss today, Padre. I came late for our appointment and then was anxious to speak with you." She clasped her hands together tightly. The priest said nothing, but the look on his face frightened her. "Señora Mejia has become very thin, and she moves with much discomfort. I was thinking we must find a way to convince her to leave this life of self-imposed punishment."

"And is not prayer the best antidote for suffering?" he asked.

"Of course, Padre. And she prays—as do I—for forgiveness. But you yourself have urged her to leave these walls."

"And where would she go? I understand she has no one left."

Guiomar clenched her fingers tighter. "I have room in my house." She looked up to see a smug smile curling the priest's lips.

"That is very generous of you, Señora. There are not many among Sevilla's great families who would welcome a Judaizer into their home. Even one as repentant as Señora Mejia," Padre Dominguez said, lifting his eyebrows. "Especially since she will have to wear the yellow *sambenito* for the rest of her life."

Guiomar swallowed the gasp that nearly escaped her. "The *sambenito*? I had thought her years behind these walls had been penance enough," she said, looking directly into the priest's cold eyes. "Not to mention her daughter's death."

Dominguez reached for an orange. "Well, I can understand your reluctance if you don't want Señora Mejia to sit at your dinner table in her robe of shame," he said. "Perhaps you can place her among the servants."

Guiomar felt the color rising in her cheeks. He was making a hypocrite of her. But she deserved it. What had she been thinking when she made the offer to Inés? She was endangering not only herself but her family. Francisco would be furious, as would her father. "Yes, perhaps. Let me think on this some more, Padre. I clearly need to consider the ramifications." She emptied the rest of the oranges onto the table. "I almost forgot," she said, pulling a small leather pouch from her pocket. "I noticed the repairs on the outer walls of the Castillo have not been completed since the flood. I worry that water will seep into the cells. Perhaps this gift can speed up the work."

He reached out his hand and accepted the pouch, lifting it to judge its weight. "We have many needs, Señora. I assume I am free to determine the most pressing and use your generous gift accordingly?"

"Of course, Padre. And, as you remember, I am sure, my husband has promised a major gift when he returns from Veracruz, which I am happy to inform you will be soon. I received a letter from him just yesterday saying he will be here by Christmas."

"I am pleased to hear your husband is returning. As for the gift, the Lord, not I, will be pleased to receive it."

"I must get home now. May I ask for a blessing before I leave?" Guiomar picked up the basket and waited.

Padre Dominguez stepped from behind the desk and approached the woman, making a small sign of the cross on her forehead. "The Lord be with you," he whispered.

"And with your spirit," Guiomar replied, making the sign of the cross and turning to leave.

Esperanza took the letter from the urchin, who ran away like a thief as soon as he handed it to her. She put it in her pocket, hoping it was not from José Marcos. The Señora would be home soon, but she was often in a bad mood after her visits to the Castillo. And who wouldn't be? Esperanza feared the Dominican and wished she could keep her mistress away from him. No doubt this unidentified letter would further disturb her. She would wait until she could speak to the Señora alone.

It had been a long time since they had spoken intimately—only once, the night she gave her mistress the previous letter from her lover. Esperanza knew her mistress trusted her. After all, the Señora had put her in charge of carrying out Doña Benita's instructions for the slaughter and inspection of animals. And Guiomar was always kind to her now. But she kept her feelings to herself. She seemed a very lonely woman, even more so now that her husband was gone. Esperanza knew what that kind of loneliness was like. She had never had anyone in whom she could confide from the moment she was ripped from her mother's arms in her village one night.

Esperanza didn't often dwell on her past. What was the point of wallowing in sadness when there was nothing she could do to change her fate? But she sometimes wondered why the Péres family put themselves in danger to maintain these strange forbidden customs. Esperanza could not see the harm in such practices—a woman bathing after she bled each month, ensuring the meat that found its way to the family table was healthy. How did these customs threaten the Church? She knew there must be more to it than she understood. But she hesitated to ask, and she doubted her mistress could give her any insight since she seemed to know so little herself.

But the Dominican frightened her. He reminded Esperanza of the priest in her childhood village, decked out in masks of wild animals, his black skin shining with sweat as he danced before a huge open fire pit. The priest was an old man who could cast spells that crippled, even killed, his enemies. Esperanza thought perhaps he was responsible for her own father's death, and she knew the man coveted her mother. The night the slave traders came to her village, the priest pointed Esperanza out, and the men grabbed her from her mother's embrace, while two village men with spears kept her from following. It was the last memory she had of her mother, screaming out in a language Esperanza no longer remembered while the priest stood watching in front of the fire.

She was thankful that the Catholic religion that Don Pedro had her baptized in after she arrived in Sevilla had gentler gods than those that ruled her former village. The Blessed Mother protected all who prayed to her. The saints each had their special powers, which she invoked as needed. And, most importantly, Jesus forgave her sins. It was altogether a kinder religion than the one of her childhood, though the crucifix that hung near the altar at Santa Ana's scared her almost as much as the village priest's masks. She learned to focus her eyes instead on the altarpiece with Santa Ana and the Virgin Mary adorned in gold, which was more beautiful than anything she had ever seen.

Guiomar removed her heavy outer garments as soon as she returned home. She pulled back the curtains and opened the large window that led onto the veranda to let in the slight breeze. Yes, she would buy a pair of canaries to keep her company and would hang them outside each day, she decided. There was no one about to see her standing there in her camisa. Her father was still resting, and Esperanza was no doubt occupied in the *cocina*.

She sat at the desk and was about to write Francisco when she reconsidered. What could she possibly tell him about her troubling visit to the Castillo? It was too dangerous to say anything, and he would be angry at her for even suggesting bringing Inés into their home. What was she thinking? The Dominican was already suspicious that her family were secret Jews, and now she had offered to take a confessed Judaizer into their home. She had fallen into a trap of her own making.

She needed to discuss this with someone. But who? Her father was too frail to worry with such bad news. He was often forgetful now, and she feared he might let something slip in conversation.

THE SILVER CANDLESTICKS

She wondered if she could approach Don Enrique, her *padrino*. She would only tell him that she made the offer out of charity, but he would doubtless tell her simply to rescind it. How could she explain that doing so might raise suspicions? Guiomar imagined that Don Enrique had his own doubts about her family's background, and who knew, he might be a Jew himself. Her father had said that many of Sevilla's best families were conversos.

She pulled a sheet of paper from the drawer and dipped the quill in the inkwell. She held it poised above the page, considering what she should say, perhaps only that she wanted to discuss something with him at his home. She began to write when she heard a light tapping on the door. "Who is it?" she called out, reaching for a shawl to cover herself in case it was her father.

"It is me, Esperanza, Señora."

"Come in," Guiomar answered, relaxing. She was not up to a visit from her father, but maybe she could talk to Esperanza. The woman had been helpful at another painful moment in her life.

Esperanza stood near the door with the letter in her hand. "This came for you while you were out," she said, walking over to the desk.

Guiomar took the folded sheet from Esperanza. There were no markings on the paper and no impression on the seal, just like the letter José Marcos had written years earlier. She slipped her finger along the folded edge and broke the seal. She read it quickly and let it drop on the desk. The contents were not unexpected after the previous day's encounter. But she would deal with it later.

Esperanza turned to go, but Guiomar stopped her. "Sit with me awhile, please," she said, motioning for Esperanza to sit on the bed. "I need someone to talk to. Someone I can speak to in full confidence," she said, taking the servant's hand in hers. "You have been very faithful, Esperanza. And you are wise. I have few friends, and with Francisco gone and my father so infirm, I have no one to rely on." Esperanza stared back, wide-eyed, as if frightened by what Guiomar might say next. She squeezed the woman's hand tighter.

"Every time you go to the Castillo, I am terrified that you will not return, Señora," Esperanza said, dropping her eyes to hide the tears that were welling in them.

"My dear, I had no idea," Guiomar said, moving to sit beside her on the bed. She put her arm around the woman, who was taller and broad-shouldered, but now shook like a child.

"He is a devil, the Dominican," she said with great anger.

It was the second time that day Guiomar had heard the priest referred to as a demon. "Padre Dominguez is no devil, Esperanza. It might be easier to fight him if he were. He is doing the job that the Church has assigned him, perhaps more zealously than others. But even he must follow the rules of the Holy Office. I cannot disappear without evidence being brought against me. And who has such evidence?" she said, turning Esperanza's face to hers with her free hand.

"I would never…" Esperanza started to speak.

"I trust you, Esperanza, or I wouldn't be speaking with you as I am," Guiomar said. And it was true. She felt a certain kinship with this woman, despite the difference in their stations. Her childhood jealousy had turned to genuine affection because of the circumstances that threw them together. "I did something foolish today, and I am not sure how to get out of it," she said, dropping her hands to her lap. Esperanza frowned, but Guiomar continued. "The woman Inés Mejia is dying. I'm sure of it. She has withered away to nothing, and they treat her like a slave."

Esperanza flinched.

"I'm sorry, I didn't mean…" Guiomar's voice fell.

"I understand, Señora. I take no offense," she said.

"I offered for her to come live with us," Guiomar said, recovering. "It was a mistake. I wasn't thinking. But as soon as I broached it with Padre Dominguez, he made it clear I was putting myself in great jeopardy. Indeed, everyone in this family."

"Can't you just tell him you've reconsidered?"

"But I must have some excuse, don't you see? Bringing a Judaizer into the house would subject the family to suspicion. She would have to wear the ugly *sambenito*, and we would be ostracized by others, not that we have such an active social life with Francisco away. But suddenly changing my mind will make me look guilty as well. I've laid the perfect trap, with me and my family the victims."

Esperanza reached for her mistress's hands. "Don't blame yourself, Señora. You did it out of kindness. You only wanted to help the poor woman who has suffered so greatly. Everyone knows her story."

"But what can I do now?" Guiomar pleaded, squeezing Esperanza's hands.

"You have some weeks before you must visit her again. You will figure it out." Esperanza stood up. "I will think about it some more. But the best thing to do now is nothing."

"I've never been patient, but I think you are right. For the time being, we can simply wait to decide. I feel bad for Inés. Perhaps we can at least send her a basket of food each week. I'm sure the guard can be persuaded to deliver it if there are some coins attached for him."

Esperanza started to leave, then turned to her mistress. "The letter, Señora…I hope nothing is wrong."

Guiomar looked up at Esperanza, who stood by the door. "It is the least of my worries at the moment," she said. Esperanza nodded and left the room, but the statement wasn't quite true. She had many worries, and José Marcos's reappearance in her life was one of them. She leaned down and picked up the letter again. "Please send word where and when I might meet you." She would do nothing of the kind. How dare he ask her to risk her reputation by agreeing to meet him? She crumpled the letter into a ball and walked to the basin, filling it with water from the large pitcher. She let the letter float until it sank, tinting the water a faint blue, like the Guadalquivir as it passes through the mountains near Jaén where she'd once visited as a child.

She held up the small mirror on the bureau and examined her face. Was it still beautiful? Francisco assured her it was, but it was José Marcos's opinion that still mattered. She put down the mirror abruptly and heard the glass crack. It was a bad omen. The letter lay at the bottom of the bowl, its message erased. But she had yet to erase her feelings, although whether anger, jealousy, or some remnant of love, she wasn't sure.

Chapter Sixteen

LA GIRALDA

Guiomar and Esperanza headed toward the bridge that would take them to the walled city. It was the same path Guiomar had walked the previous day to the gate of the Castillo, where they would stop for a few minutes to drop off the basket containing meat, vegetables, and fruit that Esperanza had prepared for the old woman.

Guiomar had considered adding a bit of pork in case the Dominican got word of the gift. But she decided against doing so at the last minute. She had no pork in the larder and didn't want to purchase it just for this purpose. She also didn't want to offend Inés, who might think it a test of some sort. Instead, she'd put in a half chicken along with more carrots and some olives and oranges.

She was glad for Esperanza's company, partly because the servant was carrying the heavy basket but also because it gave her more freedom to walk as far from her home as she liked. The rowdy men who now frequented Sevilla would be less likely to accost two women, especially a mistress and her slave. It had been many months since Guiomar had been to the town, and she looked forward to browsing in the shop windows as she made her way to the one that sold birds of all sorts in the Barrio Santa Cruz.

The trills of canaries floated through the iron gate as they passed the large house near the Castillo. Guiomar stopped. "Aren't they beautiful?" She'd figured there were at least two the day before, but now pushing the oleander branches aside to peer through the iron gate, she saw many more in cages. The two whose songs she'd heard were bright yellow, sitting in separate cages at opposite ends of the verandah. In between were others whose colors were duller. "I wonder how we will know which ones sing," she said. "Only two of these birds are making all the music. The others are silent."

Esperanza looked through the gates. "I think the singers are the males. The females make them compete for attention."

"Much like we do," Guiomar laughed. It was true. Men competed for the love of women, as José Marcos was now doing. He had given up before, when he found they couldn't marry, but something had emboldened him to try again. Perhaps it was merely lust.

At the gate of the Castillo, the guard seemed surprised to see Guiomar. He started to unlock the gate, but she stopped him. "I'm not visiting Señora Mejia today," she said, pulling a few copper coins from her purse. "Can you see to it that she gets this?" she asked, pressing the coins into his hands and handing him the basket. The man nodded. "I will send my servant here each week to retrieve one basket and replace it with another between my regular visits," she said. "And you will be rewarded for your kindness. And discretion," she added.

"I am happy to oblige, Señora," the man answered, winking at her as he looked up from the coins in his palm. She stifled her repulsion at the fellow's impertinence. There was no need to make an enemy of him.

They walked across the narrow bridge to Sevilla, wending their way toward the cathedral and the old walls of the Barrio Santa Cruz with its warren-like streets. Guiomar stopped abruptly as they turned the corner into the alley where the canaries were sold. She thought she saw José Marcos ducking into a door at the end of the short street. Esperanza reached out and tugged her sleeve. She had seen him too.

"Let's find the bird seller quickly," Guiomar said as they moved forward. The entrance was a few doors down from the one they'd seen José Marcos entering. They opened the door and were greeted

THE SILVER CANDLESTICKS

by squawks and tweets from the cages, the racket so loud that Guiomar wanted to cover her ears. An old man sat near the rear of the store, his eyes clouded, his clothes disheveled.

"May I help you?" he said, as Guiomar approached while Esperanza walked between the cages, many hanging from the ceiling and others on wrought iron stands.

"I'm looking for canaries," Guiomar said loudly so she could be heard above the din.

"You have come to the right place, Señora," he said, standing slowly with the aid of a crooked cane. "I have several breeding pairs, fresh from the Islands. The males are strong singers, and the females will lay eggs to produce chicks. Right this way," he said, leading her into a back room separated by a curtain of colorful beads.

The room was small and dark, with only a few cages hanging from chains in the crowded space. Each cage held several birds, but none were trilling like those in the gardens near the Castillo. They scratched the floor of their cages and pecked at each other. Guiomar examined them, not knowing what she should look for. "How do I know which will sing? These are quiet."

The man smiled, revealing that his two front teeth were missing, which explained the birdlike whistle in his speech. "The males won't sing if they are kept in the same cage. They must be separate from their intended mates and each other."

Guiomar studied the brighter colored birds, which she thought must be the males. One was bigger than the rest, his chest puffed up as if he could make a lot of music. He hopped around his cage, jumping from one perch to the other almost frantically.

"How about this one?" she asked, pointing to the big male.

"He's a beauty," the old man said. "You have a good eye, Señora."

Guiomar did not want to seem too eager. She wanted to strike a good bargain, though she had no idea what such a bird should cost. She should have consulted her father, who knew all there was to know about the value of things, but she didn't want to disturb his siesta.

"How much?" she asked.

"Five hundred maravedis," he answered. "And I will throw in a female for one hundred more."

She pondered the offer. It seemed like a fair bargain. The birds came from a great distance and were highly prized in Sevilla.

"How much extra for the cage?"

The man seemed taken aback that she didn't bargain. "I'll give you the cage, gratis."

He smiled broadly again, and Guiomar felt foolish that she'd probably agreed too quickly.

She thanked him and went back toward the front room to look for Esperanza and was startled when she pulled back the beads to see her talking to José Marcos. She turned, hoping they did not see her, and retreated behind the beads. What on earth had brought him into the store? Had he seen them earlier? If so, why had he not acknowledged them at the time?

The old man was putting the big canary into a small cage and a female into another.

"Ah, Señora. You will need two cages. I hope you do not think me dishonest, but I must charge you a small sum for the second cage." He looked at her, grinning stupidly as she nodded. "A mere twenty-five maravedis, is that fair?"

Guiomar was in no mood to argue, but she didn't like being taken advantage of. "I think ten would be fairer," she said. "And what if the bird doesn't sing? What recourse will I have?"

The man's smile disappeared. "I am a man of honor, Señora. If the bird doesn't sing, I will replace him. But let us not quibble over a few maravedis. I will take ten."

Guiomar hoped to stall the transaction to give Esperanza time to send José Marcos away, assuming she had not told him she was with her.

José Marcos questioned the slave to little avail. How lucky that he should happen upon the woman who could be a go-between with Guiomar! Though the servant remained non-committal, he

THE SILVER CANDLESTICKS

hoped she would convey his message that it was imperative he see Guiomar at once. But now he wanted the woman to leave so that he could conduct his business with Jorge, the store owner. He started back toward the curtain when the servant reached out to stop him.

"Señor, it would be better if you did not go back there," she said.

"Is she here?" he raised his voice in anger and excitement.

"Why don't you go the cathedral and wait? I will try to persuade her to come. It is best you do not surprise her," Esperanza said forcefully.

José Marcos considered his options. He had urgent business, a loan earning interest every day that he hoped to pay down, but he might not have another opportunity to talk to Guiomar. Could he trust this slave? He had already trusted her with information more valuable than the money in his pocket.

"I will, but I need to give payment to Jorge before he closes his shop for the day. Will you give him this?" he asked, pulling a small pouch from his pocket. "And do so discreetly? Tell him I will bring him the rest in a week. But do not let your mistress hear."

Esperanza took the pouch. "I will if you leave right now. Wait for her by the stairway to the tower at the cathedral. I cannot guarantee that she will come, but I will give her your message."

José Marcos took her hand and brought it to his lips. "I am forever indebted to you. May I know your name?"

"Esperanza."

"How fitting. You are indeed my hope," he said, staring into the servant's ebony eyes.

"What did you give the shopkeeper?" Guiomar asked when they stood outside, each holding a cage with a canary. "I saw you exchange something, and some words." Guiomar knew it must have something to do with José Marcos.

"It was from Señor Herrera. He came into the store. He recognized me, and I stopped him from confronting you there. He had business with the owner."

"What business?" Guiomar demanded.

"Forgive me, Señora. He asked me to convey his wishes to speak with you privately. I put him off by telling him to go to the cathedral and wait."

"Were you so sure I would go?" Guiomar's voice rose.

"No, Señora," Esperanza hesitated. Should she say that she hoped her mistress would not?

"He seems very desperate. Did he give you any sense of what he wants?" Guiomar thought about the letter and his words in the garden. Perhaps she shouldn't ignore him. He might have some information that could be helpful. His wife was well-connected. Perhaps he wanted only to warn her of something. She felt an uneasy nausea in the pit of her stomach.

"No, Señora, but his passion worries me," she said carefully. "I have no doubt the man still loves you, but his love may endanger you further."

Guiomar's arm hurt from the weight of the cage. The yellow bird was hopping about on the floor, making it harder to hold, so she put the cage down on the cobblestones. She was torn about what she should do. She didn't like the thought of José Marcos waiting around until it became obvious that she wasn't coming—he would sulk and perhaps turn vengeful. She could send Esperanza to convey her regrets, but that might anger him too.

She looked toward the cathedral with its looming tower, La Giralda, which had been a Muslim minaret until the Reconquista. The new belfry at the top looked out over the entire city. She had never been to the top, but the bells could be heard all over Sevilla; on some days, when the wind was just right, she could hear them faintly from the other side of the river. She thought about José Marcos's eyes, staring deeply into hers on the patio outside his sister's house. After a minute, she realized that Esperanza was waiting patiently, still holding the cage with the female while she waited for Guiomar to make up her mind. Guiomar lifted the male's cage again and handed it to Esperanza.

"Take the birds home, and I will be along shortly." She didn't wait for Esperanza to protest—not that she would think of such a thing—and turned toward the belltower, walking so quickly she could hear her own breathing.

José Marcos leaned against the arched door that led to the sloping stone walkway to the top of La Giralda. Perhaps he could entice Guiomar to accompany him up the path to the belltower where he might embrace her. No, he should go slowly. Her honor would not allow her to accept him right away. He must woo her, make her believe that he was sincerely concerned about the Dominican's intentions, all the while making her at least a bit jealous of María Luísa.

He smiled. His life had become boring, punctuated only by the thrill of gambling when he could save enough of the small allowance María Luísa gave him. He'd had to borrow money from the shopkeeper to pay his debts, and the man was charging him outrageous interest that ended up doubling or tripling what he'd borrowed if he did not pay it back quickly enough. He had a mind to denounce him to the Dominican, but then he'd lose his primary source of funds.

Guiomar entered the cathedral from a side door. She stopped near the *Capilla Real* and knelt to light candles near the gates that enclosed the chapel. The entrance to La Giralda was behind her, but she did not want to head straight there in case someone was watching. She would make her way back slowly, devoutly, stopping to say a prayer at each statue. If José Marcos observed her, all the better.

The coin she dropped in the alms box at the base of the candles echoed as it hit the metal. There were few people in the cathedral at this time of day. Light from the stained-glass windows suffused the space with hues of blue and pink, while the scent of oranges from the *Patio de los Naranjos* wafted through the small open windows at their base. She felt at home here, even though by rights she should not. She wondered what the churches of the Jews had been like when they had thrived in Santa Cruz. Santa María La Blanca nearby was rumored to have been built around a Jewish synagogue, but it lacked the colorful windows of the cathedral. She felt guilty that this place still gave her such feelings of peace and serenity. Would she ever come to view these statues as idols, as her brother had instructed her? And what would she teach her children when they were old enough?

But she had not come here to ponder her faith—she needed to tell José Marcos that he must leave her alone. She walked briskly to the back of the cathedral toward La Giralda. José Marcos stepped out from the doorway and walked towards her, smiling. His velvet britches and waistcoat were new, she noticed, in a rich blue that complemented his coloring well.

"You've come. I was afraid you wouldn't," he said reaching for her hand. She pulled away from him, annoyed.

"I can't stay long. Esperanza said it was important, so I came," she whispered, afraid that her words would echo as loudly as the coins in the alms box. "This is very awkward. Let us kneel at one of the altars." She moved back toward the statue of Santa María, and he followed. As they knelt below the Virgin, she remembered their last visit in Santa Ana and regretted she'd succumbed to meeting again. "Well, what were you so eager to tell me?" she asked, bending her face against her folded hands as if in prayer.

"You are in grave danger, my dear," José Marcos said, lighting a candle. "My wife said there are rumors that the Dominican hopes to expose you as a Judaizer."

Guiomar turned toward him. "That is ridiculous. There is no basis for such calumny, as you well know," she said hoping he'd forgotten their conversation at Santa Ana's so long ago.

"Since when were these fanatics deterred by the truth?" he asked, though he suspected there was more to the accusation than Guiomar might admit. "The point is that he is after you. I don't know why. Have you insulted him in some way?"

"He has been a guest in my house many times. He's asked me to help him with a difficult case at the Castillo, as I told you. So where is your wife getting these tales? Maybe she has other reasons to spread rumors about me," she said, not hiding the accusation in her voice.

"If you're suggesting she's jealous," he said, smiling, "she has every reason."

"She has no reason, I assure you." She pulled another coin from her pocket, dropped it in the alms box and stood up. "I must go. It would be best if you did not approach me or my servant again." She could feel her face flushing as she spoke and hoped he would not notice as he rose.

"I cannot promise you that. If your safety is at stake, I am compelled to protect you. You think because I was forced to marry another woman that I have given up my love for you?"

"Don't say such things. They are improper. You pretend to be worried about my safety. Has it never occurred to you that you imperil it every bit as much as some false accusation? We are, both of us, married. Your love is a sin—and I want no part of it. Do you understand?" She was almost breathless.

She turned abruptly and headed for the door, hoping no eyes had seen this encounter. She quickened her pace as she heard his steps following. Was he mad? Would he follow her into the street? To her home? She didn't look back but continued down the winding streets, her thoughts in turmoil. It had been a grave mistake to come. She had made matters worse by speaking to him. She could only hope that his wife would not find out. If José Marcos was a danger, his wife was much more so. And why was the woman spreading gossip about her if not out of jealousy?

But perhaps there was some truth in the gossip. She had been fearful of Dominguez's intentions all along, and now it seemed others suspected the inquisitor's intentions as well. If only Francisco's return was closer at hand, he might save her, save them all from threat of both José Marcos and the Dominican.

José Marcos slipped back into the bird seller's store. He wished that he had not paid the Jew so much of what he owed—he needed money to loosen tongues about Guiomar. But he could start with the shopkeeper, who would surely know more about the secret Jews than anyone in his own circle. The man was dozing in a chair, his snores blending into the cacophony of squawking birds. José Marcos touched him on the shoulder.

"Jorge, my friend, wake up. I have some business for you."

The old man jumped. "You could scare a man to death, sneaking up like that," he said. "I got your payment, are you back for more already?"

"It is not money I need, but information," José Marcos said. "The two women who were here earlier, do you know them?"

"The Señora is the daughter of Pedro Péres. A beauty, no?"

"Yes, I know that much. But what of the family? Are they members of your tribe?" José Marcos said, irritated.

"I have no idea what you mean, Señor, unless, of course, you were referring to me as a reputable merchant. And, indeed, her father is a merchant, though on a much larger scale than I."

"Would you tell me, if you knew?" José Marcos muttered, "I am the woman's friend. But I would like to be a better friend, if you know what I mean."

Jorge coughed up some phlegm and spat into a handkerchief, wiping his lips. "These people are very secretive, Señor."

"The Péres family in particular?" José Marcos asked.

"They don't have much to do with those who live in the old Jewish quarter. I think the family has lived in Triana for generations, which isn't definitive, of course, since many ships' captains live there. But I could ask around, see what others know—discreetly, of course."

"And I would reward you for your help. One cannot be too careful with the goings on at the Castillo these days."

"If you don't mind my asking, why don't you just ask the woman herself? If you are such good friends, I mean."

"She would just deny it. Wouldn't you?"

The old man laughed. "I would not have thought religious scruples would deter a man like you when it came to matters of the flesh."

THE SILVER CANDLESTICKS

"One has to think of one's own skin, after all," José Marcos answered. Better to let the man think he would not get involved with a Jew.

"She's a pretty woman, Señor. But I suppose no woman is worth a turn on the rack."

Esperanza hung the two cages from the portico outside her mistress's chamber. She hoped the Señora would not be too long at La Giralda. She had a very bad feeling about Herrera's interest. He was spoiled and unfaithful, first to her mistress and now his own wife. Surely the Señora would not be so easily fooled. She was glad her master was returning soon. Things were unravelling at home. Don Pedro was not himself. The Señora had already made a grave error suggesting the woman from the Castillo live with them. And now this.

"Oh, you're here," Guiomar called from the room when she spied Esperanza outside the window. "Come in when you've finished, please."

Esperanza stepped through the large opening, wiping her hands on her skirts. "I am glad you are back, Señora. How did it go?"

"The man is impossible. I cannot fathom what he is thinking, making such a fool of himself." she said, plopping down on the bed in exasperation. "I told him never to approach me again. He has no sense whatsoever. And he claims to be interested in my safety."

"Did he give you any reason why?" Esperanza asked.

"Some gossip he heard from his wife."

Esperanza bit her lip. "I feared as much."

"I'm sure it is just idle speculation. People are always accusing those they envy of being secret Jews. If there were as many Jews in Sevilla as the gossips surmised, half of the wealth of the city would be in Jewish hands."

"May I ask you a question, Señora?" Esperanza had always wondered about the history of the Jews of Spain. It was shrouded in so much mystery and fear, yet she didn't fully understand. "Why did some Jews stay and others leave?" she asked.

"Most left. But those who fled could take nothing with them, so those with the most to lose sometimes converted—or were forced to—at least that is what I've been told. It has been a long time now, over a hundred years. Even those who stayed have become estranged from their faith. There are no places of worship, no rabbis—as the Jewish priests are known—no books to teach them what they must know."

Esperanza noted that her mistress did not say "we" when talking about the Jews. The secret was best left unspoken. It was as much a protection for her as for her mistress. If it ever came to that, Esperanza could truthfully say that her mistress was a faithful Catholic as far as she knew.

"I must answer Francisco's letter now, Esperanza. Will you let me know when dinner is ready?" she asked, dismissing her before she asked any more questions.

Guiomar sat at the small desk and pulled out her husband's letter along with a sheet of paper. She tried to remember his kind face, but the memory had grown dim. She would tell him about the canaries. He would be pleased that she had company, even if it was only two birds. She would describe her visit to Sevilla with Esperanza, the crowded, noisy shop and the old man with the missing teeth. But she would say nothing of the side trip to the cathedral or Francisco's rival, lurking in the shadows of La Giralda. She felt guilty, even though she had turned away José Marcos's advances. She could see his face before her, handsome but arrogant. Thank God her parents had intervened. If she had married him, she would be the one sitting at home, unsuspecting, while he went off to some secret assignation. Guiomar could only hope that his wife was as naive as she would have been in her place. The more her thoughts turned to José Marcos, the more she hesitated to take up the quill.

Chapter Seventeen

A DEATH

Inés uncovered the basket and peered inside. Señora Péres de Armijo was a woman of her word—it was filled with good things to eat. She pulled off a piece of chicken skin, crispy and still warm. She had not tasted such a feast since before she was taken prisoner. Even when Padre Dominguez sent special meals to her cell after Paloma's death, the fare was the same as the priest's: bland and very rarely any meat.

She took a large bite out of the chicken leg, savoring it as she chewed. She would be eating like this every day if the Señora fulfilled her promise. It was almost too much to hope for.

She covered the basket and hung it from one of the pegs. She would eat the chicken slowly, but not so slowly that the meat rotted. Surely it would be good for a day or two in the cool room sheltered from the heat of the courtyard. She only had to worry about rats, but they could not easily climb the slick wall to reach the food. She wondered how long it would be before the Señora sent for her. She looked back at the basket before leaving her small room. Now she had something to look forward to after she finished her work, some chicken and maybe a few olives and an orange. She would sleep well after such a meal.

She had mopped the floors leading to the stairway to the prisoners' quarters before noon, but she always dreaded the task of scrubbing the hallway outside the cells, even though she was required to do so only once a month. It brought back too many memories. Many of the cells were empty now, most of the Judaizers were already dead or gone from Sevilla. There had been no burnings since her daughter's corpse was secretly dragged to the scaffold and set aflame. Most died from disease or wounds they incurred from the *tormentos*. No Sevillanos attended Paloma's auto-da-fé, which was held in the dead of night. Apparently, the sight of a child's burning corpse was too much for even the most hardened Jew haters.

Inés felt the bits of meat working their way back up her throat. She tried not to think about her daughter because it brought back the shame of her own accusations against the child. Her shoulders throbbed, as they always did when she recalled her time on the rack. They were after names of fellow Judaizers. Names, names, and more names, but she knew no one. Her husband and parents were dead. There was only herself and her daughter. "Paloma, Paloma," she'd called out her child's name in pain as they turned the giant wheel that separated her limbs from their sockets. And when they took her down off the horrible contraption, they asked her again. "What does she do, your daughter?" At first, she'd resisted saying more, but when they threatened to put her back on the rack, she whispered, "She helps me light the candles on the Sabbath." If only she could take back those words. If only she had let herself be torn apart.

She got down on her hands and knees at the far end of the dark hallway, where she could barely see. She heard a voice calling out, "Help me, I am dying." It was weak, but still she thought she recognized it.

She stood up, but she wasn't tall enough to look through the iron bars on the heavy door. "Is that you, Marta?"

"Yes, please help me. I cannot move my legs." Inés stood on her tiptoes, but still could not see into the cell. It had been the same the night of the deluge. Marta and the other women had lifted her up so that she could call out for Padre Dominguez. She had thought she would die that night. Perhaps it would have been better if she had. Marta sounded weak, like an old woman, not the healthy girl who'd shared a cell with her. She had been young, well-fed, and strong. But no one could last long in this place.

"I will get help, Marta. Hold on, dear child."

The men at the other end of the hallway began banging on the doors. "Help us, angel of mercy. We are dying too," one voice pleaded, while others let out whistles and yelled profanities. She nearly knocked over the bucket as she ran back down the hall.

She crossed the courtyard to the chapel. The Dominicans were praying the Hours and she hoped to find Brother Tomás there. She listened outside the chapel until she heard a break in the chanting, then opened the door and looked around. Brother Tomás knelt at the near end of the choir stall, his heavy belly pressing against the ledge of the pew in front of him on which his prayer book was balanced. She walked quietly toward him, hoping no one would notice. Most of the men had their eyes closed and heads bent against their folded hands. She hoped that Padre Dominguez did not see her.

"Brother Tomás, I need your help," she whispered, tugging at the friar's sleeve. "A woman is dying in the cells."

The friar looked up. He put his finger to his lips and slipped out of the choir stall, following quickly behind her as the monks stood again to begin chanting the prayers.

When Inés reached the cell, she called out loudly, "Marta, Marta." But the woman didn't answer. Brother Tomás looked befuddled. He had no way to open the cell, and the guard was nowhere to be seen. He peered in and saw a woman passed out on the floor, sitting in her own filth.

"I must fetch Padre Dominguez to open the cell," he said and walked off before Inés could respond. She wrung her hands. Why had she not inquired after Marta? Once she'd left the cell after the storm, she'd avoided even thinking about those she'd left behind. The young woman had been so kind to her. She should have done more. Why was she so weak, thinking only of herself? She had killed her own daughter with her weakness. Now this kind woman was dying because she had not interceded. She beat her fists against her head. She began to wail but stopped herself when she heard footsteps on the stone stairs.

"Why did you not come to me?" Padre Dominguez asked, shoving Inés Mejia aside.

"I did not wish…"

"This is no time for excuses, Señora," he said as he put the key into the lock and shoved it open. The stench was overwhelming. He picked up the hem of his robes and stepped toward her. He could detect no breathing, but he would have to get closer to make sure. As he reached out to touch her, the woman grabbed his hand.

"I must confess, Padre," Marta said, her voice barely a whisper.

"Yes, my daughter," he said, covering his face with the sleeve of his habit. He looked back at Tomás and the Mejia woman still standing in the door, their mouths agape. "Leave us. And you, Tomás, get me the ciborium, quickly."

Inés pulled back, leaning against the hallway a few doors down. She was afraid to leave the Dominican with Marta. Who knew what accusations he might force from her on her deathbed. She wished that she could comfort her, bring her fresh clothes, and remove her from the filth of the cell. How had they let this happen? Had they broken her legs? She was not even a Judaizer, Inés was sure of it. She had seen the woman pray to the Virgin devoutly every day, even when the other women taunted her for her piety. But the cells had always been filled with those who could not truly be called Judaizers.

Even she was barely guilty. Her sin had been a few rituals, which harmed no one. She had never blasphemed, never spit on a plaster saint, or touched her teeth to the host when she received communion. She was more faithful in her Catholic duties than in the ones passed down from her mother. Still, she had been unwilling to abandon those few practices she knew of her ancient faith.

But what if she had lit the candles and whispered the Ave Maria instead of the strange words that held no meaning to her? Would they have thrown her in jail? And her daughter too?

Paloma. The girl's innocent face appeared before her when she shut her eyes. Would Marta's face soon be added to her nightmares?

Brother Tomás could barely breathe by the time he reached the bottom of the stairs. He wheezed loudly as he passed Señora Mejia, motioning her off when she tried to stop him. "Here, Padre," he said, passing the ciborium to his superior, who stood next to the small window, trying to catch a breath of fresh air through the bars on the window above him.

Dominguez took the silver container with the consecrated Hosts and walked over to the dying woman. He bent low and touched her lips, which were cracked and almost blue. She opened her eyes, which showed no sign of recognition, but she parted her lips and stuck out her tongue, which was blackened. He pulled back instinctively but placed the Host on the tongue. "*In nomine Patris, et Filii, et Spiritus Sancti,*" he whispered, but he could see that the woman was dead. Her tongue stuck out obscenely, the Host on its tip about to fall to the filthy ground. He snatched it back and put it in his own mouth to avoid desecration. He was filled with rage. Better this sinner had died without absolution. Her failure to swallow the Host was proof enough that she had not repented. He turned to see Brother Tomás standing mute, tears falling down his fat cheeks.

"See to it that her body is burned," Dominguez shouted as he shoved past the friar.

"But, Padre," Brother Tomás protested, "she received the Last Rites."

"Do you dare question my authority?" Dominguez stared into the man's pig eyes. "Did you not see that the woman would not swallow the Body of Christ? She was a Judaizer who must suffer the auto-da-fé. I will see to it that her guilt not go unpunished."

Brother Tomás said nothing, but he vowed to report this irregularity to the Superior of the Order in Toledo. Dominguez went too far, first with the Mejia child and now this poor creature. He would make inquiries, even if it cost him his place in the kitchen. He had turned a blind eye for too long. Perhaps there were others in the Castillo who had doubts about his methods.

Inés pushed her back against the wall as the Dominican whisked past her, saying nothing. She walked to the cell only to find Brother Tomás closing the door. "Has she died?" she asked the clearly grieving friar. He nodded silently. She pushed open the door and saw Marta, her mouth still open and her tongue hanging out. She gasped.

"See to her, would you, Señora?" Brother Tomás asked from the doorway. "They will come for her body soon. Padre Dominguez has ordered her burned at the stake, but let us try to give her some measure of dignity in the meantime."

Inés couldn't believe her ears. How could this happen yet again? How many burned corpses would satisfy the God of the Christians? She wanted to curse the stupid monk standing in front of her, but what good would it do? He was not to blame. And the one who was could not be touched. She walked over to Marta's body and knelt, ignoring the smell and the excrement covering the ground. She reached out her hands and closed the woman's mouth, still warm as if she were alive. Poor Marta. A woman whose only sin was the belief that her Catholic faith would protect her.

Padre Dominguez returned to his casita without going back to the chapel. He must change out of his filthy clothing; the stench of the woman's waste clung to his robes. In the morning, he would call the tribunal together to sentence her. He must observe the proper procedures if she was to be burned at the stake. The image of her blackened tongue stuck in his mind. He would give his own witness to what had transpired. Brother Tomás would be less than useless, as would the Mejia woman.

He took off his outer cape and lifted the outer scapular over his head. He untied the cincture around his waist and laid it on the cot. Perhaps he would use it to scourge himself rather than his usual rope. His blood would purify the soiled hemp more than any washing. He bent and pulled the white gown forward, trying not to let the filthy hem touch his face as he removed the garment. The smell was enough to make him gag. It was disgraceful that the guard had not alerted him to the woman's condition. Through her thin camisa, he could see her legs set at an odd angle. No doubt they had fractured during the *tormentos*. *What information had she offered up?* he wondered. He would read the transcript before calling the tribunal. No reason to be caught off guard. If she had confessed her sins, all the better. If not, her refusal to swallow the Host was surely enough to condemn her. He rolled the garments into a ball and stuffed them in the laundry basket.

A slight breeze from the windows sent a chill down his spine. It felt pleasant after his exertions. He knelt next to the cot and bowed his head. "Deliver me, oh Lord, from these swine," he prayed. "Help me to purge them from the streets of Sevilla and send them to the gates of hell." He stopped himself. No, this was not why he had been sent here. Yes, he was to rid the city of sinners, but only to keep the faithful safe. His duty was to help the sinners recover their faith. But was not it also his obligation to instruct the faithful in the consequences of heresy? How could he discourage others from Judaizing if he did not show that even death could not rescue the heretic from punishment? He reached for the rope and began to beat his back, lightly at first, then harder, biting his lip to keep from calling out. The pain would purify him. He could feel the drops of blood gather and then run down his back with each successive lash. He must pay for his sinfulness. He wrenched his shoulder as he brought the rope down harder, the pain so intense he finally let go. The bloody rope lay on the floor beside him like a snake. He picked it up and threw it toward the basket when he heard the knock at the door.

"Just a moment. I am changing," he called out, wondering who could be bothering him now. He grabbed the soiled garments in the basket and wiped his back. He looked in the wardrobe for a fresh robe and put it on quickly, but he had no other cape. It would have to do. He opened the door to find Inés Mejia standing before him.

"What are you doing here? How dare you come to my room," he said, spitting his words in her face. She looked up at him, not flinching.

"I must talk to you," she said, surprised at her own temerity. She had rushed to his casita immediately after washing Marta's body. She could no longer keep silent. It was enough that she had allowed this monster to burn her own daughter. She would not allow him to do the same to Marta, who was a true Catholic.

"This is indecent. I cannot let you into my rooms. What is so important that you cannot wait until the morning and see me in my office?" He was growing impatient with this tiresome woman. He'd allowed his guilt at her daughter's suicide to cloud his judgment—and he had no reason to feel guilt over a heretic's suicide.

"It cannot wait. You are committing a grave sin, Padre," she said. "Is it not my duty to prevent you from doing so if I can?" she asked, throwing words at him she knew would sting.

"Go to my office. I will be along in a few minutes. Wait inside. And don't talk to anyone." He shut the door in her face before she could reply. He could not very well go out as he was. He held up the scapular and cape. He would have to put them on despite the muck that stuck to them. But what would he do for a cincture? He had been careless to use the rope to scourge himself. He carried it to the basin and poured from the pitcher until the basin was filled with pink water. He wrapped the damp cincture around his waist and cursed the woman under his breath.

Brother Tomás knelt in the chapel alone. He needed strength to take on Padre Dominguez, and he knew his own weaknesses all too well. He loved his sweets too much. He had trouble rising in the middle of the night to pray Lauds. His mind wandered during

Mass. He missed his family, especially his mother's cooking. He had entered the monastery rather than take to the sea with his brothers. The very thought of waves made him nauseous. His family were poor, and the Church offered him a roof over his head and two meals a day, even if they were not large enough to satisfy his stomach.

He had been lucky to land in the kitchen. His talents at baking bread kept him busy and satisfied as he would always eat the burnt loaves rather than inflict them on his fellow Dominicans or the poor souls in the dungeon. Everyone knew his secret. It was difficult not to notice that his belly kept growing while the other priests and friars remained thin. But even Padre Dominguez looked the other way because his bread was so delicious. He often added anise seeds to the dough or, when it was available, a bit of honey or the cane sugar that came from the New World. His mouth started to water just thinking of it. It was always this way. Instead of keeping his mind on his prayers, it wandered to food until the grumbling of his big belly gave him away. When it happened during the singing of the Hours, his fellow monks would smirk or poke their elbows into his side. But now, he must concentrate and ask for guidance in what he was about to do. He fingered the rosary on his belt. Surely the Virgin Mary would guide him in the right way to proceed.

He finished his prayers and returned to his cell. He sat on the cot, realizing he had nothing to write with. His mother could not read, nor could his brothers, so he normally had no need of writing materials. He wondered if he should knock on one of the other monk's cell doors. It was late and the rule of silence was being observed. But if he was to write the letter, he must do it now. If he waited, he would lose his nerve. He went next door to the cell occupied by one of the oldest priests, a man who sat on the tribunals. He rapped on the door and waited. The old priest stuck his head out. He was already in his night clothes.

"I am sorry, Padre. I have an urgent matter. I must write a letter," he hesitated, "it cannot wait." The man stood, silent, his eyebrows raised. "I have no paper or quill. May I borrow them?"

The old priest opened the door and motioned Tomás to the tiny desk beside his cot. Pulling open the drawer, Tomás took out two sheets of paper, the quill, and a small ink bottle. "I will return these in the morning. Bless you, Padre."

Tomás's hand was not elegant. He had only learned to read and write when he entered the monastery at age twelve. How should he begin? To accuse his superior of over-zealousness might strike the prior in Toledo as a testament to the inquisitor's effectiveness. It would be far easier if the priest had taken a mistress or was enriching himself at the expense of the Castillo. He opened the bottle of ink and dipped the quill, still unsure what tack to take. It was useless to accuse Dominguez of persecuting the innocent. No, he would emphasize the public burning of the corpses. The practice was uncommon, though not unheard of. There had been such a burning in his own hometown, a man whose effigy was hanged and burned alongside his exhumed and rotting corpse. But that had been many years earlier in Murcia, and the man had been an enemy of the mayor.

He would begin with the burning of the child's corpse. The event was shrouded in secrecy. No one from the monastery, save perhaps Padre Dominguez, had witnessed it. Maybe the prior was unaware it had happened, though rumors traveled quickly. But a second burning would certainly raise concern, especially if Marta had not been formally found guilty of heresy and relaxed to the civil authorities for punishment.

Brother Tomás crossed himself. He had turned a blind eye for too long, content to bake his bread, whisper his prayers, and consider himself pious when he rose from a sound sleep to attend Lauds in the chapel, with little thought of what went on beneath the floors of the Castillo.

Padre Dominguez was anxious for Prime to be over. He read the Psalm from the choir: "For strangers have risen up against me; and the mighty have sought after my soul: and they have not set God before their eyes." He must read the transcripts and prepare his arguments. Who would rise up against him? Surely not the gluttonous friar whose only interest was in pilfering bread to indulge his appetites. Inés Mejia was another matter. But he would deal with her. "Turn back the evils upon my enemies; and cut them off in thy truth. I will freely sacrifice to thee, and will give praise, O God, to thy name: because it is good: For thou hast delivered me out of all trouble: and my eye hath looked down upon my enemies."

He peered up from the prayer book to survey his flock. They were mostly weak men whose sins he knew from the confessional. The scribes were mere ciphers who sat in the room and wrote down the words of the accused while the jailer applied the *tormentos*. As for the jailer, he was a drunkard, and Dominguez suspected the man took pleasure in others' pain, not to mention his being aroused when he stripped the women before applying the ropes. There was not much to fear from this bunch. Still, he would proceed cautiously.

The transcripts were sitting on his desk when he reached his office. They consisted of only a few pages. He read:

> The woman Marta Montelongo was brought to the interrogation room and was asked whether she wished to say anything on her behalf. She was ordered to be stripped and asked again whether she wished to make a confession. "I have nothing to confess, Señores. I am faithful to my baptismal vows. I honor the sacraments. I am a good Catholic," she said before the ropes were attached to her arms and legs and she was placed on the potro. The ropes were tightened and she was asked again to tell what she had done that had caused others to bring charges against her. "I have done nothing. For the love of Christ, loosen the ropes, I beg you," she called out. The cords were tightened again. The woman screamed in pain but refused to say what she was guilty of. She was asked to name

others who conspired with her. Three more twists of the ropes were applied until she begged to be let go. "I will say whatever you wish me to. But you must give me the words. I know not what you want from me." The inquisitor informed her that any testimony she gave must be of her own free will and asked that more turns of the rope be applied, at which time her lower leg bone cracked under the pressure and she fainted.

Dominguez sighed. He had hoped for more. The session lasted some thirty minutes, with a pause at the half-way point to observe the rule that no *tormento* could be applied for more than a quarter hour. Perhaps there had been an earlier session. He must ask his assistant. After all, the woman had been at the Castillo for many months, perhaps as long as two years. He recalled that her father had also been brought in but died at the time of the deluge. They had little property between them, which had been seized to pay for their incarceration.

He would have to make a case to the judges, who could be a problem. There was not even a hint of confession, and with her property already disposed of, there was little incentive to find her guilty postmortem. His only hope was to convince Inés Mejia to turn witness against her. If the old woman could be persuaded, her testimony along with his own might be enough. But time was short. It would be much more difficult if they interred her body and had to seek an order to have it exhumed.

He reached for the last of the oranges Señora Péres de Armijo had left on her visit. As he peeled the skin, he realized he had the perfect enticement to secure the old woman's testimony. He would use her desire to leave the Castillo to make her say what he wanted. The juice from the orange dripped over his fingers, and he wiped them on his habit, still dirty from the evening before. He must order a second complete habit. It was not fitting that the head of the Inquisition in Sevilla dress like a beggar.

Chapter Eighteen

A DECISION

Inés paced the floor of her tiny room, her hands folded and head bowed. The priest had barely listened to her when she pleaded with him not to burn Marta's body three days earlier. His mind was elsewhere, and he soon left to pray the Hours. She had not been forceful enough. It was foolish to rely on the Inquisitor's sense of justice. He had dismissed her without saying a word about Marta's fate. She should seek out Brother Tomás, who was a good man. There were probably others as well, but she had little contact with any of them. She merely saw them moving about the Castillo in their robes, scurrying from place to place along the corridors like black and white beetles.

She wondered how much time she had. The priest had said there would be a tribunal. Surely that would take a while. Meanwhile, Marta's body would remain in the cell, rotting. She could almost smell the decaying flesh she remembered from her own time in the cells. A prisoner would die, and the guards would not remove the body immediately. The scent was sickly sweet, one that stuck in your nostrils, never to be forgotten.

She gagged just thinking of it, but as she sniffed the air, she realized the smell was no mere memory. She had forgotten about the chicken. She had meant to eat it after she returned from scrubbing the floors outside the cells the day Marta died, but when she returned, she had no appetite. She took the basket from the nail on which it was hanging and pulled back the cover. The odor nearly made her retch. She covered the basket again and took it out into the courtyard to dump its contents in the cesspool behind the stables.

"Señora, Padre Dominguez wishes to see you," a young friar called out as she was returning to her room.

"At this moment? I was about to start my work," she said.

"Yes. He said to come at once."

The young friar walked away quickly before Inés could ask more questions. She wondered whether she should drop the basket outside her door to air out the smell, which still lingered, but decided to bring it with her instead.

She knocked at the door to the Dominican's office, which was closed, as always.

"Enter," Padre Dominguez said, the transcript of Marta Montelongo's inquisition spread out in front of him. He had spoken with the inquisitors, who proved unhelpful, and continued to ponder how best to proceed. "Sit down," he said, motioning the Mejia woman to the chair across the desk.

Inés put the basket on the desk. "You wished to see me?" she asked.

"Yes. I had to rush our previous conversation, which I regret," he said. "I have studied the dead woman's records, and I think you could be of help to me." He eyed the old woman steadily, her face nearly as white as her hair. This would not be easy.

"Thank you, Padre. I know that you are a just man." She grabbed the basket and set it by her on the floor. The Dominican's nose twitched. "What is that stink?" he asked.

"Pardon me, Padre. I was on my way back from dumping…" she hesitated. She couldn't tell him that she had spoiled meat in the basket because he would ask how she had gotten meat in the first place. She was about to make up a story when he stood up and walked around the desk. "Let me see that basket," he said. She lifted it up, and once again the movement seemed to release the smell that still permeated the straw. He crossed his arms across his chest, standing so close to Inés that she felt the heat of his body.

"Where did you get that?" he asked, his voice angry but controlled. The basket was identical to the one Guiomar Péres de Armijo brought with her, he noted.

Inés panicked. She had been stupid to bring the basket with her. She'd thought the smell might make him think about Marta's body lying, unburied, in the cell. "It was a gift from the Señora. She gave me some extra food because she was worried about my health." The priest was still standing above her, his proximity making Inés fearful. He said nothing but went back to his chair behind the desk.

"You would like to go live in Señora Péres de Armijo's home? She talked to me about this after her last visit." He folded his hands on the desk and bent closer to the woman.

Inés was pleased that the Señora had indeed spoken to the Dominican on her behalf, but his question frightened her. "Yes, Padre. I am ready to leave the Castillo, as you have suggested many times before."

"I see," he raised his eyebrows, as if surprised. "Well then, we must try to accommodate you both. The Señora is a generous benefactress. And, I trust, a good Catholic who will keep a repentant sinner like yourself in the fold." He had found his bargaining chip. Perhaps convincing the woman to give testimony would not be so difficult after all. "There is one problem," he said, waiting to see the woman's reaction before proceeding. Her face went slack. He pursed his lips and shook his head gently. "I want to help you, Señora Mejia, but you must help me in return."

Inés felt a sharp pain in her gut. This man was not to be trusted. She wished that she had not started down this path. Marta was dead. Did it matter what happened to her corpse? Not even the fires of the auto-da-fé could touch her now. As for the Señora's offer, her generosity no doubt would put them both in greater danger.

"What is the problem, Padre? I thought I was free to leave of my own choosing. If not, then I accept my fate."

"No. You misunderstand. We must follow procedure, that is all." He had rushed forward too quickly. "It is a matter of protocol, which I have already discussed with the Señora. You have never been formally judged by the tribunal. It is a process we must complete for you to leave. Nothing really. Just your testimony and confession. Very simple. I will be on the tribunal and will recommend the lightest penance." He struggled to conjure some image that would transform his features into a look of loving kindness. His mother's face appeared but quickly faded.

He waited, but the woman said nothing. "There is an alternative. But it will require your cooperation on another matter," he said finally.

"What matter?" Inés asked hesitantly.

The priest shuffled through the papers on his desk, his eyes moving across one, reading it silently, though his lips moved. "There is some unfinished business regarding the dead woman. There is no doubt she was a heretic…"

"She was a good Catholic, Padre," Inés interrupted.

"Let me finish. That is, if you want my help." The woman was testing his patience. She looked chastened, so he continued. "I appreciate that the woman was a friend of yours. But you are in no position to judge the state of her soul. I have her testimony under questioning here. Unfortunately, she died before the tribunal could be convened to pronounce her guilt and turn her over to the civil authorities for punishment." He picked up one of the documents. "She clearly said here," he tapped the document, "that she wanted instruction in how to frame her confession." It was a literal rendering of her words, if not their intent. "But, out of mercy, she was returned to her cell without drawing up the written confession so as not to tire her after her long questioning. So now we must have the signed testimonies of two witnesses who can attest to her guilt." He paused to give the woman time to absorb what he was saying. "It is a mere formality, as I said."

Inés sat perfectly still. She feared that if she lifted even a finger, she might hurl her body across the desk and gouge out the

THE SILVER CANDLESTICKS

priest's eyes. The image of Marta lying in her own filth, the grotesque angle of her broken legs jutting through her skirt appeared before her. If there was a devil, surely this was his emissary sent to make miserable every person who crossed his path. She breathed in slowly, considering her words.

"And if I don't agree?"

"I will convene a tribunal, whichever choice you make."

She sat impassively, saying nothing.

"Do you understand, woman?" he shouted, slamming his fist on the table.

"I understand perfectly," she answered calmly, though his words were a death sentence. "There will be an auto-da-fé. Either I assist you in seeing my friend's corpse burned at the stake, or I will take her place."

Dominguez leaned back in his chair. The woman wasn't stupid. Jews rarely were. He had been too lenient with this heretic. She had accused her own daughter of Judaizing, but where would the girl have learned the forbidden practices if not from the mother?

"I need a decision," he said.

Inés felt the pain in her shoulders. She could not live through another session on the *potro*. It would be better to confess at once. She had lived a long life. Forty-three years. Or was it forty-four? She had lost count within these walls. It would soon be over. Not as she wished, perhaps, sheltered in the Armijo home. But the suffering would be at an end. It was said that those who repented received mercy from the executioner, their life snuffed out before the pyre was lit. It would be quick.

Padre Dominguez watched the woman's face. She looked almost at peace. Well, why not? All she had to do was sign a document that would allow the dead woman's corpse to be burned, as it should be. "So, you will testify against Marta Montelongo?"

Inés shook her head. "No, Padre. I will not."

It was done. She had sealed her own fate.

The priest's face turned red. It was not the answer he expected.

"You have made a grave error. I cannot protect you. Nor can I protect your benefactress who you have spent much time with recently. We must question you about Señora Péres de Armijo. She has taken too much interest in your case." He stood up and walked toward the woman, who was now visibly shaking. "I will take this," he said, lifting the stinking basket from the floor. "As evidence. Who knows what was in it. Perhaps some innocent child's flesh to be used in some ritual."

"You are the Devil himself," Inés screamed before throwing up at the priest's feet.

Guiomar opened the window to listen to the canary, whom she had named Gordito because of his round chest. The bird trilled happily, jumping about the cage to attract the attention of the quieter female, Mantequilla. She called to Úrsula, who sat on the floor playing with a wooden doll.

"Come, *m'hija*, say hello to the birds." The child looked up, her face as grave as if she were in church. Guiomar walked over to her and lifted her into her arms, nuzzling the child's neck with her nose. She felt a pang of pity. She must shower this child with love, even if it was sometimes hard for her. "Shall we say hello to Gordito, my love?" The child nodded her head willingly, if not enthusiastically.

Guiomar stepped through the large opening with Úrsula in her arms and walked up to the cage. "Buenos días, Señor Gordito," Guiomar proclaimed solemnly. Úrsula smiled. Guiomar hugged her tightly and then began to tickle her until the child started giggling.

"No, no, Mamá," Úrsula begged through her squeals.

Guiomar twirled her about until she felt she might drop her from dizziness. When she stopped, the child looked bewildered.

"Señor Gordito," Guiomar addressed the bird seriously, "should I take Úrsula inside to the nursery?" She looked at the girl's face, her eyes wide and her mouth slightly open. The bird continued to hop from his perch to the floor of the cage and up again.

"Do you understand his language, Úrsula? I admit I cannot."

"Sí, Mamá. He says yes." The child nodded up and down quickly, her eyes still open so wide that she looked astonished.

"Well, I am glad you understand him. I shall have to consult you when I am unable to translate," she said, kissing the child on the cheek. "Now let us find Esperanza and your brother," she said, stepping back into the bedroom.

When she returned from the nursery, Guiomar took out her paper and quill. She had been putting off writing to Francisco but now she must. She had given a great deal of thought to what she should say, the events of the previous week playing out each night as she tried to fall asleep. She could not let him know what she had learned from José Marcos about the gossip swirling around her.

The truth presented two dangers, the information itself, which might be intercepted, and the fact that Francisco's rival was once again pursuing her. But she must say something to suggest the urgency of the request she was about to make. She wanted her husband to come home—not in the fall, or worse by Christmas, but immediately. She needed him. His children needed him. Without him, they were...how would she put it?

Lost.

> My dearest husband, I cannot tell you how pleased I was to hear that you will return soon, or how heartbroken I am that I must wait one day longer than the number of days it will take you to cross the seas. I do not wish to worry you. My health is good, as is the children's, though my father grows ever weaker by the hour. Yet, I am sad and lonely in ways that I never anticipated when you left. I have not always been a good wife. I am painfully aware of my failings. But without you here, I am truly lost.

A few days ago, I went with Esperanza to buy a pair of canaries to keep me company. This morning, Úrsula and I watched the male, whom I have named Gordito, serenade the female, Mantequilla. They must be kept in separate cages so that the male will sing his lovely song. But as I watched them, I realized how cruel it is for the pair to be separated. Would Mantequilla not be happier to have her mate close at hand than to luxuriate in his rich song from a distance? So, too, am I happy to give up whatever worldly treasures you are amassing so far away to have you beside me now. You have been gone too long. I want you to come home at once, my dearest. I cannot bear your absence a moment longer than it takes you to sail back to me.

She put down the pen and read her words. Did they convey enough urgency? She hoped he could read between the lines. She had never written anything similar in the time they had been apart. Perhaps she should refer to the bird cages as prison cells. No, that was too much and might confirm suspicions should it get into the wrong hands.

She folded the paper and prepared the wax to seal it. Her fingers went to her throat, as they often did out of habit, rubbing the small gold pendant Francisco had given her when Úrsula was born. She put the spoon with the melted wax down, unfastening the gold chain that held the pendant. She then poured the wax on the folded paper, pressed the oval into the soft wax, and carefully removed it.

Would he recognize the design? If so, would it mean anything to him? Surely, he would recognize a departure from her common practice of affixing the family signet. If nothing else, it would signal that the message inside should be read with more than usual care. She had nearly died the night he gave her the pendant. She hoped he would remember that and know she was in danger once again.

THE SILVER CANDLESTICKS

Inés sat waiting on her cot. The Dominican had not ordered her to be taken into custody when she left his office that morning, but it was merely a matter of time. She surveyed the tiny room. She had lived here peaceably, if not in comfort, since right after the flood. Soon, they would take her back to the cells in the dungeon. She could bear that fate, though it would be worse than before because she would be alone in the dark, fetid enclosure, perhaps the very one where Marta's body lay now. But she would break under torture. She would tell them whatever they wanted to hear. She had done it before. They would ask her what Señora Péres de Armijo talked about with her. And she would tell them. Innocent things. But when they put her on the rack, she would blurt out worse. "How did you keep your faith secret?" the woman had once asked. They would twist the question as vigorously as they twisted the ropes.

Inés pulled back the thin muslin that covered the bed. She stood up, shook the cloth free and began to twist it tightly until it formed a long rope. The setting sun cast shadows across the floor from the barred window high above the table. She draped the cloth rope over her shoulder and walked the short distance to the window, climbing slowly onto the chair and then the table, grabbing the bars above her to steady herself. She pushed the edge of the twisted sheet through the bars, peering out on her tiptoes to see if anyone was in the courtyard who might observe the scene.

Had the bells rung Vespers? She couldn't remember. She tied a double knot around the bar, pulling hard to test its strength. She grabbed the twisted cloth mid-way and wrapped it around her neck, once, twice, three times, until she could barely breathe. She tied another knot, tightly, under her chin, her fingers trembling as she began to choke. She stuck her toe between the table and the wall, pushing with all her weight against the stones. The table moved, making a horrible grating noise, and the chair crashed to the floor. She felt the throbbing of blood in her temples. With a quick, violent leap, she pushed the table away. "Paloma. Paloma," she mouthed, but no sound emerged.

Chapter Nineteen

THE RUMORS

Esperanza carried the basket over her arm, hurrying along the street to the Castillo. Her mistress had instructed her to be courteous to the guard, but careful, as one never knew whether he would report what was discussed to the Dominican. She felt uneasy. *How long would this continue?* she wondered. Inés Mejia might live a long while and Esperanza hoped that the Señora had given up the wish to have the woman come live in their household. The Señora had confided that she had written her husband, asking him to return at once. This also worried Esperanza.

She clutched the basket closer and breathed in the sweet aroma of figs and dates. The Castillo tower loomed ahead, with the guard in his green britches standing slackly beside the small gate, the only color against the drab stones. The sun reflected off his helmet. It must be hot to stand all day in such heavy attire, she thought.

"Buenos Días," she said as she approached the man, who looked up with a frown. She had anticipated he would be eager to receive the maravedis, but he looked displeased.

"I have the basket for Señora Mejia," Esperanza said, extending it to him.

"It won't do her much good where she is," the guard replied, his eyes narrowing.

Esperanza pulled back her hand. "I don't..."

"She is dead. Like her daughter. A suicide."

"*Madre de Dios*," Esperanza whispered, putting her arm out to steady herself against the wall. She looked in the man's eyes. He seemed frightened, or was it just disappointment that he would not get his reward?

"Yes, it was quite unexpected. The gossip is she relapsed," he said. He leaned forward to whisper in her ear. "Perhaps your mistress saw the signs."

Esperanza stumbled backwards. "How would *she* recognize any signs?" she protested too loudly.

The guard's eyes widened. "There are rumors, girl. Surely you've heard them," he said, his lips curling. "I'll take this anyway. No point seeing it go to waste," he said, grabbing at the basket, which Esperanza held tight.

She reached into her pocket and pulled out the coins, throwing them at his feet. "Take your money. There will be no more where that came from," she said, turning away.

Esperanza found the Señora in the nursery playing on the floor with Antonio and Úrsula, who clapped her hands when she saw Esperanza.

"I must speak to you, Señora," Esperanza blurted.

Guiomar noticed that Esperanza still carried the basket on her arm. Was it the empty one? If so, she would have surely dropped it off in the *cocina*. "It is time for your siesta, children," she said, standing up. "Put them to bed, Esperanza. I will be in my room," she said, her heart beating faster as she looked at Esperanza's stricken face.

She waited in her room, pacing the floor. Something had gone wrong. She took a deep breath. Perhaps the guard had changed or he refused the basket. She must calm herself. Gordito warbled outside, distracting her. She had mailed her letter to Francisco four days earlier. It would take weeks to reach him. She must remain strong and level-headed, no matter what happened. If only she could enlist the counsel of someone wiser, her *padrino* maybe.

She had neglected him since Francisco left. She must rectify that immediately.

Esperanza opened the door without knocking. "Oh, Señora. I am so sorry to be the bearer of this news."

"What? Tell me, Esperanza. You're scaring me," Guiomar said, rushing towards her.

"Señora Mejia is dead," she said, reaching out to embrace her mistress, whose eyes opened wide in terror.

"How?" she whispered, falling against Esperanza, who steadied her.

"A suicide. 'Like her daughter,' the guard told me."

"She hanged herself?" Guiomar began to sob.

"I don't know the details, Señora. I was too shocked—and frightened—to ask. The man said she had 'relapsed.'" Esperanza stopped herself. Should she say more?

"What did he say exactly? Remember the words. It is important."

"He said maybe *you* had detected the signs of her relapse." Her mistress gasped. "I asked him how you would recognize such signs." She waited briefly, assessing the effect of her words.

"Yes, go on," Guiomar pressed.

"He said there are rumors…" she began sobbing too. "I threw the money at him and left. I know I should have remained calm, Señora, but I couldn't." Her eyes beseeched her mistress to forgive her.

Guiomar shook her head. It was worse than she expected. She had little time to prepare. José Marcos had been right. She must try not to panic.

"We must be very careful, Esperanza. Poor Inés. I fear that I may have endangered her with my silly offer. You were right about the Dominican. He is the Devil. If only I had someone to guide me. I don't know what to do."

"How can I help, Señora? I would do anything for you." Esperanza grabbed her mistress's hands and brought them to her lips, her tears spilling onto them.

"You are the only one I can completely trust, Esperanza. But I must seek out help from others as well. We are too weak to fight this alone. I am hopeful my husband will return sooner than expected, as I have implored him. But it may not be soon enough. We must consider who our allies might be. My brother, if only we could get him word. And Don Enrique, my *padrino*. I must reach out to him at once."

Jorge closed the shutters on his bird shop early. He still had plenty of time to make it home before sunset, but not if he were to collect information from the guard first. It was a dilemma. If he did not walk to the river and across the bridge now, he would have to wait until Monday, a full week from his first talk with the guard, whom he had promised money as Herrera had instructed. He did not carry money on the Sabbath, and even if he went by the Castillo after Mass on Sunday, the guard might not work on the Lord's Day. It was very complicated following the rules of two religions when he would just as well abide by neither. He grabbed his cane and pulled the heavy door shut. His wife would have to wait.

By the time he arrived at the bridge, breathing heavily and dripping in sweat, the sun was low in the sky. The guard signaled to him when he stepped off the bridge. "Buenas tardes," the guard yelled out. Jorge wished the man were more discreet. Apparently, the fellow had been waiting to transmit some information. Jorge hoped it would be worth angering his wife.

"I take it the servant delivered her basket?" he asked without returning the greeting.

"Much has happened, Señor. I thought to get you word earlier in the week, but I wanted to deliver something concrete."

"Well, get on with it, man," Jorge said, annoyed.

"The old woman hanged herself—or that is the rumor. I guess Señora Péres de Armijo didn't know because her slave came today with the basket, as arranged."

"And?" Jorge could barely stop himself from pushing his cane into the man's chest.

"I told her what happened."

"What did she say? You remember our agreement. I want information about the Señora not some suicide in the Castillo."

"Not much. I pressed her on what she observed in the household. She seemed agitated by the question. But I have more information for you. More valuable than my conversation with the pretty *esclava*, who remains, I think, a good source we must cultivate."

Jorge stepped closer to the man. "So far, you have provided nothing. Don't get greedy, my friend. You will be fairly compensated based on the information you provide. I am only the go-between, remember."

The guard grinned. "This comes from a source far closer to the truth than a slave."

"Who?"

"The inquisitor himself. Padre Dominguez," he said with a smirk on his face.

"Did you talk to him directly?" He found the idea preposterous, but he might be wrong.

"I did. He called me in to discuss a basket in the possession of the old woman the day she killed herself. He recognized it as the one Señora Péres de Armijo carried on her last visit. He wanted to know how it ended up in the Mejia woman's possession. So I told him. I thought he might remove me on the spot, but he wanted information as well."

"So, you are serving two masters, are you? Should I reduce your reward by half?"

"You misunderstand, Señor. My conversation gave me the opportunity to know the Inquisitor's mind. I am sure he suspects the Señora of being a Judaizer. He thinks she conspired with the old woman. He wanted me to get hold of the new basket when the servant came today. Unfortunately, I failed."

Jorge leaned on his cane. So, Herrera was right. He pulled out a pouch from his jacket and poured the coins into his palm, squeezing them tight. It was a dirty business. He had hoped merely to pass on gossip, harmless enough if it stopped Herrera from pursuing an adulterous relationship that would harm a woman he respected, even if the feeling was not mutual. But the inquisitor was a dangerous man. One with great power. He must be careful. He did not want to slip into the Dominican's trap as well. Jorge was a useful man to many powerful people in Sevilla, who looked the other way when it came to the purity of his bloodlines or his piety when they needed money. But the inquisitor would not be so tolerant.

"Does the Señora know she is under suspicion?"

"How would I know? The servant seemed surprised by the news of the suicide," he said, staring at the moneylender's closed fist. "She seemed frightened as well. She probably knows more than she would be willing to say in our first conversation."

Jorge relaxed his fingers and extended his hand, dropping a few coins into the guard's outstretched palm. "Do not try to cheat me, friend. You cannot be the source of information both to the inquisitor and to me. And what does he have to offer? A few years off the fires of Purgatory?" he laughed, dropping two more coins into the man's palm. "But the information you find out from inside these walls," he pulled back his hand, "that will be the most valuable information of all. Do you understand?"

The guard looked at the coins in his palm. The last two were small but gold. "I understand," he said, smiling.

Jorge turned toward the bridge again. If he hurried, he might make it home soon after the last rays of the sun disappeared beyond the horizon, missing the candle-lighting but getting to enjoy the Sabbath meal nonetheless.

José Marcos waited impatiently outside the moneylender's shop. The man did not conduct business on Saturday, but he usually sat in the shop for a few hours to keep up appearances, though he had not yet arrived. José Marcos was about to leave when he spied the bent figure turn the corner. He hoped he would have news from the day before, but he was not sure what news could be construed as good. If Guiomar was under suspicion, maybe she would turn to him for help. She had once before, though he had failed her then.

And what could he offer her? In reality—little. But in the meantime, she would be his.

"Have you news?" José Marcos asked.

"Not here," Jorge answered, putting his key into the lock. He entered the shop, opening the shutters to let in light, which set off the macaws. "Hush, my beauties. I have company," Jorge said to the large scarlet macaw who sat chained to a perch. The birds were hungry and would not quiet down until he had fed them. "Sit down, Señor," he said to Herrera. "I must attend to my birds, and then we can talk."

José Marcos fidgeted as he waited for the moneylender to finish his duties. Maybe he should buy one of these creatures for his wife. At the very least, it would give him good reason to be seen entering the shop so often. The moneylender disappeared behind the beads and returned with a large bucket of water in one hand and a burlap sack of seeds in the other, limping without his cane.

Jorge put the sack down and went from perch to perch, pouring water into the bowls. The scarlet macaw screeched when the bucket brushed against it, flapping its long wings excitedly. "*Cállate*," Roja," he said, tapping the bird's beak.

"Hola! Hola!" the bird answered, bobbing its head in rhythm.

"Can't you hurry? I don't have all day," José Marcos stood up, setting off more cawing among the parrots.

Jorge set down the pail. "I learned some interesting news from the guard," he said. "Exactly what you feared, I am sorry to say." He watched José Marcos for a reaction, but the man looked more irritated at the slow pace of his revelation than upset at what he might have learned.

"So, what did the fellow say? And how did he come by his news?"

"The old woman, whom the Señora was helping, hanged herself earlier in the week. It appears that the Señora was not informed because she sent her servant to bring the woman food. Word from within the Castillo suggests that now the Señora herself is under suspicion by the inquisitor."

"Do you trust the fellow?"

THE SILVER CANDLESTICKS

"I trust no one, Señor. But he knows that I will pay him for information. And if he provides false information, I will cut him off, not only from the reward but from access to credit when he needs it. So yes, I believe him. He will remain a good source of information as long as the money lasts."

José Marcos started to reach for the pouch inside his jacket, but the moneylender touched his arm. "Not now, Señor. Your credit is good with me."

José Marcos was baffled. The moneylender had always been happy to receive payment, but perhaps it had something to do with the man's scruples on his holy day. He extended his empty hand and patted the old man on the arm. "I appreciate your diligence. And I might throw you some business as well. How much is that big red parrot?"

"Roja? She's a beauty, no? And a good talker. I have taught her many words already, and she is young. I raised her from a chick. But let us not talk business today. If you want her, I will arrange to bring her to your home. And maybe I will have more news to impart by then. Meanwhile, be careful that you do not get entwined in this mess. The Dominican has a nasty reputation, and he would be happy to fill more than one cell in this endeavor. I don't plan to be caught up in it. And neither should you, Señor."

José Marcos considered the man's words. But what was life for if not to live to the fullest, even if it entailed danger? Especially if the danger was rewarded with the kisses of a beautiful woman.

With some trepidation, Guiomar opened the letter from her *padrino*. She read it quickly, relieved when she saw that he had accepted her invitation to dine with her on Sunday. She had made it clear it would be an informal affair, just him and her father who, she said, retired early, giving them a chance to catch up. She hoped that he would understand her wishes, and his reply clearly showed he did.

Guiomar went to the dining room and saw that Esperanza had placed the empty Sabbath candlesticks on the table for the evening meal. She picked one up, bringing it to her lips. The silver felt cool against her skin, recalling how terribly she had behaved when her mother gave them to her. It remained a deep source of shame. It was not yet sunset, but she went to the side-table and retrieved two beeswax candles, the best her husband's makers had produced, placing them carefully in the candlesticks so that they stood straight. She would light the candles and say the prayers silently before the evening meal, but it would be the last time she would do so. It was too risky.

She had carefully hidden the small book Alfonso had given her in a secret compartment in the headboard of her bed, though perhaps it was time to burn it. After the meal, she would ask Esperanza to bury the box holding her mother's candlesticks wrapped in the old lace. Perhaps someday she would dig them up and present them to Úrsula, just as her mother had done. She hoped that it would not bring as much sorrow to her daughter as it had her. By then, the Dominican might be gone, burning in the hell he claimed to save others from. Was it possible that the Inquisition itself would disappear? The madness had gone on for more than a hundred years, but it could not go on forever.

Guiomar was startled when her father shuffled into the dining room. His gait had become unsteady, his feet moving along the carpets as if he did not have the strength to lift them. "Papá, you're early. The meal will not be ready for another half hour," she said, kissing him on the cheek.

"So, I cannot sit at my own table except on your schedule?" He grabbed the chair at the head of the table and sat down.

"Of course you may, Papá. I just didn't want you to sit in that uncomfortable chair longer than necessary. Let me see if the meal can be served early."

Don Péres pointed a gnarled finger at the candlesticks. "You think I don't know why you want me to come late? Your mother used to sneak around lighting forbidden candles. I won't have it. Do you hear?"

Guiomar pulled back. His words stung as harshly as if he'd struck her. "I wasn't sneaking, Papá," she whispered, not so much to avoid being heard by the servants as not to arouse further anger. "I will put them away if you wish. They were Mamá's last gift to me. I simply light them to remember her." She watched her father's face. He seemed to have forgotten his anger already.

"You look very pretty tonight, Benita. Is it a special occasion?"

Guiomar suppressed a gasp. He confused her with her mother. His mind was deteriorating more rapidly than she realized. "Papá, it's me, Guiomar," she said, reaching out to take his hand.

"What? Of course," he said, shoving her hand away. "Is your husband going to grace us with his presence, or is he avoiding me as usual?"

Guiomar weighed her response. "Francisco is in Veracruz. But he will be back soon. Very soon, I pray."

"Good. Let us eat. I am starving," he said, smiling.

Padre Dominguez genuflected before leaving the chapel. He had prayed for guidance in how to proceed. In less than a week, he had lost two souls, souls that had been within his grasp but were snatched away by the forces of evil. Was he being punished? He had mortified his flesh to the point that it had weakened him. The welts on his back attested to his penance for the carnal thoughts and pleasures that still haunted him. What more could the Lord want? Why was he being tested so relentlessly?

And now he had a decision to make about Señora Péres de Armijo. It would be far easier to let go of his suspicions. She gave generously to the Church. She attended services regularly, was modest in her dress and demeanor, and even though her husband had been gone more than two years, he had not picked up a hint of scandal.

But then how would he know, locked inside the walls of the Castillo as much as any prisoner? He was rarely invited out. The Archbishop seemed uninterested in his efforts to rid the city of sinners, living a life of luxury in the *Palacio Arzobispal*. How often had he been asked to dine with him there since arriving from Toledo? A handful of times at most, and never alone, always in a group of parish priests.

Dominguez was so lost in his thoughts, he nearly ran into Brother Tomás, who was waiting just outside the chapel door.

Brother Tomás clutched the rosary under his tunic. "Mother of God, give me courage," he prayed silently. He had made his decision. He could not wait for an answer from the priory in Toledo, an answer that might never come. He must confront Dominguez directly, even if it meant he would be punished.

"Padre, may I speak with you?" he asked as the inquisitor stopped in front of him.

"You follow the Rule of Silence as well as you do the duty to fast, I see."

"A great sin is weighing on my conscience," Tomás blurted out.

"You want to confess? I cannot refuse, but not here. Should we go back into the chapel?" Dominguez wondered whether the man would impart information he was fearful of revealing outside the protection of the confessional.

Tomás felt outwitted. He had long since avoided Dominguez as a confessor, fearing the priest would use any information he gleaned not only against him but others, all while maintaining the seal of confession as a shield.

"No. I would rather talk man to man."

The inquisitor let out a bitter laugh. "Am I not your superior, Brother Tomás? If you have something to tell me, speak up. But do not forget your station."

Tomás rubbed the crucifix on his rosary between his thumb and forefinger, pressing so hard the corpus dug into his soft flesh. "It is our duty to save souls, Padre," he said, "and I fear we have driven the innocent to despair. Señora Mejia…"

Dominguez yanked his forearm before he could finish, the bony fingers digging in with strength that belied the priest's age and appearance. "You dare accuse me of driving the heretic to take her life? Is not her final act proof of her guilt, as was her daughter's?"

"She was an old and feeble woman, frightened that being subjected to the *tormentos* would cause her to accuse others, just as she accused her own child. Padre, can you not see how unnatural it is for a mother to accuse her daughter? Isn't this unnatural act proof enough of the Devil's hand?" He was almost breathless as he pronounced the words.

Dominguez could barely believe his ears. Here was blasphemy of the worst sort. This fat pig was saying that the Church's own methods, intended exclusively to save souls from eternal damnation, were causing some to commit mortal sins against the Holy Ghost. He had offered these women salvation, and they had refused to repent, choosing instead to despair of God's saving grace.

"Your words, Brother Tomás, cast doubt not on the Church or the Holy Office of the Inquisition, but on you. May God have mercy on your soul." He let go of the friar's arm and hurried toward his casita.

Tomás crossed himself. "Give me strength, dear Lord," he mumbled. But he knew that he was no match for Dominguez. He wanted to flee. But where would he go? And how? He had accomplished nothing by speaking directly to the inquisitor. He would need allies if he were to fight Dominguez, and there were few inside the Castillo who could be counted on. He had limited contact with the world outside—the merchants he purchased the Castillo's wheat from, the deliverymen who brought sacks of flour and other stores into the Castillo.

Only one other person came to mind. Señora Péres de Armijo. He had been sent years ago to deliver a message to her personally, and he bumped into her occasionally on her visits to Señora Mejia. Did she even know the poor woman was dead? He must endeavor to find out.

Part IV
APRIL 1597

Chapter Twenty

THE ARCHBISHOP

"Shall we take a walk in the garden, Don Enrique?" Guiomar asked as Esperanza cleared the table. Her father had already retired for his siesta, and he'd had trouble making conversation during the meal. Don Pedro insisted that he would launch a new mission to Méjico and perhaps Perú if Don Enrique could find a suitably armored ship so as not to fall prey to pirates when he brought back all the gold and emeralds he would acquire. Don Enrique humored his old partner, exchanging glances with Guiomar. Once again, her father mistook her for her mother, this time humiliating her by grabbing her around the waist to kiss her on the lips.

Now that he was safely in his room, she welcomed the chance to talk to Don Enrique about her predicament. The late afternoon was cool, the sky clouded, and a brisk breeze threatened a storm. She took her *padrino*'s arm and walked with him along the portico toward her canaries.

"Are these a new addition?" Don Enrique inquired as they approached the warbling birds.

"Yes. I bought them to keep me company. I am very lonely these days," she said sticking her finger through the cage. Gordito stopped singing and approached her finger warily.

"The life of a merchant's wife is a difficult one. Your mother, God rest her soul, suffered when your father was gone for long periods. She was subject to melancholy. I have never seen the signs in you, however." His eyes followed the contours of Guiomar's lovely face. He hoped that Francisco had proven a good husband, better than the scoundrel Herrera.

"It is not melancholy but fear that grips me," she said, guiding him to a bench near the large tree in the middle of the garden. "You know that the inquisitor has asked for my help with a woman at the Castillo, and I visited her regularly."

"I've never liked the arrangement. The man is not to be trusted. He is a zealot, as I have told you before."

"I should have listened to your advice—something my mother and father complained of regularly when I failed to listen to theirs. Now I fear I may be in real danger."

Enrique turned toward his goddaughter. Her lips quivered, and he reached out to stroke her cheek as he did when she was a child. "What has happened, *m'hija*? Why did you not come to me sooner? I will see the man removed from his post if he dares to…" He stopped, forcing himself to take a deep breath. "Tell me everything," he said, taking her hand and squeezing it.

Guiomar told the story as best she could—her visits to the Castillo, her foolish offer to take Inés into her home, the Dominican's implied threats that it would bring her own family under suspicion, Inés's suicide, and finally, the guard's insinuations that they were conversos. Don Enrique said nothing, asking no questions, seeking no clarifications. She worried that he was now suspicious too.

Finally, he spoke, softly but with passion. "It is nonsense. I have known your parents—and your grandparents before them—for many years. I have never seen a single sign that they were not true and faithful Catholics."

Tears welled in her eyes. "But what can I do, *Padrino*? I cannot fight this alone. I need my husband at my side. Is there nothing you can do?"

Don Enrique stood up, lifting Guiomar by her hands. "First, I will send word that Francisco is to return immediately. But it will take some time before he arrives. In the meantime, I will see the archbishop. The Holy Office is under his control at least nominally. There have been two suicides that we know of under this fiend's tenure. I am sure there are other irregularities. We will find them out, and it will be the Dominican who should fear his fate, not you, my daughter."

As they walked back toward the house, Esperanza appeared, somewhat shaken. "You have a visitor, Señora," she said. "From the Castillo."

Guiomar gripped Don Enrique's arm. It had begun—sooner than she anticipated. She was terrified but glad that she had her *padrino* by her side.

"Who is it?"

"The monk. The one who came before to deliver a message two years ago at Easter when your brother was here."

Guiomar looked to Enrique, her face wordlessly begging advice. He patted her arm. "Show the monk into the *sala mayor*. We will meet him together," he said to Esperanza.

Brother Tomás stood nervously as the Señora and a gentleman he did not recognize entered. Perhaps it was Don Pedro Péres, though he had imagined the father differently. "Buenas noches. Forgive me for this intrusion, but it is an urgent matter," he said, looking first at the Señora and then the gentleman.

"Sit down, please," Guiomar said, gesturing to a large chair near the fireplace. "May I introduce Don Enrique Gomez y Duran? I'm sorry, I've forgotten your name, if I ever learned it," she said as casually as she could.

"Brother Tomás, at your service," he said, bowing slightly.

"Esperanza, can you bring Brother Tomás some *café* and *pan dulce*?" She turned to Esperanza, who stood in the corner looking terrified. "Sit down, please," she said to the monk who looked like he might flee any minute. "Do you have another message for me from Padre Dominguez?" she asked, smiling. There was nothing to do but treat this visit as nothing out of the ordinary. If she showed fear, he would report it back to the priest as more evidence of her guilt.

"No, no, Señora. Forgive me, but I am here on my own. I snuck out of the Castillo to come, and I cannot stay long. If my absence is discovered, it will be bad for…" he didn't finish his sentence. "I come with bad news, I am afraid. Señora Mejia is dead," he blurted out.

Guiomar said nothing for a moment. Better to let the monk think it was news to her and she was in shock. "What happened?" she asked.

"It is too long to tell in detail. Suffice it to say that she took her own life, like her daughter. I believe Padre Dominguez drove her to it."

"That is a very strong accusation, Brother Tomás" Don Enrique interjected. "What evidence do you have to back it up?"

The monk looked toward Guiomar. "Go ahead, Brother Tomás. Don Enrique is trustworthy. Nothing you say will go beyond this room unless you wish it to."

The servant put a cup of coffee on the table next to his chair and handed him a plate with a sweet on it. His hands shook as he set the plate next to the coffee, leaving the cake uneaten.

"Señora Mejia came to me on Monday while I was in chapel. A young woman was dying in the cells. When we found her, she was lying in filth, her legs broken and useless. Señora Mejia knew the woman, I believe. When I summoned Padre Dominguez, he gave the woman the Last Rites, but she died before she could swallow the Host," he stammered, stopping to take a sip of the warm coffee. "Padre Dominguez said that her refusal to accept Christ's Body was proof that she was a Judaizer. He ordered her body left in the cell, unburied, until he could arrange to have her corpse burned at the stake."

"So, Inés killed herself because of this?" Guiomar was incredulous. She had assumed it was because the Dominican threatened the poor woman in some way.

"He wanted Señora Mejia to bear witness against the woman. The inquisitor has great power, but he cannot order an auto-da-fé before a tribunal has been convened. Apparently, the woman did not confess to heresy, even when she was subjected to the *tormentos*. I think he hoped I would testify that the Host remained on the woman's tongue. As if that were proof of anything but that the poor wretch had expired before she could swallow it."

Enrique abruptly stood up. "Do you see what folly these beliefs lead to?" he said accusatorially. "This must stop before we are all consumed by accusations and superstition."

"I think what my *padrino* is saying is that Padre Dominguez has perverted the purpose of the Holy Office," Guiomar interrupted before he could continue. The last thing they needed at this moment was to lose a valuable ally.

The monk nodded, the fat beneath his chin wobbling against his habit. "Yes, exactly, Señora," the monk agreed. "I have written to the prior in Toledo to that effect. Padre Dominguez goes too far. I have told him so to his face. He pushed Señora Mejia to commit the sin against the Holy Ghost by driving her to despair. And he has done it before—to the woman's daughter, who also took her life as a mere child." Tears rolled down his fat cheeks as the words tumbled out. He grabbed for the *pan dulce* but caught himself before taking a bite.

Enrique sat down again, controlling his temper. "Would you be willing to speak to the archbishop if I can arrange it? Are there others who might be encouraged to come forth?"

"There was a young priest who chafed against Padre Dominguez's ways, but he has left the Castillo. Padre Jaramillo. A Franciscan. He was one of two chief inquisitors under Padre Dominguez."

"Do you know what happened?" Enrique asked.

"It had to do with the girl, Paloma Mejia. I have no first-hand information. Just the usual whisperings. Padre Yañes, who is still at the Castillo, knows more. But he is even more zealous than Dominguez."

"Do you know where Padre Jaramillo is now?" Guiomar asked.

"He is in Méjico, Señora. He went to minister to the *Indios*, as I understand."

Guiomar sighed. It would be difficult to prove a case against the inquisitor with only this monk as a witness.

"He might send written testimony, if it comes to that," Enrique suggested. "But let us not detain you. We must figure a way to communicate with you without risking your discovery. Is there anyone you trust as a go-between?"

The monk frowned. "The guard at the gate near the bridge is known to do favors for the right price."

"I know him," Guiomar said. "I will send my servant if I need to get in touch with you. But be careful Brother Tomás. We do not need to endanger any more souls than necessary," she said, reaching out to take the plate with the still uneaten *pan dulce* from his hands.

Enrique sealed his letter to the archbishop. It was short and to the point. He requested an audience with His Excellency to discuss a bequest he wished to make. He wondered how much this favor would cost him. Rodrigo de Castro Osorio was known to be a greedy prelate. He had turned the cathedral into a magnificent edifice filled with gold and silver from the New World and works of art from the best artists in Spain and elsewhere.

Enrique loved Guiomar as if she were his own daughter, but the girl's father had cost him dearly, first with the loss of a ship and then with his retirement. Now he would have to spend more money to secure information and, possibly, stop the Holy Office from pursuing his goddaughter.

But it could not be helped. It was not as if he lacked the funds to live in luxury the rest of his life—and he had no heirs to inherit what remained. He rang for his servant, who appeared in the doorway immediately. "Deliver this to Archbishop de Castro, Javier, and wait for a reply. And while you are at it, go to my goddaughter's home and tell her I have posted letters to Méjico with orders for her husband to return immediately." The old man took the letter, bowed, and silently retreated.

THE SILVER CANDLESTICKS

Enrique closed his eyes. It had been many years since Benita's face had come to him. She was beautiful in her youth, even more so than her daughter. Once he had thought to seduce her when Pedro was away on a voyage. But she had been unapproachable. Was it possible that she was a Jew? Pedro, like himself, was a skeptic who seemingly had little use for religion. But he had never observed him refraining from pork or failing to work on Saturday. It was true that Pedro was good with money, but so was he. In any case, the reputation of Jews was much exaggerated, and the Church used its calumnies against them to enrich itself. If Guiomar's blood was tainted, so be it. She had done nothing wrong. She was a good girl, if a bit vain and spoiled.

After the long meal the archbishop served, Don Enrique wiped his face and pushed back the heavy chair that had grown increasingly uncomfortable during the rich repast. "Your Excellency, I have a grave matter to discuss, which might be better suited away from your generous table," he said.

Rodrigo de Castro Osorio raised his eyebrow and his goblet at the same time, and an attentive monk filled the latter with more wine. "We can retire to my study, if you wish, Enrique," the archbishop said, motioning the servers to clear the table. The two men stood up, Enrique following the prelate down a wide hallway.

The study was more intimate than Enrique would have imagined, the shelves lined with heavy tomes bound in leather, furnished only with a small desk, two armchairs facing each other with small tables at each chair's side. The archbishop removed his skullcap and placed it on the table as he sat down. Enrique's eyes involuntarily shifted upwards, and Archbishop de Castro patted down the few stray gray hairs that stood up on his nearly bald head.

"So the bequest was not your only reason for seeking my company, Enrique? I should have known there would be more to your visit. They have been too rare of late."

Enrique eyed the man, who was older than him by a few years. He wondered how the archbishop stayed so trim considering the dinner they had just eaten, but perhaps he did not indulge this way at every meal. His long narrow face was almost gaunt, the closely clipped beard giving him an even more angular appearance.

"I don't wish to speak out of turn, Your Excellency, but there is a matter I have become aware of that you may not know about. It involves incidents at the Castillo San Jorge." He stopped to observe the archbishop's reaction, but again, the prelate only slightly raised an eyebrow.

"I would not have thought you had much interest in what happened behind those walls," de Castro said. "But tell me, what has aroused your concern?"

"I came across the information while visiting my goddaughter, Guiomar Péres de Armijo. She has been assisting an old woman at the Castillo whose daughter killed herself awhile back after the mother denounced the child under torture. Now the mother has killed herself as well."

"And these suicides are what brings you here?" De Castro's voice betrayed some skepticism.

"No." Enrique hesitated. "It has to do with the inquisitor, Padre Dominguez. The man has become a zealot, not content with only rooting out heresy among the living but punishing it beyond the grave." Enrique leaned forward. "Do you remember the story of the girl?"

"I was away from the city at the time," the archbishop replied, shifting in his chair. "But the story of the burning of the child's body in the Plaza is well known." He stood up, facing Enrique directly. "It was an error—one of those things that will not be repeated," he said, locking eyes with his guest.

"But Dominguez intends to do so again," Enrique interjected.

"With the mother's body?"

"No. With another's."

"How do you know so much, Enrique?" De Castro stared hard at his guest.

Enrique felt uneasy. He had gotten himself in deeper than he had anticipated, all for the sake of his goddaughter. He should have

THE SILVER CANDLESTICKS

expected the prelate's reaction. After all, he was questioning the archbishop's supervision of his flock.

"Let me explain, Excellency." Don Enrique took a deep breath and began a recitation of what he and Guiomar had been told by the fat monk: the death of an innocent women, a devout Catholic, whose corpse Padre Dominguez intended to burn posthumously.

"But what has this to do with the suicide?" the Archbishop asked.

"Dominguez pressed the old woman to testify against the innocent Christian to justify burning the corpse. One can imagine it brought up memories of her daughter's burning."

De Castro put his folded hands to his face, his pointed forefingers touching his lips. "Well, we cannot have bodies burned in the square with no trial, and it is difficult, though not impossible, to try a dead woman. I see no reason why I cannot put an end to this matter quickly, Enrique. But I am still curious…" He leaned toward Don Enrique so that the two were within arms' reach. "What has this to do with you?"

Enrique could not avoid the question. "Not me, Excellency, but one I love as if she were my own child. I fear that Dominguez, in his fanaticism, will turn his sights on my goddaughter. He has pulled her into his web by insisting she befriend the old woman. Now he may try to shift the blame for the woman's suicide to her. He sees Jews everywhere." He looked at the archbishop's narrow face, letting his eyes settle on the prominent bridge of his nose. The gesture had its intended effect. The archbishop sat back in his chair and let his hands drop.

"We cannot have that, can we, my friend?" de Castro answered, standing up from his chair. "I will send for the priest. In the meantime, do not make yourself such a stranger. You are good company. Perhaps we can set up a hunt. I have a new falcon I'd like to try out," he said, replacing the cap on his head and moving toward the door to signal the visit was over.

"By all means. My skills are rusty, but I would enjoy riding along—and perhaps the rabbit afterwards." He bowed before taking his leave, turning at the door for a final word. "I will send my lawyer when the bequest has been set up. I don't think you will be disappointed."

Padre Dominguez received the archbishop's summons with trepidation. Perhaps he had been hasty in pushing the auto-da-fé for the dead woman. It would be best to see her remains buried quickly now, at least what was left of them after two weeks covered in lime. He had initiated no formal process, talking only with the two priests who had overseen her interrogation and the fat monk. Could he be the source of this mischief? He couldn't imagine how the man would have reached Archbishop de Castro, even if he had mustered the courage to do so. He saw the Armijo woman's hand in this. She had the connections to reach the archbishop. Perhaps her brother, the priest, had involved himself. He tapped his fingers on the desk. He would make the most of this opportunity to meet with the prelate. Perhaps he could even turn him into an ally.

    He walked across the courtyard toward the prison. It was best he dispose of the woman's body himself. He would need a couple of men to remove it and a cart to take the remains to the burial field outside the city. The fat monk could be trusted to keep his mouth shut, so long as he continued to turn a blind eye to the monk's pilfering a few extra loaves for the urchins who lurked around the walls of the Castillo. He must get the body in the ground as soon as he could so there would be nothing to discuss with the archbishop.

Chapter Twenty-One

MARIA LUISA

José Marcos walked briskly toward the *sala*, his hands balled into fists behind his back. How dare his wife summon him as though he were a servant before he'd even had time to dress properly, much less enjoy his *café*? María Luísa's imperious outbursts had increased recently, almost as if she suspected that his heart had strayed. But how could she know such a thing?

"You called for me, my dearest?" he said, forcing his lips into a smile. "Are you well?" He leaned to kiss her on the cheek, but she turned her head abruptly.

María Luísa sat upright in her chair, coldly eying this peacock of a man, his fair curls still uncombed, his face unshaved, which made him oddly more attractive to her at a time when she wished to keep him at some distance. "So, I hear you have been taking your religious duties more seriously of late. May I know what prompts this sudden devotion?"

José Marcos leaned back in his chair, trying not to betray his surprise. He must have been seen at La Giralda. But by whom? And what had they reported? "My dear, I hope I have always taken my devotions seriously. But I am not sure what you're referring to now."

María Luísa stood up, towering over him as he appeared to slouch further into the chair, his arms akimbo like he had not a care in the world. "I think you know very well what I mean. Your little tête-à-tête with Guiomar Péres at the cathedral a few days past."

"Oh, that..." he laughed lightly. "Surely you are not jealous, my love." He had not thought of what he would say if María Luísa found out about his encounter, but what was there to say? Nothing had happened. He stood up and reached out to encircle his wife with his arms, but she slid away. "This is ridiculous, my dear. I ran into the woman by accident. Actually, it was the woman's servant whom I encountered first at the parrot shop."

"Is that why I now have that screeching creature hanging outside my window? Is the moneylender now a procurer too?" She pushed her husband in the chest. *He could not treat her like this. It was enough that he gambled and spent her money on lavish clothes without ever thinking of her.*

José Marcos grabbed her wrist. "I have done nothing to dishonor you, María Luísa. I have not touched another woman since I laid eyes on you. Not that I have not had the opportunity," he added without thinking that he was only making her more jealous. "I love you, *cariña*. I am offended that you would doubt my love." He gripped her wrist tighter as she tried to pull away.

"You are hurting me." María Luísa winced. He dropped her hand instantly, but his eyes frightened her. "So how did this accidental meeting come about? I am curious how you came to be in the same place unplanned," she said, not allowing him to escape so easily.

José Marcos looked at his wife's face. Her heavy brows were furrowed, and her lips pursed, revealing small, vertical lines. He said nothing for a moment, considering his options. He could tell her the truth, that he wanted to warn Guiomar to stay away from the inquisitor after hearing María Luísa's own gossip. Or he could invent a lie and say that she had asked to see him. He cleared his throat and sat back down, again letting his arms fall off the sides of the chair.

"There has been another suicide at the Castillo, as I am sure you know," he said, drawing out his reply as he wove a story close enough to the truth that he would remember it later if necessary. "The slave approached me at the parrot shop," he stopped again, waiting to see her response. Her face did not change, her lips still firmly shut, her brow drawn together unattractively. "She asked if I would speak to her mistress and try to convince her to stay away from the inquisitor."

María Luísa let out a harsh laugh. "That is rich, *mi marido*. As if asking a married man to intervene would help if the woman was under scrutiny by the Holy Office." She took a step closer to her husband, reaching out to pat his head. "You are more of a fool than I thought," she said and turned away.

José Marco wanted to grab her again but refrained. He remained in the chair as his wife disappeared through the archway. He felt vulnerable for the first time since he had been married. This woman, who at first had relieved all his anxieties about his future, now had him in her grip. Why had he not understood when he married her that her wealth would never be his and that she would use it to control him? He was no better than one of the slaves who could be bought and sold at will, made to satisfy his mistress in any way she desired. What if her jealousy made her seek revenge, not just on Guiomar but on him? He ran his fingers through his hair. He could still feel her patronizing touch on his scalp as if he had been branded.

María Luísa entered the *cocina*, a place she rarely set foot in. Two of the servants were preparing something over the stove. She approached the older woman, whom she had often seen talking with the heavyset servant who worked in her sister-in-law's household. The woman had worked in the home of Don Pedro Péres before Guiomar presented her as a wedding gift to María Dolores. It had seemed too generous a gift at the time. Perhaps the woman was sent away because she knew too much about the family.

"Anita, may I have a word with you?" she said, wrinkling her nose at the unfamiliar smell wafting from the large pot on the hearth.

Anita turned around, startled to hear her mistress's voice. "Yes, Señora. Forgive me, I did not hear you approach." She caught the cook's eye as she wiped her hands on a towel. "We were just preparing breakfast for the servants, Señora."

"And what is that odor?" María Luísa asked, relieved that it was not something she would be expected to eat.

"It is tripe, Señora. The intestines of the goat served last evening," Anita said, hoping that she would not be reprimanded for using the offal that was sometimes fed to the pigs. Her mistress's lips tightened in disapproval.

"Next time, cook your meal outside so the smell doesn't foul the whole house," María Luísa said. "Well, are you coming?"

"Move the pot to the courtyard," Anita instructed the other woman, who stood frozen as if hoping she would not attract the Señora's notice, as she followed her mistress into the hall.

"I have often seen you speaking with the servant of Señora Herrera de Madrid," she said, studying the eyes of her own servant. It was sometimes difficult to discern whether slaves were telling the truth. She did not trust them and preferred to bring in young girls from the countryside, but they would often run away or become pregnant.

"Yes, Concha. She was from my same village. But we are not close," she added, which was partly true.

María Luísa studied the woman's face. She could see the worry spread across her brow even though her voice remained calm. "I might want to talk to Concha," she said. "Could you arrange that?" Better not to use Anita as a go-between. She suspected Concha's silence could be bought.

"Of course, Señora. I can invite her if you like." She hesitated again. "Or if you prefer, I could arrange a meeting at the market or perhaps the church?"

"I will think about it and let you know." She turned to leave. "And of course, you will say nothing to anyone," she said, looking back over her shoulder. The woman nodded.

María Luísa would get to the bottom of what was going on between her husband and Guiomar Péres de Armijo. He would be a fool to risk everything for a few moments of pleasure. She knew his eyes strayed, but she would not put up with an affair of the heart.

Concha stood in the plaza in front of the church, where a few parishioners lingered after Mass. She resented being asked to use her few hours of freedom to talk to the haughty wife of Señor Herrera. But Anita had said it would be worth her while.

"What does she want with me?" she'd asked her friend.

"Perhaps she is jealous of your former mistress," Anita had offered.

Concha shifted her weight from one foot to the other, her hips swaying. She had plenty she could tell the woman, but was it wise? Juanito would soon return home with Señor Armijo, and she must think of his future as well as her own grudges. And the Señora had recently been kind to her, giving her news of her son. She would listen to what the woman offered, but she must tread carefully.

"Concha?" María Luísa came up behind the slave, whose heavy rear end undulated like a cow in heat, she observed.

Concha turned quickly, embarrassed she'd been caught off guard. "Señora, how may I assist you?" she asked, curtsying.

"Come, let us walk together," María Luísa said, heading away from the church toward Calle Catalina. "Can I trust you, Concha?" she asked, grabbing the woman's arm. "I am in need of information, and I have reason to believe you may have the very information I seek." She dug her fingers into the woman's flesh, but her face remained placid. "I will pay you, of course. Handsomely."

Concha wanted to pull away but held her stance. "I cannot imagine that I have any information of value to you, Señora. But I will try to help in any way I can." So, it was jealousy that was driving the Señora. Señor Herrera must have strayed. Too bad he had not chosen her.

"I am curious how you came to my sister-in-law's household," María Luísa began tentatively. "Was there a problem in the Péres household?"

Concha suppressed a smile. "I hope there was no problem with me, Señora. But my mistress…" she stopped, lowering her eyes modestly.

"Yes," María Luísa shook her by the elbow, "tell me."

Concha lifted her eyes, staring at the woman who was tall and thin and much older than she had ever noticed. No wonder the lusty Señor Herrera looked elsewhere for his pleasure. But she could not imagine that her former mistress was any better in bed than this scarecrow.

"I do not like to speak ill of those who have treated me well," she said, again averting her gaze downward.

María Luísa thrust a coin into the slave's hand and clamped her fist shut. The woman looked up again, slipping the coin into her pocket.

"I am a good Catholic, Señora. I have been ever since I was brought to this place as a child. I believe in the saints and the Holy Ghost, and I do not want to burn in hell." She made the sign of the cross, kissing her thumb before proceeding. "But before Doña Benita passed away, I noticed things…" She stopped. She had been down this path before with the priest and it had gotten her nowhere. Perhaps she should try another.

"What things, Concha? Are they Judaizers?" María Luísa couldn't conceal her eagerness. She should be quiet and listen, but she felt vindicated. She had warned José Marcos, and he had ignored her wishes and tried to alert his former lover. He would pay for his indiscretion. "What exactly did you see, Concha?"

Concha wished she had stolen a look at the coin. It felt soft to the touch, perhaps it was gold. "I am sorry, Señora," she said, reaching into her pocket. "I cannot accept this," she opened her palm. It was only silver. She put her hand out. María Luísa grabbed it.

"There is more where that came from. Much more if your information proves truthful," María Luísa said, dropping another two silver coins into the slave's palm.

Concha nodded. Perhaps over time, she could earn enough to gain her son's freedom if not her own. She would have to drag out the story, give only a bit at a time. She must win this woman's confidence. Maybe she would take her into her own household.

"I do not know if they were Judaizers, Señora. But they had strange customs, which they tried to hide. After Doña Benita died, the daughter—Guiomar, you know her, I think—began to stick her nose in the *cocina*, always shooing me away so that she could talk to the servant Esperanza alone." She watched the woman's eyes, which glowed with hatred. She had hit a sore spot. "Do you know the woman?"

María Luísa nodded. "I have reason to believe she is implicated," she said. The servant stared dumbly at her. "Involved. The servant is involved."

"It is strange, Señora. My mistress was always jealous of Esperanza when Doña Benita was alive. Doña Benita favored the servant, treating her almost as a member of the family. But after her death, things changed between the two. I think she relied on the woman to teach her what her mother had failed to."

"What exactly did she teach her? Do you know?" María Luísa was growing impatient. Unless the slave could provide details, the information was worthless.

"I sometimes observed them examining the innards of the chickens to be served at the family meal. If they found a deformity, we—the servants—would eat well that night. They gave us the whole bird, not just the offal." She had not realized how lucky she had been in the Péres household until she was given away.

"But what about pork? Did they refrain from eating pork? That would be proof of their Judaizing."

Concha had often thought about the question. Pork was served in the Péres household on important occasions. She had even seen Don Pedro Péres eat it heartily, spearing a thick slice with his fancy *tenedor* and shoving the whole piece into his mouth. "They ate pork, but not often," she said. "I don't think we ever cooked it when they dined alone."

The Señora nodded vigorously. "I see. Yes," María Luísa said. "That makes sense. It helped them avoid detection." What more proof did she need? she wondered. Some had ended up at the Castillo on less evidence, especially if the accuser was a person of some standing. "I won't keep you longer, Concha. You have been helpful. But if anything more occurs to you, reach out to Anita, and I will arrange to meet you again." She turned to go, but the slave reached out as if to detain her before dropping her hand.

"There is one thing more, Señora," Concha said. "I don't know whether I should mention this, but you have been so generous, I feel I must." It was a gamble, but she sensed it was not piety that drove the woman to seek evidence against her former mistress. "Señora Péres was in love with your husband before he met you."

"And how do you know this, Concha?" María Luísa could feel her stomach tightening.

"There was talk that Doña Benita forbid her daughter from marrying him, Señora." She could see the effect of her words on the woman's face.

María Luísa should have expected it despite José Marcos's lies. Guiomar had rejected him, not the reverse. "And do they see each other now?" she asked as if it was only idle curiosity.

"I don't know, Señora," Concha answered, then added, "though I did see them speaking privately at the christening."

María Luísa wanted to strike the woman for her insolence but held back. Better to use her to get revenge on her rival. She would deal with José Marcos in due time.

José Marcos threw his cards on the table, knocking over the newly filled goblet of wine in his anger. He had won two hands early in the game, but now his winnings were gone and he had racked up more debt with the moneylender, whom he had hoped to pay back. He pushed his chair away from the table and stood, unsteady on his feet.

"Sit down, my friend. Your luck will change—and if not…" the dealer smiled, "your credit is always good with me."

The other players laughed.

THE SILVER CANDLESTICKS

"He's ruined the cards," the old man to the dealer's left complained.

"Maybe a fresh deck will change your fortunes," the dealer offered, signaling to the large *Negro* who stood near the door.

José Marcos leaned over the table toward the dealer. "Only if I brought my own cards," he said through clenched teeth.

"There is no need for that kind of talk, Señor. I run a clean game and anyone who says otherwise will lose more than a few gold pieces," the dealer answered, the smile gone from his lips. The *Negro* took a few steps toward José Marcos.

"I'm leaving," José Marcos said, pushing the man aside brusquely.

"You are always welcome back, Señor," the dealer said. "I am happy to take your wife's money."

José Marcos lunged at the man, grabbing him around the throat. But it was the cold steel of a knife at his own throat that made him loosen his grip. The menacing fellow pushed the tip of the blade into his neck until he could feel blood dripping down.

"Let him go," the dealer said, smoothing his shirt collar. The servant wiped the blade on José Marcos's shoulder and put it back in its sheath.

"I shall not forget this," José Marcos said as he stepped back from the table.

"Nor will I," said the dealer. "Perhaps it would be good to find another game, one that suits your skills better," he said, laughing as José Marcos exited through the back door.

José Marcos did not want to return home, and most of the taverns in Santa Cruz were already closed. He walked along the cobblestones, his head bowed. He inhaled, the air moist with a breeze off the river. He wanted to see Guiomar more than anything. She was in danger from his wife's jealousy and the inquisitor's zeal, but there was little he could do to protect her. Perhaps he should have agreed to run away with her all those years ago. Would his life really have been any worse if he had been with the woman he loved even though she could not provide a life of leisure? If they had fled to the New World, he might have made his own way there. Others had made their fortunes starting out with even less. He remembered the emerald ring Guiomar had shown him, enough to pay their passage to Méjico. And there was more she could have taken, she had said.

He had been a fool to reject her. María Luísa was a tyrant. He could not bear to touch her. He turned down the street to the moneylender's shop. The man kept odd hours because of his Sabbath. Perhaps he would be there. He must get more information from the guard at the Castillo, even if he could not pay for it at the moment. If he could convince Guiomar she was in danger, perhaps she would look more favorably on him. Her husband had been gone a long time, after all, and a woman familiar with a husband's desire could be awakened to her own.

María Luísa got up to use the chamber pot. She had not heard her husband return. She threw a shawl over her shoulders and walked down the long hall to his room, tapping lightly on the door. She listened for an answer and then gently opened it. The bed clothes were undisturbed. He had not come home. She walked to his armoire and opened it. She pulled his shirts down and flung them to the floor, then his britches and his coats, made of the finest velvet in rich hues, burgundy and azure and black. She had paid for every one of them so that he could dress like a dandy and seduce other women.

She kicked the pile into the corner of the room. She should open the window and toss them out onto the veranda and set fire to the bunch. It was what he deserved, making a fool of him with that Jew witch. Well, José Marcos would find that his wife would not look the other way as many women did. She would make him pay. She would make them both pay. It was nearly dawn, perhaps not too early to dress and make her way to the Castillo. Her money might not secure the fidelity of a man like José Marcos, but she suspected the priest would be more open to doing her bidding. For the right price.

Chapter Twenty-Two

A DEATH

"Come quickly, Señora. Your father has fallen," Esperanza said, not waiting for her mistress to answer the urgent knock on the door. It was barely dawn, but Esperanza had gone to check on the old man before starting her duties in the kitchen. She'd found him on the floor, his leg twisted beneath him. He was breathing, but his eyes were rolled back in his head. She was afraid to move him and placed a blanket over him before running to her mistress's room.

Guiomar did not even cover herself before racing to her father's side. She knelt beside him in her muslin nightgown, stroking his face. "Get the doctor," she screamed at Esperanza, who looked stricken that she had failed to do so already. "Papá, I am here," Guiomar whispered. She moved her hand to his leg, contorted at an odd angle beneath him as if he had stumbled over himself getting out of bed. She tried to move it gently, but her father's face seized up in agony, though only the whites of his eyes showed through his open lids. He gasped, his chest expanding and contracting, then let out a noise, a rattle in his throat, his lids fluttering for an instant. She put her head to his chest but could hear nothing. He was gone. In reflex, she crossed herself before collapsing on top of him.

Esperanza entered the room to find her mistress sobbing over the body of Don Pedro. She reached down to touch Guiomar, who grabbed her hand so forcefully she nearly pulled Esperanza to the floor.

"What am I to do?" Guiomar looked up at Esperanza's face, streaked with tears. "What am I to do?" It was a question with no answer. She was alone. An orphan now, with no one to protect her. Francisco was across a broad ocean. Her mother was buried in a crypt. And soon, her father would be too. "Help me. Please, help me," she whimpered. "You are all I have left."

Esperanza started to protest that her mistress still had her brother and her *padrino*, but instead, she helped Guiomar to her feet and embraced her. "We must send for the priest. It is important. Now more than ever."

By the time word reached Padre Dominguez that Don Pedro Péres had died, it was too late to pay a call to the daughter. Why had they not alerted him earlier? The family seemed to prefer the old priest at Santa Ana. Yet there was a time, when Señora Péres nearly died after giving birth, that he was the one she asked for. Perhaps he had played his hand foolishly, insisting that she come to the Castillo so often. Now with the suicide of the old woman, he had no hold on her.

He knelt at his prie-dieu. He would pray for the father's soul. The man never struck him as devout—whether Catholic or Jew. He remembered Don Péres stuffing a large slice of ham in his mouth when he had dined at their home. Perhaps it was for show. He had not been invited since the husband sailed for Méjico, but that was understandable. "*In nomine Patris, et Filii*," he muttered under his breath, trying to push worldly thoughts aside, "*et Spiritus Sancti.*"

He fastened the rosary back to the loop on his cincture and was about to retire to his casita when there was a rap at the door. The old lay brother stood silently in the hall and handed him the sealed letter, bowing slightly before retreating. Dominguez stared at the episcopal seal. It was an odd time to receive a message, he thought as he opened the letter. He scanned the page, which was signed by a clerk, not the archbishop. "You are hereby summoned by his Excellency to appear at the *Palacio Arzobispal* immediately following Terce." He did not like the tone of this summons—he was the head of the Holy Office in Sevilla, not some parish priest who could be ordered to appear with no notice or explanation.

He placed the letter on his desk and sank into his chair. Perhaps it was something to do with the suicide. He was glad he had given the body a proper burial, not deserved perhaps, but one for which he could not be faulted. Was the fat monk the cause of this? He dismissed the idea. Maybe it was the Péres de Armijo woman. If so, she had picked a fight she could not win. Her father could not protect her with the worms waiting to devour his body. Nor her husband, who had neither the wealth nor social standing to sway the archbishop.

He would go to the archbishop's residence as directed, but he would not be cowed. Sevilla was becoming more corrupt with every passing year. It could not all be blamed on the Judaizers, whose numbers were dwindling with his efforts. But the effect of their contamination had spread. Adultery, sodomy, prostitution, gambling, and usury were endemic, even among the supposedly upright of the city. His job of saving souls was not done, and he would not let Archbishop de Castro push him aside because he had offended a few sinners.

José Marcos received the news that Don Pedro Péres was dead with, if not outright relief, hope. Guiomar would be the man's only heir, her brother having taken a vow of poverty when he entered the priesthood—that is, assuming Don Péres had not left a substantial bequest to the Church, which he considered unlikely. Now all he had to do was woo her back while her husband was away. He went to his dresser, still in disarray from his argument with his wife, lifted out a silk shirt and held it before him in the mirror. He could not be faulted for paying his respects at the Péres home. He should ask María Dolores to accompany him. A condolence call with his sister would arouse less suspicion. But he did not want to waste time. And if María Luísa learned of it, what else could she do that she had not done already? He picked up the remaining garments and put them on the bed neatly. He would not place them in the armoire, even though it was clear that she had given orders for the servants to leave them on the floor where she had thrown them. His wife was acting like the child that her womb would not produce.

The air was cool in the late afternoon. He considered asking the stable boy to bring the carriage but decided the walk would give him time to think. What would he say to Guiomar? He imagined her sitting in the *sala mayor*, dressed in black taffeta, perhaps the same dress she had worn so many years before when they met at Santa Ana's. He regretted his decision to rebuff her. It was cowardly, as she no doubt believed. But he was younger then and believed that he could make a better match. Love was not a suitable basis for making life's important decisions. But neither was greed, he now realized. Even if he were to convince her of his love, they couldn't entirely escape. If they ran away, it would be in disgrace. They could flee to the New World, but their sordid tale would follow them. And what would she do with her children?

He slowed his pace. He was equidistant now between the Péres house and the Castillo. If he went to the Castillo, he might find the guard who had promised information. With her father gone, Guiomar might be more vulnerable to the inquisitor, especially if her riches could be confiscated. He suddenly felt the need for some wine. He turned onto one of the side streets and headed back toward the square near the church. He could calm his nerves and think before proceeding. Acting before considering the consequences had always been his weakness.

The plaza was nearly empty. Most were just rising from their siestas, and only one small cafe on the plaza had opened its shutters. The bell in the tower struck the fifth hour as he sat at a small table on the cobblestones. The waiter wordlessly brought him a dish of olives. He reached into his pocket to check whether he had taken any coins. It would be embarrassing if he could not pay for a glass of wine. He pulled out a few copper maravedis, all that was left after his disastrous loss at the tables the previous evening.

THE SILVER CANDLESTICKS

Enough for a single glass of cheap wine. He clenched his fists. How had it come to this?

He should strike out on his own, beg his wife for the money to go to Méjico on the promise he would bother her no more. Forget Guiomar. Was he a man or a beggar who must suck from a woman's tit his whole life? Disgusted, he spat the olive pit on the ground.

Esperanza turned the corner onto the plaza. She did not expect to see Señor Herrera sitting there, scowling. It was too late to turn back, but she headed across the plaza quickly, hoping he did not see her. She must make arrangements for the Mass and burial, which could not take place until Alfonso arrived from his monastery. Don Enrique had dispatched a carriage to Ronda to bring him, but it would be a couple of days at least. Guiomar had fretted that her father must be in the earth quickly, but there was no way that would happen without a proper funeral procession and Mass. It was already a problem that Don Pedro had died suddenly, without a priest to administer the Last Rites. There would be talk among their enemies that it was a sign he had sinned in some way, perhaps even that he was a Jew.

"Señorita," José Marcos called out. The servant stopped without turning. He stood up from the table, scraping his chair across the stones.

Esperanza had no choice but to talk to him. "I assume you have heard the news," she said without a greeting.

"Yes. My condolences to your mistress," he said, noting, not for the first time, how comely the *negrita* was.

"I am sorry to be rude, Señor, but I must talk to Padre Saavedra about the funeral arrangements." She nodded her head and turned her back on him before he could protest.

José Marcos's cheeks burned. The slave was insolent.

Guiomar sat beside her father's body, which looked so much smaller in death. She glanced down at her brother's secret book, open to the prayers for the dead. The instructions were confusing.

The prayers, whose words were a mystery, required the presence of ten adult men. What was she to do? She wished her brother were there to guide her. Was it like the Mass, which required a priest to consecrate the Host? She wanted to whisper the words aloud but feared that it would be a desecration. Would her father's soul not ascend to Heaven until the words were spoken by ten men?

She picked the first prayer, which the small book said should be a dying man's last words. "*Shema Yisrael; Adonai Eloheinu Adonai Echad.*" She formed the letters with her mouth, silently reading the transliterated Hebrew. Surely God could hear a woman's voice as easily as a man's, one voice as clearly as ten. "*Baruch Shem Kevod Malchuto Le'olam Va'ed.*" What did they mean, these strange words? She recognized Israel and the call to *Adonai*, the One true God, and the word *Baruch*, which was also said during the Sabbath candle lighting. She would ask her brother to fully explain their meaning when he arrived.

She traced the strange letters in Hebrew printed next to the Roman ones. When her mother died, Alfonso had been by her side, guiding her in what she must do to prepare the body. She had tried to do the same for her father, washing the body from head to toe with Esperanza, though modesty prevented her from uncovering his nakedness. Esperanza had lifted her father's torso to remove his bedclothes and put on fresh linens, which had been stored for this occasion, discarding the old, which she would burn. Guiomar looked at her father, his eyelids held down with coins. She wished to reach out and take his cold hand, but the book described the dead as unclean. Yet it also commanded that it not be left alone, as that would dishonor the person's memory.

It was all so mysterious. She knew the rituals of the Church, the anointing, the prayers. She understood them as well as any lay person could, but these rules were new to her, similar in some fashion to what the Church required—candles at the foot of the body—but different in more ways. A quick burial, no procession or elaborate ceremony with incense and music written specifically for the occasion, only the family and the community gathered each

THE SILVER CANDLESTICKS

evening for seven days to recite prayers, which she neither knew nor was permitted to intone with the men. But she had no community of believers to turn to. No one to comfort her in her grief and instruct her in the way of mourning. If only she had Francisco by her side.

"I came as quickly as I could, *m'hija*," Don Enrique said as he entered the room, startling Guiomar, whose back was turned. "I have sent word to Francisco, which should reach him before the month is out, and I have sent a carriage for Alfonso." He reached out to take his goddaughter's hand, squeezing it gently. His old partner was no longer the lion he had been in his youth but a lamb: white, silent, easy prey for any wolves who might attack him or his family.

"Your father and I were like brothers. We loved each other, but we were not always at ease in the other's presence. I regret that in recent years, we had grown apart. I let business get in the way of more important considerations...."

Her *padrino*'s voice trailed off. Guiomar had tried to be a buffer between the two men after her father retired. But in the last year, as her father's mind deteriorated, she kept Don Enrique at some distance in deference to what would have been her father's pride if he were capable of such in his diminished state.

"I have sent my servant to discuss the arrangements with Padre Saavedra," she said. "I wish to bury him as soon as possible."

"But you should not put him in the crypt too quickly, Guiomar," he said. "And what of Alfonso? Will you not wait for him?"

Guiomar looked down, shocked to realize that the small book her brother had given her still lay open in her lap. If Don Enrique had noticed, he didn't let on. She closed it, kissing it, and making the sign of the cross as if it were a prayer book. Which, of course, it was, but not the sort she should be consulting in front of anyone, even her godfather, considering their recent discussion about the Dominican. She slipped the book into her pocket and stood up.

"You are now my only father" she said, throwing her arms around Don Enrique's neck.

Yes, but could he protect her? Enrique wondered. He would do his best, but it might not be enough. She had enemies—including perhaps the most dangerous one, herself. She was careless. What if someone else had seen her little book? His aging eyes were weak, but even he could see the strange letters on the page. Who else might come across this damning evidence? The slave seemed devoted to her, but might she not trade information for her freedom? It was all the inquisitor would need to put Guiomar into his dungeons, and even Rodrigo de Castro would not stand in the way.

"I have news, *m'hija*," he said, his memory jogged. "I spoke with the archbishop. He will deal with Dominguez—but we must be careful not to give him any cause to pull back. Do you understand me?" he asked, holding her out at arms' length. She cast her eyes down, blushing. "Now fetch me a glass of wine, *m'hija*," he said, kissing her on the cheek. "I will stay with your father a bit. I have some things I need to say to him, even if he cannot hear me."

Guiomar slipped out of the room, relieved that her *padrino* would take her place by his body. Did he know the custom that the dead must be attended at all times? She must take her children to see their grandfather, though it pained her to think of their reaction.

She stopped by the nursery and found one of the servants on the floor entertaining the two boys, Esperanza's and her own, as Úrsula sat quietly in the corner, wrapping her doll in a piece of black cloth. "Don Enrique is in with the body, Blanca. Will you bring him a glass of wine? I will take the children to say goodbye to their *abuelo* now."

"If he's dead, how will he hear me?" Antonio asked, looking up.

"He is in heaven, my child, and can see and hear everything. Even better than when he was with us," Guiomar said, though she didn't believe it herself. "Now put away your toys and come with me. You too, Úrsula," she said.

The look on Esperanza's son's face made Guiomar stop in her tracks. "Would you like to come, Benito?" The boy nodded eagerly. The days ahead would be difficult as she buried her father with only Esperanza by her side each day. Esperanza had been as much a mother to Antonio and Úrsula as she herself had ever been. Now it was her turn to embrace the slave's child. She reached out to take the boy's hand. "Well, let us hurry. It is nearly time for your dinner."

Padre Dominguez sat outside the large oak doors that led to the archbishop's private office. Though he had left immediately after Terce as ordered, he had taken his time getting to the palace. Now it was he who had to wait. It had already been a half hour, as the cathedral bells alerted him. How much longer must he sit here like a supplicant? A few priests came and went. A servant walked by, carrying a large silver coffee set with only one cup. Dominguez shifted in his chair, hoping to catch the man's eye. But the priest stared straight ahead as he opened the door just enough to slip through without offering a glimpse inside.

The priest looked around at the heavily paneled walls of the anteroom, the wood carved in intricate designs. Ornate paintings in gilt frames adorned the walls. Dominguez preferred the stark Castillo with its whitewashed walls and unupholstered chairs. The life of the soul demanded sacrifice. De Castro had taken the same vows of poverty, yet he lived in the lap of luxury in a palace created for the Moors. The place still bore the arches and pillars of the *Mudéjar* style, the walls painted in the colors of the infidels. Putting a gilded painting of the Virgin on the wall could hardly sanctify this place.

"The archbishop will see you now," said the priest who had delivered the coffee, motioning him through the large doors.

Dominguez stood silently as Rodrigo de Castro put lumps of sugar in his coffee and stirred it with a tiny spoon. He shifted weight from one foot to the other, but the archbishop did not look up. Finally, he lifted his eyes and motioned Dominguez to the chair on the other side of the table.

"Sit, Padre. I would offer you coffee, but I hear that you are a man of very austere habits, which is befitting of your office. Am I right?" Dominguez nodded, his lips turning up slightly, but whether a smile or a smirk, de Castro couldn't tell. "I am sure you are wondering what matter was so urgent that I summoned you on such short notice. My apologies, but I did not do so lightly. It seems that your..." he stopped, searching for the right word, "zeal, let us say, has some wondering whether you have gone too far in your mission to root out heretics." De Castro observed the priest's lips turn upward again, this time with no mistake about their meaning. The man was as impertinent as he was smug.

"If the recent unfortunate suicide within the Castillo is the cause, your Excellency, I hope you will allow me to explain." He wondered who could have aroused the archbishop's interest in the old woman, though he suspected it could be none other than Señora Armijo. "As your Excellency knows, the woman's daughter committed suicide after the mother accused the girl of Judaizing under questioning. I hoped that the mother's soul could be saved, so I called upon another woman whom I believed could help and, in the process, perhaps aided in nourishing her own faith in the one true religion." He waited a moment before proceeding. "You must know the woman or her family. Señora Péres de Armijo, whose father was a wealthy merchant in Triana. The man died yesterday, may God have mercy on his soul."

The archbishop ran his tongue along his lower teeth, which ached from the sugary coffee. "Do you have reason to question Señora Péres' faith—or the state of her father's soul?" he said, spitting a coffee ground from the tip of his tongue onto the saucer. So Don Enrique had been correct. This zealot had the Péres woman in his sights, and the burning of this poor soul's corpse was merely an excuse to seek an intervention.

"I am concerned with all the souls under my jurisdiction, your Excellency," Dominguez replied quickly.

"All the souls, Padre? Does that include my own? And what about yours?" de Castro asked, spitting out another ground.

"My own soul I leave to Our Lord and Savior to judge. And I would not presume to judge your Excellency."

"Who said anything about judging, Padre? You take offense too easily." He could see what Don Enrique found so dangerous about

THE SILVER CANDLESTICKS

the inquisitor, who suspected heresy in every soul he encountered. "This matter has come to my attention because—under your jurisdiction, indeed your very own roof—we have had two suicides. If we are in the business of saving souls, Padre, the worst thing that can happen is to precipitate the one unforgivable sin against the Holy Ghost, which suicide is the clearest manifestation of. Do you not agree?" He stared hard at the priest, whose faint color drained from his pale face until he appeared as white as an ibis.

"No, I do not," Dominguez said too quickly and too loudly. "Begging your pardon, your Excellency, but if I erred, it was in assuming that Señora Péres would be a good influence on the old woman. Instead, she corrupted her with promises of taking her into her home and then reneging. Something I doubt you have heard from her lips."

The archbishop studied the inquisitor's face. He saw malice—the nostrils flared, the eyes dilated. Dominguez looked more like a marble death mask than a living visage. "I have not had the pleasure of meeting Señora Péres, Padre, though I knew her father as an acquaintance and benefactor of the Church. I understood that the Señora was also *your* benefactor after the flood. Am I wrong?" The priest's upper lip quivered, bringing his face to life, making it more malevolent in the process.

Dominguez realized he had misspoken, even if his words were God's truth. He could not afford to make an enemy of the archbishop, especially in the coming days, if he was to proceed against the Péres woman. "I beg your pardon, your Excellency," he said, bowing his head. "I should not have spoken without telling you the full facts of the case. I have good reason to believe that the Péres household practices the Hebrew faith. I have one living witness against Señora Péres. The other, unfortunately, was Inés Mejia, who I suspect may have taken her own life because the woman tried to reinforce her Hebrew faith. If I launch an investigation, I will ascertain whether others in the Péres household were involved in such heresy." He leaned forward in his chair. "The Holy Office does not need your permission to begin proceedings, though I would hope to have your blessing."

De Castro stood up and moved toward the insolent priest, bending over to grab the armrests on the man's chair. He could smell his foul breath and the odor of sweat emanating from his tattered woolen habit. "Be careful, Padre. You start down this road at your peril. Your evidence had better be good. I do not want to hear a word of this leaking out. Nor do I want to hear of anyone put to the rack to gain evidence. Do you understand?" He let go of the arms and stood hovering over the priest, whose skin had taken on a tint of greenish grey, as if the bile in his liver had bubbled up to his face.

Dominguez nodded, controlling the urge to scoff outright. He might not have the prelate's blessing, but de Castro himself perhaps had reasons not to step in the Holy Office's way. He looked around the archbishop's palatial office, the gilded paintings, thick carpets and fine tapestries, the heavy silver coffee setting, and the rings on the man's fingers, emeralds and rubies as big as finches' eggs. The Péres' wealth was reason enough to pursue the case with the father dead and the husband, no man of independent means, away on business. Why should their gold and silver end up in a vain woman's hands rather than in the Church's coffers? He stood and proceeded to the door, when the archbishop's voice stopped him.

"And no more burning corpses at the stake, Padre. It is uncivilized."

Chapter Twenty-Three

THE TRAP

Padre Dominguez had not personally met Señora López de Herrera before, but he knew the fleshy servant who sat next to her across the table. She had come to him years earlier with tales of Judaizing in the Péres home. Perhaps he had been wrong to dismiss her, though she seemed both sly and concupiscent, someone to be kept at a distance even if her information was useful.

Concha listened as the Señora laid out her case. "I cannot say I am surprised at your information, Señora," Dominguez said. "But we need more than the word of a disgruntled servant who was dismissed from the household," he added, eyeing Concha, who seethed at his words.

Why did the Señora not also mention adultery? she wondered. That would be enough to stir this celibate's loins. He looked like a man who paid to peek from behind the curtains at couples writhing in the marriage bed. "If I may, Padre," Concha leaned forward. "I have other information that may be of interest. Señora López de Herrera is too delicate to bring it up."

María Luísa reached out and pulled the woman back. "It is not delicacy, Padre. What this woman is alluding to is that Señora Péres and my husband were lovers before my marriage and her own. The two have been seen together recently. Perhaps it is nothing. But I suspect you will find out for yourself."

There. It was done. She could not take it back. José Marcos would pay for his wandering eye. He would not only lose her and the life she had provided, he could also be investigated by the Holy Office. He would not last five days in the dungeon, much less five minutes on the rack. She could be rid of him, the marriage annulled if necessary.

Dominguez nodded. He could not have hoped for so much. His case would be much stronger with Señora López de Herrera ready to denounce her own husband in order to ensnare Señora Armijo. And what could the archbishop do if the sins were carnal as well as heretical? He had often found the two went hand in hand. Jews seemed to have an appetite for sin. And why should they honor their marriage vows when they were entered under false pretenses? Did not the Hebrew patriarchs take more than one wife? Concubines as well?

María Luísa watched as the priest's mouth worked as though chewing a piece of tough meat. "Will I be called on to give witness against my husband?"

"There will be time to decide about that. I hope to spare you the embarrassment if possible," he answered. "We shall see."

Concha could hardly contain herself. At last she would have her revenge. And it was not only the Jew but the woman's favorite, Esperanza, who would pay. Perhaps even the slave's child.

A cold chill went down her spine. She had forgotten her own son in the heat of her anger. What would become of him? He was due back soon, but until then, he was employed by Señor Armijo. "I beg your forgiveness, Padre. There is one other matter I must mention." The priest's head jerked up, his eyes fastening on hers.

"What now?" he said, anxious to get the two women out of his office, especially the slave whose breasts swelled when she spoke.

"My son is returning from Méjico with Señor Armijo. They are expected in a matter of weeks. He may have information that would be helpful to your investigation. But if they are forewarned, he may become a hostage."

"Do you think I am an idiot, woman? I do not intend to advertise my investigation. The accused are always the last to know." He stood abruptly and stepped out from behind the desk.

"Señora," he said, bowing to María Luísa. "Thank you for coming forward. I will make it as easy on you as I can. But I have no doubt your faith will sustain you," he said, making the sign of the cross on her forehead.

"And I will not forget the Holy Office and the Church in my will. As you know, I have no children and my husband is not worthy to inherit my estate if he survives me," María Luísa said, reaching out her hand to the priest, who seemed to hesitate before taking it. Unpleasant man, she thought. But useful.

Dominguez crossed the courtyard. He could smell the baking bread, and his stomach growled. One could not always control the body, which responded to the senses before the mind could discipline it, like the tumescence that grew between his legs at the most inappropriate times. At least he had not experienced that indignity when the black-skinned temptress sat before him this time, as he had before. He must think through his plan carefully. He would need at least two witnesses against Señora Péres, but it would be prudent to enlist more than the minimum. Her father was dead, but she had other patrons, and who knew what riches her husband had acquired during his stay in Méjico. Brother Tomás would be a reluctant witness, but the fellow was none too bright and might be tricked into saying something useful.

"Good afternoon, Brother," Dominguez called out as the monk pulled a wooden paddle laden with loaves from the oven. The man turned quickly, nearly losing his precious cargo, which slipped dangerously close to the edge of the tilted paddle.

"Padre, I didn't hear you coming. Let me just tidy up here," Tomás said, removing his apron, which was smeared with grease and sprinkled with flour. The priest never brought good news, and Tomás had more than usual reason to fear his appearance. He wiped his hands on the apron and put a light cloth over the bread to keep the flies away. "To what do I owe this pleasure, Padre?"

"I have just come from an interesting conversation with two women who are concerned about the decline in our morals in Sevilla. A sad story, really. The one, a wealthy widow who has married a man whose eye wanders where it shouldn't."

Tomás slipped his hand into the pocket of his habit. The letter he had received from Toledo that morning was still unread. He was waiting until he could retire to his cell before perusing its contents. It filled him with both anticipation and dread. He had made serious allegations against Padre Dominguez, but unless the priest was a better actor than those who performed in the *autos sacramentales*, the man knew nothing of the complaints yet.

"I will pray for her, Padre, and her errant husband," he said, but felt something amiss. The priest was not known to engage in idle gossip. "You have many burdens, Padre. You carry the weight of the many sinners on your shoulders. I will keep you in my prayers too," he said. But from the look on the inquisitor's face, the words gave more offense than solace.

"Yes, well, prayers are always appreciated, but I had hoped I might get something more useful from you," Dominguez said, shooing away a fly that hovered above the aromatic loaves. "Your close friendship with Señora Mejia may be helpful to the investigation I wish to launch." The monk pulled back as soon as the words were out of Dominguez's mouth. But it couldn't be helped. He must pursue the truth.

"You know the role Señora Péres de Armijo played in the old woman's suicide. I had been willing to look the other way, to think perhaps she took her life because Señora Péres had withdrawn her offer to live in her household. But now I fear there was more to it."

Tomás trembled. Did the priest learn of his visit to Señora Péres and his warning? He had spies everywhere. Who knew whom to trust? "I don't understand," he said, the words barely audible even to himself.

"Did Señora Mejia ever say anything to you about her benefactress? Anything? The slightest detail might be important. I know you wish to clear Señora Mejia's name. Perhaps there is a way to accomplish both our aims." Dominguez put his hand on the monk's fat shoulder.

"I...I...I...don't recall her speaking of Señora Péres," he stammered. "But we only exchanged a few words, 'good morning,' 'bless you,' that kind of thing."

Dominguez let his hand drop from the shaking man's shoulder. The monk was not as big a fool as he had hoped. "And yet you were so distraught at her death and so intent on giving her a Christian burial," he said. He would throw him a bone. "I relented on the Montelongo woman as a favor to you. I ordered her interred, after all," he stared at the monk's quivering face, which showed only fear. "If anything occurs to you, a stray word or a request for a special prayer, for example, please come to my office." He snatched the cloth from the loaves. "They must cool properly if they are to form a good crust," he remarked.

Brother Tomás felt sick to his stomach as the priest turned his back to leave. Each time the inquisitor wanted to accuse a woman of Judaizing lately, Dominguez had sought his help. Was he so obviously of weak character that the priest thought he could be made to provide false testimony? He had done nothing to encourage such judgment, surely, and had resisted each time Dominguez sought to involve him in his schemes. Yet the priest continued to press. Perhaps he thought Tomás could be manipulated more easily because he was uneducated, unlike the others who served in the Castillo. Or maybe it was his wide girth. Yes, he had his weaknesses when it came to sneaking a bit of bread or savoring the scraps left by others when it was his turn to clear the plates from the refectory. But these were small sins that would not cost him his immortal soul.

He reached in his pocket and pulled out the letter he'd been carrying all day. He must face the consequences of his temerity.

We have received your complaint about the Grand Inquisitor of Sevilla, Padre Diego Dominguez. At this time, we see no reason to pursue the matter. Padre Dominguez has been a zealous defender of the One True Faith, which remains under assault by those who would hide their perfidy under the cloak of piety. His methods, though perhaps unorthodox, have saved countless souls from perdition. You would do well to follow his example. Yours in Christ...

Tomás' hands trembled as he folded the letter and returned it to his pocket. What had he accomplished, except expose himself to the wrath of his superiors? How had he imagined that the prior of the Order would take his word above Dominguez's? Now he too might become a target of the Inquisition. It did not happen often that the Church pursued Judaizers among the religious orders, especially not those who came from humble backgrounds like himself and were unlikely to be Jews in the first place. But his superiors might imagine him one of the Protestant heretics that had lately sprung up in France and elsewhere. He must be careful to give Dominguez no cause to view him as other than an ignorant fool.

José Marcos knocked on the door of the Péres house, still unsure exactly what he would say to Guiomar. He was thankful that the servant who opened it was not the haughty one who had rebuffed him in the plaza outside the Church of Santa Ana. It had been so long since he had been a guest here that the *esclava* seemed not to know who he was, but she invited him into the *sala* and said she would let her mistress know that the gentleman wished to see her.

José Marcos looked around the room, which had changed little since his occasional past visits with his sister. Too bad she was no longer as close to Guiomar since the two women had married. But many of Guiomar's friends had cut her off when she married Francisco Armijo, a union that had shocked everyone in their circle. He still stiffened at the thought of her in the candlemaker's arms. He was beneath her.

"Señor Herrera, how may I help you?" Esperanza stood in the arched doorway that led to the small room off the foyer. José Marcos spun around at the sound of her voice, frowning.

He looked at the beautiful slave who stood as tall as he, her hands folded against her skirt. "I must see the Señora," he said, refusing to convey more.

"She is indisposed, Señor. Perhaps you can tell me the subject you wish to discuss, and we can arrange a more suitable occasion."

Her mistress had been frightened when Blanca brought word of her guest. "How could he dare to come here directly? Tell him I won't see him."

José Marcos looked the woman up and down. She did not know her place. Guiomar had been too gentle with her, which served neither woman well. "It is not a matter I can discuss with an intermediary," he said, choosing his words carefully. "When I tell her, she will understand the need for discretion." He planted himself in place with no intention of leaving. "You would do your mistress a great service by telling her that I have urgent news to discuss."

The man was exasperating, Esperanza thought, but she could not afford to offend him lest it cause problems for Guiomar. "Sit down, sir. I will bring you some *café*. It may be a while since the Señora was not expecting guests."

Guiomar must be right, she thought. This move was too bold to be trivial. She entered her mistress's room to find her pacing the floor.

"What does he want?"

"He would not tell me, Señora. He says he must speak to you directly." The desperate look on her mistress's face made her add, "It could just be his vanity."

"Well, he is certainly vain. But he wouldn't risk offending his wife by coming here if his own interests were not at stake." Every time she had let him back into her heart even a little, he had hurt and disappointed her. He could claim he loved her all he wanted, but she knew she could not trust him.

"Take your time, Señora. The longer he waits, the surer we can be that he is not simply amusing himself with a flirtation. And it would not be good to have the servants see you eager to greet him."

"You are wise beyond your years, Esperanza. Certainly, wiser than I," Guiomar said, glad to have her as a friend and protector. "I think you should remain with us when we meet, even if he objects. It will provide a witness to whatever transpires. In these times, we cannot be too careful."

José Marcos finished his coffee and was beginning to be annoyed at the time it took for Guiomar to appear when he looked up to see her, radiant, in the doorway. Was it his visit that made her eyes shine so, her face flush? He walked toward her to take her hand when he saw the slave hovering behind her. "I had hoped we could have some privacy, Guiomar," he said, stifling the urge to address her even more intimately.

"It would not be…" Guiomar struggled to find the right word, "…proper. As you have warned me, I am under suspicion. I must not give the Dominican excuses to accuse me of untoward behavior."

She was always a clever girl, José Marcos had to admit. "But how do you know, my dear, whom you can trust?" he said, his eyes moving toward the servant.

"Exactly," said Guiomar.

José Marcos laughed. "I am serious, my love," he said, the words slipping out before he could catch himself. He looked furtively at the slave, who appeared nonplussed. "My wife seeks to make trouble for you. She has discovered that I am still in love with you—"

"Stop, Señor," Guiomar recoiled from José Marcos's tone. "You dishonor me with your loose talk. I am a happily married woman, as I have told you every time you have approached me." Her voice rose in anger as she considered what a danger he posed.

José Marcos fell to his knees, reaching out to grab Guiomar's hem. "I cannot help that I love you. I know I have done nothing

THE SILVER CANDLESTICKS

to deserve you, but you must believe me. You are the world to me. I would never do anything to harm you, which is why my wife is so jealous."

Guiomar looked down at his upturned face, tears streaming down his cheeks. Could it be that he truly loved her? She looked at Esperanza, whose face grimaced at what was unfolding.

"I should go, Señora," Esperanza said barely above a whisper, but before she could escape, her mistress grabbed her arm.

"No. You must guard my honor," she said, shaking herself loose from José Marcos's groveling. "Stand up, Señor. These displays insult me. You should leave. Now."

José Marcos lifted himself up slowly, his eyes fixed on Guiomar's. Was it her pride speaking or had her love truly dissipated? He could read only anger, her pupils dilated, small lines emanating from the frown on her lips. He had misjudged the situation. She would be no help to him in fleeing his overbearing wife unless he was honest. To a point, at least.

"You have put me in an awkward situation, Guiomar. I love you, truly I do, more than I have ever loved anyone. You are the only person who truly understands me. Now my love for you has made my life untenable with María Luísa, who just this morning threatened to throw my clothes from the window and has forbidden me to return. I have nothing and nowhere to go," he said, hanging his head.

Guiomar knew that she should shove him toward the door. But she had already earned his wife's enmity and could scarcely afford to make an enemy of him as well. Better to be generous in the hope that it might buy his silence. Perhaps she could even encourage him to leave Sevilla.

"There was a time when I would have done anything for you," she said, lifting his chin with her forefinger. "Do you remember?" she asked, staring into his eyes, which looked green in the late afternoon light. He nodded, but she detected no embarrassment in what should have been a shameful memory of his own cowardice. "At that time, I was willing to part with the emerald my father gave me so that we could make our way to the New World."

José Marcos shifted his weight from his heels to the balls of his feet. Guiomar would make him pay for his fickleness, but if the price was right, he would prostrate himself at her feet. Apparently it was his fate always to be a supplicant before these rich, haughty women.

"Wait here," Guiomar said, leaving Esperanza behind to watch him. She walked quickly down the hallway to her bed chamber. Pulling a set of keys from her pocket, she went directly to the wardrobe, pushing a panel that revealed a hidden drawer. She unlocked the drawer and pulled it from the chest, throwing its contents on the bed. The large emerald in its heavy gold setting rolled across the damask. She slipped the ring on her finger and put the other jewelry back in the drawer. Then she replaced it, locking it again before sliding the panel back in place.

José Marcos kept a firm grip on the ring in his pocket as he made his way to Santa Cruz. Guiomar's generosity belied her professions of indifference. If she did not still love him, she could have easily appeased him with a less valuable gift. No, it was a parting message. She could not tell him she loved him in words, but her gift was meant to convey her feelings. Too bad he had not been able to embrace her, to awaken her desire, which he had no doubt was still there beneath her cool demeanor. But the slave had insisted on staying by her side and wordlessly showing him to the door.

He was relieved the moneylender was in. He wanted to waste no time leaving Sevilla before his wife got wind of his visit to the Péres household. The old man eyed the emerald suspiciously, holding it up to a candle to see the refraction in its cut.

"I take it you have not come by this dishonestly, Señor?" Jorge asked, as if he believed he would tell him the truth.

"It was a gift. Do not try to cheat me because you doubt its provenance," José Marcos said, slamming his fist on the table. "I came by it honestly. A gift from a woman who cannot bear to see me suffer. She wishes to free me from this place," he said wistfully. "And if she was free herself, I have no doubt she would join me."

Jorge smiled. So he had gone begging to Señora Péres. Surely the woman was wise to buy him off, even if the cost was high. The emerald was of fine quality, its weight hefty as a river pebble. If he paid Herrera even half its value, it would see him to Veracruz and establish him there for some time. But the indolent young man would likely fail unless he could find some rich, neglected matron there whose favor he could curry with his looks.

"I am not sure what I can do with such a ring, Señor. Its resale will be difficult, as no doubt someone would recognize the stone. There are few this fine in all of Sevilla. Who knows, your wife might even learn of it and come banging at my door."

"I told you, I did not take it from my wife," he said, grabbing the moneylender by the collar.

"Settle down, Señor, I didn't say you did. It's just that a stone like this is likely to raise questions, so I cannot possibly give you what it is worth."

"Cheat me, will you, Jew?" José Marcos spat the words in the moneylender's face. "Perhaps I should pay a visit to the Castillo instead?"

Jorge took Herrera's fist in his hand, removing his fingers from his collar one by one. "I wouldn't be spending too much time with the inquisitor if I were in your shoes, Señor. I hear that he is as scrupulous about hunting down adulteresses as he is Hebrews. And if he can find one who is both, well, he will light the pyres himself." If the man had any feelings for the Péres woman, he would take what was offered and disappear. For good.

José Marcos stuffed the leather pouch filled with gold inside his jacket. He considered returning home for his clothes but thought better of it. He could buy some clothing near the port, nothing fancy. The money would have to last him until he could make his own way. He had heard that Méjico was a land of great opportunity. If he was lucky, he might even return to Sevilla one day in style, a beautiful woman on his arm, maybe even a wife once María Luísa died. Until then, he must be frugal and leave the cards and dice behind in the alleys of Sevilla.

Part V
AUGUST 1597

Chapter Twenty-Four

FRANCISCO'S RETURN

Francisco waited at the dock as the sailors unloaded the cargo. He watched the men lift the heavy trunks, their muscles glistening with sweat in the afternoon sun. Their ship had arrived early that morning after the three-day journey up the Guadalquivir from Cádiz, the gateway inland from the sea. He was anxious to get home to Guiomar, but he not want to act any differently than he might on an ordinary journey.

In the six weeks he'd been at sea, he'd had no word from his wife, only the mysterious letter she had sent him in Veracruz and the even more worrisome one from Don Enrique he had received en route. He had hoped that someone in the household would be checking the docks every day for his arrival, but so far none had approached him. He feared that might mean Guiomar was already imprisoned in the Castillo, but he knew the port was especially busy with a convoy from Perú bearing gold and silver for the royal mint, so perhaps she was somewhere down the docks. He paced back and forth, yelling occasionally when one of the sailor's steps did not quicken as he carried a smaller trunk down the gangplank. It was one thing for the men to struggle under the burden of silver bars, but another when the wooden crates contained maize or chocolate or coffee. The gangly youth, Juan, was one of the worst laggards.

"Pick up your pace, Juan," he shouted, catching the boy's eye. He expected to see anger or resentment, but the eyes were blank, reflecting no emotion, nothing, as dark and inert as a chunk of coal. He had considered leaving him behind to return with another ship but thought better of it when he remembered his surly mother, Concha, who still might do the family harm.

"Señor Francisco," Esperanza called out as she made her way through stacks of wooden boxes toward her master. He turned around quickly, nearly knocking over a boy who darted between cargo and sailors at high speed. She could see his look of surprise turn to relief then anxiety in the few seconds it took her to reach him.

"What news do you have?" he asked without any attempt at the usual pleasantries.

"Señora Guiomar and the children are well, Señor, thank Our Lord. And you?"

He breathed a deep sigh and broke into a smile, which made her wish the Señora could see him as the loving, good man he surely was.

"I am so happy to hear it, Esperanza. I am well and will be home in a couple of hours. I need to go by the Casa de Contratación to submit the record of my inventory, but I will be along quickly. Please tell your mistress that…that my trip was a huge success." It was better not to say anything more. If he treated his early homecoming as nothing special, it would arouse less suspicion.

Everything he did from this moment forward must be careful. He was full of questions about the household, but they would wait until he was safely in the confines of his home. Indeed, they would wait until he and Guiomar were alone and in each other's arms.

Esperanza walked across the bridge to Triana, keeping as brisk a pace as she could without drawing attention. Still, it took her more than an hour. When she entered the gate, she saw the Señora peering from the window. The door flew open and Guiomar rushed towards her.

"Is he here?" Guiomar whispered.

THE SILVER CANDLESTICKS

"He is," Esperanza smiled, reaching out to take her mistress's hands. "And he looks very well. If I may say so, Señora," she squeezed the soft flesh, "he looks quite handsome."

Guiomar laughed and pulled Esperanza to her. "You are always playing the matchmaker with me and my husband," she said, planting a kiss on Esperanza's cheek. "Did he say anything? When will he be home?"

"He is going to the Contratación first and then he will be home. He said to tell you that the trip was a success." Guiomar's forehead wrinkled in response to her words. "Of course, he first asked about you and the children. I think he was being cautious with his words and actions, Señora."

"I'm sure you're right," Guiomar replied, but still she felt a pang of—what—disappointment? "We must prepare a big meal in honor of his return. Not for tonight, it is too late. But tomorrow. Please send word to my *padrino*, and who else?" She shuddered despite the warm air. "Should we invite the devil himself?"

"Not tomorrow, it would be too soon," Esperanza said firmly. "You should plan a large dinner in perhaps a week's time. You could send the invitations tomorrow. And you are right about the inquisitor. He should be on the list if you hope to win favor with him. He would see it as an insult if you did not invite him."

Guiomar wondered where Esperanza's wisdom came from. Of course, she had been brought up in the same household and taught by the same woman. But still, Esperanza seemed wise beyond her years or experience—wiser than herself, she had to admit, feeling a twinge of the old jealousy.

"Tell the servants to prepare a festive meal for us this evening, but it will be intimate, just Francisco and myself. Now I must prepare for his homecoming, Esperanza," she said, turning to go to her room. What should she wear, she wondered? She ran her fingers through her hair. She had not washed it since her last bath after she finished bleeding the previous month. It was too late to do anything about it now. She should have been getting ready all week. She recalled how she had primped and fretted over her appearance when she was younger—and when she was in love. But didn't Francisco deserve her best?

She threw open the door to her wardrobe. She would look foolish if she chose a gown meant for a formal occasion, but she wanted to be appealing to her husband and honor him by making it clear that she cared enough to pick something special. She touched the silk of an emerald dress cut simply with a modest neckline and small buttons down the front. She pulled it from the wardrobe and laid it on the bed. It was the same green as the ring she had given José Marcos. Was he already on his way to the New World as her husband returned? There had been no news from María Dolores.

But then, why would there be? If José Marcos had indeed fled, the family would feel the sting of scandal. She had seen none of them since her father's funeral, but Santa Ana's was not their preferred church though they lived nearby. She imagined his wife, María Luísa, in her fine gowns at the cathedral when the archbishop offered Mass.

She picked up the dress and held it in front of her, observing herself in the mirror. The color was not the most flattering now that her skin had turned sallow. She pinched her cheek with her free hand, hoping color would rise, but nothing could erase the small lines that had formed across her brow or in the space between her nostrils and the edges of her lips. She smiled, which made the latter disappear into the natural fold of her cheeks. She must learn to smile more. Even if smiles made the lines deeper, they gave her face the appearance of youth, not the care-worn visage that reflected the terror she felt as she awaited word from the Castillo.

"Mamá?"

Úrsula stood in the doorway. Guiomar had not heard the door open. The child stood rigidly, waiting for permission to enter.

"Come in, child," Guiomar said, trying to stifle her annoyance at being caught in a private moment. She had tried to love this child as best she could, building a bond with her over the canaries, although it had dissipated as she herself grew bored with them.

Nothing could consume her interest for long as she struggled to keep her worry about the inquisitor in check.

She reached out to take Úrsula's small hand, kissing it as she sat on the edge of the bed, the green silk gown still draped over one arm. "Your Papá is coming home, *m'hija*! Are you happy?" The girl's sad eyes remained doleful even as her lips turned upward. "We must find you a pretty dress to wear for your Papá. He will barely recognize you, you've grown so big. And where is your brother? We must tell him the news as well."

The child reached over to stroke the rich, green fabric. She was such a taciturn child, rarely speaking except to answer a direct question. Yet she was already learning to write her letters and, according to Esperanza, loved stories before she went to sleep. Úrsula was nothing like her mother, neither in her physical appearance nor her manner. Was that why she found her hard to love? At least Antonio looked like her family, tall for his age, with the self-assured gaze that let everyone know he was special. "Let's go find him, shall we?" She put the dress down and led her daughter into the hall.

Chapter Twenty-Five

BARRIO SANTA CRUZ

*P*adre Dominguez closed the ledger and stood up from behind his table. The two inquisitors remained seated, their heads bowed. The older one fingered his rosary, the folds of his habit bunched between his knees. The younger priest, a recent addition to the Castillo, looked as if he was holding his breath, his face beginning to turn red.

"Is this all you have for me?" Dominguez tapped his long, thin finger on the ledger with irritation. Before either could answer, he bellowed, "What am I supposed to do with this? You've given me nothing on the woman. Has she no enemies you could interrogate?"

"But, Padre," the younger man raised his eyes briefly, "we have always relied on others to come forward. It has never been our practice—"

"Are you telling me what our practice has been? Remind me. How long have you been here?" Dominguez leaned across the table, shoving the book toward the priest.

"I was speaking, of course, of our Order, Padre. The prior sent me..."

"*Idioto*, you think I don't know why you were sent? To spy on me and report back to the archbishop, as if I, not the Judaizers, were a threat to the Church. Get out. Both of you," he shouted. The two men quickly rose, bowing slightly as they retreated from his office.

THE SILVER CANDLESTICKS

He could still inspire fear if not the respect he was due. He had the testimony of the lusty slave and her mistress, which could still prove useful. But he needed more. Some concrete act that someone had observed. Failure to attend Mass. Disrespect for the Sacraments. Some careless gesture or stray look at the time of the Consecration. The jaw moving after receiving communion, suggesting that she was chewing the Divine Host. It was said that some Judaizers mocked the Host by baking unleavened bread and performing their own rituals over it, casting spells on their enemies, mixing it with menstrual blood—or worse, the blood of Christian babies—and feeding it to animals.

Who knew what occurred behind the walls of the Péres household? And how would he find out? There must be a way. He would talk to the haughty López de Herrera woman again, but not the fleshy *esclava*. She was a witch, sent to tempt him in his dreams. But Señora López was both jealous and rich. He would exploit the former in pursuit of the latter. If he was lucky—but there was no such thing as luck, only Providence, he reminded himself quickly—he might fill the Castillo's coffers with the Péres woman's fortune and a good portion of Señora López's too.

He pushed back his chair, the scraping sound setting his teeth on edge. It was foolhardy to rely on other inquisitors to come up with damning testimony. He must do it himself. He rarely set foot outside the Castillo except when he was summoned to dinner at a patron's home or—he clenched his jaw at the memory—by the archbishop. There was no question that the archbishop's hand was responsible for the new priest being sent to spy on him.

He would give them no fodder for their suspicions. Everything he did in this investigation would be to the letter of the law. But nothing stopped him from investigating on his own. First, he would talk to the guard at the bridge. He had provided very little information after their first conversation, and he suspected the man had more than one buyer for the gossip he shared. Finding out who else wanted information on Señora Péres would lead him to more sources and might uncover useful information.

Padre Dominquez was not a man who enjoyed the outdoors, as his pale skin attested. He was more comfortable behind the walls of the Castillo than walking about the town, especially if he had nowhere to be at a given time. But he walked briskly toward the gate, his arms folded under his scapular. A few workmen carried stones across the courtyard, their brown faces grimacing under the weight of their burden. He had approved replacing some of the stones in the cells that had become loose in the floods a few years earlier after one of the guards alerted him that a prisoner had tried to remove them in an effort to escape. *And where would the miserable fool go?* he wondered. No doubt he had accomplices on the outside, whom Dominguez hoped to uncover, but he didn't have the chance. The prisoner had fallen ill and died before he could be questioned. Now there was nothing left to do but cover up the gaps in the wall before others got the same idea.

The smoke from the tileworks and the stench of the river, with the occasional animal carcass floating downstream, nearly overcame him. He put his sleeve to his nose to block the smell. He had become less fastidious in his habits, perhaps because he was far from the baths in the main building. It was cumbersome to heat water for the large tub that two lay brothers carried to his casita every few weeks, and he sometimes lost track of when it was time to bathe.

He opened the gate with the large key he kept on a ring attached to his cincture. The door was low, so he had to bend to exit, snagging his habit on the rotting wood of the frame. The guard stood languidly a stone's throw from the gate, resting on his pike. Dominguez wondered if it was possible to sleep while standing.

The man drew his body erect when Dominguez cleared his throat. "Too much liquor last night, Señor?" the priest asked.

"I gave up drinking long ago, Padre. It does not agree with my stomach—or my wife's temper," the guard answered, looking the priest in the eye. "To what do I owe the pleasure?"

"You remember the bargain we struck some time ago? You have been noticeably remiss in bringing me any intelligence on Señora Péres since the death of the old woman. Why is that?"

The guard shifted the pike from one hand to the other. "I have nothing to report, Padre. The woman seems to live an exemplary life. If anyone speaks against her, it may be the wife of Señor Herrera. The man is a scoundrel, and his wife is justifiably jealous. He has abandoned her, you know."

Dominguez wondered at the guard's willingness to defend the Péres woman. Perhaps she had paid a higher price than others to ensure his loyalty. "So, Herrera has left the wealthy heiress? That seems out of character, don't you agree? Unless, of course, he had another wealthy woman he hoped to seduce."

"No doubt he had hope, but Señora Péres remains in Triana, and Herrera has fled," the guard replied.

"Where do you get your information, may I ask? You seem well informed about the goings on behind the walls of Triana." The guard sucked air through his yellowed teeth, a low whistle signaling he would not let go of what he knew without further prodding and precious silver. The priest pulled out a small bag and opened it slowly. He could feel the guard's eyes boring into him as he emptied a handful of coins into his palm. It was more than he wanted to part with, but they would certainly be repaid a thousandfold if he succeeded in getting the information he wanted. He thrust his hand out toward the guard but quickly closed his fingers around the silver. "Tell me what you know, and if it proves helpful, you will get your reward."

The guard spit on the ground. "The man sold an emerald ring in Santa Cruz to one of the moneylenders a few weeks ago. Where he got it, who knows? Perhaps he stole it from his wife."

Dominguez's heart quickened. "An emerald ring, you say?" The priest remembered the Easter dinner he had attended soon after Guiomar's marriage. He had noticed the ring at the time. It was hard to forget. The stone was the largest he had ever seen, even bigger than the archbishop's ruby.

"Do you know the moneylender who purchased the ring?" he asked.

The guard looked down at the priest's closed fist. "I might," he answered with a smirk.

"If you know something and withhold it, it could go badly for you," Dominguez warned. "Especially if the matter is under the jurisdiction of my office. At the very least, I would not want a man of questionable loyalties guarding the Castillo."

The guard spat again. "You might inquire at the bird merchant's shop in El Barrio Santa Cruz. The proprietor is known to be one of Herrera's lenders."

"Let me know if you hear anything more. Send word immediately. Do you hear?" The man nodded and stretched out his palm. The priest dropped a single silver coin into it. "Don't worry. There will be more. But only if you deliver."

Dominguez disliked Barrio Santa Cruz. Its streets were dirty with dung and urine from the donkeys and horses that passed through and sent up a stench in the afternoon heat. The Jews who once lived here had mostly been replaced by pickpockets, prostitutes, and drunks. It was easy to get lost in the labyrinthine quarter, whose streets twisted and turned at odd angles, many eventually leading to the Cathedral. The bird shop was down one of the older, narrower corridors that led to La Giralda.

It was a shame, the priest thought, that the Church had not torn down the tower that had once been the minaret built by the Muslims on the site of their Great Mosque. Instead, a few years earlier, the archbishop had commissioned a statue atop the structure, which served as a beacon across the great city, visible everywhere, even from the Castillo's upper floors. El Giraldillo—the statue—was said to represent the triumph of the Church over the Muslims. But Dominguez considered the heavy bronze more pagan than Christian, its feminine figure dressed in armor that did not conceal its ample breasts.

THE SILVER CANDLESTICKS

He peered into the shop window. A large red bird with blue plumage stood on a perch just inside. Dominguez put his hand on the door handle and pushed inward, which set off screeching and cawing from all quarters. The old man sitting near the back of the room rose.

"May I help you, Padre?" the shopkeeper shouted above the noisy parrots.

The priest made his way between the cages, the noise making it impossible to state his inquiry from afar. The old man looked like a human version of his feathered wares: large-beaked with unblinking eyes.

"I have come to make inquiries about one of your customers, Señor," the priest said. "It is not an idle investigation, I can assure you, but is not yet elevated to official status. Your information might lead me in either direction."

Jorge studied the priest's face. He had not encountered the man before, but there was no doubting who he was. He stank of hatred masked behind religious fervor.

"My customers, Padre?" the shopkeeper asked. "What on earth does the purchase of one of God's most beautiful creatures have to do with the sins you seek to uncover?"

"I had in mind someone you might have encountered in your other occupation, Señor," Dominguez said, undeterred.

"I don't know what you mean," the shopkeeper responded, staring the priest in the eyes.

"Oh, I think you do. But don't worry. Usury is not high on the list of crimes I wish to investigate. At least not right now." The priest took a step forward so that he was nearly touching the man with his chest. "I am inquiring about an emerald ring, Señor, one that might have been used to secure the escape of a person—or persons—of interest to the Holy Office."

Jorge reached out his skinny arm and whistled. The scarlet macaw flapped its long wings and took flight from its perch at the front of the store. The priest cowered, his arms raised to protect his face as he moved back, bumping into cages that set off another racket. The bird landed on Jorge's outstretched arm, flapping its wings gently, then folding them against its body. Jorge leaned in to place a kiss on the enormous beak, "My beauty, it seems you have frightened the padre."

Dominguez blessed himself quickly. It was as if this winged monster were the Devil himself, garish and threatening, ready to grasp its prey in its long claws and bite off the head with its evil beak. If this moneylender kept such a demon as a pet, he too must be in the Devil's employ. "You think you will intimidate me with this display, Señor? You are mistaken."

Jorge laughed. "I had no such intention, Padre. Is she not an example of the glory of God's creation?"

"I came here for information, Señor. Do not try to divert me. Were you in receipt of this emerald ring or not?"

Jorge stroked the top of the bird's head. Herrera had put him in danger, but the way out was not to provide this priest what he wanted. He shook his head. He couldn't utter an outright lie that might come back to bite him. "I will make inquiries, Padre, but you must provide me with more details. Whose ring was this?"

"I have reason to believe it belonged to the woman Guiomar Péres de Armijo. Though it was not she herself who sold the ring, but perhaps her lover…"

"I am surprised, Padre," Jorge intervened. "I do not know the lady well, but I have never heard gossip of that sort about her, and as you might imagine, I hear many stories of the kind in my business." Jorge had made his choice—one he might live to regret. But there was something insidious about this priest that made his skin crawl. Now he must act on it, he thought. But how?

"You do know the man involved, I am told. José Marcos Herrera?"

Jorge walked toward the front of the store to put the parrot back on her perch. "I know him," he said, turning toward the priest. "He is a weak man. But with respect to Señora Péres, I had heard that her husband, Señor Armijo, has returned from Méjico with a boat full of silver. Do you think it likely she would be carrying on with

THE SILVER CANDLESTICKS

a man like Herrera?" The priest looked surprised. "Did you not know, Padre?" Jorge pressed.

"Perhaps my information is bad," Padre Dominguez said. "But tell me, how is it that you know Señora Péres? You do not attend the same..." he hesitated, lifting his eyes to the merchant's, "...church?"

Jorge thought carefully before replying. "We do not, as the Señora lives across the river and my home is in the shadow of Capilla Santa María. But the Señora bought some canaries from me a while back." He must be careful with this odious priest, telling as much of the truth as he dared without revealing anything that might compromise him. Still, he felt the need to warn Señora Péres. More importantly, he must get rid of the emerald, which would implicate him in any scheme the priest imagined. "I will ask around about Herrera, Padre. Should I send word directly to you if I learn anything of interest?"

Dominguez considered the question. He could use the guard as a go-between, but that would require him to part with more silver. "Yes, send me a note, and we will meet again. I would be interested in any information you uncover, either about Herrera's whereabouts or the Péres woman's ties to him."

Jorge measured out some seeds into a small pouch. He would deliver the seeds himself. It was a risk, but he needed to speak to Señora Péres. He went to the back room and opened the heavy locked casket hidden behind larger sacks of seed where he had put the ring for safekeeping until he could dispose of it. He had paid Herrera a fair price—enough to secure his passage to the Antilles—but the stone was worth more to the right buyer, and who better than the original owner? Especially if it meant she could evade the suspicion of the troublesome inquisitor.

He dropped the ring into the pouch and tied it with a green ribbon. Now he had only to decide on the right pretext. The trill of a robust male canary drew his attention. The fellow was a wonder, not golden like most of his kind, but red with a tufted crown.

It would fetch a pretty sum, but he might take it to Señora Péres instead, offering it to her along with the pouch. He brushed off his jacket and smoothed his grey hair in front of a tiny mirror hanging on the wall. It was a long walk to Triana, and the heat was barely tolerable, especially conveying a caged bird. He would fetch a carriage, a small investment that would be paid back in full if his plot was successful.

The stand outside the Cathedral had only two carriages, one with a broken-down mare covered in flies and a driver that looked no better than the horse. He walked to the next, open with no canopy but clean, and offered the driver a few coins to take him across the river and wait for him. The man grudgingly agreed, and Jorge lifted the cage into the carriage and pulled himself up for the drive. When they crossed the bridge that led to the Castillo, Jorge averted his face, but the brilliant canary began trilling just as they rolled past the gate.

"Hola, Señor," the guard called out as the carriage turned down Calle Catalina. Jorge waved his hand without looking at the man, who would no doubt make him pay dearly for having been seen in that neighborhood. Well, it could not be avoided. If he got the sum he wanted for the ring, it would be worth it.

Esperanza opened the door to see the bird seller standing outside holding a small cage. "Señor, are you expected?" she asked, knowing full well he wasn't.

"No, I am afraid I am not, but I hoped to speak to Señora Péres if I might. It is important," he said, arching his eyebrow to match the intensity of his tone.

"It is not a good time," Esperanza said. "Don Francisco is expected any minute."

"All the better, young lady. I would speak with her quickly before he arrives, since the matter may affect them both. It concerns Padre Dominguez," he said, watching to see if the name evoked a reaction. Still, the servant showed nothing. "He paid me a visit today about a matter," he stopped for a moment, "a matter of

THE SILVER CANDLESTICKS

the gravest importance." He reached into his pocket and pulled out the pouch. "Take this to the Señora if you will," he said, thrusting it into her hand. "Make sure she looks deep inside. I will wait outside for her reply if you prefer."

Esperanza tested the weight of the pouch and moved aside to allow the bird seller to step inside. "Wait here, and I will return shortly," she said.

Guiomar was sitting at her dressing table, touching the tiny pendant at her throat as she looked in the mirror when Esperanza knocked lightly. She jumped to her feet. Francisco must have arrived, and she was not quite ready to greet him. "Come in," she said, her voice raspy with emotion. Esperanza opened the door and stood near the threshold with a leather pouch in her hand. "Is it from Francisco?" she asked.

"No, Señora. There is a man here—the bird merchant. He says it is urgent and asked that you examine the contents," she said, holding out the pouch.

Guiomar grabbed the pouch and pulled on the green ribbon so hurriedly that the contents spilled out, small seeds scattering across the floor. She looked up at Esperanza, who said with some urgency, "Look inside, Señora." Guiomar reached in and felt the ring, which she pulled out, dropping the pouch. "What did he say, Esperanza? What were his exact words?"

"He said he needed to talk to you. I told him the Señor was due any minute and he said all the better because the matter concerned you both." She hesitated. "He mentioned Padre Dominguez's name, Señora."

Guiomar clutched the ring to her chest. "*Madre de Dios*. It has begun," she whispered. She quickly walked to the front hall, unsure of what she would say or do. Perhaps it was best simply to listen to the man. If this was a trap, the less she said the better.

She was surprised when she saw that he held a caged bird in his hand. "Buenos días, Señor," she said. "Come into the *sala*. But what have you here?"

Jorge bowed and extended his hand with the bird. "A gift for you, Señora. To add more joy to your life, I pray."

"Gracias, Señor. Would you take the bird, Esperanza?" she said, leading the bird seller into the *sala mayor*. "Please sit down. I hear you have an urgent matter to discuss."

"I know this is highly unusual," Jorge said, "but I could not wait. Padre Dominguez paid me a visit this afternoon—I assume you know him by reputation, if not personally."

Guiomar edged closer to the merchant, nodding her head. Could she trust this man that she barely knew? She opened her fist and held out the ring. "And does his visit have anything to do with this?"

"Yes, I am afraid so. Let me explain," he said, pulling out a kerchief and wiping his brow. "He came asking about you and about this ring. He accused you—no, I will not insult you with repeating his scurrilous gossip—but it involved Señor Herrera, the man from whom I purchased the ring you hold." He watched her face blanch. "I do not need to know how Herrera came to have the ring, Señora. But the thing is," again he faltered, not knowing quite how to put the matter. "I take it the ring is yours. Or so the priest said. And he claims that it was sold to secure an escape for someone—as he put it, 'a person or persons of interest to the Holy Office.'" He wiped his brow again, giving Señora Péres a moment to collect her thoughts.

"But why bring it to me?" she asked, genuinely perplexed.

"If you were to take possession of it again, perhaps it might put his suspicions to rest. As you might imagine, Señora, I took some risk coming here so soon after his visit, but I thought it might allow you to evade this overzealous prosecutor. No one need know that I was ever in possession of the ring."

Guiomar slipped the ring onto her finger. "And what would it cost me?"

Jorge cleared his throat. "I am not a rich man, Señora, or I would gladly make a gift of it. But the fact is I gave Señor Herrera two thousand maravedis and I must recoup my losses—that and whatever you think fair to compensate me for the risk I have taken today. I will have to pay off the guard at the Castillo, who unfortunately saw my carriage a short while ago. I fear he was the source of the bad information that the priest came to me with."

Guiomar could not muster such a huge sum without Francisco's help. But what would she tell him? There had been so much intrigue and suspicion, and now, finally, she hoped to prove her loyalty. What would this incident say about her innocence? How she rued the day she had fallen in love with José Marcos. It seemed so long ago, and she could not even recall what had made her love such a vain coward in the first place. Well, it could not be helped now.

"I will repay you, Señor, but we will have to trust each other. My husband will be home any minute. Will you permit me time to discuss the matter with him?"

"Of course, Señora. It affects you both, I fear. It is not my place to say so, but the sooner you can show the priest that the ring never left your finger—and never will—the better."

"I agree. Will you allow me to keep it in the meantime?"

Jorge did not like leaving the ring without collateral, but it would be best not to have it in his possession. "I trust you, Señora. Why else would I have come? Let me take my leave, and you can send the beautiful servant to my shop when you are ready," he said as he stood up.

Chapter Twenty-Six

HOMECOMING

Francisco held Guiomar in his arms. He had forgotten how lovely she was, the warmth of her body, the fullness of her breasts, her scent. "I was so frightened, *mi cariña*, when I did not see anyone at the port this morning. I feared the worst," he kissed her lightly on the lips. "I don't know what I would do if I lost you, my dear." And it was true. Every day that he worked in Veracruz, putting up with the oppressive heat, the stench, the suffering he saw all around him, he thought of his return to Guiomar. The wealth he was building would allow him to earn her respect, if not the love he longed for, and respect was the foundation of a good marriage. "Tell me what has happened. Slowly—and try to remember every detail that could be important," he said, leading her by the hand down the hall to her bedchamber.

Guiomar stepped across the threshold and immediately burst into tears. Her heart pounded in her chest. Where should she begin—the warning from the monk, her *padrino*'s efforts with the archbishop, or the visit that morning from the money lender? She feared what Francisco would say when he learned that she had given the ring to José Marcos. He would suspect the worst. Perhaps he would turn against her too. She made her way to the bed and threw herself face down on the bedclothes to stifle the scream growing in her throat. He would never believe her.

THE SILVER CANDLESTICKS

"My dear, what's wrong? Surely it isn't that bad. You are here, after all, not locked in the Castillo." He ran his hands along her arms and gently lifted and turned her to face him. "I will protect you, Guiomar. Surely you know that," he said, staring into her terror-stricken eyes.

She wiped her face with the back of her hands. "I have so much to explain," she said tentatively. "And I am worried that you will not understand my actions," she looked down, afraid to meet his gaze. She took his hands in hers and looked up again. "I have not always been a good wife to you, Francisco," she said, "but I have been faithful to you in every way." She looked into his eyes to see if he believed her, but his look reflected more puzzlement.

"I want you to understand that in your absence, I have learned how much I truly need you. But," she hesitated a moment, not knowing how to put into words what she felt, "while I did not love you as you wished when we married, I was a silly, vain girl." His face still showed bewilderment. She must say the words that mattered. "I love you now, Francisco. I truly do. I want this to be a new beginning for us if you can find it in your heart to forgive me."

Francisco squeezed her hands. "You have told me nothing that requires forgiveness. Is there more to tell?"

"Yes, much more, but it is a long story. I will try to tell it quickly, but please be patient with me. And do not make any conclusions until you know everything," she said, pulling his hands to her lips and gently kissing his knuckles. "Promise me," she asked, and he nodded.

Esperanza anxiously waited for her mistress to appear from behind the chamber door. She had asked the servants to prepare a simple meal for Don Francisco—the first time the Señora had referred to him as such. Now that Don Pedro had passed, it was natural that the husband take his place as head of the household. But the honorific surprised her, and she wondered what her master would think of it. He'd never had the pretentions of Don Pedro, but perhaps with his new wealth, he would assume them.

The *cocina* was quiet, a stew bubbling on the hearth the only sound other than those from the courtyard. She looked out the window where the sun had begun to cast shadows from the large tree. Her boy, Benito, was playing underneath. He looked up at her, the same indecipherable expression on his face that he always wore when he looked at her. The girl, Úrsula, sat next to him on a small bench, her head bowed over the doll she carried with her everywhere now, a gift from Don Enrique.

"Úrsula," she called from the doorway. "Come inside, *niña*. We have some time before dinner, and I want to fix your hair." Benito ignored her and went back to scratching at the earth with a long stick. He was practicing his letters, she was glad to see. It was important that he learn to read and write, and she was grateful the Señora had included him in the lessons the other children received every afternoon, and even happier that he absorbed them as quickly as Antonio and Úrsula.

She took Úrsula's hand and led her to the nursery. She could hear the voices from Señora Armijo's room as they passed. They were not discernible, but she did not detect anger, which bode well. Surely Don Francisco would understand her mistress's plight and the need to get Señor Herrera as far away from Sevilla as he could. But what would become of all of them, including herself and Benito, if the evil priest sought his revenge? Perhaps she would be sold and separated from her boy. Or worse, she could end up in the Castillo alongside her mistress. Their riches might protect the Armijos, but would they protect her as well?

She clutched the child's hand harder until the girl let out a small whimper. "Oh *m'hija*, I am so sorry," she said, pulling the child against her skirts and bending to kiss her. "I was not thinking of you, my child, but worrying about something else." The child smiled her forgiveness without uttering a word. She was such a sweet girl, Esperanza thought, and was pleased her mistress had begun to treat the child with tenderness. The Señora was a kind woman, though Esperanza had discovered it was not always her first instinct. It could not be helped, she guessed. A woman born

THE SILVER CANDLESTICKS

to the privilege wealth brought, and one who was also beautiful, understood her own power before she learned the importance of kindness. At least Úrsula's appearance taught her humility, which would temper the effects of her family's pride.

She dressed the child in a blue frock that did not accentuate the sallow complexion the girl had not yet outgrown. She combed her hair, gathering it to the opposite side of her face as her birthmark, and tied it with a ribbon matching the dress.

"How lovely you look for your Papá," she said, holding up a mirror so the child could see her reflection. The girl's hand reflexively went to the stain on her cheek, which she covered with her small fingers. She smiled briefly before pushing away the mirror. The birthmark was not the bright wine color it had been at birth, but it was still the first thing that attracted the eye when looking at her. Esperanza kissed the child's head. "Your father loves you very much and will be so happy to see you. Now let's see where your brother has disappeared," she said drawing the girl alongside her as they exited the nursery.

"Here you are, my lovely," Francisco said, throwing his arms open as the child ran to him. "I have not given you your presents yet, niña, but I see you already have a beautiful doll."

Úrsula blushed. "Don Enrique gave it to me, Papá," she said, as if apologizing.

"Well, a child can never have too many dolls—or dresses," he said, laughing. "Or a woman too many jewels," he added, gazing at his wife. Guiomar began fidgeting with the emerald ring, which they had decided she should not remove from her finger in the hope that word would get back to Padre Dominguez and destroy his nefarious plot. "Speaking of Don Enrique, we should invite him to dinner, as well as other friends," he said to Esperanza. "How soon do you think you could undertake a banquet?"

"We had discussed this, Señ…" Esperanza caught herself midword, "Don Francisco. Next week would be the earliest. If you will provide a guest list, I can prepare something suitable."

"Good. We will want to invite some who may not have been here in a long time," he said. "And Esperanza, Señor will do fine within these walls, even if I become Don Francisco outside." Esperanza nodded but did not meet his eyes, looking toward her mistress instead.

Guiomar tried not to be exasperated with Francisco's lack of decorum. Perhaps he was right. She had grown up differently, but if he had been raised as she was, he might not have been as forgiving of her clumsy attempts to buy José Marcos's way out of her life. Francisco had not been angry with her, but his face had expressed disappointment. How could she ever explain to him why she had loved this shallow man when she couldn't even recall what had drawn her to him in the first place? Of course, he was handsome, but it had not been that alone, more the illusion that he loved her deeply. She had tried hard to excise the memories, the sound of his voice, the way he would ask over and over if he had ever told her how much he loved her when he knew very well that he had. "But no matter how many times I tell you, I'm not sure you believe me," he would say. And why should she have believed him when he clearly did not? He was drawn by her father's money, and yes, her beauty. But that wouldn't have kept him faithful.

"Guiomar, you seem lost in thought," Francisco said, lifting her chin with his fingers. She had not even noticed that they were standing alone in the hall, Esperanza having departed with Úrsula. "I am sorry, Francisco. I am so worried...and so remorseful at how I have landed us in this predicament."

"I told you, my love. We will figure our way out of it. And if we cannot..." he put his arms around her, "if we cannot, we will leave."

Guiomar gasped. "Leave? But where? And how could we? We have the children and the servants and the house," the words tumbled out of her mouth. "We would have to give up everything you have worked for," she added, hoping to persuade him such a plan was unthinkable.

THE SILVER CANDLESTICKS

"Many families are leaving, my dear. Méjico is filled with Sevillanos, Castellanos, and others. Some men bring their families, others start new ones, marrying among the *Indios* or having children with them even when they have wives and heirs at home. The lands are vast, especially to the north, and the opportunities are limitless." He was hoping to cheer her, but her face fell the more he spoke.

"But let's not worry yet. We will talk to Don Enrique. If what you say about his relationship with the archbishop is accurate, we may have nothing to fear. Now, let us get something to eat, and we will plan for the banquet."

Padre Dominguez looked at the invitation again. So they were inviting him to feast the return of Don Francisco Armijo—a new honorific, he noted. He would attend this banquet, even if the company repelled him. He had heard nothing from the moneylender, and the guard was nowhere to be found. Well, he had other ways of getting information. He would not let go of Guiomar Péres until she was locked securely in the cells beneath him. Señora López could not be bribed into silence, nor her lusty servant.

He took a sheaf of paper from his desk drawer. "I will be most pleased to accept your generous invitation," he wrote, signing his name and blowing on the page for the ink to dry faster. He wondered who else would be at the dinner—perhaps even the archbishop. He must gather as much information as possible before he faced these people.

The large ledger on his desk contained the examinations of Inés Mejia and her daughter. He had pored over them several times, hoping to learn as much as he could about the details of their observance, but the process was frustrating. The child knew almost nothing and had hanged herself before any useful information could be extracted from her. The mother revealed only what everyone knew: the family did not touch pork. They lit candles on their Sabbath, which they observed on Friday at sundown. They bathed each month after they bled, though the girl had yet to reach the age when it was necessary. He slammed the book shut.

He decided he would send a man to the docks to see what he could learn about Herrera's disappearance. But whom could he trust? None of the priests would know their way around the rough territory of the docks. He needed a man who could drink in the taverns, perhaps a gambler who could claim Herrera owed him a debt. He could even suggest that Herrera was in possession of a valuable gem and there was a reward for anyone who found him—and the ring.

He would need money for this effort. Perhaps Señora López would pay for information about her wayward husband. He wrote a second note to the wealthy patroness laying out his urgent request: he needed someone who could trace her husband's footsteps if he was to accuse Señora Péres—or was it now Doña Guiomar Péres de Armijo, he snorted—he needed help immediately. He rang a small bell on his desk, a convenience he'd added after his visit to the archbishop's house. It saved him the unseemly need to yell.

Brother Tomás stood before Dominguez's desk, fidgeting with his rosary. The priest looked up, his face immediately turning from a mere scowl to rage.

"What are you doing here?" the priest spat out.

"I…I was walking by when I heard your bell, Padre. Brother Fabian must have stepped away," he said, his voice shaking. "I didn't want you to wait in vain."

"Well, I will deal with Brother Fabian later. Take these letters and deliver them. You have been to the one house before," he said, staring into the fat monk's face, which had turned a deep red. "The other lives in the grand house near the Plaza de Santa Ana. Ask anyone, they will point it out."

Tomás took the two letters, not daring to look down lest he display his curiosity. He had no doubt that one was for Señora Péres de Armijo. He nodded, stuck the letters in the pocket beneath his robe, and retreated as fast as he could.

THE SILVER CANDLESTICKS

By the time Tomás reached the Armijo home, he was sweating profusely. What would he say to the Señora? He must let her know that the second letter was addressed to Señora López de Herrera. He had no idea about the contents of either, though he was briefly tempted to try to break the seal on the second. But the very fact that Padre Dominguez was writing to both women was surely a dire sign.

He knocked on the door, but he could see that a great commotion was taking place. Big trunks lined the patio outside, and he could hear the servants bustling in the courtyard. Finally, the beautiful servant he had met before answered the door. She seemed surprised to see him and furrowed her brows when he gave her the letter.

"May I speak to the Señora? I think she will want to know that I have a second letter to deliver—and to whom," Tomás said as Esperanza pursed her lips. She nodded and showed him to the room he had waited in before, but this time there was hardly any space on the floor with so many trunks and boxes laid out, some of them open to reveal colorful fabric and other goods inside. He had never seen such colors in cloth, like a garden of flowers: marigold and fuchsia and lavender.

"Brother Tomás, is it?" Francisco held his hand out to the monk, who seemed not to know what to do. "Guiomar has told me about you, and the help you have so generously given her. Please sit down. I am sorry for the mess. I've just returned from Méjico."

The priest reached out for Don Francisco's hand belatedly and vigorously shook it. The Señora stepped forward. "You have a letter for me?" she asked. Tomás nodded and watched as she unsealed and read it quickly, then handed it to her husband. Though he wasn't sure it was the right thing to do, he pulled the second letter from his pocket and handed it to her. "I don't know what is in it, Señora, but I have reason to believe the addressee is no friend to your family."

Francisco took the letter from Guiomar's hand and held it up to the light. It was sealed with wax, but bore no mark that could identify the sender. It would be simple enough to open it and perhaps seal it again with a few drops of wax. But what if it looked like it had been tampered with? It could mean punishment for the monk—or worse, cast more suspicion on Guiomar.

"Did the priest give you any instructions?"

"Only to remind me that I already knew your house and that the other was easy to find near the Plaza de Santa Ana."

"He didn't ask you to wait for a reply?" Guiomar interjected.

Brother Tomás was sure the priest hadn't said anything about it, but perhaps it was implied. "I could ask her for one, if you think that would help us learn what he wants," Tomás offered.

"We will hope for the best then," Francisco said. "You will not have time to come back here after your visit, so I will ask Esperanza to meet you in the plaza so you can tell her what happened. Señora López de Herrera may write her reply out or simply give you a message to relay."

"I would offer you refreshment, Brother Tomás," Guiomar apologized, "but I fear we have no time to lose."

María Luísa stared at the note from the troublesome priest. What more did he want? She had already told him what she knew about her husband's infidelity. The cad had gone with his tail between his legs to his lover to get her help in escaping his vows. But the woman must have turned him away. José Marcos had not been seen in weeks, and Guiomar Péres was still in her hacienda. So why did the priest think he could find José Marcos now with her help? She glanced at the monk, pink-faced and sweating in the doorway. She considered sending him away empty-handed.

Tomás took a deep breath. "Is there a reply for me to give to Padre Dominguez, Señora?" He tried to avoid her eyes, but he could feel them boring into him. Finally, he looked up. The woman's nostrils flared.

"Well, don't stand there. Go in," she said, pointing to the *gran sala* and stepping aside to allow the fat monk to pass by her.

THE SILVER CANDLESTICKS

The large room was more ornately furnished than the Armijo home, with damask drapes hanging from the large windows and a large tapestry depicting a hunt at the far end. Tomás waited for the Señora to ask him to sit, but she didn't, instead leaving him alone in the room.

The monk was not used to such luxury. He could not recall ever being in such a great room. There were several chairs, plush with velvet wine-colored cushions, and two leather divans with wooden arms elaborately carved with lions' heads. The candelabra in the middle of the vaulted ceiling held two dozen candles or more, unlit with the afternoon sun pouring in from the south-facing windows, protected from the street by elaborate wrought-iron grills. He was about to examine the tapestry, which looked very old, when a servant came in and handed him a letter.

"Is there any message I should give the Padre along with this?"

"No. Just take it to the priest. And quickly," she said, pointing to the door.

The monk shuffled past her, nodding.

As agreed, Esperanza waited in the plaza outside the church. She tried to look as if she had some purpose there, studying the flowers in the pots that surrounded a small fountain, nipping the dead blooms and putting them in her apron as if she were collecting them for seeds. She heard the monk approaching from behind, breathing heavily as though he had been in a great hurry. Smiling, she turned to him. "Buenos días, *Hermano*," she said, scanning those seated nearby at the tavern. He came close and handed her the letter. She took it but had no idea what to do with it.

"You don't expect me to open this, do you?" she whispered.

"I thought about it," he said. "How else will we know what to expect?"

"It is impossible. The priest would know at once, and you would be doomed," she said, handing it back. He secreted it under his scapula.

"Did she say anything? Any hint of its contents?"

Tomás felt he had failed in his mission. He had frightened Señora Péres and had nothing to back it up. "I am afraid we will just have to wait. Señora López de Herrera left after reading the letter and sent her servant to deliver this reply."

"Please keep your eye out in case she comes to the Castillo and try to get us word. We have invited the priest for dinner next week. If you have information, please try to send it before then." She reached out and squeezed the monk's arm. "And thank you, Brother Tomás. You are a good man."

Before he could reply, she turned and walked briskly across the plaza.

Padre Dominguez returned to his casita to wait for the monk. Meanwhile, he would scourge himself in preparation. He had not done so in many weeks. Perhaps that was why the Lord had not answered his prayers to deliver the Péres woman into his hands. If he was to make the haughty *rica* suffer, he must suffer himself. God expected no less from his humble servant. Perhaps the whip would inspire visions of how to proceed. He must be cleverer than the Judaizer if he was to ensnare her in a lie or catch her in an act of heresy.

He knelt on the hard floor, lifting his robe so that his flesh touched the stone, but he experienced little pain. In the corner, he kept a small urn filled with rice. Anyone who discovered it might have assumed he hoarded the precious grain to enjoy alone, but he kept it to increase his suffering. He now spread a handful of grains in two small piles on the floor, lifted his robe, and knelt again, grinding the small particles into his knees until they were painfully embedded in the skin. He was about to loosen his robe to bare his back when he heard a knock on the door. He stood so that his robe covered the rice on the floor before telling the intruder to enter.

"I am sorry to disturb you, Padre, but I thought you would want the Señora's response as soon as I returned," Tomás said nervously, holding the letter in front of him. He took a step toward the priest, who snatched it from his hand. He turned to go, but the priest called out.

"I need you to find me some trousers and a shirt, nothing fancy. Perhaps you might take them from one of the prisoners, as long as they aren't too filthy."

Tomás tried not to show his surprise. What on earth could the priest want with such rough garb? He nodded and turned, but then stopped. "I could easily obtain second-hand clothing at the market if you prefer, Padre. I have need of some baking supplies and have to go there anyway." The priest's face showed nothing, but he assented.

"Take a few maravedis from the drawer in my desk. Whatever you think you will need," the priest said, standing stiffly in the center of the room. The monk was pleased. The ploy would allow him enough time to visit the Armijo home and advise them of this new information.

Chapter Twenty-Seven

AT THE DOCKS

During the day, the docks were teeming with sweaty men, most of them unloading cargo from the fleets returning from Perú and Méjico. Despite its inland location upriver from the coast of the Atlantic, Sevilla was now the busiest port in Europe. Fifty years earlier, King Felipe II had built the *Real Casa de Moneda* on the banks of the Guadalquivir, which minted New World gold and silver into coins used to finance much of Europe's economy. But the evening crowd at the docks was now drunk sailors yelling foul epithets at each other and passersby, cursing their mothers, their lovers, and the captains and officers who left them to do the dirty work while the selfish men went home to their wives and children.

Padre Dominguez felt naked without the heavy robes he had worn for more than thirty years. He didn't know what to do with his hands without a scapula to cover them or a rosary to finger in his nervousness. The smell of garbage mixed with spices from the barrels stacked along the quay was a nauseating combination. He combed the crowd of sailors, looking for one in particular, a mulatto of about twenty, who Señora López de Herrera had described as unusually tall and well-muscled. He felt ridiculous. How could he recognize a boy he'd never met? But the Señora had been adamant in her note: "Find the boy, Juan. He can help you in your quest for my errant spouse."

THE SILVER CANDLESTICKS

He walked along the docks, weaving in and out between the stevedores and their cargo, searching for a man who fit Juan's description. He was about to give up when he noticed a group of young men lazing against a stack of crates, smoking. One struck him as a possibility. His skin was fairer than he had imagined, but he was nearly a head taller than the others. There was a certain sensuality about him that reminded him of the voluptuous servant who had twice made charges against Señora Péres and whose image so troubled his dreams. As Dominguez approached, the boy sneered and flicked the rolled-up tobacco he was smoking onto the ground.

"Buenas noches, Señores," the priest said to the hostile stares of the men who leaned against the crates. "Do any of you know Juan of the Hacienda Herrera?"

"Who's asking?" the tall one responded, taking a step forward.

The priest pulled back but smiled. "A friend who could make it worth your while," he said lightly, but he felt uncomfortable, even scared.

"Get back to work," Juan said to the others, thrusting his chin toward the nearby ship. "I'll be there in a few minutes." The men dispersed, grumbling under their breath.

"Your mistress thought you might be able to help me," the priest said.

The boy spat out a bit of tobacco stuck to his lip. "I have no mistress, unless you mean the *puta* I left behind in Méjico, and I rule her, not the other way."

"I mean Señora López de Herrera. I assumed you were of her house," the priest said, feeling repulsed by the bravado of this young mulatto.

"You assumed wrong. I work for Don Francisco Armijo. That's his ship," he said, pointing to a medium-sized vessel whose cargo lay piled at the foot of the gangplank. "But he is not my master either. I have no master. I am a free man." The boy pulled himself up to his full height and looked menacingly down on the man before him, whose superior tone suggested he was a gentleman but whose clothes told a different story.

"I beg your pardon," the priest answered, bowing slightly.

"My mother is a servant, but not in the house of Señora López de Herrera. At least she was not when I left two years ago. I don't know the woman," Juan said, suddenly more curious than offended. After all, he had barely earned his freedom—it wouldn't be official until Don Francisco registered his status as a free man before a justice of the peace in Sevilla.

Dominguez reached to shake the other's hand. "I should have introduced myself. I am…Arturo Cháves, from Córdoba," he said, picking the name of the Inquisition's treasurer in that city. "I am tasked with finding Señor Herrera, who has abandoned his wife. I have reason to believe he may be seeking to flee to Las Indias when the fleet leaves in August. Do you know him?"

Juan's lips curled. He wished he could talk to his mother, but he had not seen her yet. His only contact with her for the past two years had been through his employer, who would pass on messages in his letters home. "I may know him," he said, not wanting to give away too much.

Dominguez grew irritated, but it would not help to alienate the young man. He was his only chance of tracking down Herrera. "I would, as I suggested, make your assistance worth something," he said. "Since you work for Señor Armijo, did you happen to know José Marcos Herrera before he married the wife he has abandoned?"

"My mother used to whisper about him in the slaves' quarters when she thought I was sleeping," he said, narrowing his eyes. "I may have seen him once or twice."

Dominguez conjured the image of Juan's mother, imagining how she might lust after the handsome Herrera. "Did you happen ever to see him in the company of Señora Péres de Armijo?" he said, pulling a pouch from his britches.

"Not after she married," Juan answered, holding out his palm.

Dominguez untied the strip of leather and opened the pouch, shaking a few coins into his own hand. "But before? When she was unmarried?"

THE SILVER CANDLESTICKS

Juan stared at the coins. Should he invent more than he had seen? "I saw them in the garden once or twice," he said. The man nodded and handed him a single piece of silver.

"That is helpful, but more detail would be better," the priest said, closing his fingers around the coins in his fist.

Juan snorted. "You want me to say I saw them fucking?"

Dominguez recoiled at the boy's vulgarity. It was a bad business having to deal with someone of this sort. "I want you to tell me the truth. No more, no less."

"I never saw them embracing, but I heard my mother talk to the woman's maid, Esperanza, in the dark. My mother is a lusty woman. She hungered for the man and was jealous of the Señora. She must've had reason to be jealous," Juan replied.

This was something, the priest thought. Not enough to charge Guiomar Péres de Armijo with adultery, but there was certainly more to this story. "Will you help me find him?" he asked, pouring the coins back into the purse and jiggling it so that its heft could be measured by the sound. "I will make you a present of this, and maybe more, depending on what you can tell me. If you lead me to Herrera, there will be gold as well as silver."

Juan grunted his assent and started back towards the ship. "Where will I find you?" he asked, turning his head back before stepping onto the gangplank.

"Send word to me at the Castillo," the priest answered. "I am friends with Inquisitor Dominguez. Just send a message to him that you have news of his friend. He will know how to find me."

Perhaps it was a mistake to direct the mulatto to the Castillo. The boy was no doubt a brute, but he was not stupid. He had essentially told him that Herrera was wanted by the Holy Office. He had to hope that Herrera could not promise the boy more for his silence than his wife was willing to pay for his whereabouts.

Guiomar approached Francisco just as he was heading out the door. "You must find Don Enrique when you are at La Casa de Contratación. My father had said he's usually there early in the morning."

"But we will see him in a matter of days, my love," Francisco replied, placing a kiss on her brow. He felt a surge of desire, recalling their lovemaking the previous evening. Guiomar had been open to him in a way he had never experienced, receptive to his embraces and his passion.

"The monk's warning yesterday makes me fear that we have less time than either of us had hoped," she said.

Francisco nodded, pulling her closer and kissing her on the lips. He'd planned to remain in Sevilla another year before returning to Las Indias, but the situation with the inquisitor made that impossible. Perhaps they could leave in the spring. By that time, he would have their finances in order, and he could perhaps sell his father's candle business. He could even sell Guiomar's home if she would let him, though so many bigger haciendas were being built on both sides of the river for newly rich merchants that it would likely not bring much.

"Do not worry, *corazón*," he said, releasing her.

"We need a plan, Francisco. I trust you and my *padrino* will devise one," she said, taking hold of his hand. But in truth, she wanted a say in what would happen, and she was not sure either man would think to ask her opinion.

Francisco walked past the rooms in La Contratación occupied by the mapmakers, who were forever adding to the sailors' knowledge of the routes across the ocean. When he got to the room where the king's clerks collected the *quinto real*, the tax owed on all goods that passed through the port, he prepared for a long argument over whether his books were in order. The inspector at the docks had disputed the weight of the silver on his ship, alleging that the scales were off by a tenth. The shameless thief told Francisco he would accept a quarter of that in direct payment or he would have to pay the full amount to the tax collectors. Francisco refused, and the inspector wrote the higher amount in the log, which he would now

THE SILVER CANDLESTICKS

have to dispute with the clerk. He was in no mood, but he was not willing to pay the crown more than its due, much less to the thief at the docks who bore the king's seal. He was about to step up to the desk when he felt a hand on his shoulder.

"How are you, my son? I heard you were back," Don Enrique said, pulling his godchild's husband into a long embrace.

Francisco was pleased that Don Enrique had found him before he had a chance to go looking. He appeared older but still in good health. "Guiomar has told me that you have kept her safe in my absence, especially since the death of her father. I cannot thank you enough," Francisco said, his voice full of emotion. "We will see each other at dinner next week. But I am anxious to discuss something before then if you have the time," he said with some urgency.

"For my goddaughter, I would do anything. And that extends to you and the children as well," Don Enrique replied. "Shall we walk? We can go along the walls of the Alcázar and perhaps find a bit of shade."

Francisco gave up his place in line and followed Don Enrique to the courtyard. "You know already that the evil priest at the Castillo has Guiomar in his sights," Francisco confided as they walked beside the wall. "Yesterday, one of the monks from the Castillo came to tell us that Dominguez is in communication with Señora López de Herrera. The woman hates my wife and has been spreading indecent gossip about her—none of it true, of course," he said. "Later, the monk returned in search of some britches and a shirt at the request of Dominguez. I can only imagine why."

Enrique stopped under a large orange tree. "I assume the monk was the same one I met with Guiomar weeks ago, which prompted my letter to you?"

"Yes. Brother Tomás," Francisco replied. "I gave him some old clothes from my old days in my father's shop. Guiomar was happy to see me part with them," he chuckled. "I think Dominguez will use them to search for José Marcos himself in the back alleys and gambling dens. I can only hope the scoundrel has already disappeared to Cádiz or Lisbon. Guiomar did her best to help him escape before the priest got his nails into him and made him confess to something that might implicate her."

He feared this made Guiomar sound guilty of covering up some wrongdoing. He reached up to break off the tip of a low-hanging branch and ran it through his fingers, stripping the leaves. The sharp smell of citrus tickled his nostrils, making him sneeze.

"You are not used to the smells of Sevilla anymore!" Enrique laughed to ease the tension. "There is no way Dominguez could find his way around that part of town, even in your old clothes. But if we want to make sure he doesn't find Herrera, we had better find him first. I can have one of my men discreetly inquire whether he still frequents the gambling dens and brothels. Meanwhile, we can check the ship manifests to see if he is scheduled to depart when the fleet leaves port."

"*Muchas gracias*. I am already so indebted to you, I can never pay you back," Francisco said, shaking Don Enrique's hand. "Now I should get back to my quarrel with the authorities. The inspector tried to cheat us at the docks."

"Well, my son, pick your fights carefully. Sometimes it is worth letting go even when your cause is just."

"But it is your money as well as my own, Don Enrique," Francisco protested.

"I didn't say you should cheat me because you have been cheated," Enrique said, with no hint of irony. "When it comes to business, I have no heart, as your father-in-law could have told you."

Francisco realized he had much to learn about the ways of Sevillian society. But he shouldn't complain. Don Enrique had enriched him enormously. So what if he wasn't willing to pay for Francisco's naivete in not greasing the right palms. It mattered little compared to saving Guiomar from the Castillo.

Juan wandered down an alley near the docks. It was very dark and stank of bilge and rotting fish, and if he was not careful, men might jump him from the narrow doorways leading into the brothels. He had been smart to leave his money with his mother. She laughed out loud when he told her that a man had approached him who sounded like a gentleman but looked like a common thief. "Did he have the face of a skeleton and eyes that looked like they could pierce your soul?" she asked. When he told her he was not afraid of such magic, she warned him that the man was a priest, not a gentleman, and in league with the Devil himself. Nonetheless, he could be useful, so Juan must do as he asked.

Juan was only interested in the gold the priest had promised. He had no wish to harm Don Francisco's family. Esperanza had been kind enough to him when he was a boy, occasionally giving him bizcochitos, and once a sip of chocolate, which he found he could enjoy almost as often as he wished in Veracruz.

Juan opened the door of one establishment. The smoke was so heavy that it was difficult to see, but in the back, a group of men were huddled over a deck of cards. He made his way past several women with heavy rouge on their lips and cheeks, their breasts barely covered with gauzy material. One fair-skinned young girl wore nothing but a flower behind her ear. The women reached out to touch his thighs, his crotch, rubbing themselves against him as he gently pushed them aside. "Maybe later," he told the young girl, who only looked at him, smiling, a gap in her teeth making her look even younger.

He entered the room where men were gambling, but didn't see Herrera. He pushed the rear door open, nearly knocking over a sailor with his pants around his ankles while another knelt in front of him. He spat, barely missing the sailors. It was one thing to engage in such acts aboard ship and another when there were women available.

It would be a long evening if he had to go through every whorehouse and gambling den near the docks. But he worked his way down the street quickly, surveying the customers in each establishment until he finally spied Herrera in a small tavern at the end of the alley. The place stank of piss and sweat but was eerily quiet. Juan leaned against a wall near the front door, pulling his pipe from his pocket.

Herrera sat at the first table, clearly drunk and in a foul mood. Juan watched as Herrera placed a large bet, but the look in his eyes suggested it was out of desperation, not because he held a good hand. The man's hair was greasy, his clothes were soiled, and he looked as if he had not slept in days.

Herrera looked up from his cards and caught Juan's eye. "What are you staring at?" he demanded, putting his cards face down and looking as if he might leap across the table.

Juan emptied his pipe on the dirt floor and stomped on the embers before answering. "No offense. You look familiar, that's all."

José Marcos wanted an excuse to leave the table. He had already lost nearly everything he got from the sale of the ring—a veritable fortune in a matter of weeks.

"We may have met before," he said. "Give me a minute to finish this hand, and you can buy me a drink." The other players placed their bets. He looked from one to the next and passed, discarding two cards from the four he'd been dealt and drawing two from the pile. He had already lost so much it was not worth risking more on this hand.

The player to his right called out, "*Primero cuarenta y nueve*," followed by a loud guffaw as the fourth man yelled, "*Maximus*." No one bid higher, and the last player turned over his cards, revealing an ace, six, and seven of hearts—a winning hand. José Marcos looked up at the young man in the corner. "It's time for that drink," he said, pushing his chair back. He would have liked to tip over the table, but what use would that be? He would just end up bloodied and no richer.

The two men left through the door Juan had entered. Juan wished they could walk back to the first brothel to see if the young *puta* was available, but he shouldn't be distracted from his business.

"So how do I know you?" José Marcos asked when they got to the end of the alley. It was so late, he wasn't sure they would find another open tavern unless they went nearer the plaza.

"I used to see you sometimes when I was a boy. At the home of Don Pedro Péres. You would come with your sister to see the Señorita, Don Pedro's daughter."

José Marcos grabbed the mulatto's arm. "Guiomar? Did she send you to find me?" he asked, squeezing hard until the man pulled away.

"Be careful, Señor." Juan said, balling his fingers into a fist. "No one sent me," he lied. "And why would Señora Péres de Armijo, as she now is known, want to do so?" He started walking again. "There is a tavern this way," he said, looking back at Herrera, who stood still on the cobblestones in the middle of the alley.

When they finally found the tavern, which was not far from La Giralda, Juan ordered a large carafe of good wine and two glasses to their table near the door. He poured the first and gave it to Herrera, who seemed impressed after tasting it.

"My luck seems to have turned," José Marcos said, raising his glass in a toast. *But what does this man want?* he wondered. The wine was too good to be wasted on a chance companion. "To what do I owe my good fortune?"

Juan drank the full glass before speaking. "I've just returned from Méjico, if not exactly rich, at least much richer than I left," he said, filling his glass and Herrera's again. "I've had enough of my shipmates. Nearly six weeks at sea, smelling their stink in the bunks each night, sharing every meal on board. I am glad to meet a familiar face, but one not too familiar, if you understand my meaning," he said.

"So, what's it like in Méjico? Are the women as free with their bodies as I've heard?" José Marcos snickered.

"Well, they're not like the petticoated bitches here, that's for sure. You need not marry them or even promise to for them to spread their legs."

"But what about the life there? What is it like to live among savages?" José Marcos asked. "Is it a place where a man might make something of himself if he has nothing?"

"You ask as if you have an interest in going," Juan responded. "I wouldn't blame you. Every man wants adventure and there is little of it here."

José Marcos sighed, "Not if you are not the first-born."

"I wouldn't know, Señor, as I have no idea who my father was, only that his skin was fair enough to lighten my blackness."

"Your mother belonged to the Péres household? Was Don Pedro perhaps your father?"

Juan shook his head. "My mother was not good looking enough to snare that old scoundrel. The man also seemed to be in love with his wife, as I recall," he scoffed.

"But are you still…" José Marcos was not sure how to put it.

"Someone's property?" Juan slammed his glass down hard. "No. I have bought my freedom with my service to Don Francisco Armijo, the one who ended up with Señora Péres' hand." Herrera's face seemed to darken. So he had struck a nerve.

"But I am done with Armijo too. I will sign onto another ship when the fleet goes out in August and remain in Veracruz, or perhaps go into the interior or farther north to the silver mines."

José Marcos was wary of sharing too much information with this fellow. But the man knew a great deal about the voyage and what was on the other side, and he could prove useful. "I have thought of going to Las Indias. I was on my way to Lisbon to set sail from there when I fell upon some hard luck," he said.

"At cards?" Juan smiled. "We've all met the same fate at the card tables, which is why I avoided them on board. I knew I had to save enough to purchase my freedom, and I will do that in a day or two."

"Do you think you could help me sign onto a ship? I thought I would be able to pay my own passage, but my money is nearly gone," José Marcos confessed. "I am not used to physical labor, it's true. But I am strong," he said, thrusting his chest out to show its contours against his shirt.

Juan poured out the last of the carafe and lifted his glass to Herrera's. "To a good voyage. I will help you, my friend," he said, downing the glass in one long gulp. He started to get up from the table. "Where are you staying now? Perhaps we could share accommodations." Herrera lowered his eyes. "I mean, of course, that you could share mine," he added quickly, though he had none to offer yet. "That is, after I visit my mother for a day or two." The priest would gladly pay to keep tabs on Herrera, and it wouldn't be long before the man would find himself in a cell in the Castillo. "Where can I find you again?"

José Marcos admitted that he sometimes slept in the alley near the whorehouse unless one of the women took pity on him and let him sleep in her armoire while she entertained customers. "Let's meet again where we found each other tonight," he said. "Perhaps my luck at the tables will have turned again. Shall we say two days hence?" His new friend nodded and was about to leave. "You forgot to tell me your name," he called out.

"Juan," the mulatto shouted as he ducked his head at the doorway and disappeared down the street.

It was nearly dawn when Juan arrived at the hacienda where his mother now worked, the home of Herrera's sister, which he had neglected to mention the previous night and Herrera seemed not to have recognized. He was awed by its size and the elaborate iron gates that guarded the entry and the decorative grates on the tall windows. A high wall extended from the sides of the house, enclosing the grounds. He walked along the wall until he came to the rear, where a small wooden door led to the slaves' quarters. It was locked, so he waited, sitting on the cobblestones outside, his back resting against the cool earthen wall, his head on his knees. He must have fallen asleep because when he awakened, the sun was already high on the horizon and he could hear voices inside. He knocked, and a young urchin opened the door.

"Tell Concha her son is here," he said, tousling the boy's hair, thick and curly as lamb's wool. The boy let him inside and he waited for several minutes until his mother appeared, wiping her flour-stained hands and forearms on her apron. She embraced him, pulling him close to her large bosom. She reeked of onions and garlic, and Juan gently pushed her away.

"Did you find him, *m'hijo*?" she asked, her voice revealing her impatience.

"Yes. I found him playing cards in a brothel across the river. He is not the man I remember," he said.

"What do you mean?" his mother asked anxiously.

"I mean, he is down on his luck. His clothes were filthy."

Concha shook her head. "He gave up a life of great wealth—his wife is even richer than his sister is now—all because he couldn't keep his big cock in his pants."

"So, should we send word to the priest?" Juan asked. "I agreed to meet him again in two days, and I told him that he may live with me until I can secure him a place on a ship."

"Who will pay for that?" Concha asked.

"I will ask the priest. It is in his interest that I keep Herrera close and learn as much about him as I can. That will take time."

"But I wanted you to stay with me," she whined. "It's very lonely here, and the new Señora is a hard mistress. I even hoped…" she stopped.

He already knew what she was going to say. "If you want me to buy your freedom, we will need whatever money the priest can provide. And even that may not be enough."

His mother's nostrils flared, as they did whenever she was angry. When he was younger, they signaled she was about to lash out and beat him with her fists. But he was too old for that now, and besides, he knew she needed to stay in his good graces.

"There may be other ways to get the money," he said. "We will see what happens with the priest." What he did not tell his mother was that he hoped to get Señor Armijo to part with even more.

The mulatto's letter was addressed to *El amigo de Padre Dominguez, Arturo Cháves*. It was written in a poor script and the words were badly spelled, which did not surprise Dominguez. But he understood their meaning. The man had found Herrera and would meet him again in two days. "I will need to pay for lodging," he wrote, "for me and him, until I get the information you seek."

The priest shook his head. The mulatto was abusing his generosity. And how did he know the young scoundrel would not take off with the money and never be seen again? But the sailor had not provided him enough information to follow up himself, which was clever, so he had no choice but to trust him. He considered attempting to meet the fellow again to take better measure of his intentions, but he didn't like the idea of sneaking down to the docks again, and he couldn't very well invite him to the Castillo. The priest took the leather pouch from the drawer and counted out thirty pieces of silver. He winced at the thought that Herrera's life was being sold for the same amount as the Lord's and put back three pieces. It would have to be enough for this greedy traitor.

Chapter Twenty-Eight
THE DILEMMA

Francisco saw Juan approaching from across the plaza. He walked with a certain swagger that no doubt attracted native women in Veracruz, where his caste was higher than theirs, but could land him in trouble here at home. The boy had entered his service to assure the silence of his troublesome mother, Concha. But he was lazy at first and later quarrelsome. Only on the return trip did Juan's behavior improve. Nevertheless, Francisco had promised the boy that he would sign the *coartado* freeing him and that was what he intended to do.

"Buenos días, Don Francisco," Juan said, bowing slightly.

"This is a big day, Juan. You have earned your freedom. I hope you will use it wisely. You will have opportunities that are closed to many who are similarly situated," he said, not sure how to phrase what he wanted to say. "What I mean is, you can choose to live here or return to Veracruz—or elsewhere. But you will have to earn your own living."

Juan felt his anger rising. Did this man believe he had not earned his own living every day of his life since childhood? He had scrubbed floors, wrung chickens' necks, emptied the chamber pots when he was barely able to carry them. "I have plans, Don Francisco," he said, barely controlling the tone of his voice. "I already obtained lodging not far from the docks. And I will join another crew soon."

THE SILVER CANDLESTICKS

"If you wish to earn some money in the meantime…" Francisco started to offer without thinking, then proceeded more cautiously. "I don't have anything presently, of course, now that the ships are unloaded. But if you need a recommendation—"

"I have other resources," Juan replied coldly.

Francisco regretted the turn the conversation had taken. He must be careful with this boy, who was now a man that could prove dangerous.

They reached La Casa del Ayuntamiento, the townhall in the central plaza. Francisco led them through the heavy mahogany doors and up the main staircase under the ornate vaulted ceiling depicting the Spanish monarchs up to Carlos V. The justice of the peace was at the end of the corridor, and there were two other men waiting to have papers notarized.

"I would like to be of some service to you, Juan. You are an ambitious young man. Let me see if I can secure you a better position when you set sail," Francisco said. Juan's expression changed, and he stood more erect, which made him taller, but oddly less threatening. Resentment bred hatred, and Francisco could not afford to make him an enemy.

Juan observed his former master carefully. Did he detect a whiff of fear? Armijo had good reason to be fearful, but it would be best not to let on, at least at this point. Maybe later it would become useful. The priest was good for some silver, but only as much as Señora López de Herrera's jealousy allowed. Don Francisco, on the other hand, stood to lose his wealth, his wife, his children, perhaps even his life if the priest ensnared the family in the Inquisition's grip. "I would gladly accept whatever help you are willing to provide," he said as the notary beckoned to them.

"How will I find you?" Francisco asked before stepping up to the desk. He signed two copies of the document, which the notary stamped and handed back to him without looking up.

"You may contact me through my mother," Juan said. "You know where to find her," he added with some resentment that his mother had been given to another household like a piece of furniture. He watched Armijo's face as he spoke, but it revealed nothing.

"Would you like your mother present when we stand before the judge?" Francisco asked in as sincere a voice as he could muster. "We could come back tomorrow, with her as a witness and any others you choose, and make it a festive occasion."

Juan sensed some trick at play. "I am not close to my mother. She gets along with no one, as you know yourself," he said, keeping his eyes on Armijo. They proceeded down an empty hall to the justice of the peace. The ceremony, if it could be called that, took no more than a few minutes. Francisco raised his right hand and swore that the manumission was permanent, after which he slapped Juan on the back and handed him his copy of the *coartado*.

Perhaps he could turn his master's good will to his advantage. "Shall we walk outside?" Juan asked. "Within these walls are too many ears."

Francisco nodded and the two went silently down the wide staircase and out into the plaza, which had yet to fill with the hordes of merchants, señoras on their way to their seamstresses, beggars, pickpockets, and others who would later fill the area surrounding the large fountain in the center.

"Let me be clear, Juan, not that you have suggested otherwise, but I intend to ensure that my copy of the document be filed in the archives at the Contratación expeditiously so that there is no question of its legality. I have no desire to deprive you of your freedom one day longer than necessary. Indeed, I am uncomfortable with the whole institution of slavery. It is an evil practice that should be condemned by every Christian."

Juan looked at the man who had personally exploited his underpaid labor for the last few years while he earned his freedom. He raised one eyebrow, which even a hypocrite like Armijo could read as a sign of skepticism. "I will accompany you to file the paper if you please. And afterwards," Juan smiled, "we can talk as men, not master and slave. I have information that I think might prove

THE SILVER CANDLESTICKS

valuable to you. It concerns a man who has been asking questions about Señor Herrera—and your wife."

Francisco kept the muscles in his face from betraying his emotion. "Absolutely. We must talk as one man to another, my friend. Let us go file the document now." He needed Juan, but he knew that, like his mother, the fellow could not be trusted.

Guiomar was frightened at what her husband told her when he returned from the Casa de Contratación, first that José Marcos had not left Sevilla as he promised when she gave him the emerald, then that Padre Dominguez had hatched a plan to use José Marcos to get to her.

"Are you sure the boy is telling the truth?" she asked. "I have done nothing improper with the man. You must believe me, Francisco," she implored. "I gave him the ring to rid him from Sevilla, not because of any affection I have for him." She reached out to take her husband's hands. "When I think back on my life before I married you, I am filled with remorse. I was a silly, vain girl, flattered by the attentions of an unworthy man. But I rebuffed him when he reached out to me after we were married and only agreed to speak with him one other time before he came to ask for help. And even that time, as God is my witness, I pushed him away. He never touched me," she said, her tears starting to flow.

Francisco lifted her chin. "I do believe you, my love. I am not telling you this as an accusation but so you understand the danger you are in. The danger we are *all* in if Dominguez gets his claws in us," he said, leaning over to kiss her forehead. "I had hoped we would have time to settle our affairs, to transfer the ownership of my father's business now that he is too old and I can no longer oversee it. But we have no time. I must make inquiries, discreetly, about what ships will leave port this month or else we will have to wait until spring, and that may be too late."

"You must talk to my *padrino*. He will know what to do and can make inquiries without exposing us. I hope he will not balk at losing your services, as he did when my father retired before my mother's death." Don Enrique could be a hard man, she knew, but she also knew he loved her as a daughter. "Perhaps I should be the one to broach it with him," she said.

"We will do it together. And the sooner the better," Francisco replied. "In the meantime, we must decide who will go with us on our journey."

"Esperanza must come. And her son. But of course, she must agree," she said, worrying that perhaps her faithful servant might not wish to do so. "And, Francisco, there is another matter to discuss. I was horrified at your description of the Africans who have been brought to Méjico."

"My dear, slavery is both much harsher in Méjico and more fluid. The Church forbids that the *Indios* be enslaved, but they are treated as badly as the slaves are, indeed much worse than slaves in Sevilla. I watched men die from the severe beatings they received."

"Then we must free Esperanza and Benito," she said.

"I hoped you would say that my love. But we must wait until we are in Méjico so as not to draw suspicion."

"And the others?"

Francisco put his hands on Guiomar's face. "*Mi corazón*, it would be better if only Esperanza and Benito accompany us. Perhaps Don Enrique can include the others in his household."

"I will ask him."

"And you have to settle the matter of their..." he wasn't sure how to put it, "their long-term status."

"I would hope that Don Enrique will free them on his death," Guiomar added. "He has no heirs to leave them to."

"You could do so yourself once we are in Veracruz," Francisco offered. "They are your property, after all," he said. He was sincere in his abhorrence of slavery, but he worried that Guiomar would have difficulty giving up this part of her inheritance.

"I will talk with him," she said, though she imagined the discussion might be more difficult than Francisco could understand. She was asking her *padrino* to take great risks on her behalf and had little to offer in return but the wealth the slaves represented.

"We must act as if nothing has changed and tell no one of our plans except Don Enrique and Esperanza," Francisco said. "The worst thing that could happen would be for that devil priest to find out in advance." He kissed her again on the forehead. He felt genuine love for her, but he worried that she would find her new life a challenge, left to do for herself what had always been done for her. It would be especially hard if they left Veracruz for the north eventually, as he planned. It would be safer there, beyond the reach of the Inquisition, which had already become active in Ciudad de Méjico. But he would bide his time before telling her the extent of his plans.

Juan jingled the coins in his pocket. Soon he would add gold to his store of silver, hidden behind a stone in his new dwelling. It was a dangerous game he was playing, deceiving the priest and leading on his former master. He liked the thought of that—his former master. He was a free man now. If he chose, he could take the priest's silver—and Armijo's gold—and simply disappear, leaving both men in the lurch. It would not be difficult to get to Portugal. With the funds he was about to receive, he could buy a horse and ride there, avoiding coaches that might give away his escape route.

But why worry about such things? The priest would surely not come forward to claim he had been cheated. His mother might suffer the consequences of Señora López's wrath, but what had she ever done for him? As for Armijo, so long as he did not disclose the whereabouts of Herrera, his family was safe, and Juan had paid for the lodging he'd share with Herrera for a month. Herrera could remain there, undetected, so long as the man was careful.

Juan knocked on the gate behind Señora Herrera de Madrid's house. As before, one of the servants let him in and went to fetch his mother. She appeared shortly, her face sweating as if she had been standing over a boiling pot.

"*M'hijo*, how handsome you look," she said, embracing him. "Did you go to Casa de Ayuntamiento?"

"What do you think? I am not the lazy boy you used to berate. I am a responsible man—one who is now free as well," he chided.

Concha looked at her son, beaming. It was true. He was not the child who left the household of Don Pedro a few years earlier. He had grown tall and muscular, a man who would attract many women and not just the *Indias* of Méjico. With his fair skin and strong features, perhaps he would land a Spanish girl of a decent home. "So, have you done what the priest asked? Is Señor Herrera safely hidden until the priest chooses to set the civil authorities on him?"

"He is. And when do you think that might happen?" he asked, hoping to pry more information from her.

"Who knows. But why do you care?" He had something up his sleeve, she could tell. He might have grown tall and more "responsible," but he was still wily. She wasn't even sure *she* could trust him. A mother's loyalty was a thing to be taken for granted, but not a child's.

"I want to be sure not to be there when it happens. But they won't find him until I tell them where to look," he said. He hoped to drag it out as long as he could. He needed Armijo's money in his hands before it was safe to disappear. He had promised Armijo he would take Herrera with him, but he had little desire to do so. It would cost twice as much to sneak both of them out of Spain and across the border to Portugal, but who knew if he could secure work on a ship there. He spoke no Portuguese and had no desire to learn, though his Spanish might be enough. It would be hard to secure one sailor's berth without greasing a few palms. Two would present more challenge and expense.

Concha became irritated. He was putting her in a bad position. She had promised her mistress that her son could find the woman's handsome husband and the priest would be angry if Juan double-crossed him. It was not out of the question that she would bear the brunt of both Señora Lopez's and the inquisitor's displeasure.

"Don't play games with these people, Juanito. They have great power, which they are not afraid to use," she said, hugging him once again. "I must return to my duties before I am missed," she said, turning to go.

    Juan watched her retreat to the back of the house. A pang of remorse hit him. She had not been a bad mother. Only in comparison to Esperanza, with whom they shared a casita at the Péres household, did she seem harsh. Esperanza treated her boy with great affection, but he was much younger, and perhaps his own mother had been kinder once, before his memories of her had fully formed. She had, after all, secured him a position with Don Francisco when he sailed for Méjico, and perhaps it was also she who put the idea of the *coartado* in Don Francisco's mind. He kicked at the dirt in the courtyard with his shoe. It was not wise to become sentimental now. He must take care of himself and let others see to their own safety. He left through the gate, knowing it was the last time he would lay eyes on his mother.

Chapter Twenty-Nine

A SUDDEN DECISION

Guiomar and Francisco rode a carriage to Don Enrique's hacienda outside the city. The streets leaving Sevilla were crowded with merchants, farmers and others flooding in to sell their goods to the sailors and hangers-on who had come in with the arrival of the fleet. Prices rose sharply as the crowds grew, with goods unloaded from the ships selling more dearly than during the months when the city was less crowded. Taffeta, chiffon, silk, even serge sold at a premium as the city's women looked to adorn themselves in the latest fashions. The men, too, now wore silk vests in bright colors with britches to match.

Francisco looked out at the sea of fancy dresses and wondered how Guiomar would adjust to a new life in Méjico. If they stayed in Veracruz, she would mix with other wealthy merchants' wives, entertaining with elaborate feasts that would include new foods, new customs, and a social structure very different than that of Sevilla. Veracruz was a city of new wealth, unencumbered by the social strictures of the Old World. Francisco was equal to any man, unlike here, where his status rested on that of his wife's family and not his own success. But Guiomar would have to learn to sit at table with men and women who had newly acquired the finery and manners that she had been born to. Many of the women could not read, and even some of the men were barely literate, though well enough versed in numbers to know how to make a profit and invest it. Still, he supposed she had suffered enough from the laws of purity in Spain not to mind the mixing of blood that took place in Méjico. Besides which, he suspected that many among the merchant class were, like the Péres family, New Christians who had reverted to their old faith on the distant shores of the New World. Perhaps she would even learn from them what her parents had not been able or willing to teach about their customs and beliefs.

The road to Don Enrique's hacienda was lined with large cedar trees, their twisted roots making it appear as if they were entering a magical realm. Francisco slowed the carriage and reached over to take Guiomar's hand.

"There is no turning back now. Are you sure you are ready to do this?"

"We have no choice, Francisco. I would stay if I thought it was safe—I would be lying if I said otherwise. But the priest will hound me until he succeeds in locking me in his dungeon."

The wall surrounding Don Enrique's estate was tall, with bits of broken glass affixed to the top, a new addition since he had last visited, Francisco noted. The wrought iron gate was open, and Francisco led the carriage up the cypress-lined path to the front of the house, where Don Enrique was standing on the patio near a large fountain.

"*Bienvenidos*," Enrique shouted as Francisco pulled back on the reins. A footman appeared from the side of the house and took charge of the horses as the couple alighted. Enrique embraced Guiomar, kissing her on both cheeks, before grasping Francisco's hand in his own to pull him close and affectionately slap him on the back.

"You look more beautiful every day, *m'hija*. I can see that Francisco has helped put the color back into your cheeks," he teased. "Come in and we will have some light refreshment," he said leading the couple through the door to his large house. Inside, a young servant held a pitcher and basin with a small towel draped over her arm so that the guests could wash, each taking turns as the girl poured water over their hands. Afterwards, they crossed the wide corridor, which led to a covered patio around which the house was built. The servants had laid out a table with a pitcher of sangria and a bowl of fruit as well as stuffed olives and a large round of Manchego.

Guiomar sat at the table, and the servant filled her glass. She put it to her lips and tasted the sweet wine. She looked up at Don Enrique, who lifted his glass in a toast: "*Salud*! May my goddaughter and her husband remain close to me for a while longer," he said. Guiomar winced. How could she ask this man who had been so good to her all her life to part with her now in his declining age? She remembered her father's last days. He had become frightened and suspicious of those around him, and on his worst days, only she could calm him. Don Enrique would have no one if she left.

"I fear it has become impossible to stay even for the few months until the fleet sails in the spring," Francisco blurted out too quickly.

Don Enrique was stunned. He looked at Guiomar's face, which had turned crimson. "What does this mean, *m'hija*?" he asked. Francisco started to speak, but Don Enrique turned quickly, "Let my goddaughter answer, please."

"It is why we have come, *Padrino*. We must leave now—with your blessing and your help. We have only days left," she said, reaching across the table to rest her hand on his. She looked pleadingly into his eyes. "I beg you, let Francisco explain. He has a plan."

Enrique leaned backwards, tipping his chair onto its back legs, which drew one of the servants to stand behind him. His habit unnerved everyone, as if he were some old fool who would land on his ass if he weren't careful. "Tell me," he commanded, turning to Francisco.

Francisco described his encounter with Juan, which had changed everything in his mind. "I don't think it's enough to get Herrera out of the picture. There are too many now who have been exposed to the lies about Guiomar and her family," he said, keeping up the subterfuge about the family's religion. "The priest has informants everywhere. The only way to remain safe is to leave—and to do so at once."

THE SILVER CANDLESTICKS

Enrique leaned forward again, clasping his hands on the table, but said nothing. Guiomar reached over and put her hands on his. "*Padrino*, I wish it could be otherwise. I have prayed that this menace would disappear, and I know you have done your best to rein in the priest, but he is obsessed with putting me in his dungeon. I don't know why—surely, I have done nothing to warrant it. But I have seen first-hand what happens to those he has condemned. He will stop at nothing. He drives innocent women to betray their children and children to take their own lives. I like to think I am strong, but who can be sure they are strong enough to withstand the rack?" Her tears fell over their hands.

Don Enrique lifted hers to his lips. "I will never let that happen—even if it means parting from you forever. But we must be practical. You cannot simply board a sailing ship—we must register your names as passengers in advance and show proof that you are not Jews if you hope to take any of your possessions with you, including your slaves and anything more than the clothes on your back."

"I hoped that you might find some captains who are willing to attest that we are good Catholics, preferably some who are not from Sevilla," Francisco offered. "I will pay them whatever is required," he added, making it clear that Enrique would not have to assume the burden.

"I will need a list of which ships are due to sail and the captains' names," Enrique said. "We will have to move quickly, and hope that there are some men from Genoa, Lisbon, or Antwerp in the mix. In the meantime, we must withdraw enough gold to ensure your safe travel without arousing suspicion."

"There is one more thing," Guiomar said. "I know I have asked much from you and now I must ask more." Her voice faltered. "It is about my household," she said, trying to judge exactly how much he would agree to do.

"You don't intend to take all your slaves with you—that would be dangerous. I know they are a part of your inheritance, but…"

"I will take Esperanza and her son, but I was hoping you might find a place for the others, four in all, two women and two men," she said tentatively. "At least on a temporary basis."

"Why not sell them? They would bring a handsome sum," Enrique offered. "And you may need the money."

"That is impossible," Francisco interjected.

"What my husband means, *Padrino*, is that I intend to free them," Guiomar said, reaching out to squeeze Francisco's hand. "Once we get to Veracruz, I will sign the *coartados* for Esperanza and her child. And the others—they have served my family for many years, and they will need a roof over their heads and food. Might you help them, *Padrino*?" Her eyes pleaded with her godfather, who softened under her gaze.

"I am a businessman, *m'hija*."

"But they are not merchandise, surely, like maize or cloth."

"More like gold and silver, which can be invested to produce more," Enrique replied.

"But they have souls, surely!"

"Guiomar," Francisco interrupted, "we are asking a great deal of Don Enrique. We need not settle the details now."

"You have married a wise man, *m'hija*," Enrique said, lifting his goblet. "*Salud*," he said, downing the glass in a single gulp. "I only wish that I were young enough to accompany you on this great adventure. In the meantime, I will make the arrangements, and you need not fear for your servants. Send them to me and you may do what you wish when you are safe in Veracruz." But even as he said the words, he knew that he was putting himself in danger. *So be it*, he thought. He had always said Guiomar was the daughter he never had. Now he held the power to give her life. A new life. Even if it meant risking his own.

Esperanza could not sleep. Guiomar had made it clear that she was free to make her own decision, but she had no experience in deciding her own fate. From the moment the men had grabbed her in her village when she was just a child to the present, she'd never had the power to decide even the smallest matter. She had been stripped of everything. Her family. Her clothing. Her name. Her language. Her religion. She could not decide when to rest her tired feet much less where to sleep or for how long. The activities of her days and nights were meted out by others, and even when her mistresses had been generous, as Doña Benita had been and Guiomar had grown to be, she was subject to their wishes and was rarely asked about her own desires. Now she must decide whether to get on a ship and sail to the New World with her son, a world as alien from Sevilla as Sevilla had been from her village. And from what Don Francisco had said, Veracruz was just the beginning of the family's long journey.

She lifted her torso, resting her weight on her elbow. Benito was asleep on the cot in the corner. His chest expanded with each breath, and she wished she could rock him in her arms as she had when he was little. But he was growing fast and would soon be eight years old. He was learning to read and write, though he would much rather spend time with the animals and the neighborhood urchins. What future did he have in Sevilla? He might grow up to be a groomsman or perhaps be apprenticed in the Armijos' candle factory. But he would not be free. As Don Francisco had explained, it was too dangerous to grant their freedom until they reached Méjico. She would simply have to trust him.

She stood up, grabbed her shawl, and quietly stepped outside. The moon was large and bright as it had been the night Benito was conceived. She had not thought of the boy's father in a long time. The man had shown no interest in her, nor in his son, in the years since he left the Péres household. After earning his release from indenture, he had simply disappeared. She had heard his name mentioned once or twice by the other servants, but she never inquired into his whereabouts.

She sat beneath the tree in the courtyard, pulling her legs up and wrapping her arms around her knees. She heard the hoot of an owl, long and mournful, then felt the powerful burst of air as it swept by her from its perch in a neighboring tree. She watched its powerful talons grasp a small rabbit that stood frozen in the yard, the whole scene lit by the full moon. The poor creature let out a squeal as the huge bird flapped its wings and disappeared behind the wall. She did not want her son to become like the rabbit, easy prey to creatures more powerful than he would ever be. Perhaps in the New World he would have the chance to become something greater than another man's property, even if the journey would be long and hard. And dangerous. But first, they had to escape the inquisitor's grip. She did not want to think about serving that evil man at dinner this evening. What if he noticed something amiss—a packed trunk carelessly left in the hall, a nervous look on Señora Guiomar's face?

She lifted her body off the ground. This was no time to think about what could go wrong. She had a full day ahead—preparing the meal, making sure the trunks were packed with her master's, mistress's, and children's clothing. Her own bag would be light, an extra camisa for herself and some trousers and a shirt for Benito. She would like to take the farthingale that Doña Benita had given her, but there would not be room and, from what Señor Francisco said, it would ill suit the climate in Méjico. They must leave for the docks the next evening with as little fuss as possible, dressed as if they were going across the bridge for a walk along the presidio. The main thing was to look as if they planned to return later that night.

It had been years since Don Enrique himself had made the trip to La Contratación to file paperwork for departure from Sevilla, but this time, only he could secure the necessary permissions. He would have to grease a few palms to expedite his goddaughter's passage on a cargo vessel that would sail the next day. But what was it worth to have amassed so much influence if not to save those you loved?

In his pocket, he carried the documents attesting to the family's *sangre pura*, which, along with Francisco's gold, had cost him the favors of three ship's captains, two from Italy and one from Portugal who had sailed in his fleet early in their careers. His word had been enough to get them to attest in writing that they knew Francisco Armijo personally, though none had laid eyes on him. But all remembered Don Pedro Péres from his days in Don Enrique's service, and the idea that he was not a pure Spaniard and good Catholic was unthinkable.

Still, Enrique wondered if he shouldn't drop in on the archbishop while he was in Sevilla. He had no appointment, but the prelate would see him, given his latest gift, a new tabernacle for one of the side altars fashioned from pure silver from the mines of Zacatecas. The mold had been cast in Méjico from a design made by one of the best silversmiths in the New World, depicting Christ and his disciples with the short torsos and legs common to the *Indios* of Méjico, their bodies barely covered in garb more appropriate to the lush jungle of the interior than Jerusalem. But Rodrigo de Castro had been delighted by the gift, and Enrique was sure he would be welcomed at the chancery.

"My friend, I am pleasantly surprised by your visit," the Archbishop said, motioning Don Enrique to sit in the familiar chairs. "Are you worried that I have hidden away your naked *Indios*?" he asked. "They are a bit scandalous," he added without waiting for Enrique to respond. "Rest assured that we are creating a new altar that will display other artifacts of Las Indias, and the tabernacle will be the focal point," he said. "No doubt the señoras of Sevilla will find reason to spend more time kneeling before it than they might if the apostles looked more like you or me," he remarked with an indulgent smile.

Enrique was taken slightly off guard. How would he now move to discuss Dominguez and his meddling? "I am glad you approve," he said lightly. "If the Church is to be truly universal, we should encourage all races to adopt Our Lord in their own image, don't you think?"

Rodrigo let out a loud guffaw. "Spoken like a believer, Enrique, rather than the skeptic I know you to be."

Enrique smiled, but the jibe made him nervous. At least it allowed him to introduce the inquisitor into the discussion. "I will be seeing your priest Dominguez this evening," he said. "Should I be nervous, your Excellency?" he said with as much joviality as the subject could justify. Rodrigo frowned.

"Dominguez is no priest of mine. If he were not sent here by the Holy Office, I would have banished him to some backwater long ago. The man is a menace."

Don Enrique was surprised at the prelate's vehemence. "Yes, I quite agree," he said, hesitating slightly before proceeding. "He has the temerity to dine at my goddaughter's table while entertaining wild accusations against her. It will be all I can do to remain civil to the man."

"Yes, I have heard that he has spies in the Herrera household. The poor wife has been abandoned by her husband, the scoundrel," Rodrigo responded, which took Enrique by surprise. But, of course, a man like de Castro would have his own spies.

"You don't believe my goddaughter is the cause, I hope," Enrique pressed.

"Of course not, my friend. But what I think and what Dominguez believes are two different matters, and unless he steps beyond his authority, there is little I can do." Rodrigo rang the little bell on the table. "It was good to see you, but I have a busy schedule, as I am sure you do as well. Thank you for visiting—and let us share a meal together soon." The archbishop rose and Enrique stood quickly, bowing before turning to leave.

"Enrique," Rodrigo called out. "It would be a shame for your tabernacle to be displayed without proper lighting. Why don't you task your artisans with fashioning a hanging lamp in the same style to adorn the altar in the nave?"

Enrique turned around to face the archbishop. "It would be my honor, Your Excellency." The visit had been unsuccessful. It would now be up to him to stop the priest if he could.

Guiomar rifled through the dresses in her armoire. She could take only a few. She would ask Enrique to allow the servants to choose among the rest, and whatever was left could be sold. She would take all her jewels, including those bequeathed by her mother, which could be used to supply their needs in Veracruz. Francisco had already arranged for Enrique to lease the furnished house out and for the income to be deposited in accounts in Ciudad de Méjico. It was Francisco's hope to move the family to Zacatecas, where the silver mines had created fortunes among the criollos who settled there. But the land he described sounded very harsh to Guiomar: arid with the thin air of the desert mountains whose flattened tabletop peaks had inspired the name *mesas*. She wished that she could consult her brother, but doing so would put him in danger. She would write him when they were at sea, though the letter might not reach him for months depending on whether they encountered ships sailing east.

She slid her fingers along the bed's headboard until she touched the small book Alfonso had given her after their mother died. She had considered burning it but was glad that she had not. She had not looked at it since her father's death. Many of the rituals it described still seemed alien to her, except for the Sabbath candle-lighting and monthly bathing instructions. She looked at the illustrations for the cutting of the male-child's foreskin and shuddered. Thankfully, Alfonso had explained that this was too dangerous while the Holy Office operated, but the illustrations would provide appropriate instruction once the madness of the Inquisition was behind them.

She had hoped to practice her faith more openly in Méjico, but she would need more guidance than these thin pages provided. At least she would be able to light the candles every Sabbath as her mother had taught her, and Esperanza would prepare the meals in accordance with the rules she had learned. She had already asked Esperanza to retrieve the candlesticks, which had been buried in the garden while her father was still alive. They were taking no other household items as Francisco had assured her more could be bought when they arrived. But the candlesticks were irreplaceable, and Esperanza would hide them in a basket of food she would bring aboard. She wished she could take some of the fine China that her father had brought back from his trading missions, but she would have to get used to the cruder implements fashioned in Méjico. There would be many things she would have to adjust to. But she had adjusted to being a Jew, and what could compare to the shock of learning that?

She knew she would not sleep this night, the last she would ever spend on land in Sevilla. She felt a strange desire to go to Santa Ana's where her parents were buried, where she had been married and her children baptized. But the sun was setting, and it would be odd to make such a visit without a reason. Perhaps she could attend Mass in the morning, which would not seem out of place, and God would certainly forgive her dual loyalty. She could ask Francisco to go with her—after all, he was giving up his home as surely as she was.

She wondered if he would tell his father that the family was leaving. Guiomar felt a pang of guilt. Her father-in-law was barely a part of her life even though he lived close by. They met at church and large family celebrations, but he had never been a guest at their social gatherings, always demurring even on the rare occasion he was invited. The class distinctions were too great, although he was now far more prosperous thanks to the success of Francisco's adventures in Méjico. Still, her children adored him and would visit him in his small house with its fine fruit trees whenever permitted.

Francisco had been adamant that the children not be told what was happening before they embarked on the ship, but that, too, gave her pause. Úrsula was especially fond of the birds, and it would be impossible to take them. Méjico had its own brilliant specimens, she knew, but none with the melodious song of Úrsula's beloved canaries, she feared.

Chapter Thirty

A GIFT

Padre Dominguez tied his cincture tightly around his waist, pulling on the rope until he could feel it dig into his flesh. He had expected to hear from his informer already, but the man had neither sent word nor appeared at the Castillo after being summoned early that morning. He wished to go to the Armijo house that evening with as much intelligence as possible about the relations between Herrera and Señora Péres. If the informer hoped to see another maravedi from the priest, he would have to provide some evidence against these Judaizers, even if it was merely that the woman had betrayed her marriage vows.

He paced the floor of his office. The wait was intolerable. He could not very well go down to the pier again in search of Herrera. But whom could he send? The fat monk had been his messenger before, but delivering notes was very different from finding the whereabouts of men who did not want to be found. He wondered whether Señora Péres had invited Herrera's wife to the dinner that evening. It would be entertaining to see the two women at the same table. But even if she had invited her lover's wife, the latter would likely not accept. Too bad, but it would provide him with more time to study his target. In the meantime, he would send the fat monk on another errand. The moneylender could do with more pressure to reveal what he knew about the ring's provenance. He would draft a note immediately.

Brother Tomás found the sun oppressive as he hurried to the parrot shop with the letter Dominguez had given him. Sweat dripped down his brow, and he reached up with a handkerchief to wipe his cheeks. He was thirsty and hungry, but he had no hope that the merchant would offer him hospitality. He slowed his pace as he wended his way through the labyrinthine streets, which were crowded with all manner of people: sailors, vendors, women baring their shoulders, and children clad in filthy rags who wove in and out of the masses, their deft fingers dipping into pockets before the wearer even noticed the slight bump against his leg.

He was almost on the doorstep of the parrot shop when a man emerged, a tall mulatto. He slowed down until he could pass. The mulatto looked directly at him, which gave Tomás a start, though perhaps he had caught the man's attention merely because it was unusual to see the black-and-white robes of a Dominican on the streets of Sevilla. He pushed the door open and was surprised by the tinkling of a bell attached to the lintel.

"Hola," he said in a raised voice when he could see no one in the room crowded with cages.

"Hola, hola, hola," echoed a large scarlet bird with a fearsome beak. Tomás laughed involuntarily—he had never encountered a talking creature—and moved closer to the big metal cage in the center of the room.

"I see you've met," Jorge said, emerging from a doorway with strands of beads obscuring what was behind it. "How can I help you, Padre?"

"I am a humble monk, Señor, not a priest," Brother Tomás replied. "Padre Dominguez asked that I bring you this," he said, pulling the letter from his pocket. "He asked that I wait for a reply."

Jorge took the missive with some trepidation. He wondered if the monk had noticed his previous visitor leaving. The letter was straightforward: Had he made any progress in his inquiries? He hesitated before giving a response to the fat monk. "Can I offer you a refreshment, *Hermano*?" he asked, buying time. "Please, sit down. I will just be a minute."

THE SILVER CANDLESTICKS

Tomás saw a flimsy chair but hesitated to sit down; it would be humiliating if it were to break under his weight. "May I look around at your birds? I have never seen anything like them."

"Be my guest," Jorge said, disappearing beyond the curtain. He pushed aside a small carpet, lifted the trap door in his storeroom and climbed down the rickety ladder. With only the light from a taper held in front of him, he moved gingerly through the trunks and other goods stored in the damp cellar to the wine rack against the far wall. He pulled out a bottle and made his way back to the ladder. He must tell the monk something that would satisfy the inquisitor while not endangering himself or, he hoped, Señora Péres. He could invent a tale that would hold off the inquisitor for a few days and, in the meantime, warn the Señora. But what?

Jorge reappeared bearing two glasses and a bottle of wine. "So, what do you think, Hermano?" he asked as the monk stood in front of the macaw's cage.

"It looks like it could take your finger off with one bite," Brother Tomás responded.

"No, my friend, she is a gentle creature," he said, opening the cage door. The large bird gripped the metal bars and pulled itself up onto the top of the cage, bending its head to be petted. Jorge scratched the scarlet cap, and the bird raised the fringe of feathers around its neck, which made it look even more frightening. The monk stepped back, almost knocking over another cage.

"Your superior had a similar reaction. I was surprised, given his daily interaction with the most dangerous of caged animals," Jorge said, looking directly into the monk's eyes. They showed fear, which he thought was a promising sign. Perhaps he was not of the same breed as the inquisitor. "So, what is your role at the Castillo? Are you one of those who administers the *tormentos*?" he asked, observing the monk's reddening face.

"No, Señor. I am a baker. I prepare the bread for the priests. And the prisoners," he added, taking the glass the shop owner handed him.

"And is it the same bread?" Jorge asked.

"If I can help it," Tomás answered without thinking that this man might report it back to Padre Dominguez, who insisted that only the burned loaves or ones that had grown stale be given to the poor men and women in the cells.

"Kindness, even to those creatures we enclose in cages, is surely something God approves," Jorge said. "Tell Padre Dominguez that my inquiries have produced no information." It was true—but only because he had failed to make any since he knew exactly where the ring was. The fat monk nodded and took the last sip of cool wine from the glass.

"Thank you, Señor. I will be on my way then," the monk replied.

Jorge studied the man's round face. There was kindness in the features, small lines around the puffy eyes, which suggested he smiled often. "Wait a moment, Hermano. I do have a bit of information to take back to the priest," he said. The monk's eyes widened with what could only be interpreted as fear. Perhaps this monk knew more than he had let on. "Tell him that I am on track to learn the whereabouts of the gentleman he seeks. I have been promised the information before the week's end."

Tomás could feel the blood draining from his face. Perhaps it was the wine. He reached out to steady himself.

"Are you all right, my friend?" Jorge asked. He was right, this monk knew more than his demeanor suggested. "You seem upset by this information. Have you suspicion who the person I am referring to might be?"

Tomás didn't know how he should respond. He had no reason to trust this man who seemed to be an informant for Padre Dominguez.

"Did you see the mulatto leaving my shop as you came in?" Jorge continued. The monk stared down at the floor. "He arrived recently on a ship with Don Francisco Armijo," he added.

Tomás looked up and met the bird seller's eyes. "Has Don Francisco returned?" he asked, speaking before he had time to consider whether it was wise.

"Yes." Jorge reached for the monk's empty glass still clutched in his fingers. "Let me pour you another glass. I think we may have more to discuss."

Tomás sighed. "I pray you will not betray me, Señor. Padre Dominguez is a hard man—and one obsessed with Don Francisco's wife."

"I know," Jorge said. "We will have to trust each other if we are to protect the innocent," he said, lifting his glass. "*Salud.*"

Juan walked along the docks until he recognized one of the men who had come with him from Veracruz. The sailor was walking up the gangplank to an unfamiliar ship, a bundle over his shoulders. "Pablo," he shouted out. "Wait, *hombre.*"

The sailor stopped as he was about to step onto the ship and turned around, frowning. Juan had beaten him at cards on the voyage, but he had done so honestly.

"Let me buy you a drink, *mi amigo*," he said.

"Why not?" Pablo answered, slowly walking down the slippery gangplank.

"Where are you off to so soon?" Juan asked. "We barely arrived a week ago."

"My luck was no better on land than at sea," Pablo said. "I lost my wages at the card tables in three nights. I am fortunate to find a ship that will set sail in two days."

"Are they taking on more men?" Juan asked.

"Are you interested?" Pablo asked.

"No, I intend to stay awhile. Armijo proved a man of his word. I am a free man," Juan said, slapping his companion on the arm. "But I know one who is interested in leaving as soon as he can. And it might prove worthwhile to one who could assist him." He was tempted to tell the man more but thought better of it. Armijo would not be happy to have word spread of his interest in seeing Herrera gone from Sevilla.

"Has the fellow any experience at sea?" Pablo asked.

Juan laughed. "None at all. I doubt he has any experience beyond the card tables or a cuckold's bed."

"I hear the crew is short-handed. But a man with no experience…that could be risky for the one who recommended him."

"And what if he showed up instead of another sailor?" Juan threw his arm around Pablo's shoulder. "You deserve more than a week on shore, *amigo*. It's the least I can do for you since I helped you go broke," he laughed, hugging the man tighter.

Juan left Pablo at the bar with a pitcher of wine, promising to meet the sailor at the pier with his replacement at dawn the day after next. Now he had only to persuade Herrera to go. He headed to Triana to collect his money from Armijo. He would figure out how to trick the priest later. He had already set the trap with the moneylender.

The house on Calle Catarina was not nearly as imposing as the one where his mother now worked for Señora Herrera de Madrid. He had remembered it as larger and more elegant. Still, he hesitated before walking through the front gate. In his years living in the small hovel at the back of the hacienda with his mother and the one she was so jealous of, and later Esperanza's own boy, he had never walked through the courtyard to the heavy door with its iron grille. But Don Francisco had declared him a free man for all the world, so why should he sneak in the back door like a servant? He reached his hand through the bars to knock loudly. He was surprised when his mother's old rival answered the door.

Esperanza barely recognized the tall young man whose smirk signaled trouble even before he asked to see her master. She asked him to step into the hallway and told him to wait. What on earth did he want with Don Francisco? She thought of warning the Señora first, but the news would only upset her as she was preparing for the evening's celebration and the family's secret departure the next day. Her master was in a room upstairs, playing with the children.

"Señor, you have a visitor—Concha's son," she said, interrupting him as he crawled on his hands and knees, Úrsula giggling on his back as she pretended to whip him. He set the girl down slowly and bent to pat her head.

"You are a cruel mistress, *niña*. I must go tend to my wounds," he said with mock sadness.

Úrsula squealed in delight, a sound rarely heard within these walls, Esperanza noted silently.

Francisco hoped that Juan was bringing good news, but the timing was certainly bad. He had promised the boy money if he managed to get Herrera out of Sevilla, but that was before he had set so early a departure date for himself and his family.

"How are you, Juan?" he asked, as casually as if the young man was a frequent guest.

"I have secured your wishes, Señor. The man will depart in less than two days on a ship sailing west," Juan said without acknowledging the common courtesies.

Francisco did not relax the muscles in his face, which kept the insincere smile on his lips. "Good," he said, remaining outwardly calm, though his heart quickened. There was only one ship leaving port the day after next—the one he and his family intended to be on. It was impossible that Herrera be aboard that ship. And yet he could not let on that anything was amiss if he hoped not to alert this troublesome young man, who would use the information to secure a reward from the highest bidder. "And what is the plan, if I might ask?" he said.

"You remember Pablo from our last voyage. He has signed on to sail with a cargo ship heading to Veracruz, but I have made him a better offer," Juan said, pleased with his own cleverness. "His place will be taken by Herrera right before the ship sets sail."

"It seems you have thought of everything, Juan," Francisco said, reaching out to shake his hand. "And what about you? Will you remain in Sevilla?"

"As soon as I see Herrera safely on the ship, I will leave for Portugal. I would rather wait out the fall and winter there and return to Méjico when the fleets leave next spring." He stood silent while Armijo seemed to mull over the information, not knowing quite how to raise the question of payment. "I will need the means to do so, however," he said, finally breaking the awkward silence that had engulfed the room.

"Of course, Juan. I will be just a minute," he said. He turned to go, but then thought better of it. "Please take a seat in the *sala mayor*, Juan. May I ask Esperanza to get you a refreshment?"

Juan grinned at the invitation. *This is what it is to be a free man*, he said to himself, for the second time that day.

Chapter Thirty-One
THE FAREWELL DINNER

"**I**s that all he said to you?" Padre Dominguez spat out the words, barely able to control his rage. He should have gone himself. But he'd barely had enough time to perform his penance before leaving for the Casa Armijo. And now this bumbling fool was complicating his decision. Should he forego his appearance at dinner and instead go to Barrio Santa Cruz to force the moneylender to tell him where Herrera could be found? Or should he be patient, go to the Armijo home, and perhaps drop a bit of gossip? He had practiced the words already: "It is regrettable what has become of Sevilla when even the best families have produced adulterers who attempt to flee to the New World when their misdeeds are discovered." He would keep his eyes on Señora Péres the whole time—or at least until he could slyly shift his gaze to her husband.

Brother Tomás considered whether he should say more. The bird merchant had given him no further information, but he recalled the tall mulatto who passed him in the street. The merchant had inquired whether Tomás knew the young man, so perhaps he had something to do with the man Padre Dominguez was seeking.

"He said nothing more, Padre, but…" the monk waited before completing his thought.

"Tell me, you fool. I don't have all day. I am expected at the Casa Armijo any minute," the priest shouted.

"There was another man who came out of the shop just as I was entering—a tough-looking fellow with skin the color of walnuts."

"And? What has this to do with…" The priest swallowed his words. It must be the lusty servant's bastard, the one he'd already paid twenty-seven pieces of silver to track the errant husband. "Was he tall, well-built, with a nasty sneer on his face?"

"I noticed no sneer, Padre, but he looked very strong."

Dominguez hesitated. He must choose his next steps carefully. He didn't want to scare Herrera off with a false move, but he needed to have a word with the mulatto. "Can you take another message for me? I know it is getting late, but," here he applied as much honey in his voice as he could muster, "there are few I can trust except you, *Hermano*."

Tomás shivered though the evening was quite warm. He would get no supper until he had walked across the bridge again and made his way down the crowded alleys to the shop with the lovely birds.

The sun would not set for another hour, but Esperanza ordered the servants to put fresh candles in the chandelier over the long dining room table. The smell of the meats roasting in the yard wafted through the open windows, making her stomach growl. She had been so busy all day that she had forgotten to eat and only remembered to feed poor Benito when he showed up in the *cocina*, his eyes wide with longing as he stared at the pots boiling on the hearth.

Everything must go perfectly on schedule. The guests would arrive shortly after sunset—twelve in all, making fourteen at table. It had been years since the house had so many guests, not since Doña Benita had sat at one end of the long table and Don Pedro at the other. She directed the other servants to place the goblets at each plate and set the silver *tenedors*, which were no longer a novelty in Sevilla, to the left and the knives to the right, with large silver spoons on the outside. Don Francisco had ordered bottles brought up from the cellar, as well as a large bottle of clear liquid he had brought back from Méjico, which he said should be served with fresh limes to quench the fire as it scorched its way down the throat.

"When they leave our table tonight," Don Francisco had told Esperanza that afternoon, "our guests will have had a taste of Veracruz, without ever suffering the dangers of the open seas." And indeed, he had given his personal attention to the preparation of the meal, which included a pork stew made of chiles and *maíz* that he had brought back with him. Esperanza worried that the heat of the dish would make everyone drink too much wine, and the evening would end with the guests staggering to their waiting carriages. But perhaps that was her master's intention.

Guiomar could barely breathe with how tightly the corset cinched her waist. She would be unable to eat anything unless she loosened the ribbons she had just painstakingly tied. She was annoyed that Esperanza was not there to help, but Francisco had insisted that her time was better spent overseeing the table preparations. She had better get used to doing things on her own, she thought, as she began relacing the ribbons, this time not pulling so tight. When they reached Veracruz, Esperanza would be free to stay with them or go her own way, and Guiomar doubted the local girls who might replace her would know how to tie a proper bow.

It was hard to believe that this was the last night she would spend in the only home she had ever known. Tomorrow they would leave in the late afternoon as if going for a carriage ride along the Guadalquivir. She was still unsure how they would get to the port from El *Arenal*, along which fashionable Sevillanos were driven in carriages when the weather was mild, though she knew that Esperanza and Benito would go after nightfall. Their trunks, four in all, would be loaded only after they were safely aboard, and Don Enrique would see to the whole business. The canaries sang in their cages, and she wondered if Francisco could be persuaded to bring one aboard for Úrsula, who would be broken hearted if she could never hear their melodies again. The new bird that the shopkeeper had delivered when he brought the emerald ring had a magnificent trill. He was longing for his mate, or at least that was the story the shopkeeper told.

She pulled on the silk dress over the corset, emerald green to match her ring. There was no chance the inquisitor could miss it as he was to be seated at her right hand, where the ring would flash every time she moved her fingers. She thought of José Marcos—though the image of his face made her wince. She no longer loved him. But he had been part of her early life, and it was not easy to simply erase the memory. Francisco was evasive when she asked him what Concha's boy wanted, but she gathered it had to do with José Marcos' fate.

She sat down at her dressing table and inspected her face in the mirror. She must look her most beautiful tonight—happy that her husband had returned, joyful at the prospect that he would be with her and the children for the coming months, curious about the lives of her guests. Become the hostess that her mother played for so many years when her father returned with the fleet. She looked around the room, which had been her mother's. Tears welled in her eyes as she thought of her poor parents buried beneath Santa Ana's—if only she could take their bones with her. But that was impossible. She would carry their love in her heart, but their bodies would remain in the church crypt. Would they be reunited in an afterlife? It was one of the most comforting beliefs the Church offered. But the little book her brother had given her made no mention of a Jewish heaven, only the duty to follow God's laws on earth.

"Are you ready, my dear?" Francisco asked as he stuck his head in the door.

"I will never be ready for what I am about to do," Guiomar said, "but I will do it anyway." She stood up, smoothing the folds of her dress. Unfortunately, the gown had been made before she had given birth, when her bosom was fuller, and it puckered at the neckline. She reached down to the dressing table and picked up the fragile gold necklace Francisco had given her on the birth of their daughter. "Will you fasten this for me, Francisco?" she asked, walking toward him.

THE SILVER CANDLESTICKS

"It is not up to the elegance of your dress," he said, as he draped the leaf shaped pendant on her breast.

"But it is dearer to me than any jewels I own," she answered.

Don Enrique stood and raised his glass. "I have been honored to be a guest at this table for more than a quarter century," he said, looking towards Guiomar, "but I can truly say that I have never had a better meal than the one we have enjoyed this evening. I salute you, *m'hija*, for preparing a delicious feast—and you, Francisco, for the spices you have introduced us to, even if I shall no doubt curse you before the night is over." He glanced at the inquisitor, whose normally ashen face was covered in red blotches, the effect of the chiles or the wine—or both. "Don't you agree, Padre?" he said, tipping his glass to the priest, who had spoken very little throughout the meal.

Dominguez wiped his mouth with the small, colorful cloth placed next to his plate. "Gluttony has never been my weakness. I am satisfied with the piece of stale bread and thin broth my Order dictates. But," he paused, dabbing at his burning mouth, "I might make good use of these—'chiles' you call them?—for the sinners in my care."

Enrique saw Guiomar's face blanch at the priest's words and let out a burst of laughter to distract the table. "I would not have guessed you are a man blessed with such humor, Padre."

The priest smiled broadly, clearly pleased with his own wit, however unintentional. The evening had not been the success he'd hoped. He had dropped several hints to Señora Péres that he missed her visits to the Castillo and hoped she would return to do more good works. But she deflected each time.

He turned to her as the servants were placing small glasses next to the plates, pouring a clear liquid into each, then placing cut limes at intervals along the table. "I don't suppose you've heard that Señora López de Herrera's husband has gone missing," he said. "I take it you were friendly with the man's sister." He watched her face, but it betrayed neither surprise nor fear.

"María Dolores and I have not seen each other in a while—since her baby's christening, I believe. It is true we were friends at the convent," she answered, knowing she must say something about José Marcos as well. "Her brother was a lost soul. I am sorry to hear that he has humiliated his wife." Perhaps she should have chosen her words more carefully. They were bound to be repeated by the priest—but she would be on the open sea by the time he could do so.

Francisco tapped the small glass with a spoon, drawing the attention of everyone at the table. "You have before you one of the great delicacies of Méjico—mezcal fermented from the agave plant and imbibed by *los Indios* in their great celebrations." He twirled the liquid in the glass and reached for a lime. "It is best to drink the draught quickly, followed by the juice of *el limón*," he said, demonstrating. "But I warn you, it is not for the faint of heart—and the señoras may refrain without insulting their host."

The priest hesitated to lift the glass. It was bad enough to eat the chiles that would no doubt trouble his bowels later, but this liquor might be the Devil's own concoction. He had heard the stories of ritual sacrifices carried out by naked warriors tearing the hearts, still beating, from the chests of their victims. Maybe those were the celebrations when they drank the agave liquor.

"I must object, Don Francisco," the priest interjected. "Has wine not ruined enough men, turning them into worthless drunkards who waste their last maravedi on liquor rather than food for their starving children? Now you introduce a pagan substitute that might endanger their souls as well?" He pushed the small glass away, tipping it over so it spilled over the table.

Francisco wanted to grab the hypocrite by the throat and throw him out the door. A man who had ruined hundreds of lives, who took pleasure in other people's pain, dared insult him in his own home! He stood up, raising his empty glass. "Pour me another," he said, nodding to the servant who stood in the corner.

Guiomar looked at him terrified, her eyes wide, her lips pursed as if stifling a scream. She twisted the emerald ring on her finger.

THE SILVER CANDLESTICKS

The whole table sat frozen, eyes averted, not daring to move, or even breathe. Don Enrique was displeased—Francisco could tell by the set of his jaw—but the man said nothing.

Finally, the priest stood up, throwing down his napkin. "I must leave at once," he said.

Guiomar reached out and touched his sleeve. "Please, Padre, do not leave in anger. My husband has been gone too long. He has forgotten his manners," she said, looking straight at Francisco. She pushed back her chair and stood next to the priest. "I will come to the Castillo in three days. In the meantime, please accept this gift to aid your good work," she said, removing the emerald ring from her finger. A murmur of surprise swept around the table.

Dominguez looked at her outstretched hand. He could barely believe his eyes. He had stolen glances at the ring all evening, angry that the emerald was on her finger and not with the pawnbroker as he had suspected. He had hoped to use it as evidence against her, and instead she was giving it to him. Was it a sign from the Lord? If so, in which direction did it point? To guilt or innocence? Perhaps it was a way to assuage her conscience. He crossed himself and bowed to her. "You will be rewarded for your generosity, Señora," he said and made his way to the foyer.

"One moment," Don Enrique called out, pushing back his chair. "Let me have my carriage take you to the Castillo." The priest stopped and turned in the archway.

Francisco sat still, head bowed and sullen, having drunk the second glass of mezcal. His eyes were glassy, and Don Enrique feared that he might say something that would further inflame the situation. The guests looked at each other, no one willing to be the first to follow the priest's path but unsure if they should continue to eat and drink.

Francisco motioned to one of the servants, who picked up a platter of fruits and began serving the guests. "There is no reason we should not finish our dinner as we began," Francisco said, "in friendship and good spirits."

Don Enrique nodded his agreement, lifting his own glass of mezcal. "Adios, Padre. My goddaughter's gift should allow you to sleep well tonight, knowing you now have the means to save many souls. I will add to her generosity with my own bequest, which you shall receive when she visits you." A promise that would never be honored by either of them.

The priest again bowed his head slightly and retreated, with Guiomar walking him to the door.

"I look forward to your visits, Señora. I have missed our talks," Dominguez said, stopping at the open door to stare deeply into the woman's eyes, the window into her soul. But he saw nothing.

Guiomar felt a chill down her spine. "May those visits guide me to become closer to Our Lord," she said, bowing her head. The touch of the inquisitor's forefinger nearly made her lose her balance.

"Bless you, my child," Dominguez said as he inscribed an invisible cross on her forehead.

Chapter Thirty-Two

AN ESCAPE

Padre Dominguez stepped gingerly from the carriage, which stopped at the guardhouse. It was not often he had traveled in such luxury. Perhaps he should order a carriage for the Holy Office. Not so grand as Don Enrique's, surely, but one that could transport him across the river to visit the archbishop or attend to the Holy Office's business at city hall. It would now be possible, thanks to Señora Péres' generous gift, which he carried in the pocket normally reserved for the consecrated host for Extreme Unction. *How much was it worth?* he wondered. Enough to start a new life for Herrera if the tales the man's deserted wife had spun were true. Jealousy was a poison that could drive a woman crazy, even when there was no cause, he thought as he approached the gate.

The guard stood waiting for him. "I was told to deliver this to you when you returned, no matter the hour," the guard said, handing him a note sealed with no mark.

"For me? By whom?"

"For Señor Cháves, the fellow said. The same as last time—to be delivered to your care."

The priest grabbed the folded paper and stuck it in his pocket before entering the gate. No doubt the mulatto wanted more money, but the priest had less interest in pursuing his quest now. It was possible that Señora Péres would become an even greater benefactor to the Holy Office. She had already showed enormous generosity, even without being prompted by accusations. Would he not save more souls by ignoring the rumors about her while her gifts made it possible to pursue even greater sinners? And her husband—well, Armijo had insulted him, no doubt, but he could be made to pay as well. What was more, the *padrino* would clearly do anything for his goddaughter. All in all, the evening had been a great success, if not exactly as he had planned.

He lit the candle in his room and hurriedly opened the note. "Meet me tomorrow evening at ten, at the place where we first saw each other. I have the information you sought and a means for you to apprehend the gentleman." He crumpled the paper in his fist. He was weary after the meal—and the wine. He must pray for guidance. Who knew what temptations the Devil had put in his way? It would not be the first time a beautiful woman bearing gifts had led a righteous man astray.

He withdrew the ring from the hidden pocket behind his scapula and laid it on the table by the candle. The stone reflected the flame's light, shimmering green, like a lagoon, or perhaps, a fetid cesspool. The priest stripped off his habit until he stood naked and fell to his knees on the cold floor, clenching his hands in prayer.

"My God, my God, why hast thou forsaken me," he cried out, striking his breast, which burned where the emerald had pressed against it. He reached for his cincture and began knotting it. "Forgive me my hubris and guide me in how to proceed," he said as he lashed his bare back with the belt, the pain from inside his chest vying with the lashes to cleanse him.

Don Enrique stood with Guiomar at the front door, bidding the last guests goodbye. Francisco had retreated to his room, stumbling up the stairs from the effects of too much mezcal. Guiomar was furious at her husband. He had endangered everything with his reckless outburst at the priest. As soon as the captain from Don Enrique's fleet had boarded his carriage, she turned to her godfather. "What are we to do? I fear Francisco's intemperance has jeopardized our plan," she said.

THE SILVER CANDLESTICKS

Enrique frowned. "Your own rashness, *m'hija*, was no less a danger to this enterprise," he said, his voice softer than his words. "You will need whatever resources you can muster to set up life in Méjico, and you may have squandered a valuable one with the priest. Do you really believe you can buy his silence?"

Guiomar's tears fell quickly, but she knew her *padrino* was right. "We have no time to waste on tears, *m'hija*. Are all the preparations ready?" Guiomar nodded, wiping at her tears with a handkerchief. "Good. I don't think we can afford to wait a moment longer. Send the servants to bed. As soon as my carriage returns, I will load your belongings and deposit them on the ship. Have Esperanza pack whatever food is left from the banquet. I am going to talk to the ship's captain. He is a man I trust and if possible, I think we should speed our departure. Please tell Francisco to be ready before dawn." What he did not tell Guiomar was that he feared Dominguez would remain a danger so long as he drew breath—perhaps even in the New World. He would need to make sure the threat was dealt with, but how?

Guiomar went to the *cocina* to talk to the servants. It was usual to allow them to eat at leisure what was left after a banquet, but she needed to convey her *padrino*'s instructions to Esperanza. She found her dishing out the extra food to the other servants and waited until they had received their portions. "Please take your dinner and retire. The cleaning can wait until tomorrow. You deserve a rest," Guiomar said to the puzzled servants, who withdrew to the courtyard and their quarters.

"Esperanza, we must move quickly, I am afraid," she said. Esperanza's eyes widened and fear distorted her usually calm features.

"What's wrong, Señora?" she asked, moving to the door to make sure no one remained in hearing distance.

"Don Enrique thinks it is not safe to stay, even for another day. He is taking the trunks to the ship and will return for us," Guiomar said, grabbing the servant's arm. "I have done a foolish thing..." her voice faltered. "But never mind," she said, composing herself.

"It is not your worry. Please gather as much food as we can easily take with us. Enough to last until we are at sea. We will depart before dawn."

"All of us?" Esperanza whispered, her voice catching.

Guiomar reached out and took her hand. "You must not worry. My *padrino* will send a cart for you and Benito tomorrow evening. In the morning, you must tell the other servants that Don Francisco is ill and that I too am not feeling well. Keep them away from our rooms. Don't scare them, but you could perhaps hint that he may have brought an illness with him from his travels. That will surely keep them at a distance." She started to leave and then thought of something else. "And bring one of the canaries with you. Its song will remind me of Sevilla, and Úrsula will have a friend."

Esperanza hugged her mistress tightly. The time had come much more quickly than she had planned. She said a prayer as the Señora departed and began scouring the cupboards for whatever could be easily transported.

Juan tapped his fingers on the table, watching his troublesome roommate sleep. Herrera slept like a baby on the cot against the wall. He envied the man's slumber. He, on the other hand, would not sleep a minute until he had the priest's money in hand. He had not clearly asked the priest to bring money, but surely, he knew that he would get no information if he did not pay up front. The question remained whether to turn Herrera over immediately or follow through on his pact with Don Francisco.

Herrera had been wary of taking on the duties of a lowly sailor—as if he had any choice in the matter. The man would be useless on board. He would spend his first days retching over the side and the next weeks nursing the blisters on his hands. Juan smiled imagining the pale skin of the gentleman peeling from the unrelenting sun, his back exposed to the elements and his chestnut ringlets plastered against his skull.

His own first days at sea had been brutal even though he had known labor his whole life, carrying wood to the *cocina* when he could barely toddle across the courtyard, shoveling manure in the barns, scrubbing the tiles in the hacienda alongside his mother. But that life was over. The money from Armijo and the priest would allow him to leave for Lisbon or some other city and sail to Méjico again in the spring. But before then, he must decide: hand Herrera over the next evening or simply tell the priest he was due to ship out the following morning?

José Marcos turned on the cot and opened his eyes. The mulatto was staring at him from across the room. José Marcos sat up. "You are awake very late, amigo. Is something troubling you?"

Juan remained silent.

"What is it, *hombre*?" José Marcos asked. "Has something happened?" He got up and walked to the window, peering down into the street. He half expected to see jailers waiting outside to arrest him, but the alley was deserted, and a light drizzle of rain reflected off the stones in the moonlight.

Juan came to the window. "Get back from there. You are a wanted man, or did you forget?" he said, spitting the words in Herrera's face. "I put myself in danger for you, and you repay me with recklessness." He pulled Herrera back, even though there was no one outside. "You will stay in this room, away from the window, until the ship is set to sail. Do you understand?" Juan stood so close to his ward that he could smell the man's scent, grown foul over the days cooped inside. Herrera nodded and retreated to his cot, turning his back to the room.

The streets by the pier were deadly silent, making the beat of the horses' hooves on the stones sound thunderous. Francisco held Guiomar's hand, cradling Úrsula's head with his other. Antonio sat opposite them, excitement brightening his eyes.

"Why are we going on a ship, *Papá*?" the boy asked. "Was this the surprise you promised me?"

"It is, *m'hijo*. And a secret too. We will board the ship and be taken to our quarters, and you must remain very quiet all day. Do you think you can manage that?"

"But why, *Papá*? I want to see the ship and watch the men work."

"You will have many weeks to do that when we are at sea, Antonio. But until we set sail, we will remain in our cabin, which is quite small and without the luxury you are used to. We will not speak above a whisper, and you and Úrsula must remain very still. You are a big boy now. I must be able to rely on you. Can you promise me?" Francisco asked.

Guiomar shifted in her seat. He was scaring the child—he was scaring her as well. How could they hope not to be detected the whole day? Francisco had argued with her *padrino* when he returned with the carriage but relented in the end. The captain had made many of the same arguments. They would be less likely to encounter trouble if they stayed with their original plan—to leave tomorrow when the ship was fully loaded with its cargo for the New World.

But it was what he had told her before her *padrino* arrived that worried her most. José Marcos would come on board just before the ship sailed. She could not stop her heart from pounding in her chest. She had hoped never to lay eyes on the man again. At least that is what she told herself every night before she fell asleep.

"Are you all right, my love?" Francisco squeezed her hand tightly.

"I will be once we set sail," she replied. "I wish we had been able to follow our original plan. I would have liked to stroll along El Arenal one last time. I would wish to see the Torre del Oro—it is a place that inspired so much fear in my mother, but she never said why, though I can guess. Tell me, Francisco, will I ever see Sevilla again?" she asked. But she already knew the answer.

"Not us, but maybe our children or grandchildren. Who knows how long this madness can last?"

They pulled up alongside the ship. Guiomar looked out at the vessel, taking in its size. It was much smaller than she imagined. *How could such a ship brave the ocean in a storm?* she wondered. And how many would be aboard? It was small enough that she knew she could not avoid seeing José Marcos over the long journey. Francisco had suggested he would be a working seaman, not a passenger. Would she see him, shirtless, hoisting the heavy sails when she strolled on the deck? And what would happen when they arrived in port? Would Francisco remain as trusting as he assured her once they set foot on land? She bent over to kiss Úrsula, waking the child, who rubbed her eyes. "We must be very quiet, *niña*," she said. But she need not worry as Úrsula was a child disposed to silence.

Francisco opened the carriage door and alighted, reaching up to take his daughter in his arms. Guiomar stepped out, carrying the heavy basket with the candlesticks, followed by Antonio with another basket on his arm, and the family silently made its way up the gangplank.

The captain waited at the top, holding a small lantern. "*Bienvenidos*," the man said, helping the family board the ship. "Your things are in your cabin. I apologize in advance. The space is cramped and dark, but when we are at sea, you will get plenty of fresh air on calm days. Let us pray those days are many on our long journey," he said, crossing himself.

Chapter Thirty-Three

WITHIN REACH

P adre Dominguez did not bother to disguise his habit as he crossed the river in a mule-drawn cart, wearing his black and white robes with the hood pulled up to partially obscure his face. He was certain the mulatto had not been fooled by his disguise the first time they met, and in any case, his identity would soon be known to Herrera and everyone else who happened to be in the vicinity when Herrera was arrested. He had already signed the papers for him to be taken into custody based on the wife's charges of adultery and consorting with Judaizers. The constables would be waiting near the tavern, ready to swoop in when the priest gave a signal.

He sat on the wooden bench next to the driver, whose tobacco smoke filled his own lungs. But it was better than making the journey on foot. With Señora Péres' gift, he would soon have his own carriage—or rather, the Holy Office would have one. As for the Señora herself, her gift had not fully allayed his suspicions. He still smarted at her husband's arrogant tone the night before. Who did he think he was, a candlemaker's son who had married above his station? Maybe the woman had grown tired of his ill manners and returned to her previous lover. And if Herrera gave evidence against her, the Holy Office would confiscate her entire estate. She parted so easily with the emerald that Dominguez imagined it may have

THE SILVER CANDLESTICKS

been a trifle among her jewels. Surely there were rubies and diamonds too, as well as stores of gold and silver.

But he was getting ahead of himself. First, he must hear Herrera's testimony, which would be put to the tribunal. The Holy Office did not accuse suspected Judaizers without evidence, which must be weighed, considered, corroborated. It might take months before Señora Péres would end up in a cell in the Castillo, though in a matter of days, she would sit across from his desk, as she promised, where he could again test her faith with his questions.

It was possible that she was innocent. In which case, he expected her faith would inspire her to open her coffers for the salvation of her soul. He hoped—no, prayed—that she was what she seemed, a faithful Catholic and a faithful wife. He had been led to think otherwise by the jealous slave, whose heavy breasts still haunted his dreams, sometimes with shameful results. But should he take the word of such a witch, who had no doubt poisoned her new mistress against Señora Péres as well? Why did the Lord test his faith in this way, he wondered, his suspicions shifting with each jerk of the wagon.

"We are here, Padre," the driver said, pulling back the reins.

The priest handed the man a few coins. "Wait for me at the end of the alley. I will come to you when I am finished." Dominguez put his sandaled foot on the sideboard and alighted the rickety carriage. He saw no sign of the mulatto, but perhaps the man was tardy. He did not want to enter the tavern in his habit, but he needed to look inside in case the fellow was there. He could barely see into the darkened room, but the mulatto's size would have made him stand out, and it appeared he was not present.

"Looking for me?" Juan asked, tugging the priest's sleeve. The priest turned around quickly and glared at Juan, who stepped back as though to give him a wide berth.

"I see you came alone," Dominguez answered.

"Did you expect otherwise?" The priest was more naive than Juan imagined. "You will get your man. But not until I get my payment, as I am sure Señor Cháves explained."

"Where is he? Take me to him," Dominguez demanded.

"That I cannot do, Padre—it is Padre, isn't it?"

The priest looked toward a figure hidden in the shadows of a doorway across the cobblestones. Was he there to rob them, or just to spy? "Yes, I am Padre Dominguez, Inquisitor of the Holy Office in Sevilla and Triana, and God's servant," he answered. "And when will you hand over Herrera?" he asked, taking the small leather pouch from his pocket and clenching it in his fist.

"I have arranged for the man to board a ship leaving Sevilla in the morning. He will take the place of a sailor who arrived with me on Don Francisco Armijo's ship last week."

"Is it Armijo's ship that is leaving?" the priest interrupted.

Juan smiled. He had hit a nerve. "No, it is a ship out of Genoa that is delivering goods to Veracruz. Herrera will board the ship when it is too late to find another, more suitable sailor. I don't envy the fellow. He'd find life on the ship very different from what he is used to. But I imagine life at the Castillo will be harder still," he scoffed. "If you come to the pier just before dawn, you will see the ship, which is called *La Perla*. I am sure the captain will oblige you by turning Herrera over. Who knows, I may present myself in his place, though I could pay my way as a passenger thanks to your generosity," he said, holding out his hand. The priest dropped the payment in his palm, which was not stingy, judging by its weight.

Dominguez stared fixedly at the mulatto. He did not trust this man now that he had the silver in hand, but there was little he could do except wait. It was still two hours before dawn, not enough time to return to the Castillo and be back before the scoundrel made his way onto the ship. It would be better to position himself on the pier. "Will I see you at dawn too?" he asked.

Juan laughed, despite himself. "What? And get caught up in your snares as well? I will send Herrera to the ship as I promised both of you—but I intend to be on my way..." He had said too much. The priest's eyes remained on him. "On my way to Mass to repent of my sins," he said, returning the priest's cold stare.

Dominguez knew that he was being mocked. He clenched his fist again, sliding it beneath his scapular so that the man would not notice. He wished he could wipe the smirk off this insolent creature's face, but that would solve nothing. He had time. More time than Señor Herrera or the man standing before him. More time than Guiomar Péres de Armijo. Soon they would all be within his grasp, in the confines of the Castillo. It had taken him years, but Señora Péres would be his. Perhaps he would install her in the room the Mejia woman had lived in…

"Are we done, Padre?" Juan stepped toward the priest, whose eyes had become opaque, almost like a dead man's.

"Do you want my blessing, son?" the priest asked, interrupted in his reverie. Juan shook his head as the bony fingers reached out. The thought of the priest's cold hands on him sent a shudder down his spine as he turned, making his way swiftly along the damp cobblestones.

Dominguez walked to the end of the alley where the driver waited. He could sit in the cart until the pier came alive at sunrise—and from its heights he could keep an eye out for Herrera. His prey was within his grasp.

Esperanza held Benito's hand tightly as they sat on the plank behind the driver. The covered bird cage rattled at her feet on the floor of the cart, but the canary remained quiet. She was pleased the Señora had asked her to bring the small bird. She had packed as much seed as she could fit into a tin, which she put with her own sparse belongings. She breathed in the night air as the cart bumped along the cobblestones. She had walked these streets many times on her visits to bring food to the poor woman at the Castillo, but never had she seen the sights from this height or witnessed the glow of the moon on the river.

Don Enrique's cart had arrived much later than she anticipated, and she had almost decided to risk the long walk, but she couldn't figure out how she would manage. Now, as she sat safely in the cart, she was glad she had trusted that the family would not leave her. Still, she held her breath as they neared the Castillo. What if the guard recognized her? The full moon cast enough light to make her face visible at close range. But as the cart turned in front of the guardhouse, she realized that they were moving so quickly and she was so high above the road that even if the guard had been looking directly at her, he would not be able to see her. As it was, the man leaned on his spear without turning in their direction, probably dozing on his feet. Once across the bridge, the driver turned along a route she had never walked, parallel to the old city's walls but leading upstream.

The galleons stood along the riverbanks. Most of the sails were down so that the wooden beams looked like skeletons on crosses, their arms outstretched to the skies, the calm river lapping the swollen sides of the ships. She pulled Benito closer to her bosom.

"What's wrong, *Mamá*?" the sleepy boy asked. She smoothed his brow with her fingertips. She was not much older than he was when she had been put into the belly of such a ship, pulled up the gangplank by the chain around her neck. She remembered stumbling and a hand grabbing her by the hair and pushing her up the rickety plank, her feet blistered from the long trek to the coast from her village.

"Nothing, *m'hijo*. Just a chill from the breeze off the river."

"How long will we be on the ship?" the boy asked, rubbing his eyes and stifling a yawn.

"I don't know, Benito." She wondered how long the trip would take. Surely longer than her childhood voyage from Africa to Lisbon, and from there to Sevilla, which had seemed to last forever. But Benito would not be chained as she had been, left to lie in her own waste, unable to block out the smell of other bodies pressed against her or the sound of their long, desperate cries.

Her heart beat faster. It was not too late to turn around. But where would she go? Could she go to Don Enrique's estate with the other slaves? No, he might turn her away, afraid she would reveal the family's escape once the inquisitor came around. Unlike the others in the household, she knew too much. Everything—from

THE SILVER CANDLESTICKS

Doña Benita's instructions to Guiomar's endeavors to learn what her mother did not have time to teach her. Could she say with confidence that if put on the rack, she would not reveal all? And what would become of Benito? She had no choice. She must go forward. Guiomar had promised her freedom once they reached the New World. She must trust her.

The driver halted alongside a ship with its sails fastened. The dock was eerily quiet, no men about, the ships along the wharf looking abandoned. The gangplank had been drawn up, and she could see no way to board the ship. Perhaps they had given up hope that she would arrive.

The driver muttered words under his breath that Esperanza could not understand. He stepped down from the cart and looked up, putting his finger to his lips. He let out a low whistle, like a night bird, then another, and waited. A lantern appeared midship, moving upwards as if from a set of stairs leading to the ship's hold. A man's head appeared, then his body. He walked quickly to the side of the ship, stooping to pick something up. The driver stood waiting on the dock as the man threw a rope ladder over the side. Esperanza wondered how they would manage the trunk up the ladder—or the cage. The work was done in silence. The man with the lantern climbed down the rope and jumped to the dock, bringing the ladder, which he secured to some rings on the wharf.

The driver motioned to Esperanza, who gently shook Benito awake. "It is time, *m'hijo*," she whispered. "Be very quiet. We must not wake the sailors." She lifted him down to the driver, then handed down the cage. The bird tweeted loudly as the cage swung from the man's hand. The driver spat, again muttering a phrase she did not understand. But the other man said something harshly to him, and he gingerly put the cage down. The man from the ship reached out to take Esperanza's hand.

"I see you have brought an extra passenger," he said, smiling. His words were understandable, though he spoke with an accent she had never heard. "We must move quickly to ensure that no one sees you board," he said, picking up the cage and walking back to the rope ladder. "You go first. Giovanni will carry the boy up. When you get on board, move away from the side of the ship and crouch down until everything is aboard, and I will guide you to the cabin," he said. "Don't worry, it will be over soon," he said, patting her arm.

Esperanza let out the breath she had been holding. "And the Señora's bird?"

He smiled. "I will carry him myself. The trunk can wait until the morning when we let the gangplank down. There are still a few supplies to be loaded, and Giovanni will make sure it gets aboard before we sail."

Esperanza started up the ropes, which swung toward the ship as she ascended. She was afraid to look down into the water, which she could hear lapping at the ship's side, and kept herself from looking over her shoulder to see the driver with Benito in his arm. Yes, it would soon be over.

Chapter Thirty-Four
DELIVERANCE

The docks were coming to life as Padre Dominguez approached the wharf at dawn. He had not slept all night, but he felt oddly invigorated. He wondered if he had been missed at Matins and Lauds. Surely the monks would notice he was not in his pew and would search for him. He had told no one he was leaving. If questioned, the guard would tell them of his late-night departure by carriage.

It could not be helped. Soon, he would apprehend Herrera as the scoundrel approached the ship, *La Perla*, which was docked a stone's throw from where Dominguez leaned against a building. He watched as the sailors let down the gangplank and began to load large wooden crates onto the ship. He watched carefully to see if he might spy Herrera, but so far, the man had not appeared. The men worked quickly, passing the crates up the gangplank, swinging their arms in unison, laughing as they worked. He could not fully understand their conversation, which switched between Spanish and, he presumed, Italian, but the words he picked up suggested images he did not want to conjure. Filth could be understood in any language from the guttural sounds and the guffaws that accompanied the shouted words. Herrera would have been at home in their company.

As he watched the men loading, he heard footsteps at his back. He slipped into the arched doorway to conceal himself as the man passed by. It was Herrera. He was sure of it. The clothes, though they looked like they had been slept in, were of good quality and richly colored, and his chestnut hair was dirty but worn in the fashion of a dandy, with long curls at the nape. He stepped out of the archway and motioned to the driver who was waiting next to his carriage. They had agreed that the fellow would approach Herrera and try to engage him in conversation before he boarded.

José Marcos reached the foot of the gangplank. "I am reporting for duty," he said to the man at the end of the line. "May I pass?"

The man looked him up and down. "Not for me to say," he replied.

A sailor on the ship yelled down, "What is it? What do you want?" José Marcos stepped back and walked where he could see the sailor better.

"Pablo asked me to come in his place. I have papers here," he said, pulling a document from his vest. He had paid Juan to obtain a forged pass to sail to Las Indias, which had cost him dearly and attested that he had worked on a ship out of Lisbon and was not a Jew.

"Wait there," the sailor called and disappeared.

José Marcos looked around him and saw a driver approaching with his cart. He stepped out of the way when the man stopped, blocking him in against the pier.

"Move it, will you?" José Marcos yelled.

"Not before I have a word with you," the driver said.

José Marcos eyed the fellow. He was big and rough. Had he encountered the man before? Perhaps he owed him a debt. He stepped back but almost lost his footing. A big black rat scurried across his shoe. He felt trapped and uneasy, but he could not afford to make a scene. His position was too precarious; he needed to get onboard the ship before it sailed, which appeared imminent.

"What do you want with me?" José Marcos shot back. "I am about to sail, as you can see." The man leaned down menacingly but said nothing. José Marcos saw a priest from the corner of his eye, his black robes moving towards him. It was the inquisitor,

THE SILVER CANDLESTICKS

he was sure of it, though he had never met the man. It would be folly to try to run. The driver would chase him down. He turned to face the inquisitor head on. "So, it is you," he said. "Am I to be detained?"

Dominguez stopped, reaching out his arm to lean on the cart. He was tired. He needed a few hours' sleep. He was too old for this. But his gesture also made it impossible for Herrera to move past him. Herrera's face was insolent, but he detected a whiff of fear. He could almost smell it. The same as when subjects were first brought into the room to be questioned by the inquisitors. They acted as if they had nothing to hide, as if their honor had been offended. But sweat broke out above their lips even as they scowled at the priests.

He dropped his arm and took a step forward. "Detained?" he asked, shaking his head slowly. "I have no authority to detain you, Señor. But I am surprised to hear that you are 'reporting for duty.' Does your wife know?" he asked, his voice as innocent as he could make it. He smacked the cart with his open palm. "Move forward and wait for me ahead," he called to the driver.

José Marcos bristled. Of course the priest had no authority to detain him. He had not violated the laws of the Church. Gambling was no sin. "She threw me out, if you must know," he answered. "I have no prospects in Sevilla, so I will work my way across the seas and, who knows, I may yet make my fortune in the New World." He turned his back on the priest and approached the gangplank, but before he could step foot at the bottom, a large officer walked steadily down the planks.

"We are not taking on any more sailors," the captain said.

"I understood you were one man short," José Marcos replied.

"You heard wrong."

"And could I book passage?" José Marcos asked tentatively, though he had only a small portion of the money left from pawning the ring after he had gambled most of it and paid Juan for the documents.

"We have no passengers on this trip," the captain said loudly.

The priest stepped forward. "It seems you will have to wait, Señor Herrera," he said. "But I would not want to see you out on the streets. We have plenty of rooms at the Castillo," he said, a grin exposing his yellow teeth, the skin stretched tight on his sunken cheeks.

José Marcos turned his back and began walking away from the pier, but he could hear the clopping of hooves on the stones behind him.

"Follow him," Dominguez said to the driver, slapping the sideboard. "I will make my way back on my own."

Dominguez watched as Herrera turned down an alley, the cart keeping pace some distance behind. It would not be the last time he saw José Marcos Herrera. Of that he was sure. As for Señora Péres, time would tell. Perhaps she had handed him the means of her own destruction with the emerald ring. Time was on his side, and now he had more resources to pursue his cause. He would wait, observing the woman closely when she came to the Castillo as promised. The *esclava*'s accusations could yet bear fruit. If the woman had witnessed odd rituals while in the Señora's household, there were bound to be others.

As Dominguez made his way on foot along the river, he failed to notice a large, burly man emerge silently as he passed a darkened doorway. Had he turned around, he might have recognized the man as Don Enrique's driver—the same one who had driven him back to the Castillo two nights earlier. But even if he did not recognize the man's face, he might have seen the thick club the driver swung in time to stop it. Instead, there was only blackness as the blow cracked his skull and he fell to the ground.

Inside their cabin, the Armijo family sat quietly, afraid to make a sound before the ship began to move downriver. The noise outside their small porthole had quieted as the last crates were loaded up the gangplank. Úrsula sat on the cot next to her mother and sucked her thumb, leaning into Guiomar. Francisco lay on the bunk, staring at the ceiling, Antonio curled up next to him.

THE SILVER CANDLESTICKS

Esperanza huddled with Benito in a hammock that hung in the corner of the cabin. The gentle rocking of the boat, though unsettling to her, had put Benito to sleep. She wondered whether they would remain in the cabin once the ship was at sea. The quarters were smaller than the casita she had lived in most of her life at the Péres household. Her mistress would have to get used to such close living with no escape, the sounds and smells of others invading her ears and nostrils day and night. She felt the ship lurch and heard a grinding sound as the galleon scraped against the pier. She crossed herself and closed her eyes. She needed to lay still and allow the rocking of the ship to lull away her fears. A knock at the door startled her from her reverie.

Guiomar stood up abruptly. "What is it, Francisco?" she whispered.

"Don't worry, my love. It is probably the captain, here to tell us that we have set sail," he said, opening the door.

The captain stepped into the cabin, his own until he decided at the behest of his friend Don Enrique to allow the Armijo family to occupy it.

"My apologies, Don Francisco. I wish the accommodations were more agreeable," he said, looking around at the six souls occupying a space designed for no more than a single person. "The man you warned me about attempted to board just as we were loading the last provisions."

"There was no unpleasantness, I hope?" Francisco asked, worried that Herrera might have made a scene.

"He offered to buy passage when I told him we weren't taking on sailors. I refused, of course."

"Good."

"But he was talking to a priest when I came down the plank. An odd fellow, white as a ghost, in the robes of a Dominican."

Guiomar let out a small gasp. Francisco turned to her, shaking his head almost imperceptibly. "And?" he asked.

The captain reached out his hand to shake Francisco's. "Nothing, my friend. It seems the priest had business with the man. Official business, I take it, since he offered him a room at the Castillo," he laughed. "It is no wonder you Spaniards are leaving your homeland in such numbers with ghouls like that priest ensnaring so many in their grip."

Francisco studied the captain's eyes. They were warm, not threatening. He sensed the captain knew more than he was saying, but that he could be trusted. "Thank you, *Capitán*. We are grateful for your hospitality. But more for your courage. My family and I leave behind much that we love, but a new world is open to us, vast and rich. Let us pray that the fear and enmity that drives us away stays here."

The captain nodded, though his passenger must know it was already too late for such prayers.

Guiomar embraced her husband. "I am so grateful for you, Francisco," she said softly once the door to the cabin closed. "We have never spoken of what has brought us to this pass…" she hesitated, unsure what more she could or should say.

Francisco kissed her forehead. "When we are safe in New Spain, I want to learn about your traditions. I cannot promise that I will follow the ways of your family, but I want to understand more about a faith that has such a tenacious hold on its people that they would risk everything to adhere to it." He did not tell her that the Holy Office had already set down roots in Ciudad de Méjico. He'd heard rumors that a family of conversos had been burned there just the year before. But New Spain was vast and uncharted, with plenty of opportunities to disappear. Once they reached Veracruz, he had no doubt he could convince Guiomar that their journey was not over.

"I am afraid I will be a poor guide, as I know so little myself," Guiomar said. She took him by the hand and pulled him toward the small porthole window. "I should say a special prayer for our deliverance," she whispered, looking out as the waves of the Guadalquivir splashed against the boat.

She opened the basket she'd brought aboard and unwrapped the silver candlesticks inside, putting them on the small desk.

"It is not time to light the candles, which we do when the Sabbath begins at sunset each Friday. But I know only one prayer and it will have to do for now.

"Baruch Attah Adonai Eloheinu…"

About the Author

Photo by Phoebe Gersten

*L*inda Chavez has spent her decades-long career in politics and the media. She is former Reagan White House official, syndicated columnist, and author of three non-fiction books. Chavez began work on *The Silver Candlesticks* after being featured on the PBS series *Finding Your Roots* where she discovered her family were Converso Jews who left Spain for the New World in 1597. Using details uncovered by *Roots* researchers as well as her own study of the Spanish Inquisition, Chavez has created a story of love and faith set in a perilous period of anti-Semitism. Chavez earned her MFA in Creative Writing from George Mason University in 2012 and lives with her husband, two dogs, and an African Grey Parrot in Silver Spring, Maryland.